Wealth Mountain

Nicholas W. Pellegrino

Wealth Mountain

Writing and Maps by Nicholas W. Pellegrino
Editing by Shaun Baines
Proofreading by J. Flowers-Olnowich
Front Cover Artwork by Sassumia
Page 363 Artwork by Suna Utsukushi

Published by Game Quill LLC

ISBN: 979-8-9874152-0-7

First Edition

DEDICATION

To those friends who inspire me to stay creative with their excitement to play roleplaying games each week in the worlds that I've designed. This book is dedicated to the players behind the Rolandians, the Sacred Six, the Tater Dülts, the Medio Crew, the Acolytes of Dawn, the Copper Crusaders, and the Adventurers of Lorien.

CONTENTS

Chapter 1

COLB TO ADVENTURE

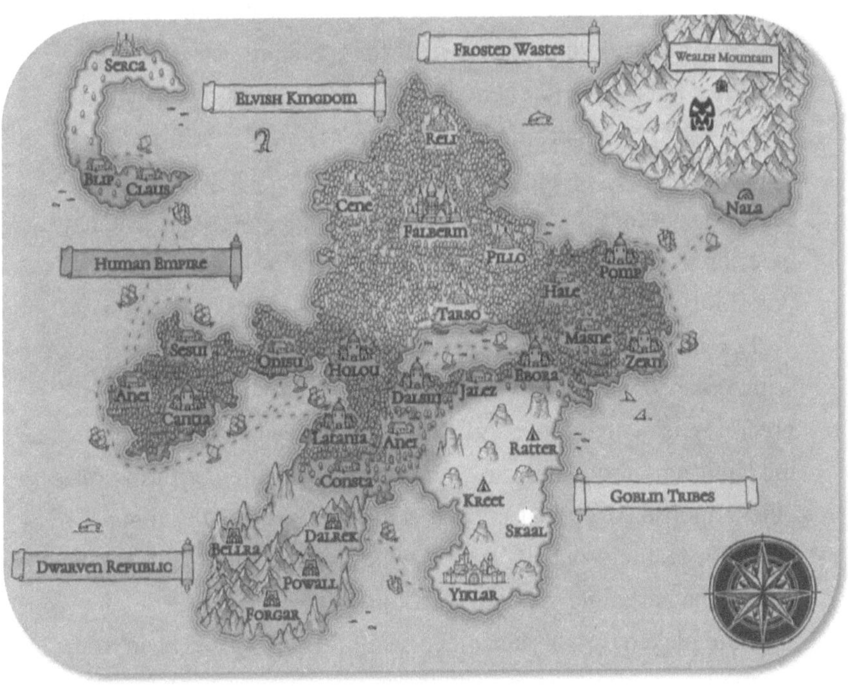

1. COLB TO ADVENTURE

It was a sunny day in Skaal. Goblin children were muddying up their cheap, ragged clothes as they played in the dirt. Spiderbats were gliding overhead, searching for their next meal. Colb, a stout goblin, 23 years of age, let out a peaceful sigh as he crammed the last toadroach into his culinary masterpiece.

Colb took a step back to admire his work. A few days ago, he had purchased a large chickengoose from Gugs, a farming goblin of the Kreet tribe. Here in Skaal, chickengoose cuisine was a rare delight. Most goblins renowned the creature for its plump, spherical hide – this is where the bulk of its nutrition comes from. However, to the more delicate goblin pallet, the best part of a chickengoose is, in actuality, its long, feathery neck. The white feathers coating the outside of the neck give it an elegant, crunchy exterior, while the inside of the tube is a blank canvas of possibility.

For this particular meal, Colb filled the chickengoose neck with crushed and boiled toadroaches. Toadroaches – a small, green insect – melt into a soft and juicy goo when boiled for just the right amount of time. By placing them inside the throat of a chickengoose, Colb had created a masterpiece for the tongue: a crunchy, feathery outside with a gooey, juicy interior. A perfect meal for a particularly wealthy customer.

Colb picked up a broken metal shield, which he had been using for the past ten seasons as a plate for customers in his tavern. He gave the shield a quick polish, and saw his beady red eyes and gnarly green skin reflect back at him through the metal. "Another excellent meal, hmmm!" Colb said to his hairless reflection, as he slid the tube of meat onto the busted shield.

The 3' 2" tall goblin carried the meal through his small, tent-like tavern. He glanced at his restaurant's fabric walls, which were decorated with a set of ragged drawings given to him by some Skaal children – the only decoration in this otherwise dull and dreary building.

Colb let out a short, anxious sigh, then tread towards the single wooden table he'd set up for customers. As he walked barefoot, his sharp toenails gripped the dirt of the unfinished floor. He hobbled along carefully, so as not to drop the precious cargo.

"Hmmm! This will taste good, yes?" Colb stated, placing the busted shield down on the mapleoak table. Across from him sat 27, a wealthy, middle-aged goblin of the Yiklar tribe. Although nobody in Skaal would have such an unusual name, number names were commonplace amongst the Yiklar goblins. To a Yiklar, the numbered name was a symbol of honor, representing great success in some aspect of the goblin business world – with a lower number generally correlating to a more important goblin.

With a number name as low as 27, the customer sitting at this table alone likely represented more wealth than the entirety of the Skaal tribe. Just one look at him verified this suspicion – 27's sharp black robe of fine silk, sinched together at the neck with a shiny purple clip, gave stark contrast to Colb's old leather uniform and dusty white chef's hat.

27 looked up at him, with a golden-yellow gaze. The goblin smiled, showing his teeth sharpened to points, as he exclaimed, "AaAaaaaahhhh, merchant! You've brought me most rarest of meals!" The goblin pulled the shield closer to himself, and inspected the stuffed chickengoose neck. The noble goblin gave the cuisine an audible sniff with his huge, green, spiked nose. "Yiklar merchants sell goods of the highest-of-quality, but only here in Skaal can I find such rarest of dining experience!" 27 exclaimed.

Colb smiled, but his body language was closed overall, as he nervously awaited 27's opinion on the meal. With his clawed hands on either side of the shield, 27 leaned forward, delicately placed his brownish-green lips on one end of the tube, and then slurped the entire thing into his mouth and down his throat in a single swift gulp.

Beads of sweat formed on Colb's brow as 27 licked his lips and scratched his chin, as if pondering the meal. After a few seconds, which felt like a few hours to Colb, 27 lifted an eyebrow, then exclaimed, "AaAaaaaahhhh, a most wonderful meal! Meal was of most excellent flavor!" Colb let out a sigh of relief, pleased to receive the good feedback. Colb cared about impressing every customer. He had feared that his work, made in a cheap kitchen in an impoverished tribe, might not be up-to-standard for such a wealthy goblin. It was nice to hear that those fears were unfounded.

"But this is most strange to me," 27 continued, "because meal was so fine and yet – yet, there exist only one single table in tavern. Why? Is culinary skill such unknown to others in Skaal, there is no need for second table? For two customers to dine at same time?"

Colb scratched the back of his head, perplexed by the question. "Hmmm, Skaal tribe is quite smaller than Yiklar tribe, yes? I serve a few travelers each day from the other tribes – like you – but I have no regular customers from Skaal. There are never enough goblins in here at once to justify second table, yes?"

"AaAaaaaahhhh, this is true, the Skaal tribe is most smallest of the goblin tribes. But, if I were Skaal goblin, I would eat here every day!" 27 triumphantly replied.

"Hmmm, but Skaal goblins cannot afford to buy fine meals every day, yes?" Colb answered, as he gestured towards a circular window cut out in the side of the tent. Through this window, young goblins of the Skaal tribe could be seen playing with a stick in the mud. "Skaal tribe has run out of goldatinum. Even Skaal children lack the Yiklar-made toys that I grew up with."

"*No!*" 27 exclaimed, shocked to his core. A loud *BANG!* echoed throughout the tent as the goblin slammed his hands down on the table. "You mean your tribe cannot afford the highest-of-quality, Yiklar-made goods that my tribe shares with world?"

"Hmmm, that's right, yes?" Colb replied as he picked up the shield 27 had just eaten off of. The dirt of the unfinished floor rolled around Colb's feet as he tread back to the bar. Colb grabbed a rag from a nearby bucket, dunked it in some peppersalt water, and began to wash off the busted shield.

"MMmMmmmm, 1 said situation was dire in Skaal, but I had no idea you were deprived even of highest-quality Yiklar goods," 27 mumbled.

"You've spoken with 1?" Colb replied inquisitively, frowning as he looked back at 27. "That sounds important, yes? It's quite a low number, yes?"

"AaAaaaaahhhh, yes, it is lowest of low numbers," 27 agreed. "In fact, 1 is extra-special name, reserved only for the leader of our tribe."

"Hmmm, what did 1 have to say about Skaal?" Colb prodded.

"MMmMmmmm, yes, well I have spoken with 1, and he shows concern for your plight, yes he does. See, while sales of Yiklar goods within Yiklar borders and even in some dwarven towns have been steady, sales with other three goblin tribes have been down, yes they have been. 1 has become concerned that other three goblin tribes are out of goldatinum to spend, yes they are, and therefore are too poor to continue purchasing of highest-quality, Yiklar-made goods from Yiklar tribe."

"Hmmm! That does match this situation, yes?" Colb replied, as he turned back to the counter and continued washing off the shield.

"*I CAN'T BELIEVE THAT*, no I cannot!" 27 shouted, pushing away from the table and standing up suddenly. His chair thumped backwards into the dirt. "To not have access to highest-of-quality, Yiklar-made goods! To have so many amazing Yiklar deals which cannot be afforded, even though they are most spectacular of deals and special of offers!"

Colb put down the cleaning supplies, but kept holding onto the shield, now a bit wary of 27's emotional outburst. "Here!" 27 shouted, as he pulled out a green bag and stuck his hand in. "Payment for meal, to get things moving, yes this is!" The yellow-eyed goblin dramatically yanked his hand out of the bag, flinging a pile of goldatinum nuggets and an electronze tooth onto the table.

Now, Colb had of course been hoping for a large tip, but this was maybe eighty goldatinum pieces and one electronze piece. That was far above the price for a single meal. He looked down at the chunks of metal, which had no adornments, but were of a roughly standardized size. "Hmmm! Meal was pricey, but not this pricey, yes? You mustn't pay such much, yes?"

"No," 27 replied defiantly, as he clipped his green bag back onto his belt. "This amount is most reasonable of deal for the food you provided. I watched as you worked, and I think I know why you really have just one table in this tavern."

27 dusted himself off, picked his chair off the ground and pushed it back into the table, then walked up to Colb at the bar. He gently pointed one of his nasty green fingers at Colb's chest, with his overgrown, sharpened fingernail lightly touching the leather uniform, right above Colb's heart. "Quality defeats

quantity," 27 whispered, looking Colb dead in the eyes. "That is the Yiklar way!" he continued, suddenly spreading his arms out in an open and friendly manner.

"You have just one table because you wish to give full focus to just one customer at a time. Each customer is so special and important to you – yes, I see it now – you are most caring and wise merchant, just like me!"

27 clapped his hands with glee, dancing a little bit as he spoke. "Hmmm! Your words are too kind," Colb replied, "I am but simple chef in smallest of goblin tribes, yes?"

"AaAaaaaahhhh, you have such humbleness as well, Colb!" 27 proclaimed.

27 leaned in closer, inspecting Colb with thoughtful eyes. The chef goblin felt warm breath on his neck as 27 muttered, "MMmMmmmm, yes, now that I look closer, I understand why Orta said I should choose you."

"Hmmm! Care to elaborate, yes?" Colb replied, taking a step back. Orta was the town elder of the Skaal tribe, and very knowledgeable about all the going-on of her people. She was 59 years old – nearly on death's door for a goblin, as goblins only lived about 60 years – which made her the wisest, most respected goblin in Skaal.

"AaAaaaaahhhh, already showing interest in my proposal before it is even spoken of! This I like, yes I do!" 27 cheered, again starting to dance a little bit as he spoke. "Let me start with this: 1 has come up with special plan, yes he has, to flood all four goblin tribes with mountain of goldatinum! Then, goblins everywhere could increase their purchasing of highest-quality, Yiklar-made goods, yes they could!"

"Hmmm, mountain of goldatinum, you say?" Colb questioned, hesitantly gaining interest.

"AaAaaaaahhhh, yes, literal mountain! And I want your help to acquire it!" 27 cheered, still dancing. "The goldatinum is hidden far away, in a secret place. I am forming a team of one goblin from each tribe to go on a most special of quest to find the goldatinum, and bring it back here! Then, all the goblin tribes could go back to purchasing of most excellently-crafted Yiklar goods!"

"Hmmm, if you know where to find such goldatinum, why tell other tribes? You could just keep all the goldatinum for the Yiklar tribe, yes?" Colb asked, confused by 27's strange plan.

"AaAaaaaahhhh, you have most wise of thought, yes you do, but your plan is not the Yiklar way! We are put on this planet to create most highest-of-quality goods, and serve them to most special and most intelligent of customers. To bring all of goldatinum to Yiklar and none of goldatinum to *customers* of Yiklar would be complete waste of purpose. No, it is the job of Yiklar goblins to protect the precious balance of product manufacturing and customer satisfaction."

27 scratched the back of his head, looking down at his feet in shame. "MMmMmmmm, 1 has recently told me that we've critically failed in an aspect of that purpose over the past few decades, yes we have. We did too much selling, and not enough buying. Too much goldatinum is tied up with the goblins of Yiklar now, and not enough is left for your tribes to purchase our items. While 1 works with the greatest minds in Yiklar to systematically shift our culture in favor of *spending* more money, I have been tasked to replenish the resources of all goblins immediately. If I complete my quick fix, that will buy time for 1 to implement the long-term fix. Together, we will protect and encourage the trading of goods for generations to come. That is the Yiklar way."

"Hmmm, I guess that makes sense, yes?" Colb stated, again picking up the cleaning supplies to finish washing the shield. "It seems a little ambitious, though, yes?"

"In my experience, 1 has a unique way of seeing the world," 27 replied. "For example, he uses his money in ways that I am not familiar with – ways that can seem wild, and indeed ambitious. However, 1 always seems to land on his feet, yes he does. He is a good goblin, and a wise one. This plan of his – the quick fix, combined with the long-term fix – I truly believe it will work, because it came from 1's most creative and intelligent mind. All I need is some goblins – like you – to help complete our part in his plan."

"Hmmm, but I'm just small chef in small tribe. Surely I would not be best choice for quest to find goldatinum," Colb retorted.

"AaAaaaaahhhh, but as I said earlier, I need one goblin from each tribe! Only in this way will every tribe have equal claim to the goldatinum, such that wealth is divided evenly among all goblin customers of the Yiklar!" 27 proclaimed, as he placed his arm on the bar table.

"Hmmm, it's alarming that you would choose me. I'm not one for traveling away from home. If you must choose Skaal goblin, surely there are better choices available than myself, yes?" Colb asked, stiffly dunking his rang into the peppersalt water bucket, trying to keep calm by focusing on his work.

"AaAaaaaahhhh, no, this is most untrue. It's no coincidence that I came to eat here today," 27 revealed, tapping a finger on his head as if to imply he thought this through. "As I said before, Orta – your tribe's elder – sent me your way. I told her of my plan, and asked who I should take with me, yes I did. She sang the praises of a tavern owner with a goldatinum heart, who feeds his fine food to the tribe's hungry children at the end of each day, even though they have not even a silvopper nugget to give in return. Orta tells me that you will bring a character to my team that no other goblin could replace. Not to mention, you are most wise goblin of business, just like me! I would want no other Skaal goblin on my team than yourself! My mind is made up, yes it is."

Colb thought for a moment about this idea. He felt pretty happy as things currently were: he was a chef in the Skaal tribe, following his passion of cooking for a living. As he considered the prospect of leaving on an adventure, Colb's eyes scanned the tavern, finally landing on the customer table, which still had an electronze tooth and some eighty goldatinum nuggets scattered all over it. *Hmmm, I could really spruce this place up with that massive tip 27 left*, Colb thought to himself. *I think I'd be fine just staying behind, yes? I could even get a real window.*

As Colb pondered these things, he kept scanning the tavern, finally landing on the circular cut-out in the tent wall. Through it, he watched as a goblin child stabbed another child in the eye with a stick. *Then again, living in Skaal is not what it used to be. Some extra goldatinum would be nice for the others around me. Perhaps I could do more for the community by going with 27 than I could by staying behind.*

"MMmMmmmm, you have much respect for your elder, yes you do?" 27 prodded. Colb gave him a nod. "She told me to choose you, Colb. She did not hesitate, no she did not."

"Hmmm, I wouldn't bring much to team, yes?" Colb worried. "Hmmm, I cannot navigate, I cannot fight. I have shield, but I use it as plate, yes?"

"Skaal is just first tribe I am checking for a teammate, yes it is," 27 comforted. He placed his gnarly hand on Colb's back for a moment, giving it a gentle pat. "I will find other goblins to navigate, to fight. MMmMmmmm, but I also need goblin to care. You would be best for that, yes you would be. Orta tells me so, and I can see it myself, yes I can."

Colb hesitated a while longer, staring silently at the impoverished goblin children playing outside. "Hmmm…" he eventually mumbled, looking back at 27. "If Orta says I can do it, then I will do it, yes?"

"AaAaaaaahhhh!" 27 shouted, his eyes welling up with joy. "This is the most wonderful of the most excellent of the most news-worthy of news!" 27 broke out into another dance as he celebrated, shaking his hips and wagging his fingers.

"Hmmm, that is good to hear, yes? I do have one request, though," Colb said, sheepishly. "May I have some time to put my affairs in order, close up shop, and prepare myself for this quest before we leave?"

"AaAaaaaahhhh, that is actually most convenient of request, yes it is, as I still need to find goblins from Kreet and Ratter before we start the adventure!" 27 replied. "How about, I will go to Kreet and Ratter tribes to pick up two more goblins, and then all three of us will meet you here in Skaal to begin the journey? That should give you one week to prepare before we come through to pick you up."

"Hmmm, this sounds most reasonable, yes?" Colb agreed, now thinking about everything he needed to do in the next week.

"Well, then it's a deal!" 27 triumphantly cried, as he started to walk backwards – still dancing – towards the door. "Best of luck with preparations and all that. I'll see you in one week, yes I will!" With a quick wave and a couple more dance moves, 27 left the tavern. Now alone, Colb stared at the money on the table, pondering what he had just gotten himself into.

Chapter 2

GATHERING OF THE GOBLINS

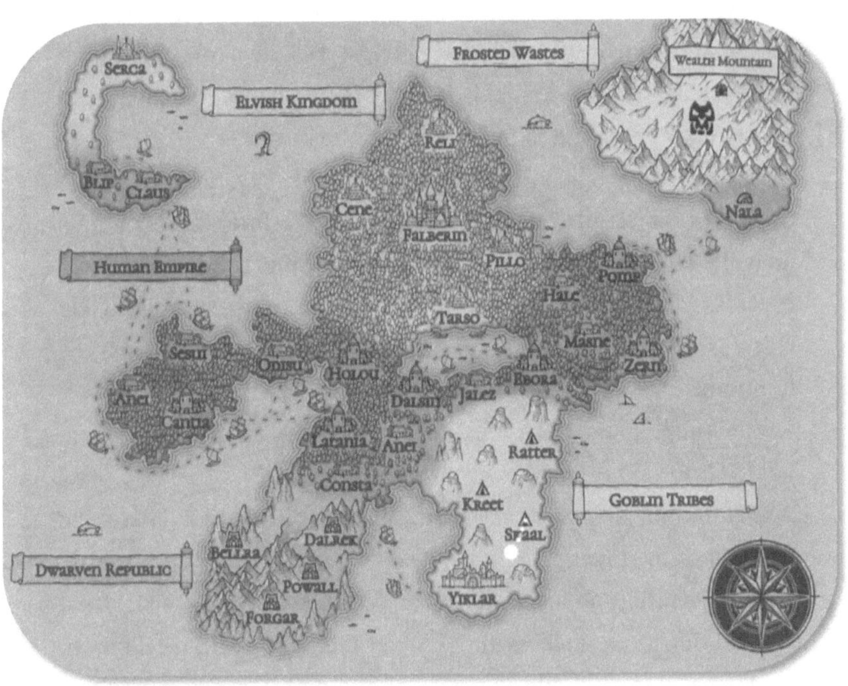

2. GATHERING OF THE GOBLINS

It had been one week since 27 first spoke with Colb about the adventure of a lifetime. Since then, Colb had been diligently putting his affairs in order. He taught his sister, Vrel, how to make a few simple recipes, such that she could run the tavern while he was gone. He also spoke with Orta, the town elder, who encouraged him and reaffirmed her decision that he was the best goblin to journey with 27. Finally, to keep himself safe, Colb invested 30 of his goldatinum nuggets into some fresh leather armor and two bright wooden shields. He gave the remaining money and one of the shields (to become a plate in the tavern) to his sister, Vrel, to aid in her upkeep of the business.

As the sun reached the highest point in the sky, Tix, one of the Skaal tribe's scouts, entered the tavern to inform Colb of 27's arrival. "Hummm, I sssssee that Yiklar goblin in the distansssssce, myesssss?" Tix announced in his usual, slithery tone. "He ridesssss in by pigeonhorssssse, along with two other goblinsssss, hummm."

"Hmmm, sounds like I should start putting on my armor then, yes?" Colb said. "Thank you for informing me."

"Hummm, do not worry of it, myesssss?" replied Tix, as he trod out of the tavern.

After putting on his armor, Colb bid farewell to his sister, and walked outside to meet with 27. Over the past week, he'd grown more confident with his decision to set out on this adventure, and even felt a little excited about what was to come. As he sauntered to the edge of Skaal territory, Colb noticed the wealthy goblin riding in on a quick, feathery steed with four stick-like legs.

As 27 rode in, a pair of goblins trailed behind him, sharing the seat on a second lanky creature. The goblin controlling the second steed was wearing a black hooded cloak, and looked to be a few years younger than Colb. Behind that young goblin sat quite the opposite – a wrinkly old goblin in a dusty, black leather jacket. He had an eyepatch over his left eye and metal rings in his very wide, long, pointed green ears.

"AaAaaaaahhhh, you look ready to travel on adventure!" 27 exclaimed as he rode up to Colb. The yellow-eyed goblin jumped off his steed, which sported a long, beak-like face. The creature stared off blanky into the distance, not seeming to notice 27 had jumped off it. "I've purchased two pigeonhorses from Kreet to speed up our travels!" 27 cheerfully announced.

Colb soon felt a mild tug on his chest as 27 pulled him in close to whisper into his ear. "And just a warning for you, I told the others that you are medic for team, yes I did. Having medic on team was best way to get them to come, and also as a chef you probably know something about herbs or whatever so I'm sure you'll be fine as team medic, yes you will be."

"Hmmm, that's not very true," Colb worried.

"MMmMmmmm, you are goblin to care, yes you are, remember?" 27 comforted. "That is all we need. You will be good as medic, yes you will be. Just relax. Go with flow, like river."

Soon, the second pigeonhorse came to a stop next to 27 and Colb, and the two other goblins dismounted. "Hmmm, okay…" Colb whispered.

"I am… medic for group, I guess, yes?" Colb announced, introducing himself. "I go by the name of Colb."

"Rrghegh…" replied the younger goblin, whose gruff dialect reminded Colb of the Ratter tribe. "Introductions are waste of time," he continued, as he pulled up the hood of his black cloak and spat on the ground.

"AaAaaaaahhhh, but I think it is good to know who we all are before we travel for long time together, yes I do. This is Drek," 27 said as he gestured to the young goblin, "of the Ratter tribe. Why don't you tell Colb what you bring to the team, Drek?"

"Rrghegh… I have knife" replied Drek, as he briefly flashed a metal dagger from under his cloak.

"AaAaaaaahhhh yes, he is holder of knife," 27 explained, "meaning, he is strong fighter. He can protect us if there is danger, yes he can." 27 then moved his gesture to the elderly goblin. "And from the Kreet tribe, this is Stibs. He is our team expert in the skills of survival and craftsmanship!"

"Hurmph. I may be 63 years old, but I'm a fighter, too!" the old goblin yelled, as he drew a sharp sword made from teeth and bones. "I carved this myself," he continued proudly, "at the Kreet cowmammoth farm, when I was just 12 years old."

"Rrghegh… you would die in seconds if fight began," Drek said in a rough voice. "You are too old to fight anymore."

"Hurmph!" Stibs replied, lifting his sleeve to reveal a muscular arm. "You think years of heavy lifting and healthy living left me frail?"

"Yes," Drek replied, narrowing his eyes. "Old is old."

"Hurmph! Say that to my face, why don't you?" the muscular old goblin shouted, raising his sword to the challenge.

"I just did!" Drek cried back, placing a hand on his dagger, and taking a menacing step towards Stibs.

"AaAaaaaahhhh, okay there is no need to begin a brawl, gentlegoblins, no there is not," 27 interjected, jumping to stand between the two. "We are here to welcome Colb – our good medic – to the team, and then continue our journey to the hidden goldatinum!"

Drek paused, now taking a moment to look Colb over with a sharp glare. "Rrghegh… whatever," Drek said, as he turned away.

Then, with a nimble jump, the hooded goblin expertly re-mounted one of the pigeonhorses.

As Colb watched Drek's acrobatic display, 27 leaned in, whispering, "MMmMmmmm, maybe you should ride with Drek this round, and I will take Stibs, yes I will. Might be good idea to keep them separate for now, to give them time to cool off."

"Hmmm, this team seems a little… disorganized, yes?" Colb whispered back.

"You know the saying," 27 retorted calmly, as a moist bead of spit flew off his tongue and landed in Colb's ear canal. "Water under bridge, and… um, under bridge is where monsters live, yes it is. So, er… when team sees those monsters, then team will figure itself out, yes it will."

27 then took a step forward, raising his voice to address the whole goblin crew. "AaAaaaaahhhh, our team is together!" he cheered. "Next – before we truly start our journey – we must go to briefing with 1 in Yiklar. He wishes to meet all of you in-person before we set off!"

With that, the noble jumped back onto a pigeonhorse, and offered a seat to Stibs, who begrudgingly took the back seat. "Rrghegh… I guess medic is with me," Drek mumbled, offering a seat to Colb. "Try not to fall off during ride."

Colb carefully climbed onto the steed. The feathers felt warm under him, and the back of the beast was surprisingly stable. As Colb adjusted himself for a more comfortable position, 27 and Drek both suddenly let out a loud "coo, COO!" and the pigeonhorses burst into a full-on sprint. Colb instinctively grabbed on tight to the feathers below him, as the wind blew into his face and the majestic pigeonhorses sprinted through the sand. The team was off, and the adventure had begun.

After a few minutes of riding, Colb started to get used to the speed they were moving. He looked out at the blank, flat wasteland of the goblin territories. Drek silently controlled the pigeonhorse, following 27 and Stibs from a steady distance. *Hmmm, this team isn't what I expected, yes?* Colb thought to himself. *It seems fractured. I worried about being too incompetent for this adventure… now I worry that all of us might be.*

Colb looked ahead at 27, who was controlling his pigeonhorse with finesse and confidence. *I suppose everything can seem like that at first, though, yes? Hmmm… I should at least try getting to know other teammates before I judge them, yes?*

"Hmmm…" Colb muttered, deciding to start up a conversation. "…I've never been to the Ratter tribe before, yes? What's it like?"

Drek remained silent, still looking in their direction of travel. Colb snuck a peek backwards, and watched as his hometribe Skaal shrunk and faded from view. "...Skaal is good home. It is place of humble goblins, yes? Small craftsmen. Everyone contributes based on their passions. It is nice place to live."

"Rrghegh…" the young goblin replied, still keeping his eyes forward as he controlled the pigeonhorse. "Talking is waste of breath. Medic wouldn't want me to waste breath, right?"

"…Hmmm, actually, I think you should talk, yes?" Colb hesitantly replied. "It would… hmmm… make your… voice stronger. To practice using voice while riding."

Drek appeared to ponder this for a moment. "Rrghegh… I've never met medic before. If that is command for good health, I guess I will tell you of Ratter." Colb leaned in, surprised his lie was successful, and eager to get a better understanding of who this teammate was. "Ratter looks like desolate place. Paths are empty and houses deserted. But this is false appearance."

Drek jolted the pigeonhorse to the left a little bit, forcing Colb to again grip the creature tightly. "...for beneath the darkness, goblins hide in every corner. We steal. We hurt. We do what is needed to survive, every goblin for themself."

"If tribe appears empty, how did 27 find you, hmmm?" Colb asked, listening on the edge of his seat.

"Rrghegh... he didn't find me. I found him. I watched as rich goblin rode into Ratter lands, wearing valuable clothes and probably holding bags of goldatinum. I ambushed him in dark alley, with knife, to rob him, yes I did. I was ready for any violent way he might respond, but to my surprise, he wrapped around me with big hug. Was extremely disturbing. I could hear snickers from other Ratter goblins in the darkness around us."

Drek visibly shivered as he recalled the embarrassment of the whole ordeal. "Then rich goblin muttered most interesting proposition into my ear, yes he did. Probably similar thing he told you and other guy. Said he had secret mission, and needed goblin that can fight if there's danger – a goblin like me. He claimed we can find big mountain of goldatinum, just for the four of us."

Colb furrowed his brow, concerned by the mismatching story. "Hmmm, just the four of us? You mean to say, to split amongst the four tribes, yes?"

"Rrghegh... that is closer to what Yiklar goblin said, yes," Drek gruffly replied, "...but certainly you do not plan to actually share mountain of goldatinum with other goblins in your tribe?"

"Hmmm, but I do? My tribe works best when we all work together, yes it does," Colb retorted, with a hint of concern.

"Rrghegh... that is waste of good goldatinum," the hooded goblin muttered back. "With my supply, I will become king of Ratter. The closest I will come to sharing of wealth is by paying other goblins to enforce my authority, and to protect my treasure from thieves."

"Hmmm… that doesn't sound like 27's vision at all, yes?" Colb questioned. "Why do you think he invited you?"

"Rrghegh… a tribe of thieves can always find creative uses for those Yiklar trinkets. A lot of us were once big buyers of that junk. I'm sure he'll gain a little of that business back once I'm rich, since I'll be hiring some servants and guards that'll need to be well-equipped," Drek chuckled.

"Hmmm… well, I suppose I wish you luck with your plan, yes?" Colb replied, deciding that he might as well avoid Drek's bad side.

"Yes. Good luck to me," Drek agreed.

The team continued to travel until dark. As the last lick of daylight dropped below the horizon, a sudden chill washed through the wastelands. With a single "coo," Drek and 27 pulled the pigeonhorses to a stop. A moment later, two flickers of light appeared as Stibs and Drek ignited torches with a tinderbox.

As the four goblins dismounted their steeds, 27 made an announcement to the group. "AaAaaaaahhhh, our progress today was most excellent!" he cheered. "We are but three hours from Yiklar, yes we are. Tomorrow we shall see the beautiful morning sunlight reflect across the most magnificent Yiklar city walls when we arrive for debriefing with 1."

"Hurmph. Worry about that city in the morning, will ya?" Stibs grumbled. "For now, we have to set up camp."

"Rrghegh… I hate to agree with old fart, but it is time to collect food and rest," Drek rudely agreed.

"Hmmm, I can help prepare food, yes?" Colb said with a hint of excitement, feeling well in his element as a chef.

"AaAaaaaahhhh, alright then, it seems we have clearly defined roles here, yes we do!" 27 exclaimed. "Stibs and I will prepare our resting place, yes we will, while you two go hunting for food."

Drek shrugged and started to walk away from the others. "Hmmm, wait up, yes?" Colb yelped, speed-walking to stay near Drek. "Hmmm, I don't have torch, after all. Without your light source, I cannot see, yes?"

"Shhh!" Drek shushed, suddenly.

Colb instinctively put his hands over his mouth, alarmed by the abruptness of Drek's response. After a moment, Colb hesitantly whispered, "…Why?"

"Rrghegh… I said to be quiet," Drek replied. "I'm listening for prey. We can't exactly see the prey since we stopped after the sun went down, can we?"

"Hmmm, I suppose not, yes?" Colb muttered.

After the duo walked in a straight line away from the campsite for a few minutes, Drek put out the torch. "Hmmm, now it is very dark, yes?" Colb questioned.

"Rrghegh… it is as if you've never had to fend for yourself," Drek grumbled back. "There is prey nearby, and we do not want them to know our position. Rrghegh… stay here."

Colb froze in place, and listened carefully to his pitch back surroundings. He could barely hear the light footsteps of Drek, tip-toeing a few feet away from him. After a moment, there was a quick swoosh of a cloak, followed by some screeching high up in the air. An instant later, Colb heard an audible *THUMP!* in the sand nearby.

"Rrghegh… food acquired," Drek announced, re-igniting his torch. Colb craned his neck to look at the ground behind his young teammate, searching for the source of the *THUMP!* he'd heard a moment ago. Sure enough, he soon spotted two spiderbats sitting in a blood-stained patch of sand, skewered simultaneously by a single dagger. Their eight legs, some of which had wings attached, curled inwards towards their fluffy brown bodies as they succumbed to their mortal wounds.

"Rrghegh… I threw knife into sky, and got double kill," Drek proudly boasted. "This will feed team for night."

"Hmmm, let's go back, and I'll cook these, then, yes?" Colb cheered. Drek picked up his dagger, with the two bodies still attached, and agreed. With Drek's torch light guiding their way, the duo returned to the camp.

However, there wasn't exactly a camp waiting for them when they arrived. What they found was 27 and the two pigeonhorses, standing before a fine mapleoak log cabin. The flat building stood 4 ½ feet tall, and covered about a 12 ft by 12 ft square of ground – more than enough space for a team of four stout goblins. It sported an intricately carved door, a triangle-shaped log roof, and four bright windows, each about 2 feet up from the ground. "Hmmm! Where did this come from?" Colb inquired.

"AaAaaaaahhhh, are you impressed?" 27 cheered. "This right here is a highest-of-quality, Yiklar-made product for luxury in camping! It is a *Yiklar Folding Cabin*, yes it is! Most portable, and most nice. Please, enter! Stibs is already inside." 27 twisted a finely carved doorknob, then opened the entrance to a large, carpeted room, with music playing inside.

Confused but intrigued, Colb stepped into the cabin. The other goblins walked in as well, and 27 shut the door behind them from the inside. Drek strolled through the interior of the building, dumped the spiderbat bodies into the kitchen, and then fell asleep face-down in a nearby beanbag chair.

"AaAaaaaahhhh, Colb, by the look on your face I'd say this is your first time in a *Yiklar Folding Cabin*. Perhaps I shall give you the tour?"

"Hmmm, I suppose you should, yes?" Colb replied, his eyes full of wonder.

27 led Colb around the cabin, which seemed to be a party space that could easily fit 30 goblins. Although the desert night had no sunlight to shed through the cabin's windows, nevertheless the whole building – with not a torch or flame in sight – was magically lit. "The cabin has sort of open-concept, yes it does," 27 announced, gesturing to the wide, wall-free space. "Although cabin's interior is effectively one room, it's split into five sections, yes it is: a room in each of the four corners, and my favorite room in the center."

27 led Colb to the middle of the cabin, which sported a wooden dance floor. A bright disco ball hung from the ceiling of the space, and seemed to be emanating a light-hearted goblin tune played with traditional crunchy, squeaky goblin instruments. "Here in the center of the *Yiklar Folding Cabin*, we have the dance floor!" 27 cheered.

27 then gestured to some couches and a table sitting in a corner of the cabin, left of the entrance. "Now, in this corner, we have the living area, which is where we sit when we feel like being alive, yes we do," 27 continued.

"Hurmph, that's right! I'm not dead yet!" Stibs cheered as he relaxed on a living area couch.

"We also have a sleeping corner, a dining corner, and – AaAaaaaahhhh, you will like this – here in this last corner is the fully functional kitchen," 27 said with a smile, turning Colb to face one of the far corners of the cabin. Colb gaped at the advanced setup. A functioning sink, fine mapleoak cutting boards, actual plates – this cabin's kitchen was ten times better than his tavern back home.

Colb walked into the cooking area, placing his hand on the cool birchpine countertops. "Hmmm, this is very nice, yes?" Colb mumbled.

"AaAaaaaahhhh, indeed, that is because it is Yiklar-made! That is why it's of such highest-of-quality! Each item is built with the finest of Yiklar craftsmanship," 27 proclaimed, breaking out into a little dance as he spoke. "Quality defeats quantity! That is the Yikar way, after all!"

"Hmmm, how did you bring all of this here?" Colb asked.

"AaAaaaaahhhh, you are asking about details of cabin! Are you interested in purchasing a fine *Yiklar Folding Cabin* of your own?" 27 inquired, still dancing. "It's only 5,160 goldatinum pieces, 4 electronze pieces, and 7 silvopper pieces!"

"Hmmm! That's extremely expensive. But no, I'm wondering how you brought this stuff with us," Colb replied. "This cabin, and everything in it, it all seems too heavy and too big to carry, yes?"

"AaAaaaaahhhh, that is not problem, because of Yiklar-made magic enchantment on cabin," 27 responded, tapping his feet and swinging his arms.

"It is just part of my purchase of *Yiklar Folding Cabin*, yes it is! With the push of a button, I can compress entire cabin and everything in it down to small piece of wood that fits in my pocket. It is a marvel of goblin engineering, yes it is!" 27 cheered.

As he spoke, he walked backwards – continuing his dance – towards the center of the room. By the time 27 had finished his thought, he was standing on the dance floor, and his movements had tripled in intensity. "If you want to buy a *Yiklar Folding Cabin* for yourself, let me know, Colb!"

"Hmmm, it seems a little expensive for me, but I'll let you know if I change my mind, yes?" Colb replied. He then pulled a crumpled chef's hat out of his pocket, donned it, and began preparing Drek's spiderbats into a nice meal for the team.

10 minutes later, Colb plated the boiled meat and carried it to the dining area. Drek's ears perked up at the sound of food being

placed on a table, and scampered from his bean bag chair to grab something to eat. The other goblins came to the table as well.

"AaAaaaaahhhh, I have missed your cooking over the last week, Colb! This is most exquisitely prepared!" 27 said as he munched on a spiderbat wing.

"Hmmm, I found some exciting spices and minerals in the kitchen, which elevated the meal, yes?" the chef replied.

"Yes!" 27 agreed.

"Hurmph, food is food," Stibs replied. Drek said nothing other than a few grunting noises as he chowed down on a spiderbat foot.

"Well, team, tonight we feast, and we rest! For tomorrow, the true quest will begin, yes it will," 27 announced to the table.

The goblins went on to finish up their meal, then settled down for the night. Drek paced around the interior of the cabin a few times, then retired to the same bean bag chair he'd been in earlier. Colb cleaned up the kitchen, then picked out a cot in the bedding area to fall asleep in. Stibs went outside to feed some breadcrumbs to the pigeonhorses and tie them up for the night, then came back in and slept on the floor with a blanket. 27 spent his time getting comfortable on some sort of hovering pad next to Colb's cot.

"Hmmm, why's your bed doing that?" Colb muttered as he sat down on his cot.

"AaAaaaaahhhh, this is a *Yiklar Floating Bed*. It feels like you're sleeping on a cloud, yes it does!" 27 cheered. The noble goblin clapped his hands thrice, to which the room's magical lighting and disco ball shut off in response.

"You certainly have a lot of magical objects," Colb observed as he stared blankly into the darkened room.

"I like Yiklar-made things!" 27 cheered.

"Seems so!" Colb agreed.

After a few moments, Stibs let out a loud snore. Drek kicked a little bit in his beanbag chair, and seemed to be quietly drifting off as well.

Colb rolled over to face roughly where he remembered 27 to be in the dark room. "Hmmm… 27?" he whispered.

"Yes?" 27 muttered back.

"I'm a little concerned that this team isn't going to be very… competent, yes? Nobody really spoke during dinner, and the two other goblins you found seem to dislike each other," Colb worried.

"It is just first day, give them time," 27 whispered. "Quality team takes time to develop, yes it does. Just because it starts like rough piece of wood, does not mean it can't blossom into high-quality *Yiklar Folding Cabin* eventually!"

"Hmmm, okay…" Colb muttered. "…good night, yes?"

"Good night, Colb," 27 replied. With that, the goblins succumbed to sleep for the night.

As the sun poked over the horizon the next day, Colb awoke to a harsh "Coo! Coo! Coo!" of two pigeonhorses screeching outside at the morning light.

"AaAaaaaahhhh, it's the beginning of a wonderful day, yes it is!" 27 proclaimed, jumping off his hovering bed. The moment the wealthy goblin's feet hit the ground, the cabin's lights and disco ball turned on, and 27 began to dance. "MMmMmmmm, are we ready to get moving?"

"Rrghegh…" Drek mumbled in reply, not getting up from the bean bag chair.

"MMmMmmmm, you know, I've been meaning to say, that is quite peculiar noise you make, Drek, and you make it often," 27 responded. "I am not sure how your throat even creates such sound, no I am not."

"Rrghegh… is Ratter dialect. To put fear in enemy's hearts," Drek grumbled, still face-down on the bean bag chair.

"MMmMmmmm, but perhaps you would yield even more fear if you were early riser as well, yes you would," 27 retorted.

"Hurmph! That's right!" Stibs announced in a crackly voice, entering the cabin from the outside. "I've been up for three solid hours now. I've packed the supplies, sharpened my sword, prepared the pigeonhorses for departure while they slept – I even had time to catch our next meal!" The wrinkled goblin proceeded to slam a bag of dead toadroaches onto the kitchen counter. "Hurmph, and look at you," he continued, walking towards Drek. "Who's unprepared for a fight now, hurmph?! I could've slit your throat before you even woke uUAUP-" Stibs failed to finish his sentence, as a rope suddenly cinched around his leg, and pulled him towards the top of the cabin. The eyepatched goblin was left wriggling upside down. "What in the-" Stibs continued, outraged, as gravity pulled his bone sword out of his sheath and towards the floor.

"...rhe rhe rhe rhe rhe," Drek snickered, finally sitting up in the bean bag chair. "Rrghegh... one does not sleep soundly without setting a few traps first. You know... in case someone thought they could slit my throat in my sleep, or something."

"Hurmph! Get me down from here! Don't touch that!" Stibs shouted, as Drek sauntered over and picked the bone sword up off the ground.

"AaAaaaaahhhh, okay, remember guys, teammates. Teammates. We're all on same team, yes we are," 27 said, gesturing for Drek to put down the sword.

While the argument continued amongst the three goblins, Colb got off his bed, and dusted off his armor. He looked into a mirror on the wall of the sleeping area, and prepared himself for the day. *A quality team takes time,* he thought to himself, as the bickering escalated behind him. *That's what 27 said. Just give them time, yes?*

A little while later, when the goblins had gotten themselves situated and Stibs had re-claimed his bone sword, the four teammates agreed to ride their pigeonhorses in the same formation as the previous day: 27 with Stibs, and Drek with Colb.

As the goblin crew began mounting their steeds, 27 clicked a hidden button under the doorknob of his *Yiklar Folding Cabin*. With a vacuum-like sound, the entire building suddenly folded in on itself, rapidly compressing towards 27's hands. After a handful of seconds, the entire cabin was gone, and only the doorknob remained in 27's grasp.

"Cabin secured!" 27 cheered, pocketing the doorknob and jumping onto his steed with Stibs.

"Hmmm, off to Yiklar for the briefing then, yes?" Colb shouted back.

"Off we go!" 27 agreed.

"Coo, COO!" Drek and 27 shouted in unison. With a sudden jolt, the pigeonhorses began their sprint, and the crew was headed south.

Chapter 3

WELCOME TO YIKLAR

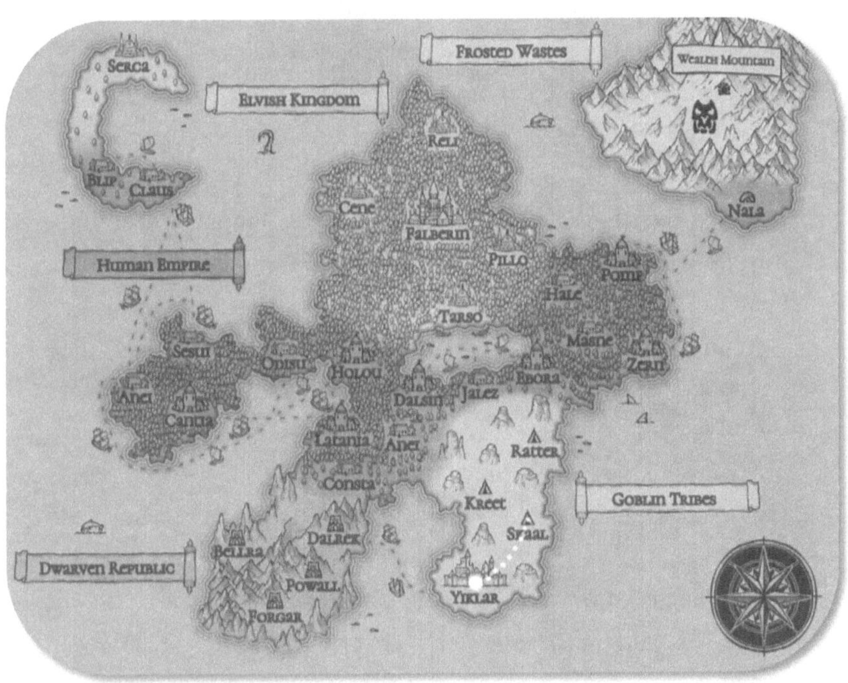

3. WELCOME TO YIKLAR

After a few hours of traveling, the goblin crew reached a beautiful city surrounded by large, brilliant castle walls. The walls were made from enormous quartzelian crystals, which had a translucent, reddish hue to them. Colb had never seen anything remotely like this back in Skaal.

"AaAaaaaahhhh, we are here! I am home, yes I am!" 27 cried out. As the goblins got closer to the city, Colb looked wide-eyed at the gleam coming off some well-polished pillars. This tribe's home was a majestic city that stood like a fortress, with a market-square town of wood and stone sitting in the heart of it. As the sun's rays flickered through the semi-transparent quartzelian walls surrounding Yiklar, a wave of rainbow-colored light sprinkled over the townsfolk. It was perhaps the most beautiful thing he'd ever seen – and quite a display of the sheer wealth held amongst the Yiklar goblins.

With a synchronized "coo" from 27 and Drek, the pigeonhorses came to a stop under a large goldatinum gate, which was wide open.

"Hurmph, why's that been left open?" Stibs questioned.

"AaAaaaaahhhh, all are welcome in Yiklar, yes they are!" 27 replied.

"Rrghegh… then why build big wall?" Drek retorted.

"AaAaaaaahhhh, because walls are beautiful, and were offered at such a reasonable price by 136," 27 replied. "He is fantastic goblin builder, yes he is!"

As the team of four dismounted their pigeonhorses, a goblin wearing a nose ring and fine studded leather sauntered up with a friendly smile. "AAAaaaaaaahhhhhh, customers!" she cheered in a singsong voice. "Welcome to Yiklar! I can tell that at least one of you is from around here – yes I can – so certainly you're aware that animals are not allowed inside Yiklar's walls?"

"AaAaaaaahhhh, I am indeed aware of such a rule! How else would Yiklar remain so clean and easy to do business in?" 27 replied. "Might you be here to sell us a solution?"

"AAAaaaaaahhhhhh, that is most wisest of observation, yes it is, as I am indeed the perfect goblin to be talking to about this!" she cheered, keeping her body language open and friendly. "I am 578, and I offer the *Yiklar Steed Holder Service*, yes I do! I can take care of your steeds for 1 goldatinum piece, 2 electronze pieces, and 1 silvopper piece per day, yes I can, or you can request 1 electronze piece and 3 silvopper pieces per hour if you're not staying for long."

"Wow! That is most reasonable of deal!" 27 exclaimed.

"Rrghegh… it's a weirdly specific price," Drek grumbled.

"AaAaaaaahhhh, Drek, that is the Yiklar way," 27 replied. "Yiklar goblins must give specific prices because we trade in specific goods! We must calculate the exact perfect deal to save you the most money while still providing the highest-quality good at a most humble of profit," 27 continued. "This does not add up to an even amount usually, no it does not."

578 agreed with 27's statement. After the other goblins pointed out that 27 technically owned both pigeonhorses, the yellow-eyed noble fronted the cost for two hours of lodging. With that, the four goblins were now on foot as they head into the main city.

"AaAaaaaahhhh, it is nice to be back in Yiklar, yes it is," 27 announced to the team. "We must head to the main tower in the center of city to meet with 1 for the debriefing that he has requested we come to. Then, we can start our journey."

As the crew walked towards an obvious large tower painted with goldatinum, Colb looked around. The Yiklar tribe was a bustling society of commerce and trade. Goblins walked around everywhere: some buying, some selling, some just having a nice day. Everyone seemed to be wearing more expensive clothes than he'd ever known, from extravagant, feather-covered costumes to simple robes of fine silk, like 27's preferred apparel.

As the crew continued to walk, Colb read the signs on various stalls set up throughout the market-city, and listened to the hustle and bustle of the crowd. Colb saw a *Yiklar Cuisine* booth, offering "fine foods for reasonable prices," which intrigued him. There was also a *Yiklar Tours* booth, offering tours of the city for 5 electronze pieces and 6 silvopper pieces. Under a sign labeled "*Yiklar News*," an older goblin handed out a small white stack of parchment to anyone that walked up to him.

"Rrghegh... check out that booth," Drek pointed out.

He gestured to a goblin calling into the crowd, "*Yiklar Dating Service* booth! Fill out a form to be matched with the goblin or dwarf of your dreams!"

"Rrghegh... with a booth like that, you could spend every night with a new partner," Drek continued with a smile.

"MMmMmmmm, I think that's not the point of that booth," 27 replied. "The *Yiklar Dating Service* is meant to help you find your one true love, yes it is."

"Rrghegh... I don't know why anyone would use it that way," Drek grumbled.

It seemed that every corner and alley in this market-city had been swiped up as real-estate for some sort of marketable scheme.

"Hmmm, what's that?" Colb asked, pointing out a section of large, block-shaped buildings just past a *Yiklar Produce* display.

"AaAaaaaahhhh, those are the *Yiklar Factories*, yes they are. That's where Yiklar goblins manufacture many of the high-quality goods that I personally sell."

"How about that?" Colb questioned further, now pointing out a brilliant tower surrounded by staircases. Young goblins in bright red robes surrounded the building, talking to each other and practicing strange movements with hammers and wands.

"AaAaaaaahhhh, that the beloved *Yiklar University*, where I learned how to be a good businessgoblin," 27 cheered. "I remember the wonderful days of memorizing the various good deals, recommended prices, and annual special offers for every Yiklar-made good. It's also where our architectgoblins learn to enchant and invent the latest-and-greatest of products."

After a little bit more walking, the goblin crew arrived at the tallest tower in the center of the market-city. "We are here!" 27 cheered. "We've arrived at the office of 1, also known as Yiklar's greatest businessgoblin!"

"Hurmph! What makes him the best?" Stibs inquired.

"AaAaaaaahhhh, this is something I have studied for long time myself, yes it is. I believe he's the best because he's created a unique business strategy which no other goblin has mastered the way he has," 27 replied.

"Hmmm, what's that?" Colb questioned.

"He calls it investing, yes he does," 27 responded. "He spends money on things, which obviously makes him lose money right now, but then somehow he knows that what he spent money on will actually bring him new, higher value in the future! I just don't understand how he knows which things to buy, no I do not. I just spent some value on storing our pigeonhorses, yes I did, but I don't expect 578 to pay me more money once we return to retrieve the steeds."

"Hmmm, that is confusing, yes?" Colb somberly replied. Colb had never spent even a silvopper piece on something that didn't seem immediately beneficial. If 27 didn't understand everything going on in the Yiklar tribe, then Colb was completely out of his element here.

While Colb stood around feeling confused, 27 knocked on the door, which was immediately opened by a pair of goblin guards. The team was then led into the tower, up three flights of stairs, and into a throne room with fine carpets and a goldatinum chair. Sitting upon the chair was a middle-aged goblin with a monocle. He had a red bag in his lap, and a fine mapleoak table set up in front of him.

"AaAaAaAaaAaAhhhhh, the team's all here!" the throne-sat goblin announced, lifting his arms to the heavens. "Allow me to give you somewhere to sit."

The goblin picked up the red bag in his lap with one hand, and dumped in a handful of coins with the other. Immediately, the bag began to magically expand. After only a second, four large chairs erupted out of the bag, each landing on the ground with a *THUD!*

Impressed, the group approached the set of magically summoned chairs, and sat down. Once they were seated, the monocled goblin clapped his hands together with a smile, and began to speak.

"AaAaAaAaaAaAhhhhh, it is good to meet all of you! Thank you for coming all this way for my briefing meeting. I believe it is good for me to physically see who is getting sent out on this mission with 27, yes it is."

1 took off his eyepiece, quickly rubbed it clean on his robe, and put it back on – squinting with his monocled-eye to get a better look at the four goblins.

"Allow me to introduce myself. I am 1, head of the Yiklar tribe," the goblin explained in a refined manner. Colb looked at his fellow teammates to gauge how they were reacting to this. 27 had bowed his head a little, as if honored to be in 1's presence.

Stibs and Drek sat comfortably, gazing around the room at the fine carpets and paintings rather than focusing on the refined goblin that was addressing the team.

"I am most excited to see this group that 27 has formed, yes I am," 1 continued. "As I am sure he explained, we are looking to flood each goblin tribe with wealth, to stimulate the commerce amongst our lands, yes we are."

1 dropped a fairly sizable handful of coins into his red sack, then pulled out a curled sheet of parchment. "AaAaAaAaaAaAhhhhh, so I will get right to the point, yes I will. Take a look at this *Yiklar Map of Finding Location*."

1 unfurled the paper, revealing a detailed map of the world. It displayed nations Colb had never even heard of – from a kingdom of elves to a strange, crescent-shaped island. "In the top right corner of the map, there is mountain, yes there is," 1 continued. "We have labeled it *Wealth Mountain*."

Colb moved his gaze to a mountain in the northeastern corner, which had a dangerous-looking skull painted next to it. "Our most spectacular oracle, 67, has seen this mountain in a vision using her most rarest *Yiklar Telescope of Extrasensory Discovery*," 1 continued. "She tells me this mountain contains more goldatinum than any of us have ever seen in our entire lives!" 1 exclaimed.

"Now, my original plan to boost our economies was to flood each tribe with my own wealth, yes it was, but I soon discovered that I wouldn't have enough to make a meaningful difference for each individual goblin," 1 explained. "The amount of goldatinum in this mountain, though – it is enough to give each goblin in every tribe hundreds of goldatinum pieces for themselves! It doesn't even have to be mined, either – 67 says it's all just loosely sitting around inside the mountain, ripe for the taking! From what some of the greatest minds at *Yiklar University* have calculated, this mountain contains the perfect amount to stimulate purchasing of Yiklar-made goods, without going overboard and making the currency worthless. Thus, your mission is to reach this mountain, divide that goldatinum into four equal piles, and bring the piles to each of the goblin tribes, yes it is."

"Hmmm," Colb replied hesitantly, looking at the map. "What is this, yes?" He pointed at the skull painted next to Wealth Mountain on the map.

"AaAaAaAaaAaAhhhhh, yes, you have most strong sense of sight, yes you do!" 1 praised. "That is another thing 67 foresaw, yes it is. She tells me there is perhaps some danger near Wealth Mountain. We have no idea what the nature of it is, no we do not. All we know is that she could hear some horrible, deep howl coming from that area when she held the *Yiklar Telescope of Prophesy* up to her ear. Her best guess was that some large beast lives in that frigid mountain range, which may pose a problem for you when extracting the goldatinum from Wealth Mountain."

Colb sat back in his seat, befuddled by 1's calmness as he explained that.

"Rrghegh... so how do we get by this giant beast?" Drek grumbled. "I want to get to the goldatinum."

"AaAaAaAaaAaAhhhhh, that is the spirit, yes it is!" 1 cheered.

"Hurmph! Let's just kill it!" Stibs threw in. "Easy solution."

"AaAaAaAaaAaAhhhhh, that is indeed the plan, if it is necessary," 1 replied.

"Hmmm... if we don't know anything about the nature of this monster, how can we feel confident we'll be able to kill it?" Colb inquired.

"MmMmMmMmMmmmm, this is good point," 1 agreed. "I do not want to send you into an unwinnable situation. This is why, I have idea to ensure you cannot be overwhelmed by any single monster, yes I do."

Drek's ears perked up. "Rrghegh… do you have some kind of super armor for us?" he asked.

"That is close guess," 1 praised, "but I was thinking of something more on the offensive. Our most excellent architectgoblin, 84, has invented a theoretical *Yiklar Spear of Irreversible Death* in collaboration with some dwarves in Bellra." 1 gestured to the map again, this time pointing out a dwarven town west of Yiklar, which sat just beyond a sizeable body of water and a mountain-ridden patch of land.

"The *Yiklar Spear of Irreversible Death* started out as simple research idea from 84, but after some tactical diplomacy and ingenuity, it's looking like it will become a reality within the next week," 1 continued. "84 requested I find someone to test out his superweapon, and I think that is good coincidence since your mission may be dangerous and require something powerful to give you an edge. If you all go to Bellra to pick up this spear – which I've already paid for – before heading to Wealth Mountain, you can use it as you see fit."

"Hurmph… how does it work? What exactly makes you say this *Yiklar Spear of Irreversible Death* is a superweapon?" Stibs inquired.

"The idea is," 1 replied, "no method, magical or not, can prevent or reverse the death of a creature that has been struck by the *Yiklar Spear of Irreversible Death*. This way, no matter how powerful some monster might be – if it can heal itself, or it's really tough, or it can raise itself from the dead – no matter what powers or magic it has, nothing will make a difference. You will be able to permanently kill any monster with one single strike! The spear will only be possible to use once, though, so make it count if you do end up throwing it at something."

"Hmmm, how are you making such a weapon?" Colb inquired.

"AaAaAaAaaAaAhhhhh, that is trade secret of Yiklar, yes it is. Just know the spear will be of the highest quality, and is unfortunately very expensive to make, so we only can offer you one," 1 replied.

"However, the *Yiklar Spear of Irreversible Death* is not the only investment I'm making into your mission today." Colb noticed 27's eyes widened at the mention of investment. "I have prepared a free, high-quality, Yiklar-produced item for each of you, yes I have, to aid you on your quest to Wealth Mountain!"

Drek leaned forward immediately. "Rrghegh… free stuff, you say?"

"AaAaAaAaaAaAhhhhh, yes, that is what I said!" 1 replied with a cheer. "First, this map, it is for you, Stibs."

"Hurmph! A map? I can just make my own maps!" Stibs grumbled, rejecting the gift.

"AaAaAaAaaAaAhhhhh, but this is not ordinary map, no it is not!" 1 replied. "It is a magical *Yiklar Map of Finding Location*! To activate it, you just hold it and say: whereami?"

"Where am I?" Stibs repeated.

"No no no, it is one word: whereami. Say that whenever you're lost, and the map will magically find your position!" 1 cheered.

Stibs shrugged. "Hurmph, alright. If you say it's magic, I suppose I'll hold onto it." The old goblin folded up the parchment and stashed it in his backpack.

"AaAaAaAaaAaAhhhhh, most good! And you," 1 turned to Colb. "For you, I have an item which will aid in your understanding of the creatures around you, yes it will." The goblin pulled out another handful of coins, poured it all into his red sack, then pulled out an amulet with a white crystal on it. He placed the item around Colb's neck. "With this *Yiklar Amulet of Open Ears*, you can understand the spoken language of humans, dwarves, and elves. Although it will not teach you their language, and so you cannot easily reply to them, this at least gives the team a set of ears which understands what's happening while you're in foreign territories."

Colb placed a hand on the pure crystal, and moved it around in his fingers. "AaAaaaaahhhh, I remember taking a class about humans as an extracurricular at *Yiklar University*," 27 cheered. "During which, I learned their native language: Hewmish! Fascinating way to speak, yes it is."

"AaAaAaAaaAaAhhhhh, perfect, then the two of you can work together to communicate with humans during your journey," 1 replied. "And when you pass through dwarf territory, or if you run into some elves, Colb will understand what they are saying as well!"

"Hmmm, thank you for the gift, yes?" Colb replied.

"Of course! It is an investment to ensure the success of this team," 1 replied. "Speaking of, my next item is for you, goblin of the Ratter tribe." 1 poured some more coins into his red sack, then pulled out a wooden hunting bow and a single arrow with a flowing, silvery color.

"*Free stuff, free stuff!*" Drek chanted with excitement.

"MmMmMmMmMmmmm, yes, this is for you," 1 continued. "A rare *Yiklar Bow of Returning Arrow*. This bow comes with a single iridhodium arrow, which is an extremely rare and expensive metal. We've enchanted this single piece of ammunition such that it will always return to you after you fire it, yes it will."

"Rhe, like boomerang?" Drek questioned.

"AaAaAaAaaAaAhhhhh, precisely – but with an absolute *guarantee* that it will always return!" 1 replied. Drek happily accepted the bow and arrow.

"Finally, for you, 27," 1 continued, turning his gaze to the team's noble. "Please present your sack." 27 opened his cloak, clicked his green bag off his belt, and placed it on the table. 1 pushed it to the side, then placed the red sack at that spot on the table instead. 27's eyes widened. "I am promoting your sack to the *Yiklar Bag of Traveling Inventory*. From anywhere in the world, you can now sell anything that is made by the *Yiklar Factories*, yes you can. Whenever you want to offer someone a good deal or special offer on an item, just drop the payment into this sack, and the product will be magically pulled straight from the *Yiklar Factories* into your bag."

Tears welled up in 27's eyes. "This… I am of such… high honored," he replied, carefully picking up the red sack.

"While you are traveling across the world for the sake of Yiklar, I thought it was only right that you should be able to spread some of our fantastic deals along the way," 1 cheered with a smile.

"Now, all of you. With your *Yiklar Map of Finding Location*, *Yiklar Amulet of Open Ears*, *Yiklar Bow of Returning Arrow*, and *Yiklar Bag of Traveling Inventory*, go! Go, and complete your quest! Pick up the *Yiklar Spear of Irreversible Death* from Bellra, then get that Wealth Mountain goldatinum for all the goblin tribes!"

"Yes, thank you!" 27 replied, crying. "We will not let you down!"

Colb cradled the white crystal hanging from his neck. It was kind of 1 to give him a gift like this. An amulet imbued with magic must not have been cheap. *Hmmm. I'll do my best not to let him down either, yes?* Colb thought to himself. *I don't want to disappoint someone so generous.*

He looked up at 1, who smiled as if he'd just read Colb's mind. *Hmmm. Perhaps that's why he requested this meeting in the first place,* Colb pondered. *After all, 27 could've just briefed us, and given us these items. I suppose 1's personal touch might've been a calculated move, to give an extra sense of importance to this mission, yes?*

Colb glanced at the shield he'd purchased back in Skaal, from a blacksmithing goblin that seemed on the verge of going out-of-business. *Hmmm, fair enough – this mission is important. I'm going to try to do everything I can to make sure we succeed. For the sake of my community in the Skaal tribe, yes?*

With that, the goblin crew hopped out of their chairs. They then descended the stairs of the goldatinum-painted tower, their heads held high as they felt newly equipped and truly prepared to start their adventure.

Chapter 4

DALREK TREK

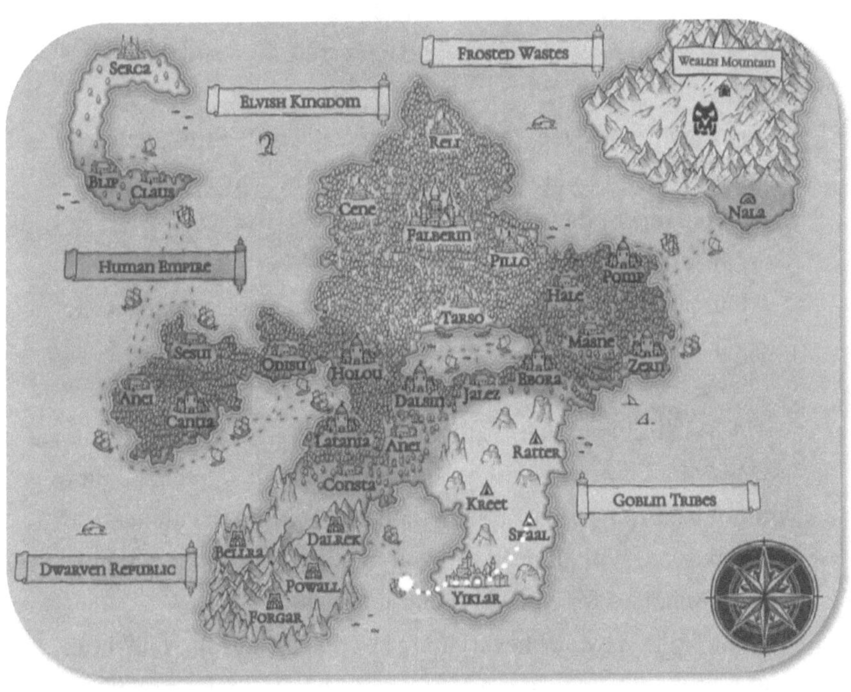

4. DALREK TREK

After the successful encounter with 1, the goblin crew went back to the main market square of the Yiklar tribe, ready to set off on the first part of their quest.

"Hurmph, Bellra's pretty far west on the map," Stibs announced. "If we're going there for the magic spear, we should start by going to the dwarven town of Dalrek by boat. From Dalrek, we can get to Bellra on foot."

"Great! I know a guy who sells highest-quality boats," 27 replied. "We'll pick up the pigeonhorses from 578, and then be on our way."

"Hurmph! Let me stop you right there," Stibs retorted. "Pigeonhorses are notoriously fearful of water. It is not a good idea to put one of those things on a boat."

"Oh… that's unfortunate," 27 replied.

"Hmmm, what if we trade the pigeonhorses for a boat?" Colb pitched. "That will give them good home, and will give us boat, yes?"

"AaAaaaaahhhh, that is true," 27 replied, scratching his chin. "MMmMmmmm, they will not be worth enough, though, no they will not be. For a highest-quality, Yiklar-made boat with magical properties, we will all need to pitch in some funds in addition to the pigeonhorses for a good purchase of boat."

"Hurmph! Why must everything be so luxurious for you? I can craft a boat with some logs and these two hands," Stibs exclaimed proudly, shoving his wrinkly, beaten hands in 27's face. "Let's trade the pigeonhorses for some raw materials, and I'll make us a boat in just a few hours. I've done it before, and I can do it now!"

27 appeared hesitant at this idea, but Colb and Drek supported it, curious to see if Stibs could really build a boat that fast.

Outvoted, 27 led the goblin crew to 949, a seller of raw materials.

"AAAAAHHHHHHH, 27! Why, you've been promoted to carry a *Yiklar Bag of Traveling Inventory*, yes you have!" screamed a short, middle-aged goblin wearing a construction hat. "What brings you to my shop, when your companions could just order products directly from you with your magic bag, yes they could?"

"AaAaaaaahhhh, yes, well, we've come to barter items for items instead of simple money-based transaction. Plus, it's nice to see a friend from *Yiklar University* again!" 27 replied.

"AAAAAHHHHHHHH, wonderful! You come to me with a custom offer, then?" 949 inquired.

"AaAaaaaahhhh, yes, it is most custom," 27 confirmed. "We have two pigeonhorses at the *Yiklar Steed Holder Service*, yes we do, and wanted to trade them for some raw materials to build a boat."

"MMMMMMMMM, that is a most intriguing offer, 27. However, I have a pigeonhorse of my own at the *Yiklar Steed Holder Service* already, yes I do," 949 replied. "I don't need two more, no I do not."

"Oh," 27 said. "MMmMmmmm, that's disappointing, yes it is."

"Hurmph! Well, what *do* you need? Maybe we can work something out here," Stibs threw in.

949 thought for a moment. "MMMMMMMMM, well, I do have a bit of negotiation problem with another goblin right now, yes I do. I could use help persuading him to see my side?"

27 nodded his head. "AaAaaaaahhhh, I can be persuasive, yes I can be," 27 cheered. "I am a merchant of high-quality goods, after all! That takes a little bit of a silvopper tongue!"

"AAAAAHHHHHHHH, sounds promising!" 949 shouted.

"MMMMMMMMMM, okay. Well, I've been having a problem with 789 recently, yes I have been. He's increased his prices on bismuthslate from the *Yiklar Quarry*. It's been making it tough for me to upsell those raw materials, yes it has been. It used to be 5 electronze per pound of bismuthslate, but now it's up to 8. Convince him to bring the price down – back to no more than 5 electronze – and I'll reward you with some wood fresh from the *Yiklar Mapleoak Farm*."

"MMmMmmmm, alright, it is deal," 27 cheered. The noble goblin stuck out his hand, shaking on the proposition with 949.

With that, 27 led his teammates to another part of the city, where a group of dusty goblins were moving rocks out of *Yiklar Quarry* and onto a wooden wagon.

"AaAaaaaahhhh, laborers of stone," 27 said, announcing his presence to the workforce. "Where might I find 789?"

Three of the goblins pointed towards a nearby straw hut, which sat precariously near the edge of a mined-out quarry hole. 27 waltzed into the hut, with Stibs and Drek trailing behind him. Colb stayed behind, nervous to enter a structure so close to a gap in the earth.

"Hmmm…" Colb muttered, sheepishly inspecting the mine from afar. "Why is that hole so wide and so deep, yes?" he asked one of the laborers.

"MmMmmmMm, we're in desert, yes we are," the goblin replied matter-of-factly. "You've got to dig deep to find bismuthslate under all this sand, yes you do."

"Hmmm, I see," Colb replied. "I go by the name of Colb, by the way. What is your name?"

"My name is 255,861, yes it is," the goblin replied, still loading chunks of bismuthslate rocks onto a wagon.

"That's a long number, yes?" Colb inquired.

"MmMmmmMm, don't remind me," 255,861 mumbled. "If I had the honor of a lower-digit name, I wouldn't be lugging rocks all day, now, would I? No, I would not."

"Hmmm, well I like your name," Colb cheered. "The high number sounds powerful, yes? It makes me feel like you could do anything you set your mind to, yes?"

255,861 rolled his eyes, and went back to stacking rocks silently. Moments later, 27 and the rest of his crew exited the hut.

"AaAaaaaahhhh, we did it, yes we did!" 27 cheered as he approached Colb.

"Hurmph! More like I did it," Stibs clarified.

"This is true, this is true," 27 admitted. "Colb, it turns out that 789 has been struggling to keep up with booming demand for his good bismuthslate business. Stibs connected him with second supplier in Kreet, which will help to alleviate that issue."

"Rrghegh… but that wasn't enough," Drek grumbled.

"AaAaaaaahhhh, yes, yes, 789 was concerned he didn't have a means of quickly traveling to-and-from Kreet – so, we made special deal! 789 promised to offer permanent preferential discounts to 949 – never to exceed 5 electronze per pound of bismuthslate – and in exchange, we yielded to him our two pigeonhorses at the *Yiklar Steed Holder Service*, yes we did!"

"Hmmm, good job!" Colb praised. With that, the team turned to walked back towards 949's shop.

Colb paused, looked back at the laborers, and checked his pockets for any goldatinum he might be able to give them. *They deserve a tip for helping us find 789*, he thought. Unfortunately, his pockets came up empty, as he'd left everything with Vrel before leaving Skaal.

He looked back toward his teammates, who seemed eager to return to 949. *Another time*, Colb thought to himself, catching up with the crew.

"AAAAAHHHHHHH, excellent, excellent, excellent!" 949 cheered after 27 delivered the good news. "Take anything you want! I'm happy to oblige!"

Stibs rubbed his hands together excitedly as he went through the scraps of wood in 949's yard. He pulled out long mapleoak poles, stout wooden blocks, and various planks from the piles. "Hurmph, you said anything I want, right? Can I take some stuff that isn't wood?" he asked.

949 nodded, to which Stibs shoved some string and some chunks of flintcoal into his backpack. After Stibs finished looting what he needed from 949's shop, the goblin crew said their goodbyes, and headed to *Yiklar Port*.

Stibs worked for a few hours, rapidly scraping together a rowboat with the planks of wood. Additionally, he carved a set of paddles with his wood blocks, string, and wooden poles. While he did this, the others left for a meal – paid for by 27 – at *Yiklar Cuisine*, which they found to be quite suitable. The chefs in Yiklar were certainly up-to-par with Colb's skill level, if not a little better. 27 still held that Colb was his favorite chef, though.

After a short while, the trio of goblins regrouped with Stibs at *Yiklar Port*. Colb handed the old goblin a packet of cowmammoth jerky when they arrived, since Stibs hadn't joined them for the meal at *Yiklar Cuisine*.

Stibs accepted the meat, then presented his shoddy, quickly-built boat to the group. It was a small 4-goblin canoe, with hand-crafted paddles. "Hurmph, not bad for only a few hours, eh?" he asked. "I didn't even use all the materials!" Stibs opened his backpack, presenting the chunks of flintcoal, some leftover string, and a couple of wooden poles that stuck out the top of the bag.

"MMmMmmmm, that boat…," 27 replied, "it… does seem to

float." 27 stared at the mass of wood bobbing up and down in the water with a face of horror. "…But maybe we should stay in Yiklar for little longer, so you have time to really polish it off, yes we should."

"Hurmph, nonsense! She's sea-ready right now!" Stibs replied, giving the side of the boat a slap, which sent a creaking sound throughout the whole thing. While 27 and Stibs spoke, Colb and Drek climbed onto the boat.

"MMmMmmmm, well it might take a long time to paddle far, though," 27 continued to stall. "Perhaps we should hire an architectgoblin to enchant the boat, so it can magically propel itself, yes we should."

"Hurmph! You haven't seen me paddle, boy!" Stibs defiantly replied, jumping into the boat. "I'm strong as a hawkbear! I'll get us across this sea no problem!"

Once again outvoted, 27 hesitantly entered the boat, and Stibs launched the team out to sea. True to his word, the old goblin paddled with rigor, moving the crew surprisingly speedily through the waters.

After a day of rowing, land was far from sight. The sun was low in the sky, and an audible grumble came from Drek's stomach. "Rrghegh… stop moving the boat. It's hunting time," he announced, standing up. The young goblin looked around at the water and sky, scanning for prey.

"Hurmph, I suppose this is good a place as any to rest for the night," Stibs agreed, stopping the vessel. The old goblin pulled out his *Yiklar Map of Finding Location*, and took a look at it.

"Whereami…" he grumbled. Suddenly, the parchment glimmered with a bright light. After a few moments, the light faded, leaving behind a white mark on the map.

The mark sat somewhere in the peppersalt sea, several miles

west of Yiklar. "Seems to work," Stibs observed with approval. "Looks like we made good progress today." He pulled the paddles into the boat as he spoke.

"Hmmm, we should order food through *Yiklar Cuisine*, or at least buy some ingredients for me to make us a meal, yes?" Colb inquired, glancing at 27's fancy new *Yiklar Bag of Traveling Inventory*.

"MMmMmmmm, this bag is not infinitely powerful, no it is not," 27 replied, patting the magical red sack. "You heard what 1 said when he gave it to me. I can sell you highest-of-quality items from the *Yiklar Factories*, but that's it. Stalls like *Yiklar Cuisine* and *Yiklar Produce* are entirely separate, independent businesses. We must be in Yiklar to purchase from them."

"Rrghegh, then we shall hunt for our food!" Drek cheered.

"Hurmph… there's signs of seagullfish in this area," Stibs observed. "We'll find 'em if we watch the waters. I'll make some seagullfishing poles with my remaining materials." The eyepatched goblin pulled the wooden poles and string out of his backpack.

"Rrghegh… no need," Drek said with a smile, pulling out his *Yiklar Bow of Returning Arrow*. "I bet I could catch way more seagullfish than you if I use this."

"Hurmph! You're on!" Stibs challenged.

Drek loaded his bow with the fancy iridhodium arrow. "May the better goblin win," he jeered.

Drek went silent, listening to the sea. Colb looked around at the waters. For a little while, things were peaceful and quiet. Colb felt calmed by the subtle wishwash of the sea. Then, as Stibs was putting the finishing touches on his seagullfishing pole, Drek suddenly fired into the water. "Hurmph, there goes your one arrow," Stibs muttered slyly.

After a moment, with a swish and a splash, the arrow flew back out of the water from where it came, with three seagullfish skewered to it. With lightning-fast reflexes, Drek caught the arrow out of the air, and slid the three seagullfish onto the floor of the boat. "Rrghegh... you were saying?" he said with a grin. Annoyed, Stibs cast his line, and the battle was on.

While Stibs seagullfished and Drek hunted, Colb started cupping some peppersalt seawater with his hands, then rubbing it into the wounded seagullfish on the floor of the boat. "What are you up to?" 27 inquired.

"Hmmm, I'm pushing more peppersalt into the seagullfish, yes?" Colb replied. "If we treat their insides with peppersalt, their meat will last us a long time."

"AaAaaaaahhhh, look at you with your fancy chef tricks! Allow me to help," 27 offered with a smile.

For the next hour, while the two goblins continued to catch seagullfish, Colb taught 27 how to boil the seawater with a cup and torch to extract more concentrated peppersalt, then use that peppersalt to treat the seagullfish into long-lasting rations. By the end of the hour, the team had accrued many days' worth of rations from 34 seagullfish: 28 of which Drek caught, and 6 of which Stibs caught.

"Rhe rhe rhe," Drek snickered, "I think there is clear winner." Stibs turned red in the face.

"AaAaaaaahhhh, do not feel bad, Stibs. It was unfair. He was using a Yiklar-made item, which is an incredibly high-quality tool, so of course he won," 27 said.

"Hurmph! My craftsmanship is just as good!" Stibs yelled, standing up. "You must've cheated!"

"Rhe rhe rhe," Drek snickered again, "just accept your loss, old goblin."

"Hurmph, at least I'm not a weak little child!" Stibs jeered back.

"Rrghegh… weak, eh? How about you and me elbow wrestle, right here, right now?"

Stibs froze, then smiled widely. "Hurmph! Let's."

27 let out a sigh as the two goblins bickered. "Quality team takes time," be muttered to himself, rubbing peppersalt over a set of rations. Colb frowned at the display, let out a sigh of his own, and went back to preparing the seagullfish as well.

While Colb and 27 worked, Stibs and Drek met at the middle of the boat. They each put one fist to their neck, extending an elbow, then approached each other until their elbows touched.

"Rrghegh… first to get pushed into the water is weaker goblin," Drek said.

"Hurmph! I know how to play the game," Stibs replied coolly.

"Go!" Drek yelled, and the two pushed their elbows into each other. With a swift motion, Stibs easily overpowered the young goblin, and sent him tumbling off the boat. Drek dropped his hands, grabbing onto the edge of the canoe as he nearly fell into the sea. He swiftly redirected his momentum, flopping back onto the boat instead of into the water. An audible crack could be heard under him as he hit the floor of the wooden vessel.

"Rrghegh… you got lucky," Drek said, standing up. "Rrghegh… why are my feet wet?"

"Hurmph! Sounds like your legs must've hit the water. That means you were pushed overboard. You lose!" Stibs announced.

"No, no, I mean…" Drek replied, looking down. The other three goblins followed his gaze to a crack in the boat, right at the spot Drek had flopped onto, which was rapidly pulling water into the vessel.

All four of them widened their eyes in a panic. "We're

sinking!" Drek yelped, rushing to a higher point on the boat. Water continued to flow in from the crack. Stibs ripped a rag off his clothes, and shoved it into the opening. This slowed, but did not stop, the onslaught of water. "Medic!" Drek shouted. "Heal the boat!"

"Hmmm, but medic is only for healing living creatures, yes?" Colb questioned.

"Rrghegh – just come up with something! We're gonna die!" Drek cried.

"Hmmm…" Colb thought for a moment. "If you spill water in the kitchen, you need a rag to soak it up," he pitched.

"Hurmph, I already did that," Stibs retorted.

"Oh…" Colb said, "...hmmm, right. How about we make another crack near the first crack? So, the water enters from the first crack, then leaks back out of the second crack?"

The four goblins looked at each other. "That could work," Drek agreed. 27 shrugged.

"Hurmph! Are you guys joking?" Stibs yelped, water now covering his toes. "That doesn't make any sense at all!"

"Rrghegh, you're outvoted 3-to-1," Drek announced, "and it makes sense to me." The young goblin kneeled at another spot on the bottom of the boat, pulled out his dagger, held it high in the sky, and crashed it down, stabbing a fresh crack into another part of the boat. Immediately, more water started flowing in from the second crack. "Wha-this just made it worse!" Drek cried.

"Hmmm, maybe the water comes in from the second crack, and flows out from the original one now, yes?" Colb theorized.

Stibs pulled his rag out of the first crack, and more water started flowing in. "Hurmph! What a surprise! That didn't work either," he jeered.

As the water level began to rise at an accelerated pace, the goblins shivered with panic. "Stop adding more water to the boat!" Drek cried out as a bead of sweat dripped off Colb's nose and landed in the canoe.

Meanwhile, 27 scanned the horizon with his eyes. "AaAaaaaahhhh, look! We're saved," 27 announced, pointing out a large dwarven trade ship in the distance.

"Rrghegh… there's no way they'll see our small boat from out there," Drek worried. "We're doomed."

"Hurmph, we just need a flare! Something to get their attention! I've got my tinderbox from home, as well as some flintcoal from 949. Does anyone have gunpowder?" Stibs shouted as he rummaged through his backpack.

The goblins all looked at 27. "AaAaaaaahhhh, yes, I do believe I can sell us a gunpowder horn for 2,210 goldatinum pieces, 8 electronze pieces, and 8 silvopper pieces."

"What?! That's so expensive!" Drek cried out.

"It is a rare gunpowder horn with special magical properties, yes it is," 27 shouted back.

"Make it cheaper!" Drek yelled.

"I can't! This gunpowder horn is normally 5,065 goldatinum pieces, 9 electronze pieces, and 4 silvopper pieces. It's already on special offer today; to stack a second custom offer on top of the current special offer is not the Yiklar way!"

"WE'RE GOING TO DIE!" Drek yelled.

"Well, what money do we all have?!" 27 shouted back.

The team pooled their money, careful not to drop their metallic nuggets into the water – which was steadily creeping up their legs. Between Drek and Stibs, they had 18 goldatinum pieces, 4 electronze pieces, and 9 silvopper pieces. Colb, having left all his money back in Skaal with Vrel, could only offer his wooden shield into the mix.

"Hmmm, I bought that for 10 goldatinum pieces, yes?" Colb pitched.

"The *Yiklar Bag of Traveling Inventory* only accepts direct money," 27 responded.

"Hurmph! Either way, we're short by a lot," Stibs worried.

The water was up to their knees now, and the boat was alarmingly close to falling completely underwater. "Where's your contribution, rich goblin?!" Stibs shouted. "Can't you pull some coins out of that magic bag?"

"AaAaaaaahhhh, yes I can, but I need to be purchasing a good in order to do so," 27 replied.

"WE ARE PURCHASING A GOOD!" Drek shouted, starting to freak out as the water approached his knees.

"No, I cannot buy from myself, that makes no sense! The bag will only summon goldatinum when I am making a deal with another seller," 27 replied.

"Oh! Idea! Colb!" 27 pointed at Colb. "Sell me those seagullfish rations we just prepared! I love to purchase your fine meals!"

Colb held out the pile of seagullfish rations, offering them to 27. "AaAaaaaahhhh, wow, what spectacular deal! You say these are only…" 27 counted on his fingers, muttering as if doing some math in his head, "…2,192 goldatinum pieces, 3 electronze pieces, and 9 silvopper pieces? What an excellent offer!"

Colb frowned. "Hmmm, that's more than my tavern makes in a whole year. I'll admit, this is a lot of food, but your offer is simply far too much, yes?"

"JUST ACCEPT IT!" Stibs and Drek yelled in unison. Colb reactively gave the pile of rations to 27, who shoved them under his arm as he summoned a fat pile goldatinum, electronze, and silvopper nuggets from his bag in response. 27 carefully poured the money in Colb's hands, and Drek and Stibs placed their money into the chef's arms as well.

"Now," 27 continued, the water starting to come in over the edges of the boat as they sank further. "AaAaaaaahhhh, customer! You say you wish to purchase our special offer of the *Yiklar Gunpowder Horn of Coralwhale Summoning*? It's normally 5,065 goldatinum pieces, 9 electronze pieces, and 4 silvopper pieces, but it's on special offer today for only 2,210 goldatinum pieces, 8 electronze pieces, and 8 silvopper pieces!"

Colb inched forward, and 27 held open his red sack. Tilting his arms slightly, Colb poured the entire pile of nuggets into the bag. They appeared to vanish as soon as they touched the inside of the *Yiklar Bag of Traveling Inventory*.

While Colb dumped funds into the sack, Stibs pulled out his tinderbox and preemptively lit a chunk of flintcoal with it. He held the ignited rock high, which ensured no splashes from the rising water might extinguish it.

"AaAaaaaahhhh, wonderful decision," 27 cheered as Colb finished pouring in the pile of currency. The noble goblin held his hand over the bag as a fine gunpowder horn with a blue wave painted on it flew out, landing in his grip. "Thank you for your purchase," he continued, frantically handing it to Colb. "Now, we just need to take a little bit of gunpowder out, and…" but before 27 could finish his sentence, Stibs grabbed the horn out of Colb's hands, dropped his ignited piece of flintcoal into it, and threw the whole thing into the sky.

"WHAT! Stibs, didn't you hear what I said it was?!" 27 shouted.

"Hurmph! It's a flare to get that dwarven ship's attention," Stibs replied.

"It's not just a flare!" 27 cried out. "It's a *Yiklar Gunpowder*

Horn of Coralwhale Summoning! It's going to get the attention of a lot more than just that ship if you use the whole thing at once!"

With a small pop, the gunpowder horn exploded in the sky, and pink glitter rained down on the goblins. Almost immediately, the water below started to tremble, and a screeching whalesong rang up from the depths of the sea. "Oh man, that thing swims fast," 27 said, sweating.

"Hmmm, what thing?" Colb asked with concern.

"A coralwhale," the noble goblin whimpered.

As the sea itself continued to shake, the goblins could only watch as a huge, spiky pink beast with massive fins launched out of the water nearby. The beast majestically flew through the air for a few moments, then on the way back down, created an explosion on the surface of the peppersalt seawater as it hit. A wave of water rose from this explosion like a wall, twenty times higher than the walls of Yiklar, and exuded in all directions from the coralwhale's landing site.

"Hmmm, I don't think we're going to be connecting with that dwarven ship in the distance anytime soon, yes?" Colb muttered, the reflection of the incoming wave glinting off his beady red eyes.

"That ship is going to be who-knows-where in a few moments. And so are we," 27 replied meekly.

"Cover your heads!" Stibs yelled as their boat started to shift from the ripples of the incoming tsunami. The four goblins all crouched down, clutching onto the wood of the boat for dear life, as the massive wave engulfed them. The coralwhale continued to screech a terrible song, and Colb experienced a sensation of being lifted into the air. Moving so rapidly and with so many sounds around him, Colb felt himself passing out, and everything went dark.

Chapter 5

EVACUATION

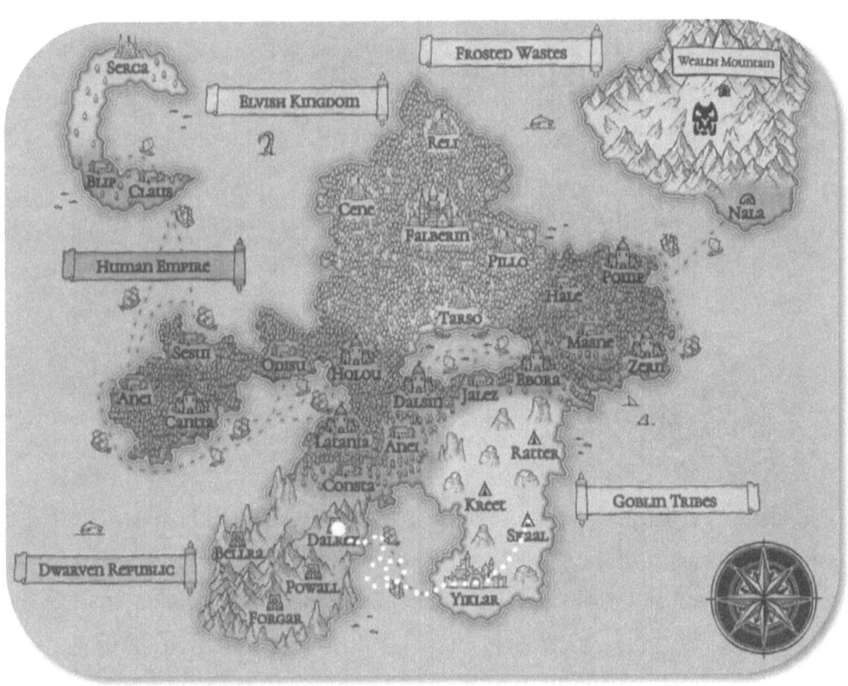

5. EVACUATION

Colb awoke with a crash, in a pile of mud and water, surrounded by broken bits of wood. He squinted into the distance, at the sun just starting to rise over some mountains. *Hmmm? Sunrise?* He thought to himself. *The last thing I remember was the tidal wave at sunset. I must have been passed out all night, yes?*

As Colb collected his bearings, he heard shouting in a language he didn't understand… and yet, as he listened harder, he realized he did understand it. "Everyone! This is a state of emergency! There is a meeting with the leaders in the town hall. The town hall! Everybody go to the town hall! Help any dwarves in need on your way there! Leave your belongings behind, and head to the town hall!" yelled a stout dwarf with a long orange beard. As the dwarf shouted these things, he banged two metal pans together loudly.

Colb looked around, feeling dizzy. He was on land, albeit sitting in a few inches of water. There were dwarves all over the place: running around, clearing rubble, and pulling each other out of flooded holes. These creatures were much taller than Colb, each standing at an intimidating 4 to 5 feet in height. Their heads were covered in hair, from their faces to their foreheads and necks. Some had trimmed their manes a bit to make visible the many metal rings attached to their hammer-shaped ears, while others didn't even bother to cut holes for their eyes to help them see.

Amongst this ocean of hair, Colb saw his three hairless companions, similarly waking up in piles of mud and broken wood. Noticing each other, the goblins huddled up. "Rrghegh… where are we?" Drek muttered, rubbing his head. "I'm still hungry."

"AaAaaaaahhhh, I recognize this place, although it's usually not so destroyed," 27 replied. "We are in the dwarven town of

Dalrek, yes we are."

"Whereami?" Stibs mumbled, pulling out his *Yiklar Map of Finding Location*. "Hurmph, he's right," the old goblin confirmed as his map magically revealed their new position. "I guess that's what we were aiming for, but how did we get here?"

27 looked around at the dwarves responding to the disaster. "We must've ridden that tidal wave from the coralwhale, yes we must have," he surmised.

"Hmmm, that would explain why the sun is just starting to rise, yes?" Colb added. "We must have been riding the tsunami all night, yes?"

"Rrghegh, that got us to the dwarf town much faster than old goblin rowing boat would have," Drek jeered.

Stibs rolled his eyes. "Hurmph, well, that's not a fair comparison, Drek. Although I've not seen one before today – er, yesterday – I've heard tsunami waves can move upwards of 500 miles per hour. Fortunately, we were in a *well-made boat*," Stibs paused to make eye contact with 27, "…built with planks of mapleoak that I specifically chose for their buoyancy. Hurmph – given the force of a wave like that, we must've been dragged west for miles. That type of force certainly would've knocked us out for the journey, but on the flip side, it also must've kept our boat at the top of the wave. Even with the couple of minor cracks, that upwards force must've ensured our boat could surf instead of sink."

"Rrghegh, if boat surfed us all the way to dwarf town… then where did boat go?" Drek mumbled, looking around.

"Amongst the rubble," Stibs replied. "It probably shattered on impact when the tsunami hit landfall. We're fortunate that nobody seems too scraped up."

"Hmmm… so, we did this?" Colb asked with dismay as he

surveyed the decimated town. "We destroyed this whole village?"

"Rrghegh, coralwhale did this," Drek corrected.

"Hurmph! The coralwhale that *we* summoned," Stibs retorted.

"Rrghegh… the coralwhale that *you* summoned with the gunpowder horn that *Colb* bought from *27*," Drek reminded. "I didn't hear *my* name in that sentence. Did you?"

"MMmMmmmm, it is not time to do blaming and complaining, no it is not," 27 threw in.

"Rrghegh, speaking of complaining – I'm still hungry," Drek whined. "When are we going to eat something?"

"Hmmm! Don't you feel bad?" Colb asked. "We decimated this town!"

"Rrghegh… we, coralwhale, Stibs, who cares what destroyed the town. Town is destroyed, that is that. I want to find food and supplies."

"MMmMmmmm, I agree with Colb. It is not good to have annihilated Dalrek, no it is not," 27 said. "We should make it up to the dwarves somehow, yes we should."

"Hurmph, it might damage our mission prospects if we're very open about what we did here," Stibs pointed out. "If we tell them we caused the tidal wave, they may seek vengeance. If we don't, maybe they'll assume this was a natural occurrence."

"MMmMmmmm, that is thing to think about, yes it is," 27 agreed. "Come to think of it, you've reminded me of something I learned in *Yiklar University*, yes you have. We were warned to be most thoughtful when selling to dwarves, as they follow sort of mob mentality at times, yes they do," the noble reminisced. "If enough dwarves latch onto the same idea, it can snowball into everybody agreeing with it. That could get *very* dangerous for us, yes it could. If just a few dwarves realize what we've done, and start telling others that they hate us, then the whole society may turn against us in mere moments. Perhaps it *would* hinder our mission to be truthful."

The noble goblin sighed. "MMmMmmmm, maybe we can help the dwarves more subtly, then. An act of kindness that won't incriminate us, but will still give some good to outweigh all the bad? Then, once we've redeemed ourselves, we can continue our quest towards Bellra."

"Hmmm, what do you think these dwarves would like, that we could give them?" Colb inquired. He scanned the carnage around him. "Hmmm, besides rebuilding their town? I'm not sure if the four of us could pull that off."

"MMmMmmmm, it's hard to say what we could do for them," 27 replied. "The eastern dwarven towns are a little bit of a puzzle to me, yes they are. Yiklar sales are low here, as opposed to in the western dwarven towns, even though both sides of Dwarven Republic are of roughly equal wealth. It makes no sense! I mean, had these dwarves simply purchased some *Yiklar Beach Sand of Protection* and sprinkled it on their shores, the tsunami would not have destroyed Dalrek, no it would not have."

"Hmmm… had we not summoned the coralwhale in the first place, this town would be fine as well, yes?" Colb reminded.

27 sighed. "MMmMmmmm – I did say not to use too much gunpowder at once while we were back there, yes I did – but it was high-stress situation for all of us. It was mistake. I don't know."

"Town hall! Everybody to the town hall! The leaders have declared a state of emergency!" an orange-haired dwarven guard continued to yell.

"Rrghegh… what is that racket?" Drek asked. The roguish goblin stuck a finger in his ear, clearing it out.

"MMmMmmmm, the popular spoken language is Dwarvish in

this place, yes it is. Your guess is good as mine as to what that dwarf is saying," 27 replied. "Colb's guess, however, will be better than all of ours."

The wealthy goblin pointed to Colb's white crystal necklace, which had begun glowing. "You should be able to understand Dwarvish, yes you should, with that *Yiklar Amulet of Open Ears* around your neck," he said.

Colb nodded in confirmation. "Hmmm, the dwarf says there's a meeting in the town call, and that someone declared a state of emergency. Probably due to the tsunami we started, yes?"

"Rrghegh, perfect! So, they're in panic. This is an excellent opportunity to loot the village," Drek pitched with glee.

27 gave Drek a look of confusion and horror. "…What? We cannot steal! Stealing is not the Yiklar way!"

"Ah, but it is the Ratter way," Drek retorted.

"We were just talking about ways to *help* them, to do something *good* to make up for the bad deed that we've done, yes we were," 27 cried out. "How can you talk of stealing from them?"

"Rrghegh, I'm hungry, and there's free stuff everywhere. Either give me some seagullfish, or be quiet while I liberate supplies from this town," Drek replied.

The goblins all looked at 27 for an answer. "MMmMmmmm… Colb had just handed me the seagullfish rations when the coralwhale appeared. They weren't properly stowed when we all passed out, so… they've been lost to the sea. We still have those toadroaches that Stibs put in the *Yiklar Folding Cabin*, though-"

Before 27 could complete his sentence, Drek proceeded to duck out of the group huddle, and sprint off towards the nearest destroyed building.

"Wha-Drek! Come back!" 27 shouted, which Drek ignored.

"*Free stuff, free stuff!*" the young goblin chanted as he

disappeared beyond some ruined buildings.

"MMmMmmmm, okay, new plan," 27 announced, placing a hand over his forehead in exasperation.

"Stibs, go find Drek and stop him from stealing. We don't need to harm these dwarves more than we already have. Colb, let's you and I go to the town hall together. You can translate whatever they're saying for me, and maybe we can figure out a subtle way to redeem ourselves before we continue our journey. Sound good?" Stibs and Colb nodded in agreement.

While the eyepatched goblin ran off to catch Drek, Colb and 27 followed the dwarven crowd to a pool of water in the center of town.

"Alright everyone, it seems the town hall was flooded. I guess we shouldn't have built it in a hole so close to the sea," a dwarf announced to the audience. This announcer stood with a group of five other dwarves. All six of them were wearing particularly shiny, goldatinum-colored armor.

The announcer's words were observed by a crowd of hundreds. "Nevertheless, I'm glad to have gathered so many of you here," the dwarf continued. "Our scouts determined that a coralwhale thrashed about somewhere in the sea last night. This has resulted in a series of tsunami waves, which will continue for the next few days."

This started a murmur amongst the crowd, which included a few exasperated sighs and cries of how cruel and unfair life could be.

"Hmmm, I feel quite guilty, yes?" Colb whispered to 27.

"MMmMmmmm, me as well," 27 replied. "What's the announcer saying?"

"Hmmm, it sounds like Stibs was right, yes?" Colb replied. "They know about the coralwhale, but as far as I can tell, they seem to think it just naturally thrashed about last night."

"As per emergency guidelines, we will be evacuating to Bellra for a week," the announcer continued. "After that, if our scouts report the waves have ceased, then we will return to rebuild our village."

"Bellra? That's where the *Yiklar Spear of Irreversible Death* is," 27 muttered as Colb whispered the translations to him.

"Yes, Lightbuckle?" the announcer said, pointing out a raised hand in the audience.

"What of my family in Powall? Have they been hit as well?" Lightbuckle called out.

"Yes," the announcer replied, "our scouts believe that Powall has also been flooded, but not as badly as us. As per the emergency guidelines, all dwarves in Powall will be evacuating to Forgar, similar to how we will all be going to Bellra. You can reconnect with your family next week, once we've all returned to rebuild." Another murmur started, and some more dwarves raised their hands.

"MMmMmmmm, this is bad," 27 whined as Colb translated the announcer's words to Goblish. "We hurt the town of Powall, too? I know this is our fault, but if only these dwarves had magically protected their shores, it wouldn't have mattered!"

"Hmmm, maybe that's how we can subtly redeem ourselves?" Colb pitched. "Offer them some of that sand you spoke about."

"AaAaaaaahhhh, that is good idea, Colb! I mean, I can't just *give* it to them, no I cannot, as my bag requires that I make a sale to summon an item… but, perhaps we could pull off that loophole again? I could offer to pay you for the service of protecting this good town, then you could turn around and purchase the *Yiklar Beach Sand of Protection* from me with my own money?"

Colb nodded. "Hmmm, that's worth a try, yes? I'm sure the

dwarves would appreciate it!"

The two goblins raised their hands, ready to pitch this *Yiklar Beach Sand of Protection* plan to the announcer. Unfortunately, their thin green arms couldn't be seen amongst the crowd of taller and wider dwarves.

"Yes, you in the front?" the announcer said, calling on a dwarf covered in yellow hair and electronze metal piercings.

"Oi, what's happenin' with the summer antlizard be'ind the volcano? It's too dangerous ta travel ta Bellra right now, innit?" the dwarf shouted.

A larger murmur broke out amongst the dwarves. Colb could make out some "that's right" and "I'd rather stay here" sentences amongst the noise.

"All right, all right, listen up," the announcer called out. "It is true, the summer antlizard still lives on the path between Dalrek and Bellra. We can't walk by it, but we feel that it would be *more* dangerous to stay in the direct path of these tsunami waves. We've decided… we're going to send in the army, and attempt to defeat it to open our path. It's a problem we needed to deal with eventually either way." This prompted a renewed explosion of worried murmurs amongst the dwarven audience.

"That's ridiculous!" a dwarf shouted from the crowd.

"Yea! How are we supposed to kill that thing?" another agreed.

"Last time you sent the army, our weapons were completely ineffective!" a third dwarf cried out.

As the announcer tried to calm the audience, Colb translated these revelations to 27. "AaAaaaaahhhh, maybe *we* can help with that!" 27 cheered. "The *Yiklar Factories* produces a line of weaponry of the highest quality. Nothing like this *Yiklar Spear of Irreversible Death* we're meant to pick up, but still some most powerful of weapons!"

"Hmmm, I heard a dwarf say that weapons are ineffective against this summer antlizard?" Colb worried.

"AaAaaaaahhhh, but Yiklar-made items are enchanted. These dwarves tend to craft non-magical weaponry, like what you might find made in Skaal or Kreet."

Colb glanced down at his simple Skaal-produced wooden shield and leather armor. "Items from Yiklar are imbued with powerful magic, yes they are," 27 continued. "Yiklar-made weapons are stronger, sharper, and generally come with some specialized effects. Equipping a whole army with Yiklar-made goods would make them undefeatable!"

"Hmmm, then it sounds like we're in a position to really help them out, yes?" Colb cheered, pointing to 27's *Yiklar Bag of Traveling Inventory*.

27 nodded in agreement, then jumped up and down while frantically waving his arms in the air. "We can help you!" he shouted. "Call on me! We can help! Let us help!"

"What's that weird sound?" the announcer questioned.

"Oi, it's a goblynn, innit!" shouted the yellow-haired dwarf from the front row. "I learn'd ta speak Goblish as an 'obby. I'm a lil' rough, but that sounded like a goblynn sayin' 'e wants ta 'elp us!"

"Hmmm, they just heard you, yes? They're talking about us!" Colb translated. "Keep going, yes?"

"Let us help you! Let us help!" 27 shouted, now with enhanced vigor.

The dwarves before them parted, opening a path to the front of the audience. The goblin duo scampered towards the announcer, hundreds of hairy faces staring them down as they moved.

"See? I knew 'et!" the yellow-haired dwarf cheered, gesturing to Colb and 27 as they arrived at the front row.

"MMmMmmmm, okay, let me do something here," 27 mumbled, pulling out his *Yiklar Bag of Traveling Inventory*. "I need a silvopper."

"The goblynn says 'e wants a silvopper piece before 'e can 'elp us," the yellow-haired dwarf announced. "Lil' greedy, innt 'e?"

One of the shiny-armored dwarves stepped forwards and pulled out a large leather bag of metallic nuggets. She removed a silvopper piece and flicked it through the air. 27 caught it, and dropped it into his magic red sack.

A moment later, a pile of parchment launched out of the bag, which 27 snatched up. "AaAaaaaahhhh, customer!" he cheered, handing the stack of papers to the dwarf that had given him the silvopper nugget. "I am from the Yiklar tribe, yes I am. My name is 27. I was… um, passing through, and noticed your plight. This is a Dwarvish-translated *Yiklar Catalog*, which lists all the magic items I can sell to you. Perhaps we can provide some magic weapons to help defeat this summer antlizard blocking your path, yes we can?"

As the yellow-haired dwarf roughly translated 27's words, the six shiny-armored dwarves crowded around the Dwarvish-translated *Yiklar Catalog*. After a minute of quickly rifling through the listings, they deliberated amongst themselves.

Colb didn't hear everything in their discussion, but he did catch a few sentences: "*I always figured these magic Yiklar items were a scam,*" "*We shouldn't just throw away a potential solution to our problem,*" and "*A leader in Forgar once told me that the Yiklar goblins are trustworthy.*"

"You have these weapons with you?" one of them asked, poking his head out of the deliberation circle. He looked at the yellow-haired dwarf. "Ask if they have the items with them."

Colb glanced at 27's red bag. "Hmmm, I can understand

Dwarvish, but I can't speak it, yes?" Colb explained. "We have as many items as you could need, and they are always available, yes?"

"Oi, right on lil' goblynn! I'm jus' like that. I can understand yer Goblish, but my speakin' it is rough – I'm glad ye can understand our Dwarvish 'ight now, yea?"

Colb nodded. "Ight," the yellow-haired dwarf continued, "lil' goblynn says they can give ya' anythin' at any time."

Given that information, the six dwarves deliberated a little more, then appeared to hold a vote amongst themselves on what they should do. The audience behind Colb and 27 watched this interaction with piqued interest. Once the half-dozen dwarves appeared to have made a decision, they all turned to face the goblin duo.

"As denoted by our unique armor, we are the six leaders of Dalrek," the shortest of them grumbled. As he spoke, he spat through the mound of matted, unkempt black hair that covered his face. "To introduce myself, I am Leader Glazeanvil: head dwarf of the army, and one of Dalrek's six highest officers. I must say, I'm not one to trust outsiders, and I don't understand your language."

One of the other dwarven leaders nudged him, causing the shortest dwarf to sigh. "Nevertheless, after discussing your proposition with the other leaders – and being outvoted – I am inviting you to join me at the front of the army on our trek to Bellra. If you can prove that your weapons are more effective than ours in a preliminary attack against the summer antlizard, then we'll purchase a bundle of them from you for our full-scale assault."

Colb whispered the Goblish translation to 27. "AaAaaaaahhhh, a wise and cautious customer, yes you are," 27 cheered. "This sounds most amiable. If you allow us to group up with our other two comrades first, us four goblins will meet you at the western end of Dalrek to set off, yes we will."

After hearing the yellow-haired dwarf's translation, the six dwarvish leaders nodded in unified understanding, and adjourned the town hall meeting.

"This is perfect," 27 said as they exited with the audience. "These dwarves are evacuating to Bellra. If we help their army defeat this summer antlizard creature, not only will we be doing a good deed to balance out our mistake, but *also* we will be getting a free escort to the very town we aimed to reach, *and* we will have convinced the leaders of Dalrek to be more trusting of Yiklar-made goods. It's a win-win-win, yes it is!"

"Hmmm, that does sound promising," Colb admitted. "Hmmm, but remember – we owe them a gift. Assuming they like the weapons, you should give them out for free, yes?"

"I'll see what I can do," 27 replied.

The duo proceeded to wander around Dalrek for a short while, searching for their companions in the wreckage. Eventually, they spotted Drek and Stibs at the western corner of the town – quite close to where they had agreed to regroup with the six leaders. The two goblins were standing next to a wooden cart full of food, valuables, weapons, and armor.

"MMmMmmmm, what is this?!" 27 exclaimed. "Where did you get these things?"

"Rrghegh… we liberated them from some rubble," Drek replied. 27 gasped, and then turned to Stibs with a look of befuddlement.

"Hurmph! I tried to stop him, but then he had some convincing arguments and, well, next thing I knew, I was helping him," Stibs said with a shrug. "We've got supplies for weeks now! Let's head out to Bellra and pick up your spear."

"No no no," 27 cried, "this is not the Yiklar way! We do not steal, we sell! Sell! We sell products and services with a focus on high quality and good deals! Stealing from a potential customer is a… a bad deal!" 27 gagged as the words 'bad deal' left an awful taste in his mouth.

"Hey, over there!" a dwarven leader shouted from nearby.

"Rrghegh… what is that dwarf saying, Colb?" Drek asked.

"Hmmm, I believe that's Leader Glazeanvil, yes? Dalrek's army is meant to meet us here," Colb replied. Stibs and Drek's eyes widened as a platoon of dwarves started jogging over to them.

"What's that cart you've got there?" Leader Glazeanvil asked as he and his small army stopped before the goblin crew.

"Rrghegh… oh no. What? What? What is he saying? This is my stuff! We found it," Drek said. "Tell them to go away."

27, Drek, and Stibs looked at Colb expectantly, as his *Yiklar Amulet of Open Ears* glowed with understanding. "Hmmm, is your translator here?" Colb asked.

"Oi, I'm 'ere!" the yellow-haired dwarf shouted from the back of the army. "Ma name's Sunbolt, by ta way! Me 'air is 'ellow ta match me name, innt dat neat?"

Sunbolt pushed his way to the front of the line until he was standing at Leader Glazeanvil's side.

"Hmmm, we feel terrible that your homes were destroyed, yes?" Colb said. "My friends here salvaged what they could from the rubble, as an act of good faith, yes? Perhaps these things will help with the evacuation, yes?"

"Rrghegh! Why did you say that?! It's not tru-" Drek started to yell, but 27 quickly grabbed him and covered his mouth before he could revoke Colb's offering.

"Oi, that's mighty fine o' you!" Sunbolt cheered, his hairy head aimed towards Colb as he spoke. "These goblynns 'ere 'alvaged some supplies fer us, now innt that nice 'o 'em?" he translated for the other dwarves.

Leader Glazeanvil furrowed his mound of black hair as he towered over Colb. "I find that unlikely," he grumbled after a moment, "but since we're here now, we might as well take our items back. Have at it, soldiers."

The leader waved his hand, to which the squadron behind him approached the cart and began looting it.

The noble goblin let go of Drek, whose lower eyelids twitched with rage. "Rrghegh… you two better watch your backs," he mumbled at Colb and 27.

After a few minutes, the dwarves stepped away, wearing their armor and wielding their weapons. The cart had been picked dry. "We are now ready to head out, dwarves." Leader Glazeanvil announced. "Let's meet up with the other leaders and townsfolk, then head to Bellra!"

A flurry of dwarves replied "Yea!" as the platoon turned and hustled away.

"You four, follow me," Leader Glazeanvil commanded.

"We need to follow him, yes?" Colb translated. Drek sat on the ground defiantly, to which Stibs grabbed him by the collar and dragged him along.

As the goblin crew followed Leader Glazeanvil and his army to the front of the evacuation lines, Colb and 27 explained the plan to Drek and Stibs.

"Rrghegh… my bow is from Yiklar, right?" Drek asked, fully laying in the dirt as Stibs dragged him along.

"AaAaaaaahhhh, your *Yiklar Bow of Returning Arrow* is indeed Yiklar-made, yes it is," 27 replied. "If you can get some good hits on this summer antlizard with it, that'll surely prove the usefulness of magic weapons to these dwarves, yes it will."

"Rrghegh!" Drek grumbled, releasing himself from his teammate's grip and standing up. "Then I'll use my arrow and slay this monster personally. Maybe show this old fart a thing or two about how fighting works on this side of the century," he jeered with a grin.

"Hurmph! Then I'll fight, too," Stibs announced. He drew his handmade bone sword, and cradled it in his palms. "I don't need magic, and I don't need inexperienced children like Drek, either."

"Rrghegh, well then – may the better goblin be the one that slays the beast," Drek challenged.

"I'll remember you said that while I'm cleaning summer antlizard guts off my sword," Stibs chuckled.

With that, the goblin crew followed Leader Glazeanvil a little further, eventually arriving at the front of four long lines of dwarves. Colb gulped at the sight of the armed dwarves behind them. *How did our mission escalate so quickly?* he thought to himself. *Whatever a summer antlizard is, I hope we can slay it before it slays us.*

Chapter 6

THE MOUNTAIN PASS

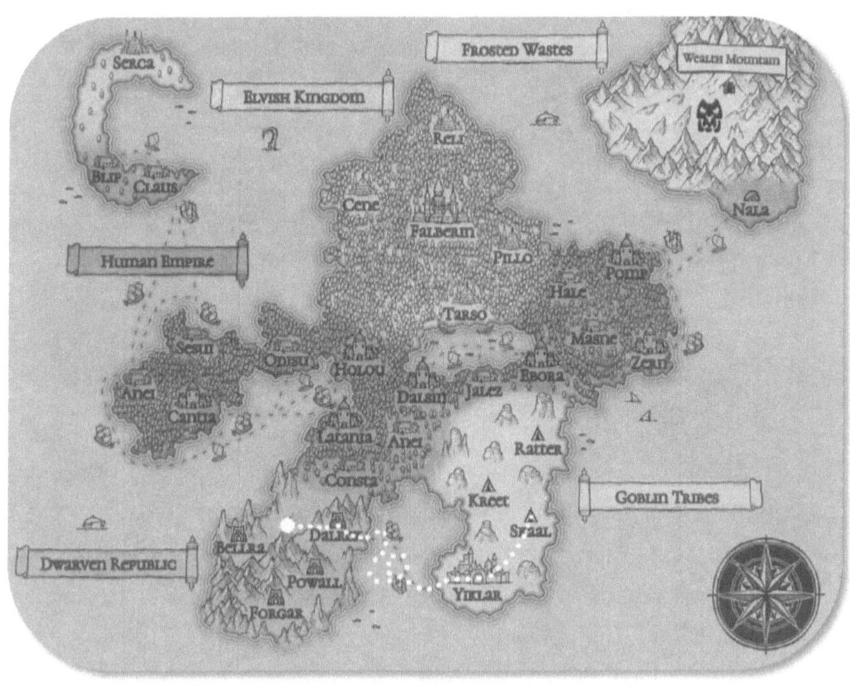

6. THE MOUNTAIN PASS

Thousands of dwarves marched out of Dalrek in four orderly lines: warriors on the two outside lines, civilians in the two middle lines. The four goblins stood at the front of the parade, standing shoulder-to-shoulder with Drek and Stibs on the outside, Colb and 27 on the inside. In front of them, Sunbolt and Leader Glazeanvil led the charge. Behind the march, a beaten town sat empty and flooded.

Colb peered at the dwarves behind him, feeling a little claustrophobic. These walls of hair marched in perfect harmony, as if they'd practiced this walk a thousand times. Colb's feet ached as his toenails scratched across the rocky terrain.

"Welcome to the army, goblins," Leader Glazeanvil said. The shiny-armored dwarf looked powerful leading the charge, marching with the Goblish translator by his side. "What are your names?"

"Hmmm, I go by the name of Colb, yes? It's nice to meet you, Sunbolt and Leader Glazeanvil, yes?" Colb cheered. "These are Drek, 27, and Stibs."

"Rrghegh… why are you telling them our names?" Drek complained as he walked. "Introductions are waste of time."

"Oi, 'eems to be Drek, Colb, 'wenty-sevnn, and Stibs, eh?" Sunbot translated for Leader Glazeanvil. "Colb 'eems ta be de only un ta understand Dwarvish."

"Then I'll get down to the plan, Colb, and you can explain it to your teammates," Leader Glazeanvil continued. "We're going to march for most of the day, then make camp in a safe zone before the summer antlizard's territory. While the other five leaders tend to the civilians, I will lead the army – and you four – into what will become our battlefield."

Colb translated these words to his friends, sweating with alarm as he considered what he was saying.

"MmMMmmm, out of wonder, what is this summer antlizard?" 27 asked.

"Oi, 'eyre wondrin' what de summer ant'izard's like, eh?" Subolt translated.

"A fearsome beast," Leader Glazeanvil replied, sending a chill down Colb's spine with his sudden shift in his tone. "It's a giant monster with an armored body. A creature that spits lava from its very mouth. Each time we throw a spear or boomerang at its hide, our weapon simply melts from the blaze it emanates."

"That will not be problem for Yiklar-made weapons," 27 confidently replied as Colb translated the Dwarvish words. "Magic is not so easily destroyed, no it is not. AaAaaaaahhhh, but I still wonder – where did this monster come from? Has it plagued you for long time?"

"We believe the beast originated from the center of a volcano, in the mountain pass between Dalrek and Bellra," Leader Glazeanvil replied as Sunbolt translated 27's words. "Half a year ago, there was an eruption. A scout said she saw it – a horrible beast launching out of the volcano's lid. Next thing we knew, our land-path to Bellra had become a territorial creature's nesting site. Ever since, all trade and travel with Bellra have required boats from Forgar in the south – quite a roundabout route, but a necessary one with an invincible monster blocking our preferred path."

Colb translated these words for his goblin crew, stuttering as he considered what they were about to face. Drek's ears perked up with interest, and Stibs muttered some analytical notes about his soon-to-be-opponent.

"Today, we are forced to send our people this way, since they may drown trying to evacuate in any other direction," Leader Glazeanvil continued. "We've decided to enact the following plan: while the civilians make camp in a relatively safe area tonight, we're going to clear their path for tomorrow. One fourth of the army will bait the summer antlizard with a preliminary attack. We expect this attack to be ineffective, but to at least draw the beast into a good position for the rest of the army to ambush it. Once everyone's in position, the main army will surprise-attack the beast, making it angry. We will then retreat southward, as far as possible – luring the infuriated summer antlizard behind us. Doing this will open the path for our people tomorrow morning, and perhaps forever if we can draw the monster southward enough that it decides to stay and make a new nest."

"Hurmph! I thought your plan was to *kill* the beast?" Stibs questioned as he heard Colb's translation.

"Oi, 'ey wanna kill it," Sunbolt informed his superior.

"Well, that's the second plan," Leader Glazeanvil said. "As I mentioned before, some of you goblins – or all of you goblins – are going to join the preliminary attack. If you prove that your weapons can actually hurt the beast, then we'll quickly distribute whatever you've got with the remainder of the army, and perhaps fight the monster during our ambush instead of just luring it south."

The goblins nodded in agreement to Colb's translation - Stibs and Drek looking competitively at each other around the thought of killing the beast, and 27 looking confident about the efficacy of his weapons. Colb's voice shook as spoke of the warlike strategy, and he absent-mindedly scratched at one of his palms with nervousness.

A few hours before sunset, the marching stopped, and the two center lines of civilians broke away to set up camp. Armed with shovels, the dwarves and five of their leaders began digging holes for their families to sleep in.

"Onward!" the sixth and final Leader Glazeanvil commanded.

"Yea!" the army cheered, following behind him and the goblin crew.

After another half-hour of marching, a horrible screeching sound started up in the horizon. "Alright," Leader Glazeanvil shouted, stopping the parade.

"Squadrons fifty-nine through eighty-four, go on ahead for the bait maneuver! Be wary of the safety of your goblin guests, although focus on your own survival first and foremost," he announced.

Leader Glazeanvil looked down at the goblins. "Time to shine, if you think you've really got what it takes," he said.

"Hmmm, preliminary attack is starting, yes?" Colb announced to his teammates.

Drek and Stibs stepped forwards, their heads held high. Stibs unsheathed his cowmammoth bone sword, and Drek drew his *Yiklar Bow of Returning Arrow*. "Rrghegh! It's about time," Drek cheered.

"Hurmph, about time to show you what a little Kreet ingenuity can do," Stibs added, brandishing his bone sword.

27 poked Sunbolt in the leg, prompting him to bend down so the noble could whisper in his ear. Once 27 had finished speaking, the yellow-haired dwarf turned to address his superior.

"Oi," Sunbolt said, speaking Dwarvish. "Dat bow is Yiklar-made. Goblynn says ta focus on de effectiveness of 'et, and ta ignore de otha' goblynn's non-magic sword, eh?"

Leader Glazeanvil nodded, which prompted Drek and Stibs to smile and hold their weapons high, as if taking this nod as affirmation for their willingness to fight. The duo saluted goodbye to Colb and 27, then head off to join the army's preliminary attack.

While a quarter of the army and half the goblin crew head off in the direction of the screeching, Leader Glazeanvil led the rest of the army towards a mountainpass in the south.

The army eventually stopped in a narrow alley between two summits. While the frontline prepared itself with shields and spears, the backline drew their bows and arrows. The group with Colb stood in the very back – a safe place for Leader Glazeanvil to dish out orders, and for the goblins to hand out magical weapons once the time came.

Colb could feel vibrations in the ground – likely from the summer antlizard stomping ever closer – but couldn't see anything of interest given his now narrowed range of view due to the mountains surrounding him.

As the army prepared their ambush, Leader Glazeanvil pulled out 27's Dwarvish-translated *Yiklar Catalog*. "Alright, merchant. Let's talk about what you've got here," he grumbled. As he and 27 spoke, Colb and Sunbolt ensured everything could be understood by everyone involved.

"I've briefly rifled through your papers here, but haven't had a chance to look at them deeply," Leader Glazeanvil continued. "Assuming your weapons are worth buying, what would you recommend? I've got tons of goldatinum nuggets with me, and the other leaders tell me I can spend as much as I want if it'll kill that monster."

"AaAaaaaahhhh," 27 replied, looking over at Colb. The chef goblin gave him a knowing side-eye. "Well, to get started… first 100 items are on me, as charitable donation," he said. "I will just need to do a quick formality with my friend Colb to pull the funds out from my personal *Yiklar Bank Account* back home, and then we will be able to buy those first hundred items for you.

Additionally, we will give you ten free pouches of *Yiklar Beach Sand of Protection* to prevent future disasters, yes we will. After we've given you those many gifts, you can start buying whatever else you want from the *Yiklar Catalog*, yes you can, if you're interested."

Leader Glazeanvil's hair ruffled with surprise. "Well, that's certainly a generous starting package, considering how expensive everything's listed for, here," he said. "Are your items so cheaply made, that you can give them away so freely?"

"MMmMmmmm – no, no, no," 27 retorted, looking appalled. "Our items are the most highest-of-quality, yes they are. I'm going to lose *much* of my fortune giving so many away to you, yes I am. It is simply because your poor town was destroyed, that we wish to assist you, yes we do."

"I just *said* I've got tons of money that I'm authorized to *spend* to kill that monster," Leader Glazeanvil replied, clenching his fists. "I appreciate your free items, but it seems strange… is some sort of scam going on here?"

"Hmmm, we've sent half our team into danger for you just now, yes?" Colb threw in. "We would not risk them for sake of scam, yes?"

"MmMMmmm, the Yiklar are not scammers, no they are not," 27 added.

In the distance, a loud "*SCREEREERRERE!*" rose in intensity. "It sounds like the preliminary encounter has started," Leader Glazeanvil huffed.

"The beast is near," he announced, raising his voice for his soldiers. "As soon as you see the summer antlizard, fire your arrows and hold your ground. Once it enters this alley, we will lure it south with a tactical retreat on my command."

"Hmmm, we should start handing out some Yiklar weapons,

yes?" Colb asked.

"Oi, da goblynns 'ant ta 'and out weapons now," Sunbolt translated.

"Listen here, goblins," Leader Glazeanvil said, his voice dropping and suddenly turning sour. He slapped the *Yiklar Catalog* onto the ground, and grabbed Colb and 27 by their collars with his two thick, furry hands. "Is this some kind of joke? You like to play with lives, eh?"

Shocked by this, Colb looked to 27, whose was staring at the *Yiklar Catalog* on the ground. 27's eyes went wide with horror.

Following the noble goblin's gaze, Colb stared down at the book, which was left open on a specific page. His *Yiklar Amulet of Open Ears* – unable to translate written words – did little to improve his understanding of the Dwarvish script before him. However, he could recognize one thing on the open page: a painted picture of the item being advertised. The image depicted blue-colored gunpowder horn, identical to the *Yiklar Gunpowderhorn of Coralwhale Summoning* that had started this whole mess.

"Is this how you get your sick laughs?" Leader Glazeanvil asked, lifting Colb and 27 a foot off the ground by their collars. "Flooding towns with your trained coralwhales, then selling us beach sand to solve the problems *you* caused? Then what – you heard about our summer antlizard problem, and thought you could sweeten your deal? Give me a hundred weapons for free, so I have to order a thousand more to equip my whole army? Are you planning to book it as soon as the fighting starts?"

He suddenly threw both of them into the ground, their backs crunching against the rocky terrain. "You want money? Here!" he shouted, pulling out a huge bag of metallic nuggets and dunking a hand into it. "Take some!"

Leader Glazeanvil pelted the goblin duo with a few handfuls goldatinum nuggets. Sunbolt watched silently, the only witness to this event – as the rest of the army was too busy preparing their positions to notice this display.

"You've dishonored the Dwarven Republic," he spat. "I have a plan to execute, and I certainly don't need you for it." He vaulted the rest of his large money sack at 27, smacking the noble goblin in the chest and knocking the wind out of his lungs.

"Wait," 27 coughed, laying weakly on the ground. He limply picked himself up, and opened the sack of money that Leader Glazeanvil had thrown at him. "Wait," he pleaded again.

While the dwarven leader turned to leave, 27 shoved his *Yiklar Bag of Traveling Inventory* into the sack, scooping up a large amount of goldatinum in the process. The funds vanished upon entering his magic red bag.

27 then aimed his *Yiklar Bag of Traveling Inventory* towards Leader Glazeanvil. With a *WHOOSH!* sound, a brown bowstaff with a rocky texture flew out from the bag. The short dwarf suddenly spun around, snatching the weapon out of the air before it could hit him.

"A *Yiklar Bowstaff of Earthquakes*, one of the best weapons ever crafted," 27 said. "Just stab it into the ground, and…"

Holding the *Yiklar Bowstaff of Earthquakes* sideways, Leader Glazeanvil attempted to snap it in half against his leg. The sturdy item held strong, smashing into his knee as if he'd just wacked his own limb with a metal bar.

The leader hissed, then ruffled his hair at 27. "Uhm…" Sunbolt muttered. "Goblynn says dat's a *Yiklar Bowstaff of 'arthquakes*. That it does somethin' if ya stab it into the ground, eh?"

"I'm keeping this for evidence," Leader Glazeanvil spat, securing the bowstaff in a leather strap attached to his armor.

"Sunbolt. Detain these two scammers, reclaim my goldatinum, and keep this whole mess out of my way until the fight is over. I'm headed to the frontline."

With that, Leader Glazeanvil stomped off, leaving Sunbolt behind with a battered Colb and 27.

"Oi, I guess et's just us," Sunbolt said, helping Colb and 27 stand back up. "I've 'ot some rope on me. Couldja tell yer buddy to turn 'round so I can bound 'im up?"

"Hmmm, he's arresting us, yes?" Colb informed 27.

"MmMMmmm, it was mistake, Sunbolt," 27 pleaded. "We did not mean to summon bad tidal waves upon Dalrek, no we did not. We wish to redeem ourselves, yes we do. Let us help."

Sunbolt scratched the back of his yellow-hair-covered head. "Uhm… I dunno, lil' goblynn. I've 'ot orders ta follow, eh?"

Colb scooped up some of the various nuggets on the ground, and handed them to 27. The noble refused them, instead offering an exorbitant amount of his own *Yiklar Bank Account* funds to Colb in exchange for the "service" of cleaning up the goldatinum mess on the ground.

"Look, we can help, and we don't even need to use Dwarven Republic funds," 27 pleaded. Colb handed the money back to him, and the noble used it to summon a handful of wands, boomerangs, shields, and daggers from his *Yiklar Bag of Traveling Inventory*.

"Hmmm, look Sunbolt," Colb said. "Magic items, yes? You can use these against the monster, yes?"

As Sunbolt started to shake his head in disagreement, a loud *"SCREEREERRERE!"* rang out. It sounded louder and closer than ever before.

"IT'S HERE!" Leader Glazeanvil screamed from somewhere in the middle of the army, as a 70-foot-tall beast stepped into view. The monster sported a reptilian head attached to a red-hot,

armored exoskeleton. The smaller army had it surrounded, and seemed to be trying to lure it towards the ambush.

Immediately, the main army let out a volley of hundreds of arrows. Each and every arrow disintegrated with a sizzle upon hitting the summer antlizard's red-hot hide.

"*SCREEREERRERE!*" it roared. It seemed angered by Leader Glazeanvil and the larger dwarven army's unexpected attack. Holding its ground with six arched, insect-like legs, the summer antlizard opened its colossal jaw towards the sky.

A sound like a screeching metal furnace rang throughout the mountain pass as a thick stream of lava fired from the summer antlizard's mouth. The molten spit arched over 100 feet high, then came crashing down upon the main army's frontline. Numerous dwarves dived out of the way, and a few met fiery, instantaneous deaths.

"*RETURN FIRE AGAIN!*" Leader Glazeanvil shouted. A new volley of arrows erupted from the main army, once more all disintegrating upon contact with the red-hot beast.

The smaller army surrounding the beast fired as well – most of their arrows evaporating upon contact with the monster's stomach. One shot, however – from a shiny iridhodium arrow – stuck into the beast's neck, ripping off a chunk of skin as it whipped around and returned to its archer.

"That was Drek!" 27 cheered, pointing out the single successful hit. The summer antlizard moaned with pain, glaring down at the group surrounding it.

"Look! The goblin's arrow worked!" a soldier shouted from the main army.

"It's true!" another said.

"Death to the summer antlizard!" a third cried.

"*STAY ON TASK!*" Leader Glazeanvil yelled. From the volume

of his voice, it sounded like he'd now reached the frontline of the main army. *"WE'RE LURING IT SOUTH!"*

Another churning, furnace-like ring echoed throughout the alley as the summer antlizard looked down. It eyed the smaller army surrounding it, and seemed ready to eradicate them with a fiery blast.

"THE PRELIMINARY ATTACK IS OVER!" Leader Glazeanvil shouted at the smaller army. *"CAN YOU HEAR ME OVER THERE? RETREAT!"*

The summer antlizard widened its jaw, red-hot liquid visible between its teeth. It took a heavy breath of air, preparing to spit. As it did so, a single iridhodium arrow shot out of the crowd below it, straight up into the beast's throat.

The summer antlizard gagged, widening its eyes and stumbling backwards. As it bumped into one of the mountain walls, Drek's shiny arrow shot out from one of its ribs, returning from whence it came.

"Hey!" a gruff soldier shouted from the backline, turning to look at Colb and 27. "Two of the goblins are right there, and one of them's holding a pile of weapons!"

"Yo!" another soldier yelled. "Hand me one of those boomerangs, will ya?"

"No, give Squadron 43 some love, yea?" another added.

"Oi, I'm 'posed ta detain these here goblynns, eh? Leader Glazeanvil 'aid no more goblynn weapons," Sunbolt shouted back.

"Oh, bugger off!" a soldier yelled. "This is a war. Give me something magic!"

"Yea!" five more dwarves agreed.

"Hmmm, it seems the backline is on our side, yes?" Colb muttered.

"AaAaaaaahhhh, their mob mentality starting to take over, but in a way favorable to us!" 27 cheered. "If we get enough of them on our side, Leader Glazeanvil's orders might not matter, no they might not."

"Oi, I'm just tryna follow de orders, eh?" Sunbolt shouted to the soldiers.

At this point, around half of the backline had begun to split their attention – partially focusing on Drek's assault against the summer antlizard, and partially looking backwards to see what Sunbolt was going to do.

"Give him a wand," 27 muttered.

Colb grabbed sky-colored wand from the pile of weapons 27 had summoned, and put it in Sunbolt's hand.

"Oi, what's this now?" Sunbolt asked, inspecting it. 27 dropped his pile of weapons onto the ground, scampered up to the *Yiklar Catalog* on the ground, and ruffled through it. Once he found the page containing a drawing of the sky-colored wand, he ripped it out and handed it to Sunbolt.

"A *Yiklar Wand of Rainfall*, eh?" Sunbolt muttered, reading the Dwarvish-translated sheet of parchment.

"Give it a shake," 27 prodded.

Curiosity getting the better of him, the yellow-haired dwarf gave his sky-colored wand a violent tussle.

BOOM! A thunderous cloud screeched as it suddenly formed in the sky, casting a shadow over the battlefield. A wash of rain drizzled down upon the army. The backline let out a collective sigh of disappointment, including "Aw," "Hey," "Now me hair's wet!" and "What a waste of time."

SsssSsSSSSSSSS! A loud sizzling sound suddenly erupted from the summer antlizard's position, as drops of rain evaporated to steam upon hitting the beast's red-hot exoskeleton.

"*SCREEREERRERE!*" the monster cried, visibly alarmed by the cooling effect of the rain shower.

"Eeeeyyyyy!" the army's backline rejoiced; their cheering now positive as they realized the benefits of Sunbolt's wand. "Give me one of those!" a bunch of dwarves shouted in unison.

Sunbolt shrugged. "Oi, 'e can't get mad at all of us, eh? Go on ahead, then," he shouted back.

With permission granted, groups of dwarves started to break away from the backline, running up to Colb to take some weapons back for their squadrons. Meanwhile, 27 summoned as many magical products as he could – using Colb's "service" of distribution as a loophole to drain his *Yiklar Bank Account* and fund this process.

"*SCREEREERRERE!*" the monster roared, Drek's arrow clipping it in the eye as rain assailed it from above. Word of what caused this rainstorm spread rapidly through the army, causing even the frontline to shout for their brethren to grab weapons for them.

Colb frantically handed out a pile of wands, each of which seemed to further empower the rainstorm upon being shaken.

"What do those white daggers do?" a soldier asked, passing up a wand and pointing at something else in the pile of weapons.

"Hmmm, what are the daggers, yes?" Colb translated.

27 quickly ripped a few pages from the Dwarvish-translated *Yiklar Catalog*, set them out in front of the weapons pile, then went back to summoning inventory from his bag.

"*Yiklar Dagger of Wind*," the dwarf muttered, reading one of the pages.

"It summons wind," 27 replied, frantically pulling a couple mirror-coated shields out of his *Yiklar Bag of Traveling Inventory* as he spoke.

"Oi, it summons wind," Sunbolt translated.

Satisfied, the dwarf took a dagger and left, only to be immediately replaced by three more dwarves poking through the catalog pages.

As dwarves started looting the weapons pile on their own, Colb looked out at the summer antlizard. The smaller army that used to surround it seemed to be retreating to join the main force – the rainstorm and Drek's *Yiklar Bow of Returning Arrow* covering them for their retreat.

"THE PLAN HASN'T CHANGED!" Leader Glazeanvil screamed from the frontline.

"WHY NOT?" some dwarves shouted back in response. *"LET'S SLAY THE BEAST! LET'S SLAY THE BEAST! WITH GOBLIN MAGIC, LET'S SLAY THE BEAST!"* they chanted. The confident words of the soldiers drowned out Leader Glazeanvil's authoritative yells. By the second, more and more dwarves seemed to be conforming to one popular opinion: 27's weaponry works.

While Colb listened to the frontline riling up, the backline seemed more frantic than anything else. Dwarves were rummaging around and grabbing weapons faster than 27 could mass-purchase them. Some dwarves had even started pouring their own money into piles around 27, having noticed that the goblin seemed to need nuggets to summon weapons.

"Hey," a dwarf said, poking Colb in the shoulder to get his attention. He was holding a sheet of paper from the *Yiklar Catalog*. "What does a *Yiklar Boomerang of Lightning* do?" he asked.

Colb repeated the question for 27, then picked up a mirror-coated shield and handed it to a nearby dwarf with damaged armor.

"MmMMmmm, it makes lightning strike wherever it hits," 27

replied, glancing at Sunbolt, the translator of his words. The noble goblin seemed out-of-breath as he dumped a fresh pile of nuggets into his bag. "We try to name these things in a way where I don't have to be asked what they all do."

As the battle raged on, Colb continued to help explain and distribute the Yiklar-made weapons. Eventually, he found himself face-to-face with Stibs, who must have returned with the retreated smaller army that had surrounded the summer antlizard earlier.

"Hmmm! You're safe!" Colb cheered.

"Hurmph, I suppose so," Stibs replied. The old goblin presented a deformed hilt to Colb. "Hurmph – I *hate* to admit this, but my bone sword isn't looking too good, here. I slashed at the beast's foot, and the blade melted like a slab of cowmammoth butter in the sun. Got anything better for me?"

Colb handed him one of the mirror-coated shields. It had *Yiklar Shield of Reflecting* engraved into it in Goblish. "I meant a weapon," Stibs said, although he accepted Colb's offering anyway.

"Take these," 27 said, tossing him a blowgun and a small bag of ammunition. "That packet contains fifty *Yiklar Blowgun Darts of Freezing*, yes it does. They are highest-of-quality! I think they'll be good for this fight, so I've been summoning a lot of them."

"Hurmph! They don't have that Kreet charm," Stibs grumbled, "…but they'll do." Armed with a new blowgun and shield, the old goblin ran off to rejoin the army. Colb watched nervously from behind the backline as the next leg of the battle commenced.

The *Yiklar Wand of Rainfall*-induced storm raged on, pelting the monster with water, and painting the surrounding mountains in a wet sheen. At the same time, a flurry of metal boomerangs erupted from the now-fully-united army. The boomerangs flew majestically through the air, then smashed into various parts of the beast's exoskeleton.

As each crescent-shaped weapon struck the summer antlizard's hide, a crack of lightning came from the storm above, striking the beast where the boomerang had hit. The summer antlizard shrieked with surprise at the sudden electric attacks.

A few minutes later, a unit of dwarven soldiers broke away from the frontline. They flanked the summer antlizard's side, firing a volley of freezing-cold darts at the creature's long legs. Wherever darts hit the summer antlizard, visible frost appeared on its exoskeleton, leaving cool, blackened scars on the beast's outer tissue.

The beast roared with pain, which only served to excite the dwarvish forces. The backline began throwing their boomerangs in an upwards curve, such that lightning continually struck the monster's back. At the same time, dwarves in the frontline started throwing white-painted daggers under the summer antlizard, which summoned great winds to cool down the red-hot abdomen of the beast. Getting hit from above, below, and from freezing darts on the side, the summer antlizard screamed in agony. One of its legs, completely black from frozen blowgun darts, began to crumple to the ground.

As the soldiers continued to pressure the monster, a short green goblin stepped out past the frontline. He walked until he was very visibly out in the open: halfway between the frontline and the dart-shooting group that had flanked the beast's side. Standing alone, the green figure raised his *Yiklar Bow of Returning Arrow*, aiming it true towards the monster's head – likely watching for a good moment to fire the final blow.

Seeing that familiar glint of iridhodium out-in-the-open, the summer antlizard started to glow red again, visibly engaged by the sight of this archer that had been hitting it relentlessly all battle. It's throat redder than anything else, the monster appeared to be bringing up all its remaining energy to the mouth for a single last-ditch attack – despite the cold rain still pouring down upon its head.

Colb watched anxiously as the beast adjusted its jaw, likely charging up to spew lava towards what could only be Drek. Colb then saw another green figure – probably Stibs, he guessed – breaking away from the group of dart-blowers, and running straight towards the very exposed teammate.

The hooded goblin pulled back his iridhodium arrow, then launched it towards the summer antlizard's face – but he was too late. Before the arrow could connect, the monster ducked straight to the ground, and released an enormous beam of molten liquid towards its attacker.

However, before the lava could incinerate the young goblin, the taller green figure jumped in the way. The green soldier stomped his feet into the ground, holding himself up with a rock-solid stance as the molten beam smacked into him instead – then deflected right back towards the summer antlizard.

"AaAaaaaahhhh, a fine display of the *Yiklar Shield of Reflecting* at work!" 27 cheered, now watching the battle beside Colb.

"Hmmm! That's Stibs, isn't it?" Colb worried. "He's going to be okay, yes?"

"Like all Yiklar-made products, the *Yiklar Shield of Reflecting* is most highest-of-quality, yes it is," 27 cheered. "Stibs will be fine! That item was a good choice to give him, yes it was."

Colb smiled, glad to have given his friend something to make them safe. "AaAaaaaahhhh, quite the preventative measure, yes that was," 27 continued, patting Colb on the back. "Why worry about burn wounds if you can avoid getting seared in the first place? Excellent work, medic!"

The summer antlizard let out a whimpering screech, no longer glowing red-hot. Although it didn't seem to be directly harmed by the lava Stibs had deflected back onto its face, the lack of heat left *inside* its body seemed to take a toll on the beast.

"FOR MAXTEN, GOD OF WAR!" the familiar voice of Leader Glazeanvil shouted. The exceptionally short, black-haired dwarf jumped out from the frontline of the army, and smacked his *Yiklar Bowstaff of Earthquakes* into the ground.

The earth began to shake violently, knocking everyone off their feet. The summer antlizard – weakened from the many attacks, and unprepared for the sudden earthquake – fell prone to the ground with a crash.

Leader Glazeanvil, however, stood standing, holding his *Yiklar Bowstaff of Earthquakes* strong on the ground. Soon, a wide crack formed in the earth from his rock-textured bowstaff, quickly growing in width and depth as it traveled towards the beast. The summer antlizard had no time to react as a ravine magically opened up under it. The monster screeched, becoming swallowed into the earth.

A plumb of dust rose into the sky, then settled as the ravine closed back up. The summer antlizard was finished, leaving nothing but a small pool of lava in its wake.

A realization that the battle was over entered everyone's minds, and a roar of rejoice exploded amongst the troops. The dwarves cheered for Leader Glazeanvil, who had dealt the final strike. *"The path is open! The path is open! By Maxten's decree: the path is open!"* they chanted in Dwarvish.

A group of soldiers lifted Leader Glazeanvil up on their shoulders, holding him high for all to see. "Let's head eastward, back to the campsite…" Leader Glazeanvil announced with a grin, "…and wake all the civilians with a grand party, celebrating our victory!"

"Yea!" the soldiers cheered.

"I think ye goblynns are off de hook," Sunbolt said to Colb and 27, watching the dwarves start to carry their leader back to the campsite. "Leader Glazeanvil won't soon forget that yer weapon made 'im an 'ero."

With that, Sunbolt gave them a nod, and head off to join the parade. Officially free, Colb and 27 rushed to regroup with Drek and Stibs.

"Hmmm, everyone is unharmed, yes?" Colb asked, looking his teammates up and down. The old goblin's *Yiklar Shield of Reflecting* was covered in soot.

Stibs and Drek nodded in agreement. "Rrghegh… I'm good," Drek grumbled. "Thanks to… rrghegh… Stibs, you did good out there," the young goblin spat, staring at the ground.

"Hurmph, looks like that dwarven leader won our bet," Stibs said, patting Drek on the back. "He was the one who dealt the final blow. I guess that means neither of us is better than the other – equals on the battlefield, so to speak."

Drek shrugged. "Rrghegh… I suppose so," he agreed, glancing at the blackened *Yiklar Shield of Reflecting* attached to the old goblin's arm.

"AaAaaaaahhhh, well I'd say we've officially redeemed ourselves for our mistake, yes we have," 27 announced to the group. "…which means, we're no longer guilt-obligated to travel with the army. Given that… I feel comfortable saying I'd rather go to bed than party with them right now, yes I would. What do we think about traveling westward a bit, then setting up the *Yiklar Folding Cabin* for the night?" he pitched.

The other three goblins nodded in agreement, exhausted from the strain of battle. And so, the crew trotted off in the direction of Bellra, eager to leave the battlefield behind them.

Chapter 7

MAXTEN'S MIRACLE

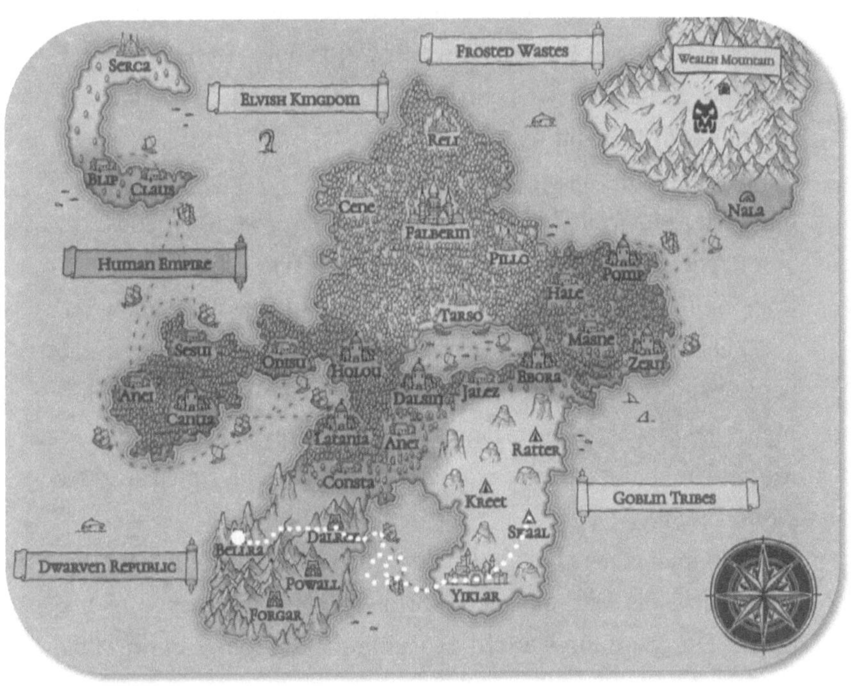

7. MAXTEN'S MIRACLE

As the goblin crew started trotting in the direction of Bellra, Colb looked back at the dwarven army. They were marching eastward – back to the temporary civilian campsite – with Leader Glazeanvil held high upon their shoulders in a parade of gratitude. A few squadrons trailed at the end of this display, working together to transport their wounded and fallen at a more leisurely pace.

The general mood of the dwarves seemed overwhelmingly upbeat due to their victory, however Colb could not help but feel uneasy seeing the charred remains of the few that had been blasted by chunks of lava during the battle.

"Hmmm, this has gotten little too real for me, yes?" Colb muttered as he trotted in a different direction, with his friends.

"Rrghegh," Drek replied gruffly, "this is way of survival. Stop thinking like medic and start thinking like soldier. We won."

"Hmmm, I guess so," Colb responded, twiddling a wand between his thumbs. The chef goblin looked down at the cool blue object held by his gnarly fingers. It was a leftover *Yiklar Wand of Rainfall* he'd found on the ground of the battlefield, which seemed worth keeping.

Colb then glanced over at Stibs, who had his new blowgun kit strapped to his belt, and new mirror-like shield strapped to his back. "Do you think we will be fighting more things during this journey, hmmm?" Colb asked the group.

"Hurmph, it's a long way to Wealth Mountain from Bellra," Stibs replied, pulling out his *Yiklar Map of Finding Location* to show Colb. "There could be anything in our way. We need to keep our guards up."

"Hmmm," Colb replied solemnly, his voice a bit quieter than

usual.

After some more walking, with Drek and Stibs lighting torches to illuminate their hike as the night darkened, the goblin crew eventually came upon a flat, open area.

27 pulled the brown doorknob out from his pocket, to which the other three goblins nodded in immediate silent agreement. And so, while the dwarves likely threw a party in the campsite they'd backtracked to, the goblins silently enjoyed a bag of dead toadroaches together in their *Yiklar Folding* Cabin, then peacefully succumbed to a little well-deserved rest.

In the morning, Colb awoke to see that Stibs had been awake for some time. The old goblin had gotten up early to forage outside the cabin, and had returned with a bundle of wild rosemushrooms before Colb had even opened his eyes. Once the chef goblin was up, he sautéed the squishy plantfungi in some grapeolive oil from 27's kitchen cabinet, then served them to the others for breakfast.

As the goblins finished up their meal, they heard the dwarven army marching nearby. "Hurmph, I guess they got an early start," Stibs mumbled. "Shall we join them?"

27 and Colb exchanged a glance. "MMmMmmmm, I guess we could?" 27 said.

"Hmmm, Leader Glazeanvil figured out we're responsible for the coralwhale, yes?" Colb informed the team. "Hmmm, but Sunbolt said we should be safe, since we redeemed ourselves with the summer antlizard, yes? Hmmm, even still, I'm not sure we should risk joining them."

"Rrghegh… let's trail them in the shadows," Drek pitched.

"MMmMmmmm, okay," 27 said. Stibs and Colb nodded in agreement as well. The goblin crew then hopped out of the *Yiklar Folding Cabin*, safely shrunk it down and stowed it away, then proceeded to trail a quarter mile behind the dwarven parade as it marched to Bellra.

The walk took the entire day, with the dwarven refugees finally reaching the village about an hour before sunset. When the goblins arrived behind them, they observed the refugees listening to a welcome speech, delivered by one of Bellra's dwarven leaders: a muscular fellow covered in hair that had been dyed bright red. His only visible facial features were his pale, pearly, spherical nose poking out of his mounds of hair, and his hammer-shaped left ear, which he'd shaved around to show off an anvil-like earring.

"*HOH*, for those of you that haven't met me, *I'M* Leader Boldpass of Bellra," the dwarf announced. Leader Boldpass spoke with vigor, putting particular emphasis on certain words without a clear reason as to why – a style of dwarven dialect, Colb supposed. "*WE* welcome you, to Bellra, brothers and sisters!" Leader Boldpass was standing on an exceptionally tall stone, speaking out to the mass before him. Around the stone, eleven other dwarves stood silently, all wearing matching sets of brilliant armor. Colb recognized the six leaders of Dalrek amongst them – including Leader Glazeanvil – and presumed the other five to be leaders of Bellra, same as Leader Boldpass.

The four goblins slid behind an old wooden cart near the refugees, deciding it best to keep a low profile for the time being. While Stibs pulled out his *Yiklar Map of Finding Location* and discussed next moves with 27, Colb continued listening to the bellowing voice of Leader Boldpass.

"*OUR* scouts informed us of what's happened in Dalrek, and so *WE'VE* dug spare sleeping holes to account for your presence," Leader Boldpass announced in Dwarvish. "*PLEASE*, make yourselves at home, *GOOD* friends from the east."

"Rrghegh… what's that guy babbling on about?" Drek muttered to Colb.

"Hmmm, his speech pattern's a little strange, but he's one of Bellra's leaders, yes?" Colb replied. "He's welcoming the refugees, yes?"

"Rrghegh… he should be welcoming *us*. We almost died slaying summer antlizard, and we didn't get anything in return."

"Hmmm, we received forgiveness for destroying Dalrek, yes?" Colb said. "I know we're laying low, but in theory, all is forgiven, yes?"

"Rrghegh… fine, we'll count that as reward from Dalrek, but Bellra still owes us too. Having that path available is probably just as good for them as it is for Dalrek," Drek spat. The young goblin seemed grumpy after walking all day. "We should ask that leader with the red hair for some goldatinum!"

"Hmmm, I think we shouldn't push our luck, yes?" Colb replied. "I think we should just grab the special spear we came for, then leave for Wealth Mountain, yes?"

"Hurmph, easier said than done," Stibs threw in. Colb and Drek looked over at the old goblin, who presented his *Yiklar Map of Finding Location* to them. "First of all, it's getting late, so we should rest now and figure out the spear thing tomorrow morning," he grumbled. "Second of all, Wealth Mountain is here." He pointed to the top-right corner of the map. "…and *we* are here," he continued, pointing to Bellra in the bottom-left portion of the map. "There's a lot of water between us and Wealth Mountain, which is something we'll have to deal with."

"MMmMmmmm, and I am not getting another boat that was made in an hour, no I am not," 27 added immediately.

"Rrghegh… so let's demand free boat from red-haired dwarf leader," Drek pitched. "Reward for fighting summer antlizard. For helping Bellra by clearing trade route."

"Hurmph, that's not a bad idea," Stibs replied. "I'd rather just get some supplies and make a boat, but if we have to keep the *whole team* comfortable…" he glanced at 27, "…then I could see that working as well."

Colb shook his head in disagreement, but stopped when he saw 27 nodding at the idea. "*Free stuff! Free stuff!*" Drek started chanting softly. Colb let out a sigh, acknowledging he'd been outvoted on the matter.

As the dwarves of Dalrek dispersed, settling into their new temporary homes, the goblin crew popped their heads out from behind the wooden cart. Like Dalrek, at least 80% of the buildings in this town were built into underground holes. It seemed that all the dwarves liked to sleep underground, and preferred to hold meetings and other business interactions beneath the soil as well. The few above-ground buildings included stone bathhouses, army training grounds, and flat tents under which dwarves appeared to be doing a strange form of yoga.

A little further back, some dwarves were wearing cheaply made armor and battling with foam sticks. A small crowd of dwarves cheered them on from the sidelines. "Rrghegh… what are they doing?" Drek asked, pointing out the odd display.

"Hmmm, I don't know, yes? I could go listen with my crystal, yes?" Colb pitched.

"Hurmph, let's stay on task, goblins," Stibs butt in.

"MMmMmmmm, Stibs," 27 replied, "it's okay. How about you and I go scouting for a secure area to set up the *Yiklar Folding Cabin*, while these two investigate that crowd? We'll meet back here in an hour to grab Colb and Drek, then turn in for the night at the cabin. Tomorrow morning, we'll have fresh minds to locate the *Yiklar Spear of Irreversible Death* and acquire a boat, yes we will."

The goblins all shrugged in agreement. With that, 27 and Stibs set off to scout for a good place to make camp. "Rrghegh… alright, Colb," Drek mumbled. "Let's go – it's time to eavesdrop."

The goblin duo carefully made their way over to the odd performance, and hid in a nearby sleeping hole that gave them a good view of the action. Colb's *Amulet of Open Ears* radiated with light as he listened to the Dwarvish voices, which sounded higher-pitched – perhaps, younger – than the voices he was used to from the soldiers of Dalrek.

"Have at thee!" a dwarf with silvopper-colored hair yelled, stabbing a foam stick into another dwarf's parchment armor. Colb translated a play-by-play to Drek as he listened.

"Aaauhg," the stabbed dwarf replied, the foam rod now getting tangled in his sticky brown beard. "How could you, a lowly servant, defy me, the great tyrant king of the dwarves?"

"I am no servant to you," the first dwarf replied, as other dwarves started surrounding his opponent. "I am Maxten, and I am a servant to dwarvenkind." The other dwarves pulled out foam sticks of their own, and pointed them menacingly towards the tyrant king. "Through war, we now end your tyrannical rain. Let the new Dwarven Republic last longer than the Dwarven Kingdom!"

Another dwarf stepped forward from the group. "Look around you as your empire halls, erm- falls, you dirty king. Know that Maxten will become worshiped as the god of war upon his death. Through his miracles, our republic will thrive forever."

"Rrghegh… Maxen? God of war? Some dwarf was screaming about that during the summer antlizard fight," Drek mumbled.

"Hmmm, I think this is a historical reenactment of some sort, yes?" Colb noted.

"Nooooooooooo…" the dwarven king cried, as the dwarves surrounding him began to beat him senseless with their foam sticks.

"Thus end the events of the great war, which concluded 2,086 years ago today," a young, yellow-haired dwarf announced to the nearby hairy crowd that had been watching. She absent-mindedly twirled part of her bright beard in her fingers as she spoke. "Maxten, who eventually became known as our dwarven god of war, still looks over us from beyond the grave. He looks over Bellra, our leaders, and indeed the entirety of the Dwarven Republic."

The announcer stepped back, and was replaced by a much more nervous-looking dwarf. This dwarf looked down at a sheet of parchment, and started stiffly reading from it. "Maxten's story tells us that no enemy is too powerful for a dwarf to overcome." This dwarf's voice sounded a bit dry, and their performance was a little bland compared to the yellow-haired presenter before them. "However, not every society can surpass overwhelming odds like a dwarven one. Thus, with the perfect Dwarven Republic created, Maxten spent his final 86 years of life assisting *other* societies that were in need of dwarven might. Even beyond death, he continues to do this: providing a miracle for allies of our good Dwarven Republic once each century."

Colb and Drek exchanged a glance. "Miracle?" Drek questioned.

"Hmmm, that's what they said, yes?" Colb replied with a shrug.

The dwarf let out an audible sigh, then stepped back as a third speaker approached the crowd. This dwarf had bright, purple-dyed hair styled in such a way that his head looked like a furry ball covered in spikes. "Almost one thousand years ago, Maxten's miracle empowered an ancient human to defeat an insanely overgrown autumn giraffeworm that threatened their society. As a result, the Human Empire remains friendly with the Dwarven Republic to this day," the dwarf announced. "Tomorrow, Maxten's miracle will strike again: this time, for the benefit of the Goblin Tribes, whose investments into Bellra have done much to improve our way-of-life."

Drek's ears rose with intrigue. "The goblins are a people of knowledge," the announcer continued. "As inventors, they wish to empower a weapon of their own creation with Maxten's might. Such a gift will allow them to someday overcome an otherwise insurmountable foe – and we give it willingly, as thanks for their many, many gifts to the city of Bellra."

Hmmm, I see what 27 meant when he said the western side of the Dwarven Republic was more receptive to the Yiklar, Colb thought to himself. *These dwarves of Bellra seem to have a much more favorable opinion of goblins than those of Dalrek, yes?*

The purple-haired dwarf then stepped back in line with the other two speakers. "Look to the skies tomorrow morning, and be witness to the power of Maxten," the three dwarves announced in unison.

The dwarven crowd produced a modest applause, as the actors continued to slap the king around with their foam sticks.

"Hmmm, now the crowd is applauding, yes?" Colb translated.

"Rrghegh… that part I could tell for myself," Drek replied. "That miracle sounded like it might be for us?"

"Hmmm, it did sound like that," Colb agreed. "I guess we'll find out tomorrow, yes?"

The two goblins watched the dwarven actors take a bow, then disperse with the crowd. The duo then hopped out of the hole, and looked up at the sun. Seeing they had a little time left, they snuck over to the dwarven bathhouse and cleaned themselves off in a secluded corner.

"AaAaaaaahhhh," 27 proclaimed when the crew reunited at sunset. "We've found a most spectacular place for the *Yiklar Folding Cabin*, yes we have!"

"Hmmm, where might that be?" Colb replied.

"Hurmph – we just put it, like, behind a hill," Stibs clarified.

"AaAaaaaahhhh, and we purchased some food for the night!" 27 cheered, presenting a medium-sized burlap sack full of food. "I think Leader Glazeanvil has been keeping quiet, yes he has been, because the dwarves of Bellra seem to *love* us! We got fantastic deal on this food, yes we did – which is good, because my pockets are *bleeding* after giving away all those weapons, yes they are. I'm… actually running little bit low. We should be careful about any more big spending, yes we should be."

With that, the goblin crew head over to their campsite and activated the *Yiklar Folding Cabin*. They then piled into the dining area, where they enjoyed a meal of fresh mangonuts, chewy rosemushrooms, fried iguanafrogs (a dwarven delicacy, which intrigued Colb quite a bit), and some classic daisywheat bread buns. During the feast, Drek discussed the play he'd witnessed to 27 and Stibs. Colb smiled, pleased that dinner wasn't just the four goblins silently chewing today.

After the meal, the goblins rested, eager to seek out the *Yiklar Spear of Irreversible Death* next morning – and thus complete a major milestone in their quest.

An hour before sunrise the next day, the magical lights within the cabin suddenly flashed on. "Rrghegh…" Drek groaned, sounding unhappy to be awake.

"Aaauh, wha-?" 27 mumbled from his *Yiklar Floating Bed*.

"Aah, good morning you four!" spouted a cheerful goblin voice from the cabin's entrance.

"Aaah, good morning indeed!" agreed a similarly joyful,

deeper goblin voice from the same place.

The goblin crew rolled from their sleeping positions to face the front door, which had been opened. Two young goblins with pink-colored eyes were poking their heads through it.

"I'm 83!" shouted the first goblin, smiling through a pair of thin-framed glasses.

"And I'm 84!" the second goblin continued, scratching his electronze nose ring as he spoke.

"We're sister and brother by blood," 83 announced, "and of course, are goblins of the Yiklar tribe as well, yes we are. I don't believe we've met," she continued, looking at 27.

"I'm the primary Yiklar merchant for the Dwarven Republic."

"...and I'm a blacksmith from the *Yiklar Factories*, but 1 sent me out to work on special, extra-rare item here in Bellra," 84 added.

"Hur… Hurmph? Who are these?" Stibs blurted, sitting up and rubbing his eyes.

"AaAaaaaahhhh, 83 and 84!" 27 exclaimed, jumping out of his bed. He began to dance in a smooth jig the second his feet hit the floor, to which 83 and 84 started bobbing their heads in synchrony.

"Hmmm," Colb mumbled, picking up his shield and wand from a bedside table. "84, you are maker of the *Yiklar Spear of Irreversible Death* we need, yes?"

"Aaah, sort of, yes!" the goblin agreed, still just poking his head in through the cabin door under his sister's. "So far, I have crafted the most classic, high-quality *Yiklar Spear of Armor Piercing*, yes I have," he clarified.

"Which is worth 52,086 goldatinum pieces, 3 electronze pieces, and 1 silvopper piece," 27 and 83 recited in unison.

"Aaah, yes! However, the *Yiklar Spear of Irreversible Death*," 84 continued, "is not normal Yiklar-made item, no it is not." 27

nodded in agreement, unable to recall a pre-set price or any special offers for such an item.

"This is because," 84 explained, "our leader 1 has arranged for the dwarves of Bellra to give my *Yiklar Spear of Armor Piercing* a little bit of a boost using rare magic."

"AaAaaaaahhhh," 27 said, rubbing his chin. "So you're taking a most exquisitely high-quality Yiklar-made weapon, and enhancing it further with the most rarest of magic? To create an item not usually available within the Yiklar inventory?"

"Yes, most precisely," the siblings agreed in unison.

"It's an experiment," 83 continued, "…but in theory, the enchantment will create a powerful weapon that can overcome any foe – although it will work only once, yes it will!"

"Aaah, this is most true," 84 agreed. "If you use the spear to strike any creature that could've been defeated another way, then that most rarest of magic will have been wasted," the siblings warned in unison.

"Rrghegh… you guys are creepy," Drek muttered. The Ratter goblin then shoved his face back into the bean bag chair, as a demonstration that he wasn't ready to wake up.

"Aah, but we must get moving now," 83 responded, wagging her finger. The siblings continued to bob their heads in alignment with 27's dance as they spoke.

"Mmmm, yes, the leaders of Bellra will be enchanting the spear very soon, and we think you should be there for it," 84 agreed. "It will give you a better understanding of the power contained within this most flawless-of-quality item."

"Rrghegh, is it Maxten's miracle?" Drek mumbled into the beanbag chair.

83 and 84 both did a double-take with surprise. "That's some impressive historical knowledge you've got there!" they cheered

in unison.

"Rrghegh, I'll get up if you stop talking at the same time like that. It's unnatural," Drek complained. The siblings silently nodded in synchrony, then pulled their heads out of the cabin, shutting the door behind them.

Once the goblin crew had gotten ready for the day, 83 and 84 met them outside. The synchronized duo led the goblin crew to a building of metal and stone, built into a deep dwarven-dug hole. The six goblins climbed down, entering the building from a hatch within the roof. They were greeted by a dozen hairy dwarves in shiny goldatinum-colored metal armor. The goblins instantly recognized them as Dalrek and Bellra's leaders.

27 and Colb glanced at Leader Glazeanvil cautiously. His hair-covered head twitched a little bit as he faced them. The *Yiklar Bowstaff of Earthquakes* was still attached to a strap in his armor.

"*WELCOME*, good goblins," Leader Boldpass cheered. His extreme emphasis on the word "*welcome*" came off as a bit jarring to Colb.

"I see six goblins, not two," one of Dalrek's leaders muttered. "Leader Glazeanvil, those are the four goblins that assisted your army, correct?"

"Hrm..." Leader Glazeanvil mumbled.

"Sorry, I didn't catch that," the Dalrek leader replied.

"Yes..." Leader Glazeanvil confirmed. "Those are the goblins that sold me this bowstaff, which *I* used to vanquish our foe."

"That's great," the Dalrek leader cheered. "And now that we're visiting Bellra – and it's been too long, by the way," he continued, shaking hands with Leader Boldpass. "We see that the relationship between our people and those of the Yiklar tribe goes much deeper than we knew."

"*HOH*, indeed!" Leader Boldpass agreed. "*OUR* town has seen great advancements thanks to investments from the leader of Yiklar." 27's ears perked up at the mention of investment. "*THAT* goblin, the one named… well, 1 was his name, I suppose. *HE* was the first one to believe in good Madrock, who quickly became the best blacksmith in town after 1 helped him open his store."

"*AH*, and don't forget Thorthurin," another Bellra leader agreed – his emphasis-ridden dialect similar to that of Leader Boldpass. "*WITH*out 1's help, Thorthurin would have never been able to open the good Drunkblade Tavern, *WHICH* is where we hold all of our town meetings now." The other leaders of Bellra all nodded in agreement.

Colb looked at 27. He could tell that gears were turning in the noble goblin's mind, intrigued by this opportunity to understand how 1 used investing – a foreign concept, for certain – to convince Bellra's leaders to share such powerful, once-per-century magic with the Yiklar tribe.

"*WE* could go on and on about how 1 has transformed this good village with his wealth," Leader Boldpass interjected, "*BUT*, better yet, we have come today to repay that debt in the best way we know how."

"And *WE*, have come to *WATCH*!" a leader from Dalrek threw in. A couple other Dalrek leaders chuckled, perhaps amused by their companion's imitation of Bellra's odd dialect.

Without further ado, Leader Boldpass pulled out a glass orb, which was just a little bit shy of the size of Colb's head. A glittery blue dust fluttered around inside the glass, twisting and turning within the spherical prison. Listening a little closer, Colb could make out a dwarven chant "Maxten, Maxten, Maxten…" very faintly emanating from the orb.

"*THIS*, is the miracle orb of Maxten, god of war," Leader Boldpass announced to the group. The eleven other leaders, along with 83 and 84, dropped to a knee to show their respect. "*MAXTEN* was the greatest dwarf in our culture. *HE* led a revolution which changed our society for the better."

Seeing the others, Colb, 27, and Stibs kneeled. Drek continued to stand, looking mesmerized by the floating blue particles within the glass sphere. "*ONCE* per a thousand years, this orb glows again, such that we may ask a favor – a miracle – from the spirit of the long-deceased Maxten. *HE* was a selfless dwarf, throwing himself into his cause for the benefit of those he cared about."

Colb thought back to the play he'd seen with Drek. In his mind, he could only picture Maxten as a young dwarven actor beating another actor senseless with a foam sword.

"*THEREFORE*, we the dwarves of Bellra, holders of Maxten's Miracle Orb, have chosen to give this millennium's miracle as a *GIFT*, to the good goblin 1, who alone brought great prosperity to the dwarves of Bellra."

With this, 84 stepped out of the room for a second, then returned carrying a black spear painted with a swirling white pattern. He kneeled, holding what could only be a *Yiklar Spear of Armor Piercing* up to the red-haired dwarf.

"*MAXTEN*," Leader Boldpass announced, holding the orb close to the spear. "*WE* wish to imbue this weapon with your miracle. *PLEASE*, make it such that this weapon will irreversibly kill the next creature it is stabbed into. *PLEASE*, make it such that the creature slain by this weapon, can never come back! *NOT* by soul magic! *NOT* by any magic! *MAKE* it such that not even another miracle could undo a death caused by this spear! *NEXT* time these goblins face an insurmountable enemy, *LET* your infinite power shine through this weapon! ...and as you enchant this spear, *PLEASE* show us some of that famous showmanship of yours, for your followers to enjoy?"

As Leader Boldpass finished the last sentence, the blue glitter drained out of the orb, leaving it as an empty glass sphere. Explosive sounds started erupting from outside, high in the air.

Colb looked up, towards the sound. A sunroof window revealed the sky had shifted into a mirage of thousands of different shades of blue, all swirling and exploding together. The firework-like display shifted and glowed, swirling into a violent vortex.

Like a tornado, the swirl of blue color touched down to the very sunroof window Colb was looking through, shattered it, and absorbed the glass fragments. "*MAXTEN, MAXTEN, MAXTEN*" hordes of dwarves chanted from above-ground, becoming audible after the window had been broken.

 The rippling blue vortex flowed into the room, then rabbitbeelined into the *Yiklar Spear of Armor Piercing*.

After a few over-stimulating minutes of color and light, the vortex finished fully flowing into the spear, and the dwarves above-ground quieted their chant. "Now *THAT* was a show!" Leader Boldpass cheered. The eleven other leaders began singing a religious song, rejoicing in what they'd just observed.

Colb looked at the now *Yiklar Spear of Irreversible Death*, which had turned dark blue in color. Once the ceremony was over, 84 sheathed it, and handed the weapon to 27. The six goblins then climbed back up and out of the building to debrief together aboveground.

"Hurmph, why didn't we use the miracle to directly summon a bunch of goldatinum for our tribes?" Stibs questioned. "Or at least, use it to directly irradicate whatever monster 1 was worried about being near Wealth Mountain?"

"Aaah, those are not the types of miracles Maxten likes to grant, no they are not," 84 replied.

"Mmm, Maxten has made it clear that his miracles exist to

empower lesser creatures to fight against insurmountable odds," 83 continued. "*Lesser creatures* referring to non-dwarf societies, in his opinion."

"Mmmm, of course, that's not very logical," 84 whispered. "Goblins are just as good as dwarves. The idea that only dwarves can defeat insurmountable odds is archaic."

"However, it's not like we were going to let them give this miracle away to the humans, no we were not," 83 added.

"Not to mention, from a manufacturing perspective, this experiment was very cool, yes it was!" 84 cheered.

"By treating Bellra, home of Maxten's Miracle Orb, especially well ever since he became leader, 1 was able to…" 83 and 84 said in unison, trailing off as they realized Drek was glaring at them.

"You can finish the sentence, sister," 84 said.

"No, you may – I insist," 83 replied.

"…1 was able to ensure they would choose *us* for the miracle gift this century," 27 finished, scratching his chin. "I don't know how he comes up with these plans, no I do not."

"That's why he's the best," 83 cheered.

"And a *fantastic* goblin to work with for engineering research," 84 added. "This experiment was *most* interesting! If you guys end up using it against a monster, be sure to tell me how it turned out! Miracles are such a fascinating research topic, yes they are! Such rare magic!"

27 nodded, patting the sheathed spear endearingly. "I'll be sure to inform you personally!" he cheered.

With the *Yiklar Spear of Irreversible Death* secured, the goblin crew made their way to the port north of town, which was built into a cut out between two mountains surrounding Bellra.

When they arrived, the goblins looked out at the peaceful peppersalt tides, which beckoned them onwards to the next leg of their adventure.

"Rrghegh… we forgot to ask for boat," Drek noted.

"Hmmm, I remembered, but I didn't say anything," Colb replied. "I think that would've been pushing our luck with Leader Glazeanvil, yes?"

"Hurmph! It's no problem. I can get us over this ocean," Stibs cheered. "I just need to find some wood."

"MMmMmmmm," 27 groaned.

Chapter 8

SAILING INJURY

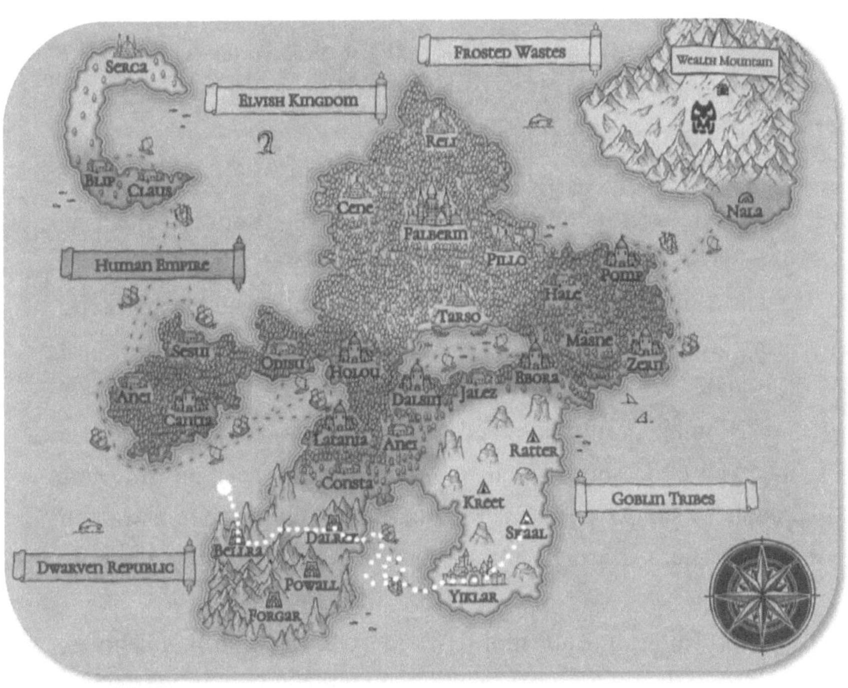

8. SAILING INJURY

"MMmMmmmm, apologies, but I'd rather not get in another handmade boat," 27 worried.

"Hurmph, then you're welcome to buy one for us," Stibs grumbled.

"Well – I am little bit low on funding in my *Yiklar Bank Account*, yes I am," 27 confided. "I went frantic buying items during the battle, yes I did, and... to be honest, I lost track of what I was spending. By the end of the battle, my personal funds had wholly depleted, yes they had, and I'd already let Sunbolt take back Leader Glazeanvil's money. With all that in mind... well, there's not really anything left."

The other three goblins gave the noble a surprised look. "Rrghegh, you're broke?" Drek chuckled. "You? Richie rich goblin?"

"MMmMmmmm – I was one single goblin purchasing literal army worth of goods, yes I was!" 27 retorted. "Of course it cost fortune!"

"Hmmm," Colb mumbled, scratching his chin. He noticed a dwarven trade ship, which floated peacefully near the shore. A couple of sailors were loading boxes onto the wooden-and-cloth vessel. "Let's ask them for a ride," he declared, pointing out the sailors.

Not waiting for a response, Colb trotted over to the dwarves, who were dressed in leather armor not unlike his own. "What?" a heavy-set dwarf asked, as Colb stopped in front of him.

Colb's *Yiklar Amulet of Open Ears* glowed with understanding as he stared up at the dwarf. "Hmmm, do you speak Goblish?" Colb asked.

"I-I don't know what he's saying," the sailor responded,

looking at his companion. The second dwarf shrugged as well.

Colb glanced back at his crew, who appeared to have followed behind him. "Hmmm, show them where we want to go on the map, yes?" he said. Stibs pulled out his *Yiklar Map of Finding Location*, displayed it to the dwarves, and pointed at the Frosted Wastes in the northeastern corner.

"What, you want to go there?" the sailor guessed. Colb nodded. "Are you asking us to bring you?" Colb nodded again. "No," he grumbled, then went back to stacking boxes.

"What did he say?" 27 asked.

"Hmmm, he's not interested, yes?" Colb said, feeling disappointed.

"Hurmph, try being persistent," Stibs pitched. "I know sailors – they like the path of least resistance. If we keep bugging him, eventually he might decide that saying yes is easier than saying no." Stibs walked up to the dwarf, and again displayed the map.

"What? Go away," the sailor grumbled. Colb just stared back at him blankly, while Stibs continued to hold the map out.

"What does he want?" the sailor asked his companion.

The second, thinner dwarf set down a box and walked up to the goblin crew. "That's a nice map," he said. "Nothing's labeled in Dwarvish, but I can tell where things are just by the drawings. Did you four make this?"

Colb shook his head. "Well, then what do you want?" the second dwarf asked. Colb pointed at their trading ship, which looked like it was just about ready to set sail.

"You want our ship?" the second dwarf chuckled. "No can do, little guy." Colb shook his head.

"I think they wanted to hitch a ride. They're looking to go all the way here, but I already said no," the first dwarf grumbled, pointing at the Frosted Wastes on the map.

"Oh, we're not going that far, buddy," the second sailor replied. "We're going to Cantia, then down to Forgar, then back here." He traced their path out with his thick finger on the *Yiklar Map of Finding Location*.

"Hmmm, they're going to Cantia," Colb observed. "That's closer to the Frosted Wastes, yes?"

Stibs turned the map back towards himself, and stared at it. "Hurmph, that's true," he replied. "If we go there, we could then make some more progress by land."

Stibs turned the map back to the dwarves, and pointed at Cantia. "You want to go to Cantia, now?" the sailor guessed. Colb nodded. The dwarf shrugged. "Alright."

"Really?" the first sailor questioned.

"Yea, why not? We're going there anyway," the second dwarf responded. "Plus, didn't Shieldbell say a goblin gave her the money to start this whole operation? Plus, Maxten just gave his miracle to the goblin tribes, didn't he? Helping goblins must be good luck!" The first dwarf shrugged in agreement. With that, the goblins had their ride.

The four travelers climbed onto the dwarven tradership, which was respectably large for having just a two-dwarf crew. It was pulled by a series of three sails and sported a catcrow's nest high up in the sky.

After they finished packing some finals sets of boxes, the two dwarves set sail. The heavy-set dwarf manned the steering wheel, while the other climbed up the catcrow's nest to navigate. Colb, 27, Stibs and Drek sat on the frontmost deck of the ship, feeling the wind on their pointed ears as the ship whisked them out on the peppersalt sea.

After they'd been traveling without a word for a few hours, Colb decided to start up a conversation. "Hmmm, you know what humans are like, yes?" the chef goblin questioned 27, who had been monotonously tapping the ship's deck with his sharp set of claws.

"MMmMmmmm, only what I could garner from a class I took at *Yiklar University*," 27 replied, glancing at Colb. "Although Yiklar goods are enjoyed across the goblin and dwarven lands, we've never broken into the market of humans or elves. The rest of this trip is going to be quite foreign land for me, yes it is."

"Hmmm, you do know how to speak with humans, though, yes?" Colb inquired.

"Yes," 27 replied, "I did learn Hewmish in my studies, yes I did. I suppose some part of me wondered if they'd ever be potential customers of Yiklar. However, we were warned that they can be dangerous, unpredictable creatures."

"Hmmm, how so?" Colb questioned.

"MMmMmmmm, from what I have heard – and again, we are headed farther north than I have ever gone, so I am out of my element here, yes I am – but from my studies, I've learned that the humans find us disgusting," 27 responded. "When Yiklar goblins approached them in the past, they spurned our items and threatened us if we didn't leave, yes they did."

"Hmmm, that doesn't sound very nice," Colb muttered.

CREAK! A large wave bumped up against the boat. "We're on course," the dwarf announced from up in the catcrow's nest, "but the waters are getting a bit bumpy."

"Aye," the ship's captain shouted back.

"MMmMmmmm – what are they saying?" 27 asked.

"Hmmm, the waters are getting a little bumpy, but we're on course, yes?" Colb answered.

"AaAaaaaahhhh, I see," 27 replied. "Erm… what were we talking about again?"

"Humans not liking goblins, yes?" Colb reminded.

"AaAaaaaahhhh, humans, yes," 27 continued. "If I am remembering correctly – and again, I may not be – I believe humans and elves are at odds, as well. Now, elves I understand even less than humans, you must keep in mind, but, it just goes to show that the humans aren't very friendly, no they are not." Colb nodded his head as he listened to his friend's words. "I've sometimes dreamed of being the goblin to finally break into the human market, yes I have… however, being spurned and threatened doesn't sound most pleasant, no it does not."

27 scratched his head, as if pondering the problem. "But… you never know. I think Yiklar products are quite fantastic, yes I do. I've always thought, if I ever met a human, that I'd try to be the first goblin to sell them something. The first goblin to convince them that we aren't an enemy, and they can receive most highest-of-quality items if they'd just give us a little trust. Plus, once humans see how wonderful Yiklar's products are, there's no way they could continue to dislike us!"

"Hmmm, well if that's your dream, then you should give it a try, yes?" Colb agreed.

"Making some sales would help with our money issue, too, yes it would," 27 noted. "A kickback from each sale goes straight to my *Yiklar Bank Account*."

CREAK! Another wave plunged into the side of the boat, knocking the sailor in the catcrow's nest off his feet. "*WOAH!*" he shouted, falling over the edge of the high-up vantage point.

Stibs jumped to his feet, his wrinkly ears perking up at the sound of danger. "Hurmph, I've gotcha," he shouted, hustling to get under the catcrow's nest. The dwarf tumbled down one of the ship's masts, plummeting to the deck – where Stibs dived to catch him. A sharp *CRACK!* echoed throughout the vessel as the dwarf landed on the old goblin.

The ship's captain and the rest of the goblin crew rushed to the scene. "Rrghegh… did the boat just crack?" Drek cried out in fear.

"Not… catastrophically," Stibs replied from under the dwarf, as if holding back tears.

The captain lifted his companion off the old goblin, who laid on the ground gritting his teeth. "I'm okay, I'm okay," the dwarf assured. "Thank you for breaking my fall," he cheered.

"Hmmm, he says thank you, yes?" Colb translated.

Drek kneeled next to Stibs, helping him sit up. The old goblin's right leg had been smushed into the deck, and was trapped between two planks of wood.

"He squished your leg!" Drek shouted angrily.

"…My leg," Stibs replied. "It hurts."

"You're still okay?" the captain asked his companion. The thinner dwarf nodded in reply. "Go drop the anchor," the captain ordered, to which his companion rushed to another part of the boat.

"I'm going to go below-deck, and try to cut this goblin's leg free, alright?" he announced. Colb nodded, then kneeled to investigate the crushed limb.

Stibs winced as Colb poked at the wounded area. "Medic…" he mumbled through grit teeth. "Please fix this. It's like my leg's on fire."

Colb looked around at the others expectantly, then remembered that he was the medic. "Hmmm," he replied, looking at the misshapen limb. "I do not see any fire, yes?"

"Hurmph, it just feels… really hot. I think… this is the worst pain I've ever… experienced… Fix this… please."

"Hmmm," Colb replied. He poked the damaged area some more, which made Stibs wince and grit his teeth even tighter. The old goblin's ankle had twisted in an angle atypical to how a leg normally should look. "I think… I will need some medical supplies to fix this, yes?" Colb pondered aloud.

"You… you don't have any?" Stibs asked. "Aren't you a medic?"

"Hmmm… I didn't bring any," Colb replied. "I guess I didn't realize I'd need to bring something like that," he continued, glancing at 27.

"MMmMmmmm, well no reason to argue about who doesn't have supplies, or who said someone was a medic when they weren't, or anything like that right now," 27 defended.

Stibs suddenly hissed, as the ship's captain shoved his leg up out of the crack. "I didn't even have to use my saw!" the captain cheered, his voice audible through the newly created crack to below-deck.

The captain and his crew member then returned to the head of the ship. "Thanks for protecting my crewmate," the captain said. "We'll call it even for the free ride, how about that?" he chuckled.

The other dwarf presented a small box to the goblins. "Here's our first-aid kit, if you need it. And yes, thanks again for helping me. I'm going to start being more careful about staying up there when the waters get turbulent."

"Hmmm, perfect, yes?" Colb cheered, accepting the box. Unable to understand Goblish, the two dwarves simply nodded at Colb, then head back to their posts. They hoisted the anchor, and set sail once again.

Colb popped open the small kit, and poured out the contents: two white rags, and some dusty rosemushroom chunks.

"Hmmm, this is kind of a sad medical kit," Colb observed. He picked up a rosemushroom chunk, dusted it off on his armor, and fed it to Stibs. "Do you have anything better, 27?"

"MMmMmmmm, the Yiklar tribe does not produce healing supplies, no it does not," 27 replied, patting his *Yiklar Bag of Traveling Inventory* as he spoke. "Not that we're swimming in funds right now, anyway."

"Rrghegh… maybe humans will have medical supplies?" Drek pitched. He looked worriedly at crushed limb of the friend that had saved his life just the other day.

"AaAaaaaahhhh, I suppose we could search for human medical supplies once we reach Cantia," 27 replied. The noble goblin scratched the back of his bald head anxiously. "MMmMmmmm… but that's assuming we can find a way to pay for it, and that the humans don't find us undesirable and attack," he worried.

"Hmmm, every goblin is different, yes? As is every dwarf, yes?" Colb said. "Perhaps, if we find the right humans, you could find someone to do business with, yes?" Colb pitched.

"AaAaaaaahhhh, although I am worried – the optimism I appreciate, yes I do!" 27 cheered. Stibs wriggled on the ground in pain. "…it's worth shot, yes it is," he continued, looking down at the pained friend.

"Hmmm, Stibs, you should rest until we get to Cantia, yes?" Colb ordered. "I'll make some rosemushroom stew, then we'll find better medical supplies in human city, yes?"

Colb wrapped the two white rags around the goblin's injured limb, then led a hobbling Stibs down to the ship's lower level, where he could rest away from the action. The chef then whipped up a rosemushroom soup in the ship's rudimentary kitchen, to feed both Stibs and to provide dinner for everyone else at the end of the day.

The next morning, while Colb was giving Stibs company below-deck, Drek rushed into the room. "Rrghegh… I spotted land in distance," Drek announced. "…may I?" he continued, reaching for the *Yiklar Map of Finding Location* sticking out of the injured goblin's backpack.

Stibs nodded, looking tired and pained. "Rrghegh… what was it? Wherearewe? Whereami?" Suddenly, the map glowed, flashing Drek in the face. He dropped the parchment and rubbed his eyes.

Colb picked the map up off the ground. "Hmmm! We're very close to Cantia!" he cheered, seeing their latest position magically marked on the parchment. "We'll find some human medical supplies for you, yes?" he promised, looking at Stibs.

"Rrghegh… you should go take look with 27. I'll stay here with Stibs," Drek said.

With that, Colb gave back the *Yiklar Map of Finding Location*, and climbed above-deck to peek out over the water. In the distance, he saw a forest-filled shore, upon which structures of black bismuthslate bricks and brown mapleoak wood blanketed the landscape. Wherever there weren't buildings or trees, humongous patches of clovergrass – short, green plants unlike anything he'd seen in the Goblin Tribes or Dwarven Republic – spread far and wide. *Hmmm, wow!* he thought to himself.

"Hmmm, this is the Human Empire?" Colb asked, walking up to 27. "I see a lot of structures, yes? It's more advanced than I was expecting, yes?"

"AaAaaaaahhhh, indeed!" 27 replied. "There are many buildings, yes there are. And these humans must like to trade, if the dwarves came all this way to ship goods for them. Maybe we *will* be able to find someone I could do business with? Someone to sell us human medical supplies?"

"Hmmm, I hope so, yes?" Colb replied. He thought about Stibs, who had stayed silent but was clearly in pain all night. The white rags and rosemushroom soup had not done nearly enough to fix his leg. "I hope so."

Chapter 9

THE SPECIFIC STORE

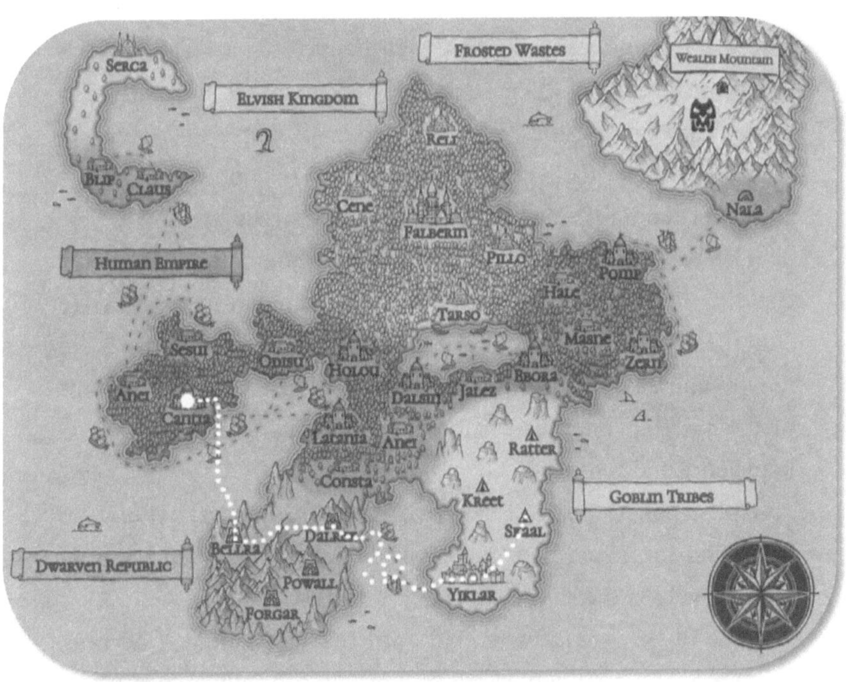

9. THE SPECIFIC STORE

It was raining when the team reached port in Cantia. The crystal-clear drops chilled the bald heads of the goblin crew. Colb put on his chef's hat, and Drek pulled up his hood to keep dry.

"AaAaaaaahhhh, the Human Empire!" 27 announced to the team as Stibs hobbled off the boat with an arm supported by Drek. "I have not been in a human city before, no I have not," 27 continued. The goblins surveyed the streets, which were paved in bismuthslate: a common stone, smooth and black in color, with natural rainbow designs subtly etched into it – a feature which could only be seen when sunlight bounced off it at a particular angle. The buildings of this town stood in all shapes and sizes, yet were uniform in their material – mapleoak wood, in this case – and had been built along a precise grid-like street layout.

The wet roads were empty, save for a couple human guards standing in the rain. The guards wore chainmail armor, and were equipped with sheathed metal swords. Their pale faces were mostly hairless, save for puffs of brown or black hair on the tops of their heads. They had smooth, rounded ears, and both stood between 5 and 6 feet tall.

Colb looked back at the two dwarven sailors, who were hesitating to unload their boxes. The chef goblin tilted his head inquisitively at the ship's captain.

"We're not going to unload until the rain's gone," he said. "You four are free to go wherever you'd like, but the two of us are going to wait out the weather for now." The captain then saluted goodbye, and head below-deck.

"Farewell," the second dwarf said. "Tell your friend thanks again for catching me." The sailor then followed his captain down the boat's stairs.

"Hmmm," Colb said, dismounting the ship and catching up with the goblin crew. "The dwarves are waiting out the rain, yes? I don't think we should wait so long, though, since Stibs needs medical supplies as soon as possible, yes?"

"I… I am not sure where to find merchant amongst these large creatures, no I am not," 27 muttered. He looked over at the two human guards, standing taught in the rain with weapons at their sides.

"Hmmm… let's just try random buildings, yes?" Colb pitched. "If something goes wrong, we can just run away, yes?"

"MMmMmmmm, I guess that's better than doing nothing, yes it is," 27 agreed with a shrug. The noble then pulled the *Yiklar Folding Cabin* doorknob out from his pocket, and tossed it to Drek. "MMmMmmmm, I need to make money somehow, and then Colb needs to find medical supplies, so why don't you two set up camp in nearby forest while we explore Cantia?" 27 pitched.

Drek nodded in agreement, still supporting Stibs by his left arm as he caught the *Yiklar Folding Cabin* doorknob. The old goblin silently grit his teeth. Try as he might to look tough, Colb could tell his eyepatched companion was struggling to withstand the immense pain coming from his leg.

While Drek and Stibs set off to build a campsite, 27 and Colb trotted towards the nearest human-made structure. "Hmmm, instead of random buildings, we could also ask those humans for directions, yes?" Colb questioned as his wet chef's hat began to sag over his face. He pointed at the chainmail-wearing guards standing in the rain.

A guard turned, noticing Colb's pointed finger. He drew his sword, and tilted his head cautiously at the goblins.

"MMmMmmmm, I think we should start by speaking with

unarmed humans, just to be safe, yes I do," 27 replied. The duo proceeded to scamper down a nearby path, particularly avoiding the guards.

The two goblins eventually ended up at the entrance to a randomly-chosen building, which contained a basic wooden door. "I have no idea if this is a shop, no I do not," 27 muttered. The two looked forwards at the doorknob, which was eye-level for their short figures. Colb shrugged and turned the knob with his small, clawed hand.

"Hmmm, only one way to find out, yes?" he said.

Colb pushed on the door, and it creaked open, revealing a dusty room lit by a fireplace. An elderly human woman sat knitting in a rocking chair, with an obese catcrow sleeping at her feet. Colb looked at 27 expectantly.

"Hmmm, you're the one who speaks human, yes?" he whispered.

"MMmMmmmm, yes," 27 whispered back. The noble took a step into the room, and raised his arms in a welcoming gesture.

Colb's crystal necklace began to glow as 27 announced his presence in Hewmish. "AaAaaaaahhhh, human! Might you be a merchant of medicines, or someone interested in purchasing highest-of-quality goods?"

The elderly woman looked up suddenly, her body starting to quiver as she let out a startled yelp. Her catcrow jumped to its feet, looking similarly surprised, and began to hiss at the intruders while menacingly fluffing up its feathers. The woman slowly reached for a nearby bell, then started ringing it violently. 27 and Colb took a step back from the odd display. "MMmMmmmmm, is... is that a yes? A no?" 27 asked.

Stomps came from a nearby staircase as an adult human with a ginger-colored beard rushed into the scene. "Hey!" he shouted.

"AaAaaaaahhhh, yes, hey-hello!" 27 cheered back.

"Get out of our house!" the human yelled back, pulling a sheathed sword down from a display above the fireplace.

"AaAaaaaahhhh, we did not know this was a house, no we did not. Could you direct us to your merchant of medicine?"

The man drew a thin metal sword out from the dusty sheath, then pointed the tip towards 27. "MMmMmmmm, I… I see you are armed now, yes you are," 27 continued, retreating to be in line with Colb. The two then stepped back into the rain, and Colb carefully pulled the door shut in front of them. The moment it clicked into place, the two goblins scampered down the street without looking back.

"MMmMmmmm, that…" 27 mumbled a few minutes later, out-of-breath. "Random building was not best plan, no it was not. The humans seemed to get violent, just as I feared, yes they did."

"Hmmm," Colb gasped back, scanning their surroundings. They were now in some sort of city square, standing on stone roads connected around a large fountain. "What about that, yes?" he pointed towards a wooden post with symbols displayed on it, which was jammed into the ground next to the fountain. "That could be some sort of map, yes?"

27 narrowed his eyes, approaching the sign. As the noble squinted at the symbols on the wooden post, Colb noticed a shiny glint of metal sitting in the fountain behind it. "MMmMmmmm, yes, this is Hewmish writing. Kind of like how we list names of things in Yiklar items catalog," 27 surmised.

While the yellow-eyed noble spoke, Colb jumped into the human-made fountain with a splash. "Hmmm, I see silvopper piece in water, yes?" he announced after a moment, picking up a circular coin and showing it to 27.

"By the walls of Yiklar!" 27 exclaimed, jumping into the

fountain as well to take a closer look at Colb's discovery. "This is no silvopper piece… it is work of art, yes it is," he cheered, inspecting the front of the coin.

"A regular silvopper piece is just a blank nugget, yes it is. This is quite the opposite! Some human must have carefully carved it into a most excellent circle, then further sculpted their face into it. This must be worth quite much!"

Colb nodded, pleased at his find. "I'm not sure why someone would throw their artwork into the fountain, no I am not," 27 wondered aloud.

"Hmmm, perhaps we could sell this to artwork merchant, yes?" Colb pitched.

"MMmMmmmm, yes, I suppose we do have right to sell this artwork now, yes we do." 27 replied. "During my studies of human, I learned of a law called finders-keepers. It states that any item which is lost or thrown out – such as this small work of art – becomes owned by whomever finds it."

Colb clapped his hands with delight. "Hmmm, this is very good, yes?"

"MMmMmmmm, yes," 27 agreed. The duo stepped back onto the road, now soaking wet from both the fountain and from the rain. "As for this," 27 continued, taking another look at the symbol-covered pole. "My Hewmish reading is not the best, no it is not. But I do recognize this word." He pointed at a two-word sentence. "The second word is store. I am not sure what this first word is, so I do not know what kind of store, but at least it is not a house, no it is not."

The goblin moved his gnarly finger across the "?e?er?? Store" sign to an arrow. Colb and 27 followed the arrow with their eyes, eventually landing upon a black bismuthslate brick building with the same "?e?er?? Store" symbols above the door.

"AaAaaaaahhhh, the store!" 27 exclaimed, beginning to dance in the direction of the building. Colb followed behind, toying with the silvopper coin in his fingers.

"AaAaaaaahhhh, merchant!" 27 shouted in Hewmish as he confidently burst through the door of the building. "We saw your sign, yes we did, but could not understand the first word. Might this be an art store, or a medicine store?"

A gruff woman with metal earrings looked up from her book. She sat behind a large wooden desk covered with scrapes. The walls of the building's interior were lined with shelves containing everything from leather journals to metal armor. "It's a General Store," she muttered, narrowing her eyes at the two goblins.

"Oh," 27 replied with surprise. "That is odd concept, yes it is," he mumbled, scanning the shelves. "Where I come from, every store is quite specific. We have *Yiklar Produce*, *Yiklar News*, *Yiklar Quarry*... I, myself, am a merchant of the *Yiklar Factories* – a magic items store." The human frowned as she continued to glare at the goblin duo.

"AaAaaaaahhhh, but a General Store?" 27 continued. "You mean to say, you're sort of a *Yiklar Everything* store? Or, *Cantia Everything*, I suppose? How can you be an expert in what you're selling, if you're selling with such variety?"

The woman remained silent, putting down her book and sitting up in her chair. She watched the goblins like a hawkbear.

27 sauntered up to a shelf full of pet supplies, and pointed towards a bag of seeds that was too high for him to reach. "What is that?" he asked, still speaking in Hewmish.

"Seeds, for feeding canaryparrots. They cost half a brick," the woman replied.

27 tilted his head, visibly confused.

"They're 30 coins," the woman clarified.

"What's a coin?" 27 asked.

"…Get out of my store," the human grumbled.

"MMmMmmmm, that is not nice thing to say, no it is not," 27 replied, cautiously scanning the woman. Colb inched his way closer to the shop's entrance, prepared to make a quick escape at the first sign of danger. The human simply narrowed her eyes further, and spat in a nearby bucket without taking her gaze off the goblins.

"MMmMmmmm, well, from what region were these seeds produced?" 27 questioned.

"I dunno. Is this just a ruse so you can steal from me? Nasty goblins," she spat back.

"Well!" 27 said with surprise. "That is even *less* nice thing to say, yes it is. Plus, how can you not know where your products were grown? Why do you give them such confusing pricing? These are reasons why General Store is not good idea. You have too many products to be expert in each one, yes you do."

"Goblins are ratty, sneaky little things. You probably don't even have any money," she replied.

"AaAaaaaahhhh, well… we *usually* do, and right now we have many nice things for sale!" 27 countered. "We have nice Yiklar-produced items, yes we do, and fancy piece of artwork as well."

Colb held up the silvopper coin for the woman to see. "That's one coin," she sneered. "That's barely worth anything. Like I said, you'd need thirty of them just to pay for that bag of seeds."

"*That* is a coin?" 27 replied with amazement.

"Get out of my store," the woman grumbled.

"Okay, okay," 27 replied, his hands up in surrender. Colb pocketed the silvopper coin, and the duo stepped back into the street, shutting the door behind them.

"Hmmm, that didn't go well either, yes?" Colb observed.

"No, but we learned some things," 27 said. "We learned that humans aren't very good at business, with this General Store nonsense… and I guess that they use fancy artwork as currency."

"There they are!" a nearby ginger-bearded man suddenly shouted, with a finger pointed at Colb and 27. "Those two goblins broke into my house and scared the daylights outta my ma!" The goblins looked over at the commotion. It was the same man they'd seen holding a sword to them before, and he was pointing them out to an armored guard. The guard nodded at the ginger-haired civilian, drew a rapier, and began to advance towards Colb and 27.

"MMmMmmmm, this does not seem good, no it does not," 27 muttered. The goblin duo looked around for a quick escape, eventually landing their eyes on a dark alley around the side of the general store. They nodded in silent agreement, and scampered towards it.

On the way to the alley, 27 tripped, slipping on the wet bismuthslate road. Colb quickly helped him up, tugging on the noble goblin's rain-soaked robes to help him stand. "Thank you," 27 huffed, as the duo fled into the darkness.

They soon found themselves facing a wall: the alley was a dead end. "Heh," the guard muttered from behind them. His body blocked the only exit. "Looks like you two stumbled into the wrong city," the guard announced in a menacing tone, brandishing his rapier as he spoke. Shadows of raindrops reflected into the alley as some dim sunlight glinted off the sharpened blade.

As Colb's *Yiklar Amulet of Open Ears* translated the man's Hewmish, it glowed softly, better illuminating the alley. This revealed an old rug and a couple trash cans sitting nearby.

"I don't know what to do, no I do not!" 27 cried out to Colb, his voice racing. "*Yiklar University* was right! Every single human we've encountered has been a disaster!"

"Let's make a booth, yes? With the trash cans," Colb pitched, pointing out the objects nearby. 27 tilted his head, looking confused. "Like the booths back in Yiklar, yes? When things are going badly, the best thing you can do is follow your heart," Colb recited. "That's a motto from Skaal. It's the Skaal way, I suppose, yes?"

"Follow my heart?" 27 questioned. His confusion from Colb's statements seemed to be overpowering his fear from moments ago.

Wet stomps echoed through the alleyway as the guard began his approach, weapon drawn.

"Earlier, you said that it was your *dream* to be the first goblin to sell something to a human, yes?" Colb explained. "You said: once humans see how wonderful Yiklar's products are, there's no way they could dislike us. So, follow your heart, and maybe we'll get out of this. That is the Skaal way, yes?"

"I wanted to start with a nice human. One that wasn't armed," 27 retorted.

"It's now or never, yes?" Colb replied, his voice sharp as it competed with the falling rain. "Hmmm! Don't let anything stop you, yes? I believe in you, and we have no other options right now anyway, yes? You have to make this guard like us, or he's going to skewer us both!"

SHING! SHING! the guard clinked his sword against his armor menacingly. He was now only a few feet away from the goblins. "Alright," 27 agreed with a nod.

The goblins both immediately knocked over a couple of trash cans, forming them sideways into a sort of crummy table. This sudden motion made the guard stop, holding his rapier defensively.

Colb threw the old rug over the whole thing like a tablecloth, and 27 unclicked the red sack from his belt, which he placed gently onto the newly built structure.

"Um, okay," the guard responded in Hewmish, clearly unsure of what they were doing.

"A good booth needs a table and chair," 27 muttered in Goblish.

"Hmmm, I'll be the chair, yes?" Colb decided. The chef goblin dove onto his hands and knees behind the makeshift table. He angled himself so his eyes could peek over the garbage cans, allowing him to watch 27's interaction unfold with the guard. 27 shrugged, sitting down on Colb's back.

"AaAaaaaahhhh, customer!" the well-dressed goblin announced in Hewmish, holding his arms out in a wide, welcoming manner. Colb's *Yiklar Amulet of Open Ears* illuminated the alleyway as 27 spoke, giving a soft and comforting ambience to the makeshift booth – although, he could feel the goblin secretly shaking with fear on top of him.

"I am 27: that is my name, yes it is. Welcome, good human, to the specific store!" 27 announced.

The guard did a double-take, his eyes wide with surprise. "Um," he replied, holding his rapier steady. "…you can speak Hewmish?"

27 nodded. The guard blinked blankly at 27. "…specific store?" he asked.

"Yes!" 27 replied, jumping up and starting to dance. "At the specific store, you can purchase very specific, high-quality, Yiklar-made goods from the *Yiklar Factories*, yes you can! You will find good deals, with very specific prices, here at the specific store – assuming you're… not here to kill us or anything."

The guard lowered his sword, and his face displayed an expression of pure befuddlement. He rubbed his eyes and gave himself a little slap, as if he were trying to wake up from a dream.

"Specific store is much better than general store, yes it is," 27 continued, patting the outside wall of the general store. "As I said, we have high-quality goods, for most reasonable of prices."

"Look, I'm just…" the guard stopped for a moment, as if collecting his thoughts. "Goblins aren't welcome in this city. I'm gonna have to dispose of you." The human lifted his rapier and pointed it towards 27.

"AaAaaaaahhhh, I see you are man of sword, yes you are," 27 continued. Colb noticed a bead of sweat drip off his yellow-eyed friend as the noble stared down the tip of the rapier. "Perhaps you would like to purchase even better sword, yes you would?"

"I think you'll find this does the job quite well," the guard threatened, moving the tip closer to 27's face.

"MMmMmmmm, I see," 27 replied, sitting back down on Colb, and thus moving his face a little further away from the weapon.

"Hmmm, try getting the conversation away from weapons, yes?" Colb whispered.

"AaAaaaaahhhh, that is good idea, yes it is," 27 muttered in Goblish, wagging a finger with approval at Colb. The well-dressed goblin looked back up at the guard. "Are you man of… entertainment? Do you like to play games?" he pitched, switching back to Hewmish.

The guard paused, then retreated his sword a little bit. "…What do you mean, games?"

"AaAaaaaahhhh, yes, games! Games are fun, yes they are!" 27 cheered. Colb could feel the well-dressed goblin's body slightly relax on his back – perhaps feeling a little more confident now that he seemed to have captivated the guard's attention. "Today, the *Yiklar Factories* has a special offer on the *Yiklar Dice of*

Guaranteed Seven, yes they do. It's a set of dice, whose numbers will always add up to seven, yes they will! You could make many fun games with this, yes you could!"

"Ha!" the guard scoffed. "As if."

"AaAaaaaahhhh, yes, yes, it is if indeed!" 27 cheered. "If you want to try them yourself right after your purchase, you can return for full refund if you are not satisfied. However, no customer has ever been unsatisfied with a purchase from the specific store!" Colb nodded in agreement from below, hoping to add some credibility to 27's claims.

"Heh," the guard scoffed. "They always add up to seven, huh? So, if I brought them gambling, I could use them to cheat?"

"Well, they are not intended for stealing, no they are not," 27 worried.

"But it would work?" the guard asked.

"I-I suppose..." 27 muttered.

"How do they work?" the guard questioned.

"They are magic," 27 explained matter-of-factly.

The man paused for a moment. "...Is the magic detectable?"

27 glanced at Colb, then at his magic red bag. "I... I don't think other humans would be able to tell," he said.

The guard sheathed his sword. "...Alright, I'll bite. How much for the dice?" Colb let out a sigh, pleased that the guard had stowed his weapon.

"AaAaaaaahhhh," 27 replied, sounding relieved as well. "The set of two dice are normally 82 goldatinum pieces, 8 electronze pieces, and 3 silvopper pieces, yes they are. However, the *Yiklar Factories* has a special offer going on today, where they are just 38 goldatinum pieces, 4 electronze pieces, and 6 silvopper pieces!"

"How much is that in coins?" the guard asked.

"Um…" 27 muttered. Colb pulled the silvopper coin out of his pocket, and handed it to 27, hoping it would somehow be of use. The noble goblin flicked it around in his hand, feeling the weight, then handed it back to Colb.

"I'd say one coin is equal to one silvopper piece. With the special offer, the *Yiklar Dice of Guaranteed Seven* are 38.46 goldatinum, which is equivalent to 3,846 silvopper pieces, so… that would run you 3,846 coins."

The guard looked taken aback. "That's more than I make in a week!" he cried.

"AaAaaaaahhhh, well that is price of high-quality goods! You can always get immediate refund if you wish to return them, yes you can."

The guard appeared to ponder this for a moment. He tapped his sheathed rapier with his hand as he thought, making Colb and 27 share an uncomfortable look.

"Alright," the guard eventually replied. "You're lucky I have a block on me. But, if these dice don't work, I'm going to kill you and take my money back." He unstrapped a leather bag from his belt, and started rummaging through it. After a moment, he placed a pile of silvopper onto the table: one massive ingot, four small ingots, and six coins.

Each of these currencies sported a detailed image of an elegant but stern-looking woman: the same human that was on Colb's coin. "Who is this person, with her face on everything?" 27 asked.

"It's Empress Cognemi, leader of the Human Empire. Where are the dice, huh?" the guard replied.

"What are these ingots?" 27 questioned, gesturing to the pile of silvopper before him.

"It's what you asked for," the guard stated. "It's 3,846 coins." He pointed at the massive ingot. "One block, which is worth 3,600 coins," he said. The guard then moved his finger to the smaller ingots. "Four bricks, each worth 60 coins, or 240 in total," he continued. "…and six coins."

27 did some quick math in his head, then shrugged, scooping up the pile of silvopper and dropping it into his red sack. "We'll give it a try," 27 cheered.

The *Yiklar Bag of Traveling Inventory* paused for a moment – taking a little longer than usual – then eventually spit out a pair of wooden *Yiklar Dice of Guaranteed Seven*, which 27 caught out of the air and handed to the man.

The guard accepted the dice, and inspected them carefully. "These are slightly smaller than regular dice…" he mumbled. "…but otherwise, don't seem too suspicious."

The guard rolled them onto the makeshift table. "6 and 1," 27 cheered, looking up at the man.

"Yeah," the guard replied. "Got lucky." The man picked them up, then rolled them again.

"4 and 3!" 27 observed.

"Huh," the guard responded, scratching his head. The human rolled the dice a few more times, then finally pocketed them, looking satisfied that they really were magic.

"You are pleased with purchase!" 27 exclaimed.

"Yeah, I guess they do work," the guard replied. "I'm going to test my luck with the boys at the casino tonight."

"AaAaaaaahhhh, and you are not thinking to kill us anymore either, no you are not? You are big fan of specific store?" 27 asked.

"It's a guard's job to kill you," the man replied. "I don't think I'm going to *need* a guard's wage anymore after I play with these dice tonight. Good luck with whatever you're up to." The man then waved them off, walking out of the alley.

As he left, 27 shouted, "Remember, quality defeats quantity. That is the Yiklar way!"

"Hmmm, you did it!" Colb cheered as 27 jumped off him and stowed the *Yiklar Bag of Traveling Inventory*. "We're not dead, yes?"

The two goblins laughed together in disbelief. "AaAaaaaahhhh, he seemed unsure about the dice at first, but did enjoy his purchase in the end. Perhaps there is some hope in getting human market interested in Yiklar-made goods, yes there is!" 27 cheered. "…Although, I don't think he plans to use his purchase in a most Yiklar-approved way…"

"Hmmm, this was a plan of the Skaal way, yes?" Colb comforted. "You followed you heart, yes? You made the sale, and we're safe! That's what matters. What the guard does with those dice is his business, not ours, yes?"

27 nodded. "Thank you, Colb," he said. "Thank you for believing that I could do that."

Hmmm, it was the only plan I could think of to avoid imminent death, yes? Colb thought to himself. The chef goblin then smiled, patting his friend on the back. "Hmmm, I'm proud to have watched you live out a dream of yours, yes?"

The goblin duo held their heads high, proud of the successful sale – and of avoiding imminent death – as they stepped out from the dark alley. The rain had slowed to a drizzle, and the afternoon sun was narrowly poking through some clouds.

"MMmMmmmm, it seems that all human money is carefully carved artwork, yes it does," 27 observed. "However, silvopper is silvopper, no matter how it is molded. The *Yiklar Bag of Traveling Inventory* seemed to accept it, so I should've gotten my kickback from the sale," he continued.

"Hmmm, how much is that?" Colb asked.

"Standard merchant kickback is 7.42 percent of selling price, yes it is," 27 replied. He seemed to be doing some calculations with his fingers as he spoke. "So, we should have 2 goldatinum, 8 electronze, and 5 silvopper from that sale. Which would be equivalent to 285 coins in Human Empire money."

"Let's see… I'll pay you 240 coins for the service of getting some medical supplies for our good friend, Stibs," 27 continued. The noble goblin proceeded to summon 4 small silvopper ingots – bricks, the guard had called them – from his bag.

Colb nodded, pocketing the metals. "If you can find seller, hopefully that will be enough money to get something decent," 27 said. "I'm starting to wish the *Yiklar Factories* produced healing items; that would be so much easier than trying to find something from the humans…"

"Hmmm, I'll be okay," Colb replied. He looked around at their surroundings. The fountain looked pretty, sprinkling water in the center of the open streets. "The place next to us was a human store, yes? Maybe there are more stores around, yes?" he surmised.

"AaAaaaaahhhh, that is possible, yes it is," 27 agreed. "In Yiklar, booths like to be near other booths. It is convenient for the customers, yes it is. Perhaps there's more humans nearby that would be willing to do business with *me*, as well?"

"Hmmm, perhaps," Colb replied. "Now that you've made one sale, I'll bet you can make more, yes? Perhaps you can earn more funding for the team, while I look around for medical supplies, yes? It's probably not a bad idea to rebuild your fortune as much as you can, yes?."

"AaAaaaaahhhh, that plan would allow us to get more done today, yes it would," 27 agreed. "That sounds like good idea, yes it does. Let's split up here, and regroup at the *Yiklar Folding Cabin* this evening. It shouldn't be too hard to find, no it should not be. The cabin's quite large, and we know generally which direction Drek and Stibs went before setting it up, yes we do." Colb nodded in agreement. With that, the goblins split up, going off on their separate missions.

Colb looked around at the other buildings in the city square. Unable to understand any of the Hewmish symbols labeling things, Colb decided to pick a nearby shop at random, and cautiously entered it.

As Colb waltzed into the structure, he was faced with a clump of vertical strings of beads blocking his path. "Come in..." cackled the voice of a human woman from beyond the beads. Colb's amulet glowed faintly as it translated the Hewmish for him. "...I've been expecting you," the alluring voice continued.

Hmmm, Colb thought. *That's an odd thing to say.* Colb cautiously pushed through the beads, ready to bolt at the first sign of danger. He found himself in a dimly lit, purple-carpeted room. He looked up at a woman in silky black clothes, covered in goldatinum jewelry. She sat behind a clear crystal ball, which was slightly smaller than Maxten's Miracle Orb in Bellra, but just as spherical.

The woman seemed harmless so far, so Colb climbed up onto a bench, looking at her as he sat down. She stared back at him from behind her crystal sphere, her black mascara and hooded robe giving an aura of mystery about her. "*Ah!* When I investigated the *stars* this morning, I could *sense* that I'd see someone not from this city today," she proclaimed, her voice smooth and sing-songy. "*Nay* – someone not even from this *empire*. I believe that *prophecy* was that I'd be seeing *you*."

Colb shifted in his seat. Indeed, he wasn't from Cantia, nor was he from the Human Empire. This woman really did seem to know what she was talking about. "Now, my *crystal ball* here knows your *future* – that is what you've come to *hear* from me today, correct?" she prodded.

Colb shook his head in disagreement. "*Oh*, well I see you've got a nice *crystal necklace* there," the woman continued without missing a beat. "Might you be a believer in the *power* of my…*healing crystals?*"

Colb nodded with excitement. It seems he'd found someone selling medical supplies on his first try! "*Ah!* Yes, I could *tell* that you were someone of *strong* will and body. Someone who wants to *heal* themselves and *those around them*," the mystic woman majestically sang. Colb continued to nod, pleased that she recognized him as the medic he was supposed to be for his team. "*And* have you brought *payment* to procure some of my *great healing crystals?*"

Colb took out the four metal ingots 27 had given him, and plopped them onto the table.

"*Ah!* Three bricks for my *half-dozen healing crystals set*, and one more as a tip! Very good," the woman replied, scooping up the ingots. She pulled out a small wooden box with six brightly colored stones inside, and handed it to Colb. "*Here* is a *pamphlet* as well, to *help* you use these correctly," she sang, handing Colb a white sheet of paper written in Hewmish symbols. It boasted a hand drawn diagram of a human, which seemed to depict how to use the stones. Colb nodded thanks, hopped out of his seat, and walked away into the drizzling rain.

The wet goblin sauntered to the edge of the city, proudly holding his box of human medical supplies. He moved a bit into the nearby forest and searched for the others. "Hmmm, Drek? Stibs? I am here with medical supplies, yes?" he called out.

He walked a little deeper into the forest, eventually noticing the *Yiklar Folding Cabin* crammed into a small clearing between some trees. Colb waltzed over to the structure, and let himself in.

27 was still nowhere to be seen, but Stibs was lying flat on the dance floor in the center of the room, with Drek sitting on the ground next to him. "Rrghegh… find anything?" Drek asked.

"Hmmm, I did, yes?" Colb muttered as he placed the wooden box down next to the old goblin's swollen limb. Stibs remained quiet, scrunching his face in pain.

Colb started poking the wounded area, which made Stibs wince. As the old goblin cringed, Colb noticed that his friend's jaw was tightly locked shut. *Hmmm, that's probably not good for his teeth, yes?* Colb pondered.

"Rrghegh… can… can I help?" Drek asked shyly.

"Hmmm, could you find something for Stibs to bite onto in the kitchen?" Colb replied.

While Drek scampered off to search, Colb poured out the six colorful stones onto the floor. "Hmmm, these will heal you, yes?" he said to Stibs.

"H… I hope so," the old goblin groaned through grit teeth. Colb looked through the set of gemstones. They varied in color, from the darkest black to the clearest green. He sorted them by hue, then started looking through the mystic's instruction sheet.

Drek came back holding an old piece of cowmammoth jerky and a scrappy bit of leather cloth. "Rrghegh… which one do you want in your mouth?" he grumbled.

"Jerky," Stibs replied, opening his mouth. Drek slid the black rectangle of meat between the old goblin's razor-sharp teeth, which clamped down onto it.

"Hmmm, we need to figure out what this paper says, yes?" Colb announced, presenting the Hewmish instruction sheet the mystical seller had given him.

"Rrghegh… I will help," Drek responded. Colb nodded in

approval at Drek's sudden willingness to assist him.

Colb set the instruction parchment down on the floor, next to the six healing crystals. Drek squinted at the sheet. "Hmmm, it's in Hewmish, yes?" Colb explained. "Once 27 gets back, he can help us translate it – but for now, maybe we can get started by looking at the picture, yes?"

The duo sat down around Stibs, and stared at the page. It contained a diagram of a naked human, with the six rocks placed directly on the skin, across different points on their body.

"Rrghegh... alright, Stibs," Drek said. "Get naked."

The old goblin shook his head. "Hurmph... pulling pants down... over my broken leg... would hurt," he complained.

"Hmmm," Colb muttered. "Maybe this just means... the stones need to touch the skin directly? We can work around his clothes, yes we can. Best not to hurt him, yes?"

Drek shrugged. "Rrghegh... you're the medic," he conceded. The young goblin picked up two black materials from the half-dozen on the ground. One looked staggered like flintcoal and speckled with goldatinum flecks. The other looked glazed and rounded, with purple crystals protruding from the otherwise black and glass-like surface.

Colb stared at the diagram. "Hmmm, put them on his chest, yes?" Colb ordered.

The young goblin shrugged, then placed the two rocks on the eyepatched goblin's chest. "Hurmph..." Stibs mumbled. "That's... tourmalpyrite... and... um... obsidethyst... I think..." The piece of cowmammoth jerky stuck on the old goblin's upper teeth when he opened his mouth to speak.

Drek's ears perked up. "Rrghegh... you know about these? Will they heal your leg?"

"Hurmph..." Stibs grimaced, visibly pushing through pain as

he tried to focus on speaking. "I… didn't know… they were… more than… just rocks…"

Colb picked up a rosemushroom-colored crystal, and placed it on the old goblin as well. "That's quartzelian…" Stibs muttered. "A… common rock…"

"Hmmm, that's all three for placing on the chest, yes?" Colb announced, looking over the diagram. "Do you feel better?"

Stibs shook his head, and one of the rocks rolled off his jacket. Drek snatched it up, then shoved all three rocks down the old goblin's shirt.

"Rrghegh… now they're touching your skin, and won't fall off. How do they feel?"

"…Cold," Stibs mumbled.

"Hmmm, let's apply the rest, then ask again, yes?" Colb pitched. Drek nodded, picking up a yellow-orange rock covered in green specks.

"That's… agatrine…" Stibs mumbled.

"Hmmm, touch it to his foot," Colb announced.

"Rrghegh… which one?" Drek asked, looking over Colb's shoulder, at the diagram. The picture showed the agatrine placed under the human's left foot, with root-like vines drawn coming out of it.

"Hmmm, left leg," Colb muttered. "No, wait. Right leg," he corrected. "I think the human's left leg is broken in this diagram, yes?"

"Rrghegh… because of the vines?" Drek asked.

"Hmmm, I think those might be bones that ripped out of the skin, yes?" Colb surmised. "So, put that stone on the right side for Stibs, since his right leg is broken, yes?"

Drek slipped his hand into the boot of the injured leg, and pushed the agatrine down the inside of the old goblin's sock. Drek then picked up the final two healing materials: a smooth green stone covered in glossy, rainbow-colored specks, and a fine-cut, reddish-blue crystal.

"Hurmph…" Stibs mumbled. "That's… jabadorite… and… a rubiamond?" The old goblin furrowed his brow. "Those… are pretty rare…"

"Rrghegh… only the finest for you," Drek replied. "Where do I put these?"

"Hmmm… on his third eye?" Colb said, squinting at the diagram. A third eye had been drawn over the human's forehead, and the final two rocks appeared to be sitting on its pupil.

"Rrghegh… he doesn't even have second eye," Drek observed, glancing at the old goblin's eyepatch.

"Hmmm, then glue the rocks to his forehead," Colb decided. Stibs shakily pointed towards his backpack, and opened his mouth. As usual, the jerky remained lodged in his upper teeth while he spoke.

"Hurmph… I've got plenty of glue in my bag," he mustered before clamping his teeth shut again. Drek dropped the rocks, and scampered over to the backpack. He dug through it, eventually pulling out a small jar full of a brown mixture. It was labeled "tree sap + dung."

"This?" he asked. Stibs nodded solemnly. Drek popped open the jar, stuck his finger in, and pulled out some of the mixture. He rubbed it onto the old goblin's forehead, then Colb finished off the process by squishing the two remaining crystals into the gunk.

"Hmmm, there you go," Colb said. "Feeling better now?" Stibs slowly shook his head. "Hmmm… maybe you will in the morning, yes?" Colb hoped.

Stibs nodded, then shut his eyes – apparently resigning to lay where he was for the rest of the night. Drek threw a blanket onto the old goblin, then crawled over to his favorite bean bag chair.

Colb sat by the cabin door, waiting for 27 to show up before he went to bed. *Hmmm. Where is he?* Colb thought. *Stibs isn't feeling better. I don't think I did a good job as medic, yes? If only 27 were here, he could translate these instructions. I must've done something wrong, yes?*

Colb waited and waited, but the noble goblin never did come back for the night. Eventually, his eyes heavy, Colb succumbed to sleep right where he sat on the floor.

Chapter 10

GIRL IN THE TREE

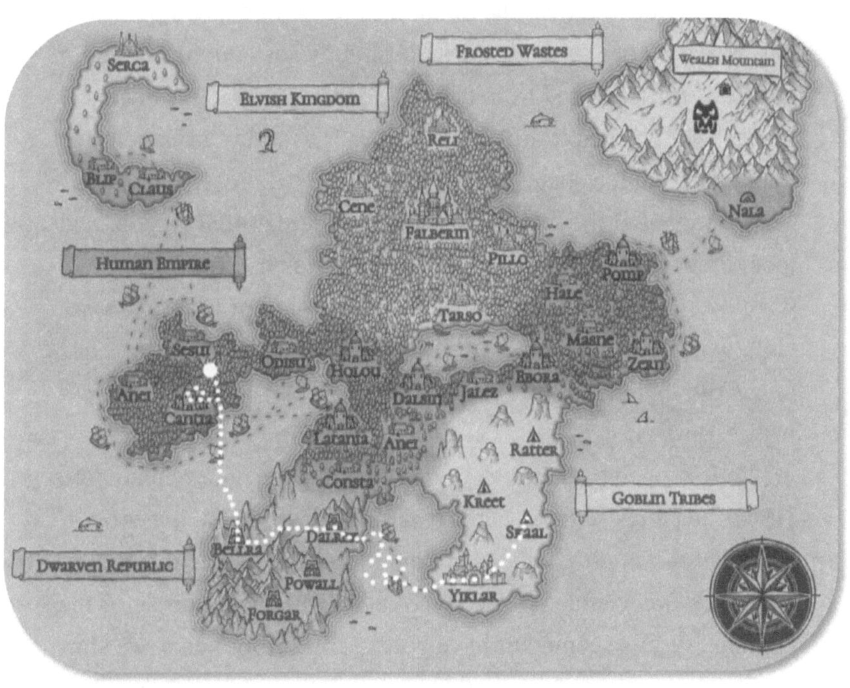

10. GIRL IN THE TREE

Colb awoke with a start, upset he'd fallen asleep before 27 came back. Colb glanced around the cabin. He could only see Stibs and Drek, snoring away. *Hmmm, Stibs usually wakes up earlier, yes? He must need extra rest today,* Colb thought. *Hmmm, but where is 27, yes?*

Colb stepped outside to see what time it was. The sun had fully secured the sky; it was at least two hours past sunrise. The rain had entirely ceased over the night, leaving behind a damp must in the forest. The ground quaked slightly as mighty autumn giraffeworms surfaced from their flooded burrows in the distance. Spiderbats chirped with joy overhead as they searched for toadroaches in the shade of the dense mapleoak trees.

Colb inhaled the cool, misty air of the unfamiliar region, and looked out towards the human city. As far as he could tell, there were no signs of 27 coming back to the cabin last night. *Hmmm,* Colb worried. *I hope he didn't run into some humans that... hurt him,* Colb thought. *Someone needs to go into the city to figure out what happened, yes?*

Colb stepped back into the cabin, shutting the door behind him. He surveyed his options. Stibs was still asleep on the dancefloor, a blanket thoroughly twisted around his waist and shoulders. Part of his leg was visible: still very red and swollen. A couple of the healing crystals seemed to have gotten loose from under his shirt during the night, and had landed on the floor around him. Drek was blanketlessly curled up in a perfect circle upon the beanbag chair in the sleeping area. Neither of them seemed ready to get up for the day.

Hmmm, Colb thought to himself as he gathered the fallen crystals around the eyepatched goblin. *His leg is still swollen... I knew I must've done something wrong. Poor Stibs… I should let him keep sleeping, at least; maybe that will help his leg, yes?* He looked over at Drek, who seemed knocked out as well. *Perhaps I should let them both sleep, yes? I'll find 27, then come back in an hour to make a meal for everyone.* Colb finished collecting the gemstones that had fallen off Stibs, and placed them in a pile on the floor, next to the Hewmish instruction sheet.

Colb then headed out of the *Yiklar Folding Cabin*, and to the city. With the rain gone, the dried-off wood of the mapleoak buildings looked to be a lighter brown than they were yesterday. The smooth bismuthslate roads looked the same: black from some angles, but a brilliant rainbow-color from others.

Cantia's city streets were bustling with morning activity. Loud clanks of metal against metal came from a blacksmith's studio. A pair of human seagullfisherman shouted about their latest catch in the streets. A group of short children marched into a school with stressed looks on their faces. Truly, the city was alive this morning.

Colb hid in the shadows, aiming to avoid another dangerous encounter with the humans. He sneakily searched the town for what felt like days, looking for a lick of green skin amongst the crowds of pale humans. Finally, after three hours of searching – which was much longer than he'd planned to be out – he heard 27's telltale "AaAaaaaahhhh" come from the window of a nearby tavern.

Colb grabbed the bottom edge of the windowsill, hoisting himself up for a view inside. Within the building, he saw a party of human nobles, sharing pints of beverages with 27. These dozen men and women were covered in fine robes of blue, red, white, and purple silk. They were cheerfully chatting in Hewmish, and 27 seemed to be the center of attention. Piles of silvopper ingots sat upon the table, and as Colb's *Yiklar Amulet of Open Ears* glowed, he could hear the conversation was about making purchases from 27.

Colb awkwardly climbed in through the window, landing flat on his butt upon the wooden floor inside the building. He scanned his surroundings, then snuck between the legs of waiters to reach 27's table.

"…So a normal king-sized bed is 76 inches, by 80 inches," a well-dressed man with a white beard and brown eyes was saying to 27 as Colb reached their table. "…but I like to sleep on a perfect square, right? So, can you make this… *Yiklar Floating Bed* of yours in 80 inches by 80 inches?"

"Yes, of course," 27 replied as he noticed Colb walking up to the table. "AaAaaaaahhhh, Colb! Everyone, this is Colb! He is traveling companion of mine, yes he is. We are on an adventure."

The human group all shifted in their chairs to look at the goblin. Now, Colb had looked directly into the sun only a few times before, but the searing burn of these 24 unfamiliar eyes beaming down upon him felt like that same sensation. Colb stepped back, sweating from the attention. "Hmmm, we… it's morning, 27. It is time to leave… yes?" he mumbled in Goblish.

"AaAaaaaahhhh, ye-what? Wow! It is morning already? I am so sorry – I had no idea, no I did not. I am so sorry, yes I truly am, but I must be going," 27 announced to the table.

The noble goblin shoved a pile of silvopper into his *Yiklar Bag of Traveling Inventory*, then pulled out a map. He slapped it onto the table, and circled the Yiklar tribe with a nearby quill and ink. "This is where I am from, yes it is," he announced to the humans. "If you wish to purchase more highest-of-quality goods, for example that custom *Yiklar Floating Bed* for you, Alton, or those custom *Yiklar Spectacles of Extracting Secrets* for you, Miranda," he continued, gesturing to the respective humans as he named them, "then you can just send somebody here to meet with my tribe. In fact, maybe we could even set up trade route through Consta or Dalsin, yes we could."

The humans nodded in approval, and scooted out of the booth to give 27 room to exit. "Always remember: quality defeats quantity. That is the Yiklar way," 27 cheered as he regrouped with Colb. "And thank you very so much for your purchases!" As the duo exited, 27 stiffly danced his way out the tavern, to which the humans laughed and clapped with glee.

With his friend physically closer, Colb could tell 27 hadn't slept the entire night. The circle of skin around his eyes had turned from healthy green to a sticky brown, and the goblin's usually fluid dance moves were now rigid and slow. "Hmmm, perhaps we should take some more time to rest before leaving, yes?"

"AaAaaaaahhhh, nonsense, Colb," 27 replied as they set foot onto the cool, bismuthslate road. "It is morning – late morning, yes it is, so we should be on our way, yes we should." 27 let out a wide yawn, then the duo marched off towards the hidden campsite. "I made many deals!" he cheered. "It's not the fortune I used to have, but it'll be enough to make a highest-of-quality purchase or two of our own when we need to, yes it will be."

Colb led the way to a narrow section of nearby forest, where Drek and Stibs were waiting in an open clearing. Stibs sat on a nearby rock, twiddling the *Yiklar Folding Cabin* doorknob in his palm. His leg still looked twisted and swollen, but he seemed to have higher spirits than the day before. Drek, on the other hand, looked exhausted. He was flat on his back in the middle of some mud, panting while holding a dagger and a large stick. A massive, beastly cowmammoth thrashed nearby, tied to a thick mapleoak tree.

"Hurmph! Took you two long enough," Stibs announced from his sitting place.

"Hmmm, it took me three hours to track down 27, yes?" Colb replied apologetically.

"Hurmph, it's no trouble. While you were gone, I taught our young hunter here how to catch a steed. This thing should be able to carry all four of us." Drek let out a long, winding wheeze from his spot in the mud.

"Hurmph, he's a little out of breath from the experience," Stibs chuckled, "but I think it'll be well worth it to have this cowmammoth, considering I can't walk at the moment."

"Hmmm, you still can't walk?" Colb asked.

"Hurmph… my leg's actually feeling worse today, not better," Stibs replied.

Colb looked up at the eyepatched goblin's forehead, and noticed the two rocks had been removed and the glue cleaned away. "Hmmm, did you pick up the instruction sheet before closing the cabin?" Colb asked. "We can do better treatment now, since 27's here to translate the Hewmish writing, yes?"

Stibs and Colb glanced at 27. The noble goblin seemed too out-of-it to even notice the large cowmammoth struggling against its bounds nearby. "Hurmph, he looks exhausted," Stibs observed.

"It is not problem," 27 announced, unable to keep his eyes open as he spoke. "Just… just carry me, and keep going, yes you should," he mumbled, leaning heavily onto Colb's shoulder.

"Hmmm," Colb muttered sadly, looking at 27.

"Hurmph, you heard the leader," Stibs agreed. "We should get moving. I think the treatment failed, but we can try again, with 27, another time. For now, these two are much too wiped out to do anything useful, and I'm hurt. So, it looks like you're taking the reins, Colb." Stibs gestured to the large, tusked beast that had been lassoed and tied to a tree. It was covered in rough white fur, broken up with various patches of brownish-black skin. It thrashed about, trying to undo the rope's knots with its long trunk.

A nervous gulp rippled down Colb's green neck. "Hmmm, is this… like when we were riding pigeonhorses? That was a little outside of my comfort zone, yes?"

"Hurmph, it's nothing like riding a pigeonhorse," Stibs replied, giving Colb some momentary relief. "…It's much more difficult than that." Colb's face turned frozen with fear in a heartbeat. "The cowmammoth is a bigger, more brutish animal. Hurmph, the ride will be bumpier, and of course the big difference is that it's wild. Those pigeonhorses had been tamed specifically for riding, whereas this beast has…" Stibs trailed off, seeming to notice the terror building up in Colb's eyes. Meanwhile, 27 slumped more of his weight onto the chef goblin's side. "Hurmph, but I'll help you figure it out," the old goblin reassured.

A few hours later, with lots of instruction from Stibs, Colb had managed to calm down the animal, build a saddle for it, put the saddle on it, and get the whole goblin crew onto the mount. He'd also retrieved his instruction sheet and dozen healing crystals from the *Yiklar Folding Cabin*, stored them all back in their box, and given the set to Stibs to keep in his backpack.

With the cabin back in doorknob form, and the goblin crew mounted upon the beast, it was time to set out. Colb sat at the head of the cowmammoth, with Stibs behind him. Drek and 27 sat sleeping behind Stibs, securely tied to the saddle. The beast poked through a pile of berries Colb had set before it with its large, white tusks. It was picking out all of the blue ones, staining its teeth with color as it munched down on them.

"Hurmph, now that the steed's been calmed by the wild tallyberries, it'll let us ride for a few hours before it realizes how much it doesn't trust us. It's time to cut the rope," Stibs instructed. With a shaky hand, Colb slowly sawed off the wicker rope around the creature's stomach, strand by strand. Stibs twiddled his fingers impatiently while Colb carefully completed the task.

Once the rope was cut, the cowmammoth didn't seem to notice, and continued to chow down on the berries. Stibs pulled out a seagullfishing pole, threaded it with a rotten applecarrot from deep in his backpack, and held it out to Colb. The steed stopped chewing the berries, and began smelling the air with long, deep breaths.

Colb accepted the pole, and slowly extended it in the opposite direction of the human city. The cowmammoth turned, raising its face into the air and aligning itself towards the smell. Then, with some loud stomps, the steed began to accelerate, eventually entering a full sprint towards the food. Colb held on for dear life, focusing all his willpower into keeping the applecarrot steady and forward. "Hurmph, feel that wind on your ears!" Stibs cheered as they rode along.

After two and a half hours of traveling roughly northeast through the forest, the cowmammoth suddenly stopped running, and began to cower. "Hmmm, what's… what's going on?" Colb asked with a whisper, still aiming the seagullfishing rod forwards. "…Did the tallyberries wear out early?"

"I don't think so…" Stibs muttered. The cowmammoth started shivering anxiously, and began slowly retreating backwards. "Hurmph, I have a bad feeling in my gut," Stibs said. "Let's dismount, then figure out what's going on. We don't want anyone tied to the saddle if the cowmammoth starts to panic and thrash around." Colb hopped off the creature, then helped Stibs dismount. The duo then cut Drek and 27 free to pull them off as well.

As they were setting their sleepy companions onto the ground, a loud *CRAW!* echoed throughout the forest. The cowmammoth immediately broke into a sprint in the opposite direction of the sound.

"Take cover!" Stibs shouted, waking up the others. Stibs hopped over to a nearby tree with his good leg, and Colb followed, dragging Drek and 27 with him.

"Rrghegh… what's happening?" Drek asked as he watched the team's saddled cowmammoth flee into the depths of the forest.

A moment later, Colb felt a popping sensation in his ears, as a thick shadow covered the forest. Above him, up in the sky, an enormous brown bird – adorned with sharpened claws that were bigger than Colb's arms – flew by, aiming in the direction of the cowmammoth.

"Hurmph! That's a hawkbear," Stibs whispered to the team.

"MMmMmmmm, I have little bit of ache in head, yes I do," 27 mumbled, scratching behind one of his ears. "Is hawkbear a danger to us?"

"Yes," Stibs replied sharply, keeping an eye in the direction it flew.

"Hurmph – from what I've read about them, they're solitary creatures, and very territorial. We should keep moving as fast as possible, and pray we get out of its hunting area before it comes back."

The crew moved northward swiftly by foot. Drek and 27 snapped back to reality as they realized the danger of the situation. Stibs hobbled along using a mapleoak stick as a crutch. As the goblins proceeded, the forest's leaves popped and crinkled under their bare toes.

After half a minute of progress, something in the forest caught Drek's gaze. "Rrghegh… I see purple human nearby," he announced, pointing slightly westward. The eyes of the other three goblins followed his crooked finger towards what appeared to be a human girl, perhaps 11 or 12 years old, climbing up a thick mapleoak tree. She looked to be an inch under 5 feet tall. Her skin was a soft purple, and she wore a light white cloak held together by a couple of belts. Two bright pink swanraven feathers stood out in her otherwise dark blue-black hair. The tree she climbed was strange as well: it seemed to have frost marks all over it, which was atypical to see considering the warmth in the forest at this time of year.

"Hurmph, she must not realize the danger she's in," Stibs grumbled, looking back towards where the hawkbear had flown.

"Hmmm, we should warn her, yes?" Colb posed to the group.

"Hurmph, go give her a quick warning, but then we all need to keep moving. We're not safe sticking around for a conversation," Stibs replied.

27 and Colb broke off from the group, walking towards the tree. The others kept their eyes on the sky, wary of the flying beast.

"MMmMmmmm, human girl!" 27 shouted up the tree in Hewmish. The purple preteen stopped her climbing, and looked down at the goblins. Her nose was smaller than Colb had expected, and her eyes were wide and blue. Her purple ears were sharp to a point.

"I have no idea what you just said," she called back, then continued climbing.

27 did a double-take at her reply. "MMmMmmmm, I am clueless to what that was, but that was most certainly not Hewmish, no it was not," he said to Colb. The noble goblin shook his head with a baffled expression.

"Hmmm, she said she didn't understand you, yes?" Colb replied, a little confused.

27 snapped his fingers, pointing at Colb's necklace, which had started glowing. "AaAaaaaahhhh, well she's not speaking Hewmish," he said, "but it looks like your *Yiklar Amulet of Open Ears* can understand her, yes it can."

"Rrghegh… stop taking so long," Drek hissed at them from far away. The girl looked out at Drek and Stibs, then back down at Colb and 27.

"Hurmph, that thing could be back any second," Stibs added.

Colb took off his amulet, looked the girl in the eye, then chucked it up towards her with all his might. She reactively reached out and caught it with one hand. The edges of the necklace became coated with frost the moment they came into contact with her purple skin.

Colb mimed putting a necklace over his head, and the girl complied, placing the *Yiklar Amulet of Open Ears* over her neck. "Hmmm, try now, yes?" Colb whispered to his noble friend.

"It's far too dangerous to be here, yes it is!" 27 shouted up the tree. "There's a hawkbear coming to kill us all!"

The girl tilted her head, then replied something in her unfamiliar language. Without his amulet, not even Colb could decipher the meaning of her words. She seemed to read their confused looks, and resorted to pointing towards the top of the tree she was climbing. 27 and Colb stepped back, then looked up at a wicker nest above the purple girl. It held an enormous brown egg with white specks on it, which admittedly looked rather delicious.

"Hurmph, what's taking so long?" Stibs asked, hobbling over to the duo with his crutch. Drek followed closely behind, his *Yiklar Bow of Returning Arrow* drawn and preemptively aimed towards the sky.

"Hmmm, I think she's trying to get that egg, yes?" Colb replied, pointing at the nest in the mapleoak tree.

"Rrghegh… that's a big egg!" Drek observed.

"Hurmph! Too big," Stibs worried. "That looks like a hawkbear egg… which means we're right in the center of the beast's territory. Hurmph – *this is incredibly foolish* – we need to move away *right now*," Stibs sharply whispered, but it was too late.

No sooner did Stibs finish his sentence, than a piercing *SCREEE!* echoed throughout the air. The goblin crew felt a chill as an enormous shadow blocked out the sun. They slowly looked up to see a massive, fur-covered hawkbear flapping above them. It clutched a dead cowmammoth in its sharpened teeth, and looked furious to have found five small creatures going after its egg.

Chapter 11

NEST OF THE HAWKBEAR

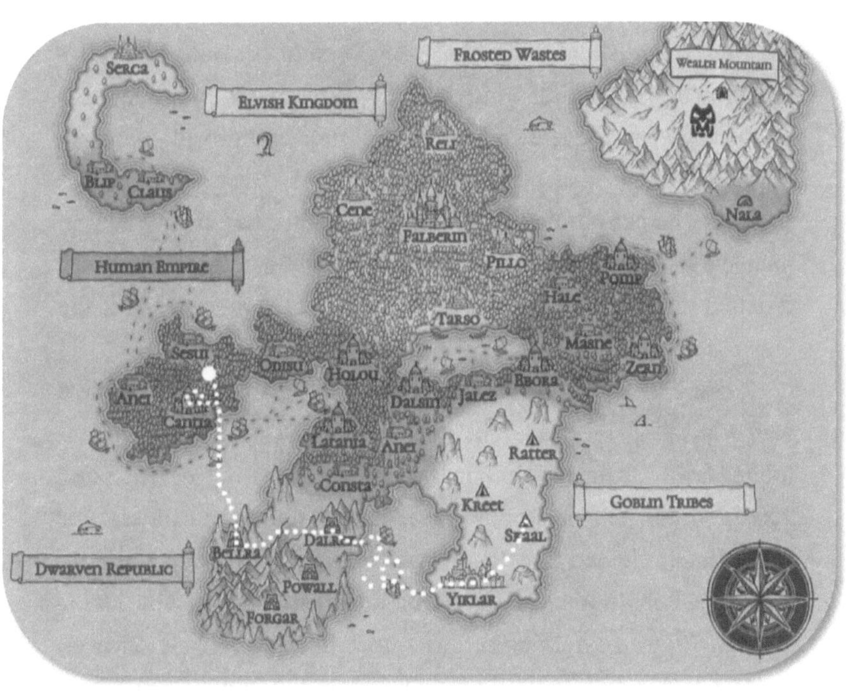

11. NEST OF THE HAWKBEAR

The hawkbear screeched through the cowmammoth in its mouth as it descended from the sky. The creature's high-pitched battle cry left an uncomfortable ringing in the ears of the goblin crew. 27 and Colb helped Stibs hobble towards cover, as Drek fired his iridhodium arrow towards the monster. The arrow clipped the fur of the beast, not even drawing blood, before flying back to the hooded goblin. Drek caught his arrow, then dove for better protection behind a nearby mosstulip-covered rock.

The ground shook from the sheer force of pressure waved by the hawkbear's beating wings as it descended, narrowing its eyes at the girl on the tree. The purple preteen looked alarmed, retreating down to a branch where she could get a more solid footing. The beast quickly repositioned to face her, lifting a talon menacingly. The goblin crew stared from their hiding places, terrified to watch the girl die but unable to take their eyes off the encounter.

Raising its hooked claw into the sky, the beast started to take a swipe at the girl's head. The girl reactively closed her eyes and looked away from the threat, holding her arms out defensively. The goblins felt a popping sensation in their ears as air immediately flowed towards the girl's open hands, collecting into a cloudy, bubbling, clear liquid mass over her palms. The *Yiklar Amulet of Open Ears* on the girl's neck became entirely encased in frost as this magical ball of matter grew and grew.

The hawkbear paused, looking confused by this display, but still furious at the trespasser. It ultimately decided to finish swiping at the girl – but an instant before its talon could make contact with her head, the strange ball between the girl's palms erupted into a ray of clear liquid with a twinge of pale blue to it.

The beam, which was speckled with solid white chunks, filled the air with mist as it blasted into the hawkbear's face. The force of the attack launched the girl backwards into the trunk of the mapleoak tree, and knocked the hawkbear off-balance as it attempted to remain airborne.

The girl's head smacked into the wood, leaving behind a circle of frost, and knocking her unconscious. As she fell limp, rolling off the mapleoak branch, Drek dived out from his hiding spot to catch her.

The purple preteen plummeted downwards, eventually landing in Drek's arms. The hooded goblin hissed as if he'd been hurt, then quickly carried her to cover behind the mosstulip-covered rock he'd jumped out from. Upon reaching cover, Drek threw her limp body to the ground, and the clovergrass around her started turning blue. The young goblin held a hand over the back of his neck, and looked to be in pain.

SCREEE! the hawkbear shrieked from above. Part of its wings had turned purple from the elf's attack, and it was flapping them frantically as if in a state of panic. After a moment, the cowmammoth fell from its jaw. As the steed's frostbitten body hit the forest floor, it shattered like it were made of glass. Chunks of frozen cowmammoth meat covered the nearby trees. Horrified, Colb could see the fur around the hawkbear's face turning a sickly whitish-purple.

Looking pained, Drek took off his hood and scrunched the fabric up against his neck like a bandage. The young goblin then drew his *Yiklar Bow of Returning Arrow*, and fired a shot towards the hawkbear's heart. The iridhodium point went straight through the hawkbear, as if the beast were made of paper. The beast's skin crunched like fall leaves, then its torso shattered to pieces – killing it instantly.

The goblins covered their heads with their hands as frozen chunks of hawkbear meat blanketed the battlefield. *THUMP! THUMP! THUMP!* the heavy pieces of flesh made sounds that echoed throughout the forest as they smacked into the dirt.

Colb looked up, conflicted by the scene before him. On one hand, the carnage covering the forest was shocking and unnatural. On the other hand, this scene felt reminiscent of the annual Skaal farmer's market – bits of raw meat displayed everywhere he looked, ready for him to purchase and cook up at his tavern.

"Rrghegh… Colb!" Drek cried, catching his returning arrow. "I need medic," he mumbled, pulling his scrunched-up hood off his wound.

Colb and Stibs rushed over to Drek, while 27 followed behind – keeping his expensive cloak off the ground as he carefully tread around the hawkbear and cowmammoth remains.

Drek revealed a sizeable blister forming on his neck, which was surrounded by bluish skin. "Rrghegh, don't touch girl," Drek grumbled. "Her clothes are safe, but her uncovered skin is *so cold*. Her bare hand touched my neck when I caught her, and now it hurts…"

"Hmmm," Colb muttered, inspecting his surroundings. "We should get everyone out of here before addressing this, yes? There might be another hawkbear nearby, yes?"

Stibs perked his ears, and looked up at the sky. "Hurmph… I think we're alright. From what I've read, hawkbears are very isolated creatures. They meet for a day to mate, then go off on their own to make a nest. Since there's already an egg in that tree, I'm thinking we're past that point, so the mate should be long gone."

"AaAaaaaahhhh, that's our survival expert!" 27 cheered as he caught up to the others. "Is it safe enough to set up the *Yiklar*

Folding Cabin for a while?" He started feeling his pockets, then looked alarmed to find them empty.

"Hurmph, I think that'll be okay," Stibs agreed. He pulled out the *Yiklar Folding Cabin* doorknob, and tossed it to 27, who let out a sigh of relief as he caught it. "We've got someone unconscious, Drek is injured, and well… my leg still feels like it's on fire. Let's go inside for a bit and try to solve some of these problems."

27 glanced around, pointed out a nearby clearing, and headed over to unfold his cabin in it. Drek followed closely behind, again scrunching up the fabric hood on his cloak and holding it over the injury on his neck.

"Rrghegh, don't touch girl," Drek reminded as he walked off with 27. "If you want to bring her to cabin, drag her with a stick or something."

Colb and Stibs looked down at the child. Her mouth was slacked open a little bit, with a small stream of snow dribbling out like drool.

Colb grabbed a stick, and lightly jabbed at her face. The end of the stick instantly turned blue, and became covered in a thick layer of frost. Colb and Stibs inspected the stick, which was so cold that it felt chilly when held even a few inches away from their rough, green skin.

"Hurmph… try a fresh stick, and just touch her clothes," Stibs pitched. "Like Drek said."

Colb tossed the stick to the side, and the tip of it shattered upon hitting a nearby stone, starling the duo. "Hmmm, you don't think that's going to happen to Drek, do you?" Colb worried. "Drek's not going to shatter, yes?"

Stibs grimaced. "You're the medic," he said. "You tell me."

"Hmmm," Colb muttered nervously. Deciding to focus on one

task at a time, the chef goblin picked up another stick, and poked at the girl's white dress. The stick seemed to be fine.

Colb dropped the stick, then looked around for one with more of a hook-shape to it. Once he found one, he carefully hooked it around a loop in her dress.

"Hmmm, off to the cabin, yes?" Colb muttered, tugging to drag her along.

"Hurmph, is that going to work?" Stibs questioned.

"Hmmm! Actually, it's working pretty well," Colb replied. Her body moved across the ground like a chunk of ice sliding along a countertop. "I think she's pretty slippery, yes?"

"Hurmph, or the ground is slippery," Stibs theorized, hobbling along as Colb pulled her. "She's leaving behind a thick layer of frost wherever you drag her."

The duo continued to walk, with an icy path forming under the girl as they went, until they reached the *Yiklar Folding Cabin*. 27 opened the door for them, allowing Colb to drag the purple girl inside.

"MMmMmmmm, maybe don't bring her into my dancing area," 27 said, watching as the girl's head and hands frostbit the cabin's flooring. Colb dragged the unconscious body into the living area, then let go of the stick.

"Hmmm," Colb said, surveying the work before him. Stibs was still limping, the mysterious girl was unconscious, and an injured Drek had curled up into a ball on a beanbag chair. "Stibs, give the human medical kit to 27, yes?" Colb requested.

Stibs took the box of shiny rocks out of his backpack, and handed it to the noble goblin. Colb pointed at 27. "Hmmm! 27, that medical kit has instructions written in Hewmish. Translate them, and figure out how to fix broken legs, yes?" he ordered.

Colb then pointed at Stibs. "Hmmm, Stibs! Get a torch, light it, and hold it near Drek's neck. Try to warm him up so he doesn't shatter from being too cold, yes?" he commanded.

Stibs and 27 nodded. "Hmmm, while you two do that, I will go outside and collect some meat, then cook it in the kitchen, yes?" Colb declared. "If the girl was going after that egg, she must've been hungry, yes? The smell of a fresh meal might wake her up, yes?"

Their jobs made clear, the three goblins split off and went to work. After a couple of hours, Colb plated his meal in the cabin's dining area. For the main course, he'd prepared hawkbear steaks covered in peppersalt and drizzled with a secret toadroach stomach acid sauce recipe. For drinks, he'd whisked cooked cowmammoth stomach lining together with crushed hawkbear eyes to create a stringy, savory, meaty liquid blend.

Drek waltzed up to the table, took a portion for himself, and began to eat. Stibs followed closely behind him, holding a lit torch close to his neck. Drek's wound still looked swollen and blistered, but his skin was back to a cheerful green, and he seemed to be acting more chipper.

Colb grabbed a portion of hawkbear steak and a stone cup of meat-liquid, and brought it to the living area. He cautiously placed the meals next to the purple girl's nose, then stepped back to see if she'd react to the smell.

"Rrghegh," Drek grumbled between bites of hawkbear meat. "If she ever wakes up, we should add that girl to our team."

Colb looked at Drek with surprise. "Hmmm, I'm surprised to hear you suggest that after she hurt you, yes?"

"Rrghegh, she didn't hurt me – I caught her. Just like Stibs caught that sailor from the catcrow's nest," Drek countered. He stole a quick glance at the old goblin as he spoke, smiling slightly as if proud to have mimicked the eyepatched hero's actions. "Plus, she killed a hawkbear without even *looking* at it!" Drek continued. "Rrghegh, I'd rather her be with us than against us."

"Hurmph, that's a good point," Stibs agreed.

"MMmMmmmm, this mission is meant to be one goblin from each tribe, yes it is," 27 countered, looking up from his sheet of Hewmish parchment. He was sitting on his *Yiklar Floating Bed* in the sleeping corner of the cabin, where he'd been working away on translating the Hewmish writing. "The vision for this mission is four goblins: one to care, one to fight, one to navigate, and one to lead. What does mysterious purple girl add?"

"Rrghegh… like I said, she can fight," Drek replied.

"Drek, *you* are already our goblin to fight, yes you are," 27 retorted.

"Hurmph! If I've learned one thing on this trip, it's that there's no benefit in fighting alone," Stibs countered.

Colb gave the girl a worried glance, pushing the plate of hawkbear steak closer to her nose.

"MMmMmmmm, well let's put it to a vote," 27 said. "I say it's not best idea to expand the team."

"I vote yes," Drek and Stibs said at the same time.

"Rrghegh… that was creepy," Drek grumbled, shivering.

"What do you vote, Colb?" 27 asked.

"Hmmm, well, we should see what she thinks, yes?" Colb interjected. "Who's to say she even wants to join us, yes? Let's get her to wake up, then figure all that out."

Colb went silent, quietly staring at the girl. She didn't seem to be waking up, even with a delicious-smelling meal right under her nose. "Hurmph… that's fair," Stibs admitted, going silent as well.

After a few minutes, Drek piped up with an idea. "Rrghegh… try feeding her," he said.

"Hmmm, won't she choke?" Colb countered.

"Give her the liquid stuff," Drek replied, downing a glass of mixed-meat-juice as he spoke.

Colb picked up the stone cup of liquified cowmammoth stomach lining and hawkbear eye. "Hmmm, okay," he muttered. Colb carefully lifted the stone glass over the purple preteen's open mouth, and dripped a couple small drops into it.

HICC, BEUGH! the girl immediately coughed, then retched as the mixed-meat-juice touched her tongue. Her eyes snapped open, and she pushed off the ground, bumping into a couch. The leather cushions cracked like mirrors as her frigid hands grabbed onto them, stabilizing her fall.

"Hmmm, we're here to help, yes?" Colb said. Her frozen *Yiklar Amulet of Open Ears* glowed as Colb spoke. She looked back at him, petrified like a chickengoose caught in a cage. Colb carefully set the mixed-meat-juice down on the floor, then pushed the plate of hawkbear steak towards her.

She muttered something in an unknown language, looking down at the steak. She seemed interested in it, but without his *Yiklar Amulet of Open Ears*, Colb couldn't understand what she was saying. He thought for a moment, then snapped his fingers upon coming up with a solution.

"Hmmm, 27?" Colb said, not taking his eyes off the purple preteen. "You would be willing to pay me to be translator, to talk to her, yes?" he asked.

"MMmMmmmm, I suppose that would be useful service for you to do," 27 replied, "but you don't know her language, no you do not. Plus, I'm not swimming in funds, although I do have some from business with the humans. How much would you want me to pay you?"

"Hmmm, I want you to pay me the price of another *Yiklar Amulet of Open Ears*, yes?" Colb responded.

27's ears rose at the idea of a sale. "AaAaaaaahhhh, I like the way you are thinking now, yes I do," 27 agreed, summoning a pile of silvopper ingots and coins from his red bag. 27 jumped off his *Yiklar Floating Bed*, and walked over to Colb. The girl stared at him carefully, her eyes darting back-and-forth between the approaching goblin and the meat on the floor.

"I will pay you this pile of human currency – equivalent in value to 104 goldatinum pieces, 9 electronze pieces, and 2 silvopper pieces – to be our translator with this mysterious girl, yes I will," he said, handing the cash to Colb.

27 spun in a circle, until he was facing Colb again. "AaAaaaaahhhh, customer, I see you've brought me the exact price of a ready-to-go, highest-of-quality *Yiklar Amulet of Open Ears*, yes you have! Would you like to buy one?" Colb nodded, handing the money right back to 27, who dumped it into his bag. 27 then pulled out a magic amulet from his *Yiklar Bag of Traveling Inventory*, and placed it over Colb's neck. "I'll give you two some space to talk, yes I will. Enjoy your purchase," he cheered, dancing a little as he backed out of the living area.

Colb looked into the girl's wide blue eyes. "Hmmm, this is food for you, yes?" he said. "I cooked it nicely for you, too, yes?"

Her frost-covered *Yiklar Amulet of Open Ears* glowed faintly as she listened to him. "Um… how can I trust you?" she muttered. Colb's brand-new amulet similarly lit up as it translated her speech for him.

Colb thought for a moment, then sat on the floor, and scooched a little closer to her. The ground where the elf had been laying felt cold beneath his leather armor.

The goblin picked up the hawkbear steak, took a bite out of it, and swallowed. It tasted truly magnificent – a unique meat, that had been a rare delight to work with. Colb then drank some of the rancid meat-mixture, which was similarly a spectacle for the tongue. He placed the steak and cup back down, and pushed them closer to the girl.

"Hmmm, I just showed you that they're safe to eat, yes?" Colb said.

The girl cautiously let go of the couch, and reached forwards to grab the stone plate. It turned blue with frost as she pulled it towards herself. Without taking her eyes off Colb, the girl pulled a white pair of mittens out from a pocket hidden inside her dress, and put them on. She then picked up the steak with her covered hands, and ripped a piece off with her clean, white teeth. As she chewed the meat, it made crunching sounds as if she were chewing ice.

She looked down at what she'd eaten with a frown. The girl then picked up her stone plate, and scratched the side of it along her meal, wiping Colb's toadroach-sauce off the meat. The girl then took another bite of the now plain steak, and looked to be more satisfied with the taste.

"Hmmm, I go by the name of Colb, yes?" Colb introduced himself. "Behind me are 27, Stibs, and Drek. You have a name too, yes?"

"Um… I do," the girl replied, taking another crunchy bite of the meat. The more she ate, the more comfortable she started to look. "I am Kashmir."

"Hmmm, what language are you speaking, Kashmir?" Colb asked.

"The… same language as you?" she replied.

"I'm speaking Goblish, yes?" Colb said. "The four of us are goblins, and we gave you a magic *Yiklar Amulet of Open Ears* so you can understand us, yes? It's translating what I'm saying for you. To understand you, I've got one on, too." Colb gestured to his magic item.

Kashmir looked down at her own frost-covered necklace. "I'm… speaking Elvish," she said. "Because I'm an elf."

"Hmmm, you're an elf," Colb repeated so his friends could hear it. "And… and we're goblins. Is… is that okay? I've heard that humans and elves are… at odds, sometimes… but goblins and elves, we can get along, yes?"

"I don't know," Kashmir shrugged. "I've never even seen a goblin. You're from really far south, right?"

"Hmmm, yes we do live quite south from here," Colb answered. "I've never met an elf either, yes? Are you from the Elvish Kingdom?"

Kashmir nodded. Colb noticed his small, beady red eyes reflecting off the surface of Kashmir's beautiful, sky-like blue eyes as he spoke to her.

"Hmmm, what brings you to the Human Kingdom, yes?" Colb asked.

"I'm heading to Jaiphione's Crescent, because I'm needed there!" Kashmir cheered.

"Hmmm, Jaiphione's Crescent? Where's that?" Colb inquired.

Kashmir took a sip of the mixed-meat-juice, made a face, and put it back. "Ugh! What is this?"

"Hmmm, it's a blend of cowmammoth stomach lining and hawkbear eye, yes?" Colb answered.

"Eww," Kashmir replied.

Colb felt a little insulted, but decided to press on. This young elf reminded him of the children back in Skaal; they certainly had no filter when sharing their opinions. "Hmmm, tell me about Jaiphione's Crescent, yes?" Colb pressed. "You sound excited about going there, yes?"

"Have you ever seen an owlvulture, or a ladybugmoth?"

Kashmir questioned. Colb shook his head. "They're beautiful creatures. Especially the ladybugmoth – it's a fluffy bug with red, polka-dotted wings! Very cute," Kashmir cheered.

"Hmmm, do these creatures live in Jaiphione's Crescent?" Colb guessed.

"They do! And many more do, too," Kashmir cheered. "And you won't find them anywhere else. About 45,000 years ago, an elf named Jaiphione established a crescent island as a safe haven for hundreds of fragile animal species. All those creatures would've gone extinct if Jaiphione hadn't stepped in. That was her last great act before she passed away. Ever since her death, we elves have been protecting that island, and worshiping Jaiphione as the goddess of nature – and now, she calls upon *me* to save it!"

Colb nodded. Listening to this young elf *definitely* reminded him of the goblin children back home. Their stories would often get twisted around to center on the child telling it – which is exactly where this tale seemed to be going. Young Skaal goblins were savvy to find some greater life purpose for themselves – as such, phrases like "my destiny" and "I was chosen" came up often.

Kashmir continued with her story. "My father told me that, just 30 years ago, humans started invading Jaiphione's Crescent. He said they're killing off all the rare creatures, because they're stupid and they don't understand Jaiphione's mission."

"Hmmm, I see, yes?" Colb replied with a nod. *I guess the elves and humans really are at odds, yes?* he thought to himself.

"My father tried to get Queen Eylbella to declare war on the humans, but she refused, and… eventually… um, punished him," Kashmir said. She continued chewing on her steak meal as she spoke. "Soon, I realized it was *my* destiny to run away from home, and get the humans off Jaiphione's Crescent myself!"

"Hmmm, interesting," Colb muttered. "Do you know how to

find this Jaiphione's Crescent?"

"Of course," Kashmir replied. "I visited it once when I was 132 years old, so I know what it looks like. Plus, I strategized my route on a map before I ran away. I just need to find a human town called Sesui, and then I can enact my plan to get to the island."

"Hmmm, you just said you're… what age did you say?" Colb asked.

"I said I was 132 years old when I last visited Jaiphione's Crescent. Right now, I'm 482 years old," Kashmir replied.

"Hmmm! Alright," Colb agreed with a chuckle. *Hmmm, kids will be kids!* he thought to himself. "That's quite impressive, yes? I'm only 23! People don't tend to live past 60, yes?"

"Hurmph, I'm right here!" Stibs grumbled from the dining area. "In the Kreet Clan, we've got goblins pushing 70! Hurmph, that's what happens when you build up some muscle and live a little healthier."

"Hmmm, the elf says she's 482 years old, yes?" Colb said with a smile. He hadn't realized how much he missed talking to children, with their sporadic claims and fun stories.

"Elves live to around 4,000 years old," Kashmir snapped. "What, you don't believe me? My father was 2,210!"

"Hmmm, it's just hard to fathom you're so old, yes? You remind me of the children from my tribe," Colb chuckled.

"AaAaaaaahhhh, you know, Colb – humans can live for a whole century," 27 threw in, having listened to Colb's side of the conversation. "I think dwarves can live for something like three or four centuries. Maybe she *could* be 482, yes she could be?"

"Hmmm, she just said elves can live for 4,000 years, yes?" Colb replied. "Pretty impressive!"

"AaAaaaaahhhh, 4,000 years, eh? That is long time, yes it is…" 27 muttered. "…but the math kind of works out, yes it does.

If she's only 482, that would make her… what, 12% of the way through her life? No wonder she looks like child!"

"Okay, well," Kashmir grumbled in an annoyed tone. "When I say that I'm 482, I really mean that I'm almost 483. My age-up day is just a few months away. I'm closer to 483 than I am to 482."

She looked at Colb expectantly, who relayed her reply to 27. "You know, I believe it," 27 said with a shrug. "Elves are big mystery. We can't assume how long they live, or how fast they mature, no we cannot."

Kashmir nodded in approval, put the last bit of steak in her mouth, then took off her mittens. "Where am I?" she asked suddenly, looking around.

"Hmmm, this is our *Yiklar Folding Cabin*," Colb replied. "We set it up in the forest for shelter, yes? We haven't left the hawkbear's nesting area."

"Ohhhhh yea, that place with the egg," she muttered. "I guess I should've realized someone would be protecting it." Kashmir stood up, and immediately bonked her head on the ceiling, leaving behind a circle of frost.

"Hmmm! Don't hurt your head again, yes?" Colb said, gesturing for her to sit back down. "You bashed your skull so hard earlier, it knocked you out, yes?"

"Oh yea…" Kashmir mumbled, rubbing the top of her head and sitting back down. "Why is your ceiling so low?"

"Hmmm, because it's made for goblins, yes? You're much taller than we could ever dream to be, yes?" Colb replied. Colb furrowed his brow, worried about the elf's safety after taking such trauma back on the mapleoak tree.

"Hmmm, you should stay right where you are, yes? At least for now. Hmmm, don't put too much strain on your body, yes? Would you like some more food?" Colb offered.

The girl nodded. "Hmmm, was the hawkbear steak okay? Would you like more of that?" Colb asked.

Kashmir nodded again. "I'll eat anything that isn't endangered," she said. "Except for insects, I hate the taste of insects. I also won't eat things that aren't food... like stomach lining and eyes – *eugh!*"

"Hmmm, your definition of food is different than mine, yes?" Colb chuckled, walking over to the dining area to plate another hawkbear steak. As he wiped his secret toadroach sauce off Kashmir's steak, Colb glanced at Stibs. "Hmmm, Stibs? Does your map say anything about a... human town called Sesui, or an island called Jaiphione's Crescent?" he whispered.

"Hurmph... hold this," Stibs muttered, handing his torch to Drek. The young goblin accepted the torch with one hand, while slurping down a fresh glass of mixed-meat-juice with the other.

"Heh! That's easy," Stibs said, showing Colb his map. "Whereami," he said, forcing Colb to shut his eyes as the map blinded him with light.

"Hurmph, sorry about that... but check this out!" he pointed to a white mark on the map, which indicated their current position: only a few miles southeast of the human town, Sesui.

Colb looked a little bit above Sesui, and saw a crescent-shaped island to the north. It wasn't labeled Jaiphione's Crescent on the *Yiklar Map of Finding Location*, but it certainly seemed to align with the elf's story.

"Hmmm, I think she wants to visit that crescent island, yes?" Colb said. If we bring her to Sesui, she says she can go the rest of the way.

"Rrghegh, what about her joining our team?" Drek asked. "You said she should decide, so go ask her."

Colb nodded, then brought the steak over to Kashmir.

"Hmmm," he said, placing the stone dinnerware on the ground before her. "You're a bit of a fighter, yes?" Colb asked.

Kashmir shrugged, putting her mittens back on and taking the steak. "I just close my eyes, and whatever's trying to hurt me goes away. I figure I'll do the same thing against the humans, and they'll leave Jaiphione's Crescent alone!"

"Hmmm... you do know that you basically killed this hawkbear, yes?" Colb asked.

Kashmir tilted her head. "No, I made it go away, and knocked myself out in the process."

"Hmmm, if you made it go away, then how are you eating it, yes?" Colb countered. She looked down at the meat in her hands, and furrowed her brow. "You're quite powerful... I think you would hurt a lot of humans if you did that to them, yes?" Colb said.

"Well..." she muttered. "The hawkbear wanted to hurt me, and the humans want to hurt Jaiphione... so I guess that would be okay," she rationalized, taking a bite of the steak.

"Hmmm... I think the humans *don't* want to hurt Jaiphione, yes?" Colb retorted.

"Why?" Kashmir countered, tilting her head the other way.

"You said yourself that they're stupid, and they don't understand Jaiphione, yes? Maybe it would be better to talk with them, tell them the story you just told me – then, maybe they will understand, yes? Instead of hurting them for no reason?" Colb pitched.

"Well, it wouldn't be for no reason," Kashmir muttered.

"Hmmm, but if they don't know they're doing something wrong, then they would think you're hurting them for no reason, yes?" Colb countered.

"You sound like Queen Eylbella," Kashmir huffed, putting

down her steak and crossing her arms.

"Hmmm, who is that?" Colb asked.

"She rules the Elvish Kingdom, and suppresses our freedom," Kashmir grumbled. "She executed my father for speaking out against the humans, and made me an outlaw for running away from home."

"Hmmm! She *executed* your father?!" Colb exclaimed. "…and she made *you* an outlaw?"

A child? Colb thought. *Hmmm… or at least, a child in elf years? I'm still not sure how her age works, but making an outlaw out of such a young elf seems cruel. Let alone killing her father!*

"Defying Queen Eylbella's wishes is a crime of treason," Kashmir clarified. "Last week, she banned my whole family from even thinking about the crescent ever again, because she was mad that my father wouldn't stop trying to rally a war against the humans. By running off to save Jaiphione's Crescent, I'm sacrificing myself for the greater good."

"Hmmm, it's sounding like this all happened very recently?!" Colb observed. "Are… are you okay?"

"I will be, once I finish my father's work," Kashmir replied. "I won't be welcomed back in the Elvish Kingdom after what I'm doing, but helping Jaiphione and finishing my father's efforts is a greater purpose than anything I could do back home."

"Hmmm, so this is a one-way trip for you, yes?" Colb realized. Kashmir nodded, eyeing the steak she'd put back on the floor. "What do you plan to do after you save the crescent, yes?"

"Um…" she muttered.

Hmmm. She didn't think that far ahead, did she? Colb thought to himself. *Even if she really is old on the outside, I'm definitely speaking with a child.*

"…I'm going to stay on the crescent, and defend it forever,"

Kashmir decided. "That way, the humans will never come back."

"Hmmm," Colb muttered, pushing the plate of steak closer to Kashmir. The elf picked it up and began eating. "What if instead, you came with us? We're on an adventure, and could use your help, yes? If we come across another hawkbear, it would be great to have someone that can make it go away like you can," he said. "Hmmm – again, not to make *humans* go away like that, but perhaps to keep us safe from the big monsters. Think about it, yes?"

Kashmir shrugged. "Okay, I will," she said, and continued eating.

Deciding to give her some space while she ate, Colb sauntered over to 27 to discuss the healing crystal situation. "Hmmm, you've made progress on the translations, yes? We can heal broken legs now, yes?"

"AaAaaaaahhhh, well I've made progress, yes I have," 27 said, looking through his notes. "But… many strange things are in here, yes there are. Grounding yourself to the earth? Burying stones in peppersalt to recharge them? Aligning rocks with the moonlight? Not to mention, I think the stones all do the same thing, yes they do, and they're just described in a roundabout way to *seem* different."

He picked up three different stones, and showed them to Colb. "The quartzelian *blocks* negative energy, yes it does. Obsidethyst *shields* you from negative energy, and the tourmalpyrite *grounds* negative energy away from you. There is no difference? It's nonsense!" 27 exclaimed.

"Hmmm," Colb muttered, taking the three stones. "Maybe it's just complicated, because it's medicine, yes?"

"MMmMmmmm, well, why don't you give them a try?" 27 said. "The instructions say that all injuries are caused by negative energy that floats around the universe – whatever *that* is – and that these energies coincidentally flowed into Stibs at the exact moment that his leg was crushed under the weight of a dwarf. By that logic, removing the negative energy will fix the leg. Why don't you hold those three stones next to Stibs, and see if it fixes him?"

Colb nodded. He started to walk away, then stopped. "Hmmm, by the way – is it okay if Kashmir joins us? I offered her the option, yes?"

"MMmMmmmm, if she wants to, then I suppose I've been outvoted," 27 replied. "So, sure! I try to be a leader of open mind, yes I do try to be."

Colb smiled, then walked over to Stibs. He held out the three stones, and touched them to the old goblin's leg. Stibs hissed at the sudden contact with his swollen area. "Hmmm, is it working?" Colb asked.

"Hurmph… not immediately," Stibs grumbled.

"Hmmm, hold onto these, and sleep next to them tonight, yes? They should block the negative energies affecting your leg," Colb declared. Stibs nodded, accepting the stones.

"Rrghegh… can I have stone? For my neck?" Drek asked.

"Hmmm… yes," Colb agreed. Stibs handed the tourmalpyrite to Drek.

The young goblin pocketed the stone, then let out a small yawn. "Rrghegh… I'm tired," Drek announced. "Time for sleep." He walked off to his beanbag chair, and with Colb's permission, Stibs put out the torch he'd been using to warm up the young goblin's neck.

Over the next hour, waves of exhaustion from the previous day caught up with everyone. The party of five gradually ate and finished up their dinners, then turned in for the night.

Before going off to bed, Colb approached Kashmir one last time. "Hmmm, sleep well, yes?" he muttered. The goblins had decided she should rest in the living area – both to protect the rest of the cabin from her freezing skin, and because Colb didn't want her skull bashing into the ceiling again if she tried to move somewhere else.

"Hmmm, give that head of yours some rest – and think about what I said today, yes?" Colb whispered. "Maybe, if you talk to the humans nicely, you could help them understand whatever they're doing wrong… and after that, if you're not welcome home, you'll always have a place adventuring with us, yes?"

"Um… okay, I'll think about it," she replied, curling up and falling asleep.

Colb smiled. *Hmmm, she really is just like the goblin children in Skaal*, he thought again. *It feels good to take care of her. She's a little extreme – wanting to kill humans, and all – but kids can be naïve like that. It sounds like her heart's in the right place, and ultimately, that'll be enough to guide her in life, yes?*

Colb looked over at Drek and Stibs, who seemed to be best of friends after the summer antlizard experience. *Hmmm, it's like 27 said: a good team needs time – and he was right! Perhaps, with some time, Kashmir will find the purpose she seems to be seeking… a way she can make the world just a little bit better, yes? One that doesn't involve killing humans, hopefully.* With that, Colb sauntered off to the sleeping area, and succumbed to a little well-deserved rest.

Chapter 12

STOWAWAYS

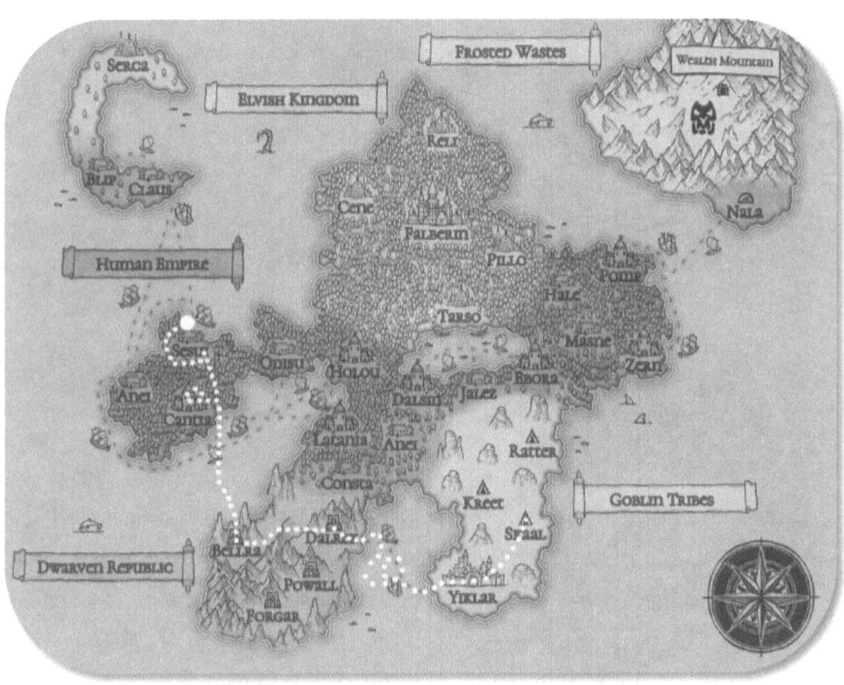

12. STOWAWAYS

In the morning, 27 jumped out of bed, looking well-rested and excited to begin the day. Drek remained sleeping on his beanbag chair, as usual, and Colb let out a wide yawn, slow but eager to get moving.

Kashmir and Stibs were already awake, both sitting in the living area. A light mist formed in the air as Kashmir twirled her fingers around absent-mindedly. Colb walked up to her, and tilted his head.

"Hmmm… we have to go northeast," he announced. "You want to go north, yes? To the crescent island?" The girl nodded. Colb looked around at his teammates. "Hmmm, what if we accompany her to the island, since we need to go north eventually anyway?" he pitched.

"Hurmph, that seems fine," Stibs declared. "We could take a boat over the northern tip of the Elvish Kingdom from that island, which might save some time." 27 nodded in agreement as well. Drek continued to lay quietly on his beanbag, but at this point, he would be outvoted either way.

Colb looked at the elf, tilting his head slightly to mirror how she was sitting. "Hmmm, we could help you get to Jaiphione's Crescent, and perhaps help you try talking to the humans, instead of hurting them, yes? Then, you could choose to stay there, or you could head eastwards with us if you wish, yes?"

"Um… okay," she replied, tugging on her hair nervously. She looked at Colb. "Are we ready to leave, then? I'm bored from waiting around."

Colb translated her words to 27, who gave Kashmir a thumbs-up in agreement. The goblins quickly packed up their things, disabled the traps Drek had set around himself, pulled Drek out of the beanbag chair, and finally closed up the cabin once everyone was outside.

"Hmmm, Sesui is to the north, yes?" Colb said once everyone was ready to leave. Stibs confirmed that information with a nod.

"AaAaaaaahhhh, I suppose our newest member should lead the way, yes she should!" 27 announced.

"Um… okay," Kashmir said, turning to walk north. "We'll go to Sesui, then sneak onto a boat. Try not to be seen; I heard that hundreds of guards live in this town. If just one notices us, they might call upon their whole army, and then we'll be screwed… but, if we do sneak onto a boat without being seen, it'll be the fastest way to Jaiphione's Crescent." Hearing Colb's translation of her words, the goblins nodded, then began to follow her. However, they all stopped when they heard Stibs call from behind.

"Hurmph… I'm… I can't really walk. My leg's still too jacked up. I can move a little if I use a stick as a crutch, but I'm going to slow you guys down," he grumbled to the team.

"Hmmm, but the human medicine has been helping, yes?" Colb replied.

Stibs scratched his chin. "Hurmph… I… eh, it really hurts. I think they're helping, but I still can't walk."

"Hmmm, let's pause and try to fix your leg again, yes?" Colb responded, walking back over to Stibs. The old goblin pulled the two stones out of his pocket, and gave them to Colb. Drek handed his tourmalpyrite back to Colb as well. The chef goblin pulled out his healing crystals kit, and passed the instructions to 27.

"Those rocks aren't magic," Kashmir said from behind him, watching Colb poke through the contents of the box.

"Hmmm, these are healing crystals, yes? They have magic properties, yes?" Colb countered.

Kashmir shook her head. "Those are just rocks and stuff you

can find underground. There's nothing special about them."

Colb looked up at her, confused as to why she sounded so sure of herself. "Hmmm, do you happen to be medic?" he asked.

"No," she replied. "But I can sense magic. The cabin, for example. And that bag," she continued, pointing at the red bag on 27's belt. "Or that magic map from last night. Those things all have magic radiating from them. They're clearly enchanted. Obviously, I've got a lot of magic radiating from myself, as well."

She then tapped one of the gemstones in Colb's hand, leaving a little pile of frost behind as she pulled her finger away. "But these are just polished gemstones. They're basically worthless." She took the wooden box out of Colb's hand, causing it to crack under her frosty grip. "Your rubidium isn't even real; it's just a quartzelian that's been dyed reddish-blue."

"Hmmm, this cannot be, yes?" Colb replied, furrowing his hairless brow. "I… I received these from human medic, yes?"

"Humans are stupid," Kashmir replied. "Elves, dwarves, and goblins have all been around way longer. I don't think you should even consider humans a civilized species. They probably just sold you a bunch of rocks that they thought were magic, but really, I don't think any humans even understand what magic is."

"Hmmm," Colb mumbled, accepting the cold box back from Kashmir and glancing at the gemstones inside. "Did these help you at all, yes?" he asked Stibs again.

The eyepatched goblin let out a big sigh. "Hurmph, as far as I can tell, I still can't walk… you're a medic, so what gives?"

Colb dumped the six stones onto the ground, then kicked some dirt over them. "Hmmm… I'm sorry… I failed," he muttered.

"MMmMmmmm, what— what is wrong?" 27 asked.

"Hmmm, Kashmir says these are not magic at all, yes?" Colb mumbled, staring down at his feet. "And they aren't healing Stibs, yes?"

"MMmMmmmm," 27 replied uncertainly. "I cannot verify or deny her opinion, no I cannot. My tribe does not deal with healing magic. This is outside of my expertise, yes it is."

"Hurmph, we don't need magic for every little thing," Stibs grumbled. "Why don't you just do some… I don't know, regular healing? Or something?"

Colb sighed. "I'm… not very good medic," he whimpered. "I am chef, and goblin to care… but I don't know much about healing."

Everyone went silent. Kashmir cringed, taking a step away from the awkward situation.

"Hurmph, Drek's still alive," Stibs said after a moment. "He still has a blister, but you got his skin to turn green again when it was blue."

"Rrghegh… blister seems better this morning, too," Drek added.

"AaAaaaaahhhh, and you helped Kashmir wake up, yes you did," 27 added. "You cared for her, and helped her get some rest." 27 glanced at Stibs and Drek. "Look, team… it's my fault for setting your expectations so high with Colb, yes it is, but you can *see* that he is goblin that cares. This is what makes him good medic, yes it is. I'm sure, if you give him *time*, he will find a way to heal your leg, Stibs."

"Hurmph… fair enough," Stibs agreed.

"Give team time, and it will work itself out," 27 said. "Every goblin – and elf, I suppose, perhaps – will fall into their role, yes they will, if given enough time. Just as I'm sure your leg will be healed in due time."

Drek walked over, then draped one of the old goblin's arms around his shoulders. "Rrghegh… in meantime, I can be second crutch, helping you walk well."

"Hurmph, thanks," Stibs replied, looking down at Drek with a slight smile.

"Rrghegh… just try not to touch my neck blister while I'm helping you," he added.

Kashmir looked at Colb. "It's still going to take him too long to travel anywhere, even with a walking stick and a goblin to help him," she complained. "We'll need to be able to move fast if we're going to sneak onto a boat without getting caught."

"MMmMmmmm, what is she saying, Colb?" 27 asked.

"Hmmm, she thinks we… might be too slow if Stibs is moving by foot, even with Drek and his crutch, yes?"

27 thought for a second, then snapped his fingers. "I have idea!" he announced. The noble pulled out his *Yiklar Folding Cabin*, activated it, and ran inside. Moments later, he stepped back out the door, pulling a magically floating slab of stone with him.

"We could just push him on my *Yiklar Floating Bed*, yes we could!" 27 announced as he deactivated the cabin again.

"Hmmm, that is great idea, yes?" Colb replied with excitement. Kashmir shrugged and nodded, seeming pleased by the quick solution.

For the next few hours, the goblins proceeded after Kashmir by foot, working together to push along the floating slab with their injured friend upon it. Eventually, they reached the border of a bustling human village called Sesui. The buildings of this settlement were made of bismuthslate brick and mapleoak wood, and thus looked similar to the structures of Cantia.

"This is Sesui, a human town," Kashmir whispered as the goblins joined her at the forest's edge. "Stay hidden while I look around." Colb repeated her instructions to the others. The trio of goblins proceeded to hide Stibs and the *Yiklar Floating Bed* behind a large tree.

Colb peeked out from the hiding spot, and watched as Kashmir skipped towards the town, keeping her head low and treading elegantly. Her footsteps made virtually no sound at all as she danced through the leaves. Her purple skin blended her in with the shadows cast from the clouds above.

After a couple dozen minutes, Kashmir came back. "I found the ports," she reported to Colb, who translated her words for the rest of the group. "If we follow this forest around to the western edge of town, we'll be right next to a merchant ship that's just finished reloading. It has two guards, but they're facing away from the boat. If we're quiet and fast enough, I think we can sneak around behind them and get onto the boat undetected."

With that, Kashmir proceeded to carefully lead the goblin crew around the perimeter of Sesui. As they traveled through a particularly narrow part of the surrounding forest, 27 winced upon seeing his bed get scratched up by some tree branches. The group eventually arrived at the ports, where water sloshed and splashed against the human-made ships and wooden docks. Kashmir pointed out the closest boat, which was quite large, and had two chainmail-wearing humans guarding it. "See that ramp?" she whispered to Colb, pointing out a wide wooden plank draped between the boat and dock. "We need to go up that, and then enter the door on the left. It'll bring us below-deck, where the humans just finished loading all their supplies. I snuck a peek down there through a window, and it's just a cargo hold, so they probably won't check it again until we arrive at Jaiphione's Crescent. That makes it a perfect place to hide while we hitch a ride. I'll guide you past the guards and onto the boat; just follow my lead."

Colb nodded, then repeated the clarified plan to the others. Stibs gave a thumbs-up from his seat on the *Yiklar Floating Bed*.

Drek narrowed his eyes, looking wary of the two armed humans next to the dock.

Kashmir led the goblins along the edge of the shore. They tread quietly, careful not to alert the set of human guards – who were staring out at the town itself, and not back at the boat they were guarding.

Kashmir slipped behind the guards, and gestured towards the dock. Pushing the *Yiklar Floating Bed*, the goblin crew tiptoed to catch up with the elf – until they heard a *clink! clink!* sound of a can falling over.

Kashmir's eyes widened. Colb looked at her, then looked down at the ground. The elf had knocked over a metal container of liquid that one of the guards must've left by his feet. Kashmir looked at the guards, who didn't seem to have noticed the sound. She slowly bent down, picking up the can and placing it back where it was. Her fingers left some frost behind on the metal cylinder as she set it back into place.

Suddenly, one of the guards started to speak. The goblins froze, and Colb's *Yiklar Amulet of Open Ears* glowed, translating their Hewmish words. "It's a bit of a cloudy day, innit?" the guard said.

The other guard sighed. "What do you want me ta say to that, Eddy? Huh? Where am I supposed ta go with that? It's cloudy? Yea, it's cloudy. It's always cloudy."

Colb looked at his fellow goblins, who seemed petrified with fear. He mouthed the Goblish words: *'It's nothing. Keep going.'*

"Geez, I'm just trying to make conversation," the first guard mumbled. "And you know what, I did. That's interesting, whatcha said there. It is always cloudy. I'd say it's cloudy about 90, maybe 95% of the time. That's a bit strange, innit? Why do you think Sesui's weather is so often uninteresting?"

"Are you seriously tryin' to make me talk to you about the

concept of something being uninteresting? Geez, Ed, get a grip. Our job is literally to just stand around. My whole life is uninteresting," the second guard grumbled.

The goblins continued to push their *Yiklar Floating Bed*, holding their breath as they got close to the guards – and breathing a shallow sigh of relief as they stepped onto the dock.

As 27 and Drek pushed the *Yiklar Floating Bed* the rest of the way onto the boat, Colb looked back at Kashmir. She was suddenly side-stepping a human arm, as the first guard turned around to grab his drink off the ground. The guard lifted the drink, then turned back to face the town. He didn't seem to notice Kashmir or the goblins.

"What the-" the guard exclaimed.

"What? What?" his companion asked.

"Here's something interesting for ya," the guard replied. "I had a beer in here, but now it's completely frozen! Just two minutes ago it was fine. How'd that happen?"

Kashmir grimaced, and tiptoed away from the guards, catching up with Colb.

"Aw, come on, you're not supposed to be drinkin' on the job," the second guard replied. "I'm gonna have to tell Gary about this, man."

"You are *not* going to tell Gary about this," the first guard replied, glaring at his partner.

Kashmir caught up with Colb, and the duo snuck onto the boat, leaving the quibbling guards behind. Once they caught up with the others, the group pushed the *Yiklar Floating Bed* over to a wooden door.

"MMmMmmmm, this door has lock on it," 27 observed.

"Rrghegh… I got this," Drek announced, cracking his knuckles. He pulled out his dagger, slid the sharpened tip into the keyhole, then slapped the hilt of the knife with a quick blow. The lock split open. "Lock is picked," he announced proudly.

The group continued forward, carefully sliding the floating bed down a stairway and into the cargo hold. When they all reached the lower part of the ship, 27 surveyed the space. "AaAaaaaahhhh, cargo area is quite big!" he cheered. "Whole cabin could unfold down here!"

With that, he pulled out his *Yiklar Folding Cabin* doorknob, and activated it in the least-cluttered area. The 12 ft x 12 ft x 4 ½ ft building barely managed to squeeze open, displacing some barrels of cargo as it unfolded. The *Yiklar Folding Cabin*'s door was positioned such that it faced the staircase the group had just descended.

"This space isn't that big," Kashmir grumbled. "Your cabin only fits because it's *so* small." She pulled open the door with a frosty hand, and ducked down as she entered.

Everyone piled into the cabin behind Kashmir, then 27 shut the door behind them. The party of five let out a collective sigh of relief, pleased to have successfully boarded the island-bound ship without causing too much trouble for themselves. They were safely on their way to Jaiphione's Crescent: another step closer to Wealth Mountain for the goblin crew, and the ultimate destination for Kashmir on her current quest.

Chapter 13

THE QUARTZELIAN PIRATES

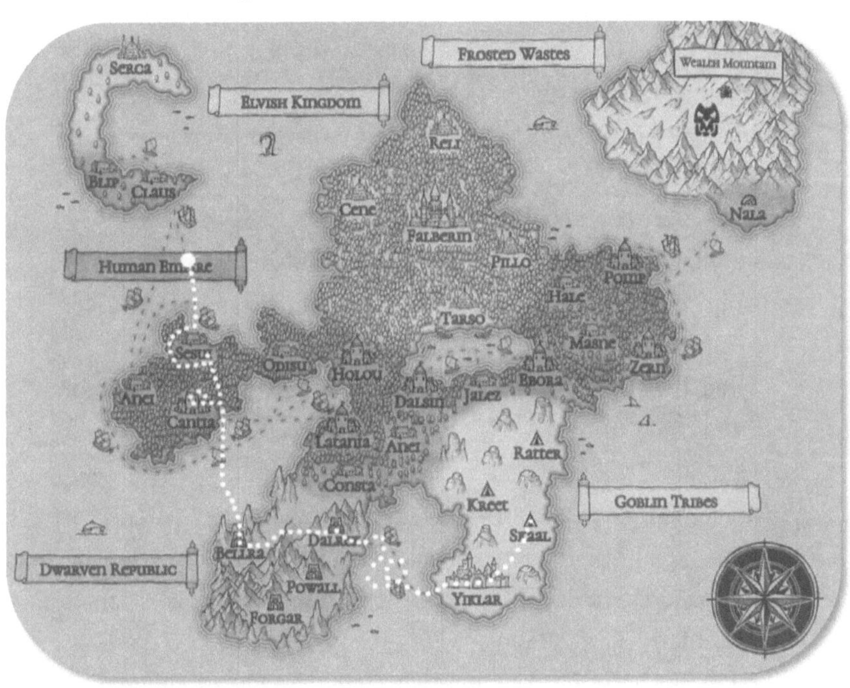

13. THE QUARTZELIAN PIRATES

As the day turned to evening, footsteps could be heard along the upper deck. It sounded like the human crew returned and was prepared the start the night's journey. While the party of five waited patiently and quietly within their cabin, the boat lurched forward, and headed out to sea.

After a few hours of smooth sailing, the goblin crew began to turn in for the night, with a sleepless Kashmir and Stibs keeping first watch in case anyone outside got too close to the cabin.

Colb stared up at the ceiling as he lay in bed, feeling the tide of the ship sway in a rhythmic pattern. He wasn't feeling seasick, but the constant movement was making it hard to fall asleep. Colb then looked to the side, where 27 had reclaimed and peacefully fallen asleep upon his *Yiklar Floating Bed*. The floating slab was stable, magically counteracting the back-and-forth movement of the ship. For the first time since 27 had shown it to him, Colb wished he had one of those beds of his own right now.

Tired, the chef goblin looked back up at the ceiling, waiting for his exhaustion to overwhelm the annoying pushes of the waves beneath him. Eventually, he succumbed to sleep.

Sometime later, Colb's ears perked up to the sounds of clanging metal from the upper deck. Now awake, he sat up in bed, and scanned the interior of the cabin. 27 and Drek both sat up as well, similarly alerted by the noise.

"Hmmm, what are the sounds upstairs, yes?" Colb mumbled. Kashmir rushed into the bedroom area, speaking rapidly in Elvish. She was holding a hand over her head, careful not to bump it on the ceiling as she crouched and ran over. The elf appeared to be very alarmed. Stibs was standing by the cabin door, leaning against the wall and holding his crutch at-the-ready like a defensive weapon.

"MMmMmmmm, I am wondering what those sounds are as well, yes I am," 27 agreed with a yawn.

"Hmmm," Colb muttered. The chef goblin hopped out of bed, pulled his *Yiklar Amulet of Open Ears* out from his pile of leather armor, and donned it. "What's going on up there, yes?" Colb asked Kashmir.

"Oh, good," Kashmir replied, seeing Colb had put his necklace back on. "We… we think the ship's being hijacked, and the crew is being killed."

"Hmmm! That seems very bad!" Colb replied with surprise. 27 gave him an exasperated look. Colb noticed this, and began translating everything Kashmir was saying.

"We heard another boat start approaching ours around half an hour ago," she continued. "After a little while, Stibs said he heard some boards clanking above us, and some shouting began. We think that sound was the other ship boarding ours. A minute ago, the shouting turned into sword fighting, which we can still hear happening right now."

"Rrghegh… should I start cutting people as well?" Drek asked. Colb jumped with surprise, then turned around to see Drek brandishing a knife behind him. "I got out of bed when I heard word of fighting," the young rogue explained. "Rrghegh, sounds like job for goblin with knife, if you ask me… perhaps it is job for elf with magic as well?"

"MMmMmmmm, there is no reason to start freezing and cutting humans, no there is not," 27 announced. "There is probably good explanation, yes there is. Perhaps our ship's crew has… has swordfighting club, yes they do. And other ship came by to have friendly midnight dueling session, yes they did."

BAM! The door to the lower levels of the ship slammed open, moments after 27 finished his sentence. Everyone rushed to the cabin's front window to see what was happening.

A group of bearded men in red coats and tight breeches rushed down the stairs. They held rapiers covered in blood. A couple wore eyepatches, and a few others had wooden peg legs. With the door now open, the squawking of a canaryparrot could be heard from the main deck.

"Eyepatches, peg legs, a canaryparrot…" 27 mumbled to himself. "AaAaaaaahhhh, these must be pirates, yes they must be! I remember this from my studies of human culture. They are treasure hunters, yes they are. They must be here to request good deals from the merchants of this ship!"

"Aye, why's there a tiny house in the cargo hold?" one of the pirates questioned in Hewmish.

"Hurmph, or they're here to steal the treasure these merchants have below deck," Stibs grumbled. Drek backed up against the wall next to the cabin door, mirroring Stibs. He held his dagger at-the-ready to stab the next human to enter the cabin.

"AaAaaaaahhhh, well either way, the humans in Cantia were quite keen on my good deals, yes they were," 27 replied confidently. "If these pirates are lovers of treasure, then offering them some most fantastic of deals will certainly put us in their good graces, yes it will! Here, let me show you." With that, he stepped forwards, and pushed open the door. Four bewildered pirates double-taked with surprise as a goblin stepped out from the small house.

"AaAaaaaahhhh, customers!" 27 announced in Hewmish. The other goblins exchanged worried looks. While Stibs and Drek continued to hold their positions around the door, Colb grabbed his shield and defensively stood in front of Kashmir.

"I see you have found our… um, shop, yes you have!" 27

cheered. "Welcome, my pirate pals, to the specific store!"

A pirate suddenly lunged forwards and took a swing at 27. Moments before the blade hit, Drek reached out past the door, grabbed the noble by the legs, and pulled him back into the cabin.

"AaAaaaaahhhh," 27 announced, immediately stepping out of Drek's grip and into the open again. "I see you are big fan of sword, yes you are. But… can it cut through metal? AaAaaaaahhhh, because we have special offer on *Yiklar Shortsword of Metal Cutting* today, yes we do."

The pirate before him stepped forwards, then carved a slice across 27's robe in a single swift motion. 27's eyes widened at how close the blade got to his torso, as his robe drooped from the newly made hole. "Aye, we're not wastin' time heya. We've got plenty of swards alreadae."

"AaAaaaaahhhh, you may have high quantity of swords, but *quality* defeats quantity. That is the Yiklar wa-" the noble started to reply, but he was cut off as the pirate grabbed 27 by the throat, pulling him up off the ground. Colb watched through the open cabin door with horror as 27 dropped his red bag to the ground, and began thrashing his little legs in the air under the pirate's grip.

"The lot of you," the pirate said, looking at Colb and Kashmir through the door of the *Yiklar Folding Cabin*. "Get out of yer' weird little house right now, or we'll cut yer' friend's 'art out." He brought the tip of his rapier menacingly over 27's heart. The other three pirates stood behind him, watching the interaction with curious interest. 27's eyes were wide – they looked about ready to pop out of his head – and he let out a loud gulp.

Drek leaned out the cabin door, and chucked his knife into the pirate's kneecap. "*Augh!*" the man yelped with surprise, dropping 27. The noble immediately grabbed his red sack off the ground, then scampered back into the *Yiklar Folding Cabin*. The pirate turned to the others, hands over the hilt of the small knife now stuck in his leg.

"Aye, stop standin' around and kill every last one of 'em in that little store!" he shouted, wobbling away from the cabin's entrance. The three pirates nodded, then carefully advanced on the cabin.

As one of the humans poked his head through the cabin's door, Stibs smacked him with his crutch. This set the old goblin off-balance, knocking him to the ground as his bad leg failed to keep him upright. Drek dived to Stibs, catching the eyepatched goblin to cushion his fall.

The pirate winced at the attack, but soon continued his advance. He dropped down to a crawl, and inched into the room, sword at-the-ready. The pirate's two companions smashed a couple of the cabin's windows, then pushed their arms inside, ready to swipe at anyone that came too close.

"They're going to get us," Kashmir whimpered into Colb's ear. The chef goblin sweat, his wooden shield the only thing he had to stop these three pirates. "I need to make them go away," Kashmir muttered.

Colb glanced at 27, whose neck was covered in unusually dark green marks from being choked. The noble looked to be frantically scanning the cabin for options, but seemed desperate, as if he was coming up with nothing.

"Hmmm…" Colb muttered. He watched as Drek started dragging Stibs towards the kitchen, away from the crawling pirate and his swinging rapier. "Hurting people is not always the answer, yes?" he whispered to Kashmir. "Hmmm… but to keep our friends safe, you can make these pirates go away."

Colb stepped around Kashmir, positioning himself behind her. He held his shield up against her back, ready to keep her steady so she wouldn't accidentally hurt herself.

Kashmir let out a slow breath, which looked like smoke as it froze some particles in the air. She then closed her eyes, looked away, and held out her open hands towards the pirate.

Everyone's ears popped as air rushed to the elf's palms, colliding together into a bubbling sphere. After a moment, two thin beams of misty liquid erupted from it, blasting the crawling pirate directly in his eyes.

"*AyyeAH!*" the human shouted, rolling over and putting his hands over his face. Colb pushed his feet into the ground, holding a strong stance as he pinned his shield against the purple elf's back. The force of the powerful beam thrust Kashmir into him. Colb's wooden safeguard made a crackling sound as part of the elf's bare neck touched it, but the chef goblin held strong, keeping Kashmir stable as she attacked the human.

As the pirate rolled to the side, writhing in pain, Kashmir's freezing beam continued straight: now shooting out the open door, and freezing the staircase that led up to the main deck.

Meanwhile, Drek took out his *Yiklar Bow of Returning Arrow*, and took out a pirate in one of the windows. Seeing his two companions go down, the third pirate backed off, and called up the stairs for reinforcements.

"Hmmm, we should get out of here now, yes?" Colb announced to his friends.

"Rrghegh, where would we go? We are on boat," Drek called out. The sound of a dozen new feet stomping onto the main deck of the merchant ship could be heard from above.

Kashmir's freezing beam faltered, then ceased. The elf opened her eyes, and looked at the fallen pirate before her. Seizing this momentary lapse in the battle, the third pirate fled up the staircase – struggling as he climbed the icy steps.

"Hurmph, we need to get above-deck," Stibs announced, standing up with Drek's assistance. "We're completely cornered in this cargo hold."

27 carefully stepped around the blinded pirate, who was still wriggling around on the cabin floor. The noble goblin then stepped into the cabin's entrance, grabbed the doorknob, and clicked the hidden button on it. With a *WHOOSH!* the cabin, and all the furniture inside, collapsed in on itself, warping and deforming as it all sucked into the doorknob: leaving behind only the team of five, the two downed pirates, and the equipment they all were holding.

Colb looked around. He was now sitting on the wooden floor of the cargo hold, in an open space with some barrels and crates lining the walls. Above a nearby stack of crates, Colb noticed a circular window. Through it, a second ship – probably a pirate ship – was visible.

"Hmmm, we could escape through that window, yes?" Colb suggested, pointing it out.

Drek scampered over to where Colb was pointing, climbed the stack of crates, and popped the window open. Peppersalty sea air wafted into the cargo hold.

Drek stuck his head out the window, and looked up. "Rrghegh, the pirate ship has ropes along the side. We could hop out and grab them to escape from here," he pitched. "I hear lots of voices coming from our ship's main deck, but the pirate ship sounds empty. I think most of the pirates have boarded this boat. It may be safer on their ship than staying here."

As soon as he said that, a couple of pirates came tumbling down the stairs. "Aye, why arr' these stairs covered in ice?" one exclaimed as his head smacked into the ground. They both had blood-covered rapiers in their hands.

Drek pulled out his *Yiklar Bow of Returning Arrow* and fired at the two humans. His iridhodium arrow clipped a pirate in the ear, then pierced the other one in the neck as it magically returned to its archer. "Rrghegh, let's get out of here!" Drek ordered as he caught the arrow.

The goblins and elf quickly made their way over to Drek, who kept the pirates at bay with his *Yiklar Bow of Returning Arrow* while they climbed the crates.

27 made it to Drek first, and put his arm out the window. The pirate ship had been anchored right next to the merchant boat, so he didn't have to reach far to grab one of the many ropes hanging along the side of the wooden vessel. Once he had a solid grip, the noble goblin slipped out the window and began to climb up.

Stibs soon followed behind. Although he was crippled in one of his legs, he had no issues climbing the ropes with his superior upper body strength.

Up next was Kashmir, whom Colb had encouraged to go before him for her own safety. The purple elf accidentally shattered the first rope she grabbed with her frosty grip – but was able to climb a different one by donning her pair of white mittens before touching it.

At this point, when it was just Colb and Drek left in the cargo hold, about half a dozen pirates had piled into the lower deck: each slipping on the icy stairs as they entered. Drek's shiny iridhodium arrow had been keeping them at bay, but now their numbers were starting to overwhelm him.

The roguish goblin fired off one more shot, then jumped out the window, grabbing onto a nearby rope. His arrow cut through a pirate, curved around, then flew out the circular window after Drek – who caught it and stowed it in his cloak.

Colb looked at the pirates, upset about the destruction his

friends had caused to them. *Hmmm… this is going to make Kashmir think fighting is okay*, he thought to himself.

"Rrghegh… grab a rope!" Drek called out. Colb turned, and saw the young goblin staring at him on the other side of the window. "They're coming for you!"

Colb looked back, only to see a rapier flying right towards him. He instinctively lifted his wooden shield, blocking the thrown sword. "Hmmm, yes," he agreed, reaching his arm out of the window.

Colb grabbed onto one of the rough, scratchy ropes. With Drek by his side, he climbed his way up, onto the pirate ship above.

When he arrived at the pirate ship's main deck, Colb surveyed his surroundings. The area appeared to be deserted; all the pirates must have gone onto the merchant ship, not expecting anyone would board theirs during the attack.

This wooden vessel had been entirely painted black, and a sharp skull-and-crossbones design was carved into every post. A white-painted wooden plank stood out along the edge of the ship. It had been positioned like a sort of bridge between the pirate ship and the merchant ship, and must have been the connecting piece used by the pirates for their attack. Stibs pushed the white plank into the water, thus cutting the pirates off from returning to their vessel.

The goblins looked at the merchant boat they'd just escaped from. It appeared to have been completely overrun – all the human sailors had been slaughtered, and about a dozen pirates were searching for loot above-deck. The pirates were so busy ransacking the merchant boat, they hadn't yet noticed their own vessel had been hijacked.

"Rrghegh… let's claim this boat and sail away," Drek pitched. "I don't see anyone left to save on that merchant ship, so I think it's best if we just leave. Does anyone know how to sail this boat?"

"Hurmph, survival expert here, right?" Stibs replied. "I'll bet I can figure it out."

"Rrghegh… then Stibs is captain. Any objections?" Drek declared. Nobody replied. "Good. If it's okay with the captain, I'm going to check the lower deck for any threats while the rest of you help Stibs."

Stibs nodded. Drek drew his bow, and head down into the lower decks of the pirate ship: ready to execute any threats that might loom.

"Hurmph, my first order as captain: someone cut all the ropes along the edge of the ship, so none of those pirates can climb on-board like we just did."

Her *Yiklar Amulet of Open Ears* glowing with understanding, Kashmir pulled off her mittens, and began touching all the ropes along the edge of the pirate boat – freezing and snapping each one off in the process.

"Hurmph… nice. 27, find the anchor and pull it up. Colb, find the steering wheel and hold it steady. I'll hoist the sails and do everything else we need to get this ship moving. We'll meet with Colb at the steering wheel when we're done."

"Hmmm, aye, aye, yes?" Colb replied. The three goblins then split off to complete their respective tasks.

Colb found a spiked wooden steering wheel at the back end of the ship, and held it steady against the peppersalt tides. As he did so, he carefully watched Kashmir, wary for her safety. *Hmmm, we're not out-of-the-woods yet, yes?* Colb thought to himself.

Sure enough, he was right to think so. After only a few moments, the pirates along the merchant ship started yelling. From what they were saying, Colb could tell that they'd realized their own vessel was being stolen. They began loading crossbow bolts and firing them towards the pirate ship.

"Hmmm! Get behind me, yes?" Colb shouted to Kashmir. He pulled out his shield and held it firmly over his face with one hand, while still keeping the steering wheel steady with the other.

He heard a *Yelp!* from Kashmir, followed by a loud *Whoosh!* sound. Within a second, Colb felt pressure across his arm as the elf smacked into his shield. Colb soon realized she was firing another beam of freezing liquid out at the pirates.

Hmmm, this power of hers always propels her backwards, Colb thought to himself. *She must've positioned herself in front of me because she knew I would catch her on my shield, yes?*

Not wanting to betray this trust he'd apparently built up with the elf, Colb widened his stance, balancing himself to take on the force of the elf's power. After about half a minute, she stopped firing, and dropped to the ground.

"Aye, there are elves on our ship!" a pirate shouted.

"Aye, stay away!" another pirate cried out. "You'll all die if you engage an elf! Let them take our ship; there's enough loot downstairs to buy a new one. It's not worth losing more crew!"

Colb looked down at Kashmir. She was curled up on the ground, tiny globs of snow forming around her eyes. "Hmmm, are you crying?" he asked. "Are you hurt?"

Kashmir rolled over, showing him a crossbow bolt that had lodged in her shoulder. It had cut through part of her dress, and pierced her skin – and, of course, had immediately become covered in frost upon touching her.

"Hmmm," Colb worried. "I'm not sure I can touch you to help. Can… can you take it out?"

Kashmir looked at Colb with her snow-covered eyes, then looked sadly at the crossbow bolt in her shoulder. With an uncovered hand, she wrapped her fingers around the tip of it, and tugged. The frigid crossbow bolt broke into shards, which crumbled to the ground. In their place, Kashmir had an open wound, through which a viscous clear liquid started pouring out rapidly.

"Hmmm, is… is that water?" Colb asked.

Kashmir shook her head. "It's blood," she whimpered. "The humans shot me…"

At this point, 27 had made his way back to the steering wheel. "MMmMmmmm, I heard some crossbow firing, but it sounds like they stopped, yes they did?" 27 asked.

"Hmmm, they decided to retreat," Colb replied rapidly. "Do you have water or something, yes? Kashmir is bleeding, I want to clean around her wound, yes?"

27 patted his pockets, then pulled out the *Yiklar Folding Cabin.* "MMmMmmmm, one moment," he replied. The goblin jogged over to a more open part of the deck, pushed the button to unfold his cabin, and when inside. After a moment, he jogged back out, holding a stone cup.

"Water from the kitchen," he said, handing the cup to Colb. The chef goblin accepted the cup, and poured it over Kashmir's wound.

"Hmmm, I think it's good to clean it first, then we'll try to cover it with something, yes?" he said. To his surprise, the water itself covered her wound. As it poured onto her skin, it froze, creating a blanket of ice that stopped her bleeding.

"MMmMmmmm, ice directly on the skin does not seem good," 27 observed.

Kashmir wiped the snow off her eyes, and inspected her arm. She sniffled, then whispered, "…ice is fine on my skin, I mean look at me." She cracked a small smile, touching the ship floor to leave behind a frosty handprint. "It feels better. Thank you."

Colb smiled. *Hmmm, as team medic, I finally feel like I've done something right*, he thought to himself.

Suddenly, a large sail with a skull-and-crossbones design on it unfurled, and caught the wind. Colb held the steering wheel steady as he felt the pirate ship lurch forwards, off to the sea.

"Hurmph, we're on our way," Stibs grumbled, hobbling over to take Colb's place at the steering wheel. "I'm worried those pirates might follow us with their merchant ship, though. They'll probably want their ship back, so we'll just have to sail faster than them."

"Hmmm, there's no need to worry about them," Colb said. "It's still *not always* the right answer to attack people," he continued, looking at Kashmir. "Hmmm, but in this case, Kashmir's attack scared the pirates enough to decide we're not worth fighting, yes? I think I heard their captain shout an order to leave us alone, yes?"

Stibs and 27 looked down at Kashmir, and nodded with approval. "Hurmph, nice going, kid!" Stibs praised.

Kashmir got up from the ground, softly rubbing a hand over her ice bandage as she stood. "Um… thanks," she muttered. The elf then tugged on her dress, inspecting the tear caused by the crossbow bolt.

Hmmm, although I'm thankful for our safety, and angry that the pirates hurt Kashmir, Colb thought to himself, looking back as they sailed away from the hijacked merchant ship, *I'm getting nervous about how violently that interaction went. I fear Kashmir will hurt innocent humans on Jaiphione's Crescent, yes? Not every person deserves to be frozen like that.*

Colb then looked forwards, at the promising seas ahead. *Hmmm, but then again, I'm glad to be going with her. Perhaps I can lead her down the right path when the time comes, yes?* With the wind blowing on his ears, a cool peppersalt smell wafting across the deck, and a fresh new boat to carry the team, Colb started to feel like everything was going to turn out just fine.

Chapter 14

VITRA'S LAB

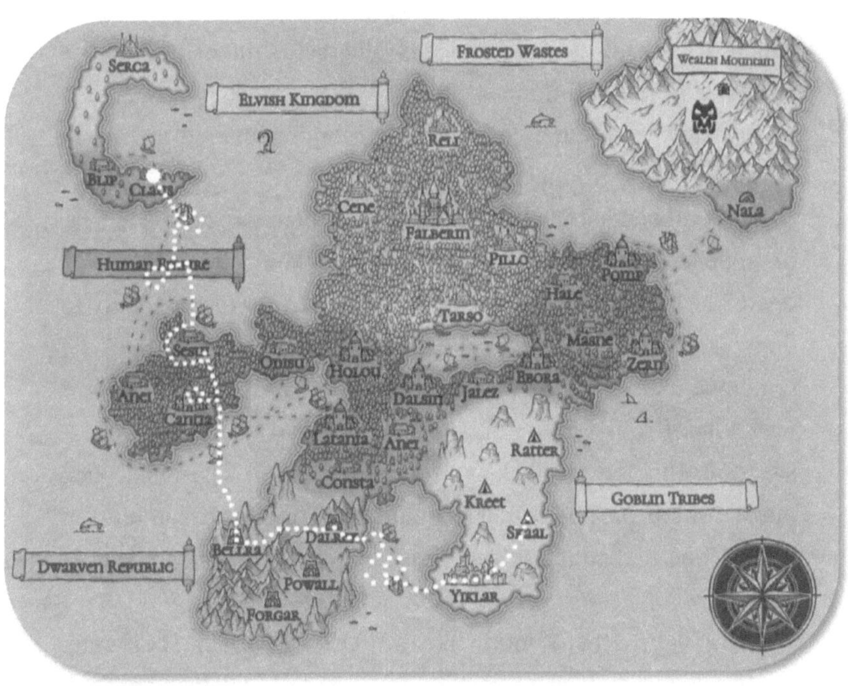

14. VITRA'S LAB

As the crew set sail northwards aboard their new pirate ship, Drek returned from below deck with a small but substantial treasure chest. "Ayerrghegh, aye found some plunder in the captain's quarters," Drek announced in his best attempt at a scratchy pirate voice. The goblin proudly dropped his chest on the ground near the rest of the crew, making a loud *THUMP!* as it hit the wooden deck.

"Rrghegh, and there's no more pirates below deck," Drek added. "The ship is ours, and this plunder is mine! It'll be the perfect start to my fortune as king of Ratter."

"Royalty is a dumb concept…" Kashmir muttered in Elvish. "Being rich doesn't make you a good leader…"

Drek rubbed his hands together with excitement, unable to hear or understand what the elf said. "Rrghegh, time to crack this open," he cheered. The young goblin reached for his belt, only to draw nothing. "…Oh yeah. I left knife in pirate kneecap," he remembered.

Kashmir rolled her eyes, and walked up to the chest. "Here," she said, flicking the lock with her bare finger. The metal lock made a sharp sizzling sound as a thin layer of frost began to form over it. She flicked it a second time, and it shattered as if made of glass.

"Rrghegh… that's more like it," Drek cheered. The young goblin quickly swiped away a few frigid bits of lock that were still in the way, then flipped the chest open.

The moonlight illuminated the contents of the chest like a spotlight to a stage. The crew of five looked with awe at the small fortune before them. Around a thousand goldatinum and iridhodium coins were scattered within the chest, with some reddish-blue rubiamonds and bluish-green sappheralds sprinkled into the pile as well.

"Hmmm, that's a lot of money, yes?" Colb exclaimed.

"AaAaaaaahhhh, that is more than even I currently have, yes it is," 27 noted. "These coins are interesting, too, yes they are. Quite different from the silvopper standard that we've seen elsewhere in the Human Empire."

Colb squinted at the coins in the moonlight. They were similar in shape and size to the basic silvopper coins from Cantia, but had a bearded pirate etched into them instead of that stern-looking Empress Cognemi woman.

"Rrghegh... that's how you know it's criminally-acquired wealth," Drek said with a grin. "You think Ratter goblins keep our currency in carefully portioned nuggets like the other tribes? Sure, sometimes – but we also trade in raw ore, and jewelry, and polished gemstones. A criminal takes whatever they can get their hands on, and doesn't follow the rules. Silvopper must've been too cheap for these guys, so they invented their own, better currency. Rrghegh, these pirates aren't so bad – it's almost a shame we had to fight them off and steal all their stuff. Almost."

Colb winced at the reminder of what this crew had done. *Hmmm, stealing? Fighting? Killing?* he thought. *We're not being a very good influence on Kashmir...*

"MMmMmmmm, now that you mention it, I am not sure how I feel about this stealing of ships and coins," 27 worried.

"Rrghegh... don't worry about it," Drek countered. "I'll keep this treasure, and we'll say Stibs owns this ship since he's captain. Your hands are clean."

"MMmMmmmm... alright," 27 muttered. The noble suddenly let out a little yawn, triggering Kashmir to yawn as well. "It's the middle of the night, yes it is. Let's travel tiny bit further – to get a safe distance from the pirates on the merchant ship, so we'll be long gone if they change their mind about leaving us alone – then drop anchor and go back to sleeping?"

Everyone agreed, exhausted from the midnight scuffle. The team sailed north for about an hour, then dropped anchor and turned in for the night. While the four goblins got comfortable in the *Yiklar Folding Cabin*, Kashmir elected to sleep out on the deck, underneath the stars.

The next morning, as the sun peeked over the horizon, the party of five divided into three groups. Kashmir sat on the main deck with Drek, watching him count the plunder in his treasure chest. 27 and Stibs sat at the ship's helm, plotting their course to a human town on Jaiphione's Crescent called Claus, and preparing the ship to set sail. Colb went off on his own, exploring the pirate's quarters below deck.

The base of the ship was split up into a series of rooms. Most were bedrooms, containing nothing more than useless human clothes and cushioned beds. The finest of the bedchambers, which must have been the captain's quarters, had been ransacked by Drek the previous night. Colb looked around briefly, then left, assuming Drek had already found anything of value.

Eventually, Colb came across a room with no beds, instead containing a full dining set. He climbed onto a tall wooden chair, then peeked his head over to see what he could find on the table. He discovered it to be covered in plastic chips, along with a set of dice carved out of bone. A couple of goldatinum coins were scattered amongst the chips, which Colb took and pocketed for later.

In another room, he found barrels and barrels of dried meat and stale daisywheat bread. He picked through them, eventually pulling out five strips of preserved salmonsnake meat and bringing them up to the main deck.

"Whadja find?" Kashmir called out to him as he climbed out of the lower deck. Colb held up the long bodies of meat he'd found. "Interesting," she called back.

Colb sauntered back into the cabin, then prepared a meal in the kitchen. He stuffed some leftover bugs into the long salmonsnake bodies, then boiled them as if preparing his famous stuffed chickengoose neck recipe – making sure to leave one salmonsnake bug-free for the picky elf. When he was done, he patrolled around the boat, giving a stuffed salmonsnake to each member of the party.

27 was the most delighted to receive one, slurping it up in a swift motion and smacking his lips with joy. Stibs and Drek accepted the meals as well, but chewed them slowly while focused on their tasks at hand. Kashmir took hers with a mitten-covered hand, biting off pieces and crunching on them as she watched Drek organize his various precious gems. Colb sat on the ground next to her, silently chewing his meal as he, too, observed the young goblin.

A few minutes later, 27 regrouped with the others. "AaAaaaaahhhh, sailors! Are we ready to leave?" the noble asked. Everyone nodded, which made 27 start dancing with joy. "AaAaaaaahhhh, wonderful!" he exclaimed. "Once you've finished your meals, meet with Stibs at the steering wheel, and we'll get this ship on the move!" The goblin clapped his hands with delight, then shimmied away.

Once they finished eating, everyone regrouped around Stibs. The old goblin divvied out some jobs, from pulling up the anchor to tying ropes and hoisting sails. Working together to complete these tasks, the crew found themselves on the move in no time. With the *Yiklar Map of Finding Location* as his guide, Stibs steered the ship in the direction of Claus: a human town at the nearest shore of Jaiphione's Crescent.

As they got close to the port, their foreboding, blacked-painted pirate ship seemed to alarm nearby human sailors. Seagullfishermen and other trading ships parted frantically to make way for the dangerous-looking vessel. At one point, Colb heard a Hewmish voice shout, "Flee for your lives! It's the Quartzelian Pirates!"

"MMmMmmmm, I think the skull and crossbones painted over our sails gives a bad first impression, yes it does," 27 observed.

"They'd better run," Kashmir mumbled, rubbing her palms together. "They don't belong on this island."

"Hmmm, now hold on there, yes?" Colb said, rushing to the elf's side. "We should *never* attack someone, unless our lives are in danger and we have no other choice, yes? Remember the plan: let's try *talking* to the humans. Help them understand why this island is so important to you, yes?"

Kashmir rolled her eyes. "Fine… but make sure your shield's ready to catch me if there's no better way to make them go away for good…"

With a soft *THUMP!* the pirate ship bumped into the human-made port. Drek lowered the ship's anchor, which almost immediately hit the ground upon splashing into the shallow waters. Stibs pushed an old wooden ramp over the edge of the ship, connecting it to the dock. Using the ramp, the team of five disembarked.

"AaAaaaaahhhh, another small human village!" 27 cheered, looking around at the bismuthslate brick and birchpine wood buildings. "I don't see any guards, or scary pirates, no I do not. This seems like most nice place to make quick pit stop before we sail off to Wealth Mountain, yes it does."

The group sauntered through the deserted port, taking in their surroundings. It seemed like a dulled down version of Sesui, with a population smaller than any human town they'd seen so far.

As the crew took a few steps into the village of Claus, Kashmir's pointed ears suddenly perked up. "I see a human!" she exclaimed, lifting her hands.

"Hmmm! No no no," Colb cried out, jumping in front of Kashmir and holding his shield as high as he could to block the tall elf. "These humans are just living their lives, yes? We don't know if they're a danger to us, yes? Some humans can be nice, and might stop hurting animals if you just explain your feelings to them, yes?"

"AaAaaaaahhhh, humans can be most excellent customers, too!" 27 added.

"Some *humans* scammed you with a pile of worthless rocks, and fired a crossbow bolt into my shoulder," Kashmir grumbled. The elf narrowed her eyes at Colb, but lowered her palms in obedience with his plea.

Colb stole a glance backwards, to see what Kashmir had noticed in the first place. What he saw was a human woman staring back at him. She looked intrigued by Kashmir and the goblins. Colb looked back at Kashmir, then lowered his shield. "Hmmm, she doesn't look dangerous, yes? Let's try talking to her, yes? 27 can speak Hewmish."

Colb stepped back in line with the rest of his crew, and 27 took a step forwards. The five travelers cautiously looked over the human before them.

Standing about half a foot taller than Kashmir, the woman towered over the goblin crew. She sported puffy green hair and wore a pair of matching green spectacles over her light face. From her chest downwards, she was covered in white-painted plate armor with a shimmering, purple hue. A small winter foxferret stood on her shoulders, wrapping its long, fluffy white body around the human's neck like a scarf. She held a small yellow duffle bag in her hands, and looked completely fascinated by Kashmir.

"Well don't let him stop you," she said in fluent Elvish. "What were you going to do with your hands just then?"

"MMmMmmmm, do… do you speak Hewmish?" 27 asked.

"Of course, I do," the woman replied, switching to the language of humans. "I was just speaking in Elvish, because I was addressing the elf."

"Hmmm, can you speak Goblish?" Colb asked. He looked at the *Yiklar Amulet of Open Ears* around Kashmir's neck. "All five of us will understand you if you speak in Goblish, yes?"

"Ah, then Goblish I will speak, yes I will!" the woman cheered, switching to the language of goblins.

"Stop showing off and tell us who you are," Kashmir spat.

"Hm, it's an exchange of information that you want?" the human muttered. "Well, show me what your powers are, and I'll tell you who I am."

"Why?" Kashmir asked.

"Humf, because I've never seen a purple elf before!" the spectacled woman exclaimed. "Most of your people don't come around Claus often, but your innate magic is most fascinating to me, yes it is."

Kashmir huffed at the human. "You want to see what I can do, huh?"

"Hmmm, Kashmir, don't hurt her, yes?" Colb warned.

Ignoring Colb, Kashmir opened her palms and pointed them at the human. The elf took a quick breath, then rapidly closed her eyes, looked away, snapped her head back towards the woman, and opened her eyes again.

This quick succession of movement activated her power for only a brief moment: allowing Kashmir to hold her ground without Colb's assistance, while sucking some air into her palms and launching a pebble of clear liquid at the human. The projectile harmlessly splashed against the woman's armor, then dissolved into mist.

"Ah, wow!" the green-haired lady cheered. She pulled out a notepad, flipped to a fresh page, and began jotting some thoughts down. "Hm, now *that* was cool, if you'll pardon the pun. So cool! You can make liquid nitrogen, yea?" she exclaimed.

The crew of five looked at her, a little confused by the human's excitability. "Argh, wait. It was a bit too opaque to be just nitrogen," the woman continued. "Hm, I noticed some white specks in it. That could've been dry ice, considering it burst into mist at the end. The bluish tint might've been oxygen..." She snapped her fingers. "Ah, I suppose you just froze the air, didn't you? You made a little ball of frozen air, and threw it at me! Excellent," she cheered, jotting down some more notes.

"Hmmm, are... are you hurt?" Colb asked.

"Me? I'm fine. Lucky me, my armor's impervious to things like that," the woman replied. "Hm, although in this particular case, the contact was so brief and my body temperature is so much higher than the boiling point of liquid air, that an insulating vapor layer would've kept me safe either way." Colb furrowed his brow, confused by the woman's scientific words.

As the green-haired human kept scribbling down some Hewmish symbols, the winter foxferret on her shoulder let out a soft sneeze, firing some snow out of its nose and onto Kashmir's dress.

After a moment, the odd lady suddenly flipped her notepad

shut, and looked over the goblins. Then, making eye contact with Kashmir, she finally introduced herself. "My name is Rachel Miranda Vitra. Hm, but most people just call me Vitra, yes they do. I'm an alchemist, working on some restorative projects here in Claus with my associate, Borin Aluvin Swornhammer."

Kashmir gave the woman an inquisitive look. She reached out her hand, and quickly poked the human's armor with a bare finger. In response, Vitra's chestplate lit up for a moment, creating a protective purple field around her entire body. The winter foxferret on her shoulder yipped in friendly retaliation.

"Ah, your cold powers won't hurt me with this armor on, no they will not," the woman repeated. She pulled a small vial of water out from her duffle bag, then tapped it against her chestplate. The water within the vial immediately froze solid.

"My armor's enchanted to freeze anything it touches, yes it is, as well as to protect me from anything dangerously cold," Vitra explained. "It's a very useful tool for potion-making."

Kashmir frowned at the human. "Where'd you get that armor? Did a goblin sell it to you?" The elf glared at 27, who gave her a baffled look in return.

"Wha-Why are you mad at me? She may speak Goblish, but you're still speaking Elvish. I-I don't know what you just said, no I do not," 27 cried defensively.

"Ah, she asked if a goblin sold me this armor, yes she did," Vitra translated. "Humf, and the answer is no. We made this armor ourselves," the woman explained. "Borin's a blacksmith. He crafted the armor, and then I enchanted it with a potion made from some of Bitty's fur sheddings." She pat the winter foxferret on her shoulder, who sneezed out some more snow in response to the attention.

"Now that you mention it, word travels pretty fast in the

Human Empire, and I did hear some goblin was selling magic items to nobles in Cantia, yes I did!" Vitra exclaimed. "Quite an unusual story. I heard it happened just the other day. Was that one of you guys?"

27 nodded, reaching for his red *Yiklar Bag of Traveling Inventory*. Kashmir put an arm out, gesturing for him to stop. "Why are you here?" the elf muttered, narrowing her eyes. "You really think I'd believe a human understands magic well enough to enchant armor like that? And what kind of experiment are you doing? Are you hurting the endangered creatures on this island?"

"Oh no, I'm helping them, yes I am!" Vitra replied.

"Maybe you think you are, but humans need to get off this island," Kashmir grumbled.

"Hmmm, let's hear her out, yes?" Colb pitched. "Vitra has done nothing to harm us, and her armor seemed to surprise you, yes? Maybe she can surprise you again?"

Colb felt a warm, hopeful feeling in his gut. *Hmmm, this human seems a bit strange, but friendly,* he thought to himself. *She seems to like elves – a rare trait for humans, from what I've seen so far – and she claims to be helping the animals that Kashmir cares about. Maybe Vitra is the key to teaching Kashmir a little empathy for her enemies, yes?*

"Hmmm, could you show us how you're *helping* the endangered creatures of this island?" Colb asked.

"Hm, I suppose I can!" the woman cheered. "What scientist doesn't love talking about their work? Follow me." The woman turned, gesturing for the crew to trail her through a nearby patch of clovergrass. 27, Drek, and Stibs all shrugged and went along with it. Kashmir gave Colb a dirty look, but he replied with an encouraging smile. Kashmir sighed, rolled her eyes, and followed the others. She kept her palms close to her chest as she walked, as if ready to attack with her air-freezing power at a moment's notice.

"We're actually fairly close to my lab, yes we are," Vitra announced as they followed behind her. Bitty, the small winter foxferret on her neck, audibly purred when she said the word 'lab.'

The group eventually came upon a circular building made entirely out of silvopper – quite unlike the other buildings of Claus, which were made of black bismuthslate bricks and light birchpine wood. "Hm! Don't touch the walls once you're inside, yea?" Vitra warned as the group approached the odd building's entrance. "They've been enchanted just like the outside of my armor… so, they'll give you frostbite if you touch them, yea? Bitty and the purple elf can do whatever, though."

The green-haired woman walked up to a vault-like door, which was attached to some sort of complex locking mechanism. Vita flipped a handle down and to the right in an awkward L motion, twisted a couple cogs around, then pushed a button. She tugged on the door, which let out a soft *click!* before creaking open.

This revealed a wide room full of a thin, transparent mist. Clouds of this fog poured out of the lab as the group stepped into the building. The winter foxferret on Vitra's shoulder squealed with joy, jumping down and rubbing its body against the interior walls of the room. A *clank! clank!* sound came from the back of the laboratory, as if someone were banging two pieces of metal together.

Colb shivered at the sudden change of temperature upon walking into the building. The walls of the room, which Bitty was furiously rubbing her body against, had the same purple hue and white-painted pattern as this human's peculiar plate armor.

"Ah, welcome to Vitra's Lab!" Vitra announced to her guests. "The 'Vitra' part refers to me, yes it does," she added fondly. The four goblins visibly shivered again, and Kashmir stood normally as if nothing were different between this room and outside.

As he rubbed his arms to keep them warm, Colb took in his surroundings. Vitra's Lab was split into two halves. The closer half, which contained the lab's entryway, was filled with disorganized, human-height desks covered in books, papers, and bubbling vials of liquid.

Colb stood on his tip-toes to look at the contents of a nearby table. It was covered in mangonuts, many of which had been half-hazardly chopped and crushed. Under the table, a short cauldron sat filled to the brim with some swirling purple liquid.

The other half of the lab, at the opposite side from the entryway, appeared to be a blacksmithing studio. That dimly lit section of the laboratory sported a tough furnace, a variety of different anvils – some of which were covered with hammers – and a large pile of loose scrap metal shoved into the corner.

"Colb," Kashmir suddenly murmured under-her-breath. "Could you ask the short one if he thinks his iridhodium arrow might pierce the human's armor? Or, if he's a good enough shot to hit her in the head?"

Colb sighed. *Change takes time*, he thought. *Just like good team takes time, yes? I should try pushing her in the right direction.*

"Hmmm, let's hear about the human's restorative experiment first, yes? She might be doing good thing for the endangered animals of this island, yes?" Colb whispered back. Kashmir gave him an annoyed look in response.

Clank! clank! sounds continued to fill the room. "Oy, Borin!" the woman shouted in Dwarvish. "We've got visitors!" The clanking stopped, and a muscular dwarf stepped into view. He stood at just over 4 feet in height: shorter than Kashmir, but taller than all four goblins. He had dark skin, but not much of it could be seen under his mounds and mounds of well-combed hair. Indeed, only his spherical nose popped out from the mop of brown hair covering his ears, eyes, mouth, and everything else on his head. As if that weren't enough, he also sported a wide, brown beard that went down to his stomach.

Below the beard, he wore a dwarf-fitted, half plate version of the same magic armor as Vitra. He carried a blacksmithing hammer in one hand, and held a clamp with a red-hot metal tube of some sort in the other. He hiccuped, then touched the red-hot tube to his chestplate. With a sizzle and a pop, it cooled to a metallic gray almost instantly upon touching his armor.

"They prefer you speak Goblish, yes they do," Vitra added, switching back to the Goblish language.

"Uh… hello," he burped. His voice was much rougher than Vitra's, and his Goblish pronunciation sounded a bit off. "I make things," he stated matter-of-factly. "Then, Vitra does the magic. To the things that I make, that is."

"Here," he burped, holding the clamp out to Vitra. She opened her hands, to which he opened the clamp, dropping the metal tube between her palms. "That's a thing I made," he explained. "I made it at Vitra's... um… return," he said.

"Mm, at my *request*," Vitra corrected.

"Ah... yes," Borin burped. He awkwardly scratched the back of his hairy head, looking a little uncomfortable. "My… Goblish isn't very good," he repeated. "What brings you here?"

"Hmmm, Vitra says that her work is assisting the animals of this island, yes?" Colb said. "We were hoping to see an example of that."

"Ah… well, that tube's perfect for that," Borin replied. "Assuming Vitra finished the… the… um… what's the Goblish word for… uh… the pedal-plant?"

"The flower," Vitra finished. "Ah, I did finish the flower, yes I did!" she cheered. Vitra inspected the metal tube Borin had given her. "That's a good idea, Borin!"

Vitra smiled at the five travelers. "Hm, you guys want to see a live experiment, yea?"

Colb nodded. "Hmmm, that sounds great!" he encouraged.

"I'll… um… leave you all to that," Borin muttered. With a couple of stomps, he turned around, then retreated back to his anvil on the other side of the room.

"Mm, he's not much for words, no he isn't," Vitra confessed as she toyed with the metal tube Borin had given her. "But he makes up for it in spirit, yes he does!"

A loud sizzling sound filled the lab as Borin poured a couple red-hot potions together at his workstation on the other side of the laboratory. "And by that, I mean he makes good stuff! Let me show you what the two of us have been working on, yea? We need to step outside for this particular experiment, though, so out you go."

Vitra shooed the group back out the lab's entrance. The four goblins jumped out immediately, happy to get beneath the warmth of sunlight. Kashmir rolled her eyes aggressively, clearly showing the human that she didn't like being pushed around.

"Hmmm, come on outside Kashmir, yes?" Colb called out. "Give the experiment a chance, yes?" Kashmir reluctantly followed Colb outside.

Hmmm, I've definitely built up some rapport with Kashmir, yes? Colb thought to himself, proud of the accomplishment. *She stepped outside, even though she's clearly anxious about Vitra. I hope whatever this experiment is can calm her worries.*

As the group of six stepped out of the lab, the winter foxferret launched itself onto Vitra's leg, then climbed up her armor and back onto her shoulders. "Hm, you're a cute little girl, Bitty," Vitra cheered. "Fun fact about winter foxferrets: they're native to the Frosted Wastes," Vitra announced.

Bitty sneezed, sprinkling some snow in front of the woman. "Here's another fun fact for you," she continued as she shut the complicated laboratory door behind her. "Winter foxferrets shrink when they're relaxed, and grow when they feel stressed, yes they do. My research suggests this is the smallest they can be, and that means I'm taking good care of her!"

Vitra lightly patted the small creature's head with two fingers. As she did this, her armor brightened, placing a protective field around the alchemist's hand. "They're a little too cold to pet normally, yes they are, but I can touch her no problem if I keep this armor on!"

Kashmir looked down at her purple, ice-cold hands, then at the four goblins. Colb caught eye contact with her, and gave a comforting smile. *Hmmm, I suppose she can relate to that little creature,* he thought.

"Hm, let's get to the experiment, then, yea?" Vitra continued, pulling a potion out from her duffle bag. She held it up for the others to see. It was a glass bottle containing a frothy pink liquid. "You," she continued, pointing at Stibs. "Who are you? You look strong, yes you do. Do you smith?"

"Hurmph, only if you count woodworking," Stibs replied. "The name's Stibs."

"I do count that, Stibs!" the green-haired woman cheered. "Might you have a hammer available?"

Stibs nodded. He slowly took off his backpack, with Drek helping to stabilize him as he did so. Stibs then pulled out a stone hammer with a wooden hilt. Leaning on his crutch, he hobbled over to the woman, offering it to her.

Rather than accepting the hammer, Vitra frowned at the old goblin. "Mm, is something wrong with your leg?" she asked.

"Hurmph, it's broken," Stibs grumbled, still holding out the hammer.

"Ah, want me to fix it?" Vitra replied.

Stibs stepped back slightly in surprise, then looked at Colb for a medic's approval. Colb shrugged. "Hurmph, I guess you can try if you want," he mumbled.

She placed her vial of frothy pink potion down on the clovergrass, then rummaged through her bag some more. After a moment, she pulled out a luminescent yellow potion with bits of ladybugmoth wings floating on the surface. Kashmir's eyes turned furious upon seeing the concoction.

"Here," Vitra continued, pouring some potion into a syringe. "It's a healing potion of my own design." Without giving Stibs a moment to react, she stabbed the syringe needle into his kneecap, injected the potion in, and pulled it out.

"Hurmph! Ouch!" Stibs yelped, pulling his leg away. He whipped his wooden crutch at her in retaliation. It shattered like glass upon slapping her armor.

"Ow!" she said, stepping back reactively. Bitty sneezed some snow at the old goblin in retaliation.

"Why... wait. Hurmph!" Stibs spoke softly as he realized he was standing fine on his own. The four goblins all looked down at his leg. Where it had been swollen and deformed just moments before, it now looked just like his healthy leg. "Hurmph! I... I think I can walk again!" Stibs continued. He stomped around, then jumped up and down a few times.

"Hmmm! That's great," Colb said. "Hmmm, but are you okay?" he continued, looking at the woman.

"Ah, yea I am. I just said 'ow' from surprise... my armor

totally froze and destroyed your stick, so I didn't actually feel anything," Vitra cheered.

Meanwhile, Kashmir had quietly walked around and behind Vitra. She picked up a frozen shard of the now-shattered crutch, and held it towards the back of Vitra's head. "Get out of the way," she shouted at the winter foxferret covering the woman's neck. Bitty turned, sneezed some snow at the elf, then let out a wide yawn.

"Hm?" Vitra murmured, turning around. Before she knew it, she was looking down the center of a cold wooden shard. "Woa! Why is this happening?" she questioned.

"Stop pretending to be good," Kashmir sneered. "I saw what's in that potion. You killed a ladybugmoth to make that! Those things are endangered!"

Vitra slowly put her syringe down, and retrieved a bubbling, orange-colored potion from her duffle bag in its place. "No…" she replied, switching from Goblish to Elvish, and taking a step back. "They are not endangered, and I did not 'kill' one to make my healing elixir."

"I could see its wings floating in your syringe!" Kashmir cried out, taking a swing at the woman.

Vitra quickly uncapped her orange potion, and splashed it on Kashmir. It sizzled, then popped as it hit the elf's dress – making a small, fiery explosion that knocked both Kashmir and Vitra off their feet.

"Hmmm! Don't fight," Colb cried out, jumping between them. He held his shield towards Vitra, keeping Kashmir safe behind him.

"She tried to cut me with a sharp piece of stick – what was that about?!" Vitra countered, switching back to Goblish. The woman gave the other three goblins a look of befuddlement, as if checking to see which side they would take. "I appreciate your interest in my work, but I can't do anything if you're going to attack me?!"

The door of the laboratory creaked open, and Borin stepped out. "I hate this door," he mumbled, fumbling to shut it with the complicated locking mechanism. "Oy, who set off an explosion, huh?" he bellowed in Dwarvish.

"I was just starting to show them the experiment, and the elf swung at me!" Vitra exclaimed.

"Of course she did," Borin said, walking over to stand next to Colb. "She's an elf; I was surprised to see her visiting our lab in the first place. Elves don't *like* us, remember? And for good reason."

"Oh…" Vitra mumbled, standing back up. "I forgot about all the tension that brought us here in the first place."

Vitra adjusted her spectacles, cleared her throat, and started speaking in Goblish so everyone could understand her. "Hm, I've heard you elves care a lot about the creatures on this island, yea?" Vitra said, looking at Kashmir.

Kashmir stood up, patting off her burnt dress. "You hurt me!" she shouted. Colb looked back at Kashmir, unsure if he should continue standing in-between her and Vitra.

"I'm sorry," Vitra said. "I was so excited to learn about your powers, and your apparent interest in my work… I forgot about all the politics of this area, so I wasn't ready when you attacked me. I reacted offensively, and that was wrong."

"Hmmm, she didn't want to hurt you," Colb observed, looking at Kashmir. "She's apologizing, yes? It looks like she wants to talk, instead of fighting more, yes?" Kashmir narrowed her eyes.

"Around 30 years ago, a group of sailors discovered this island," Vitra explained. They quickly informed the empress, who sent some scientists to map it out. Those scientists discovered this to be a sanctuary of rare, never-before-seen creatures… a carefully balanced, and extremely delicate ecosystem."

"My father says that you humans *ruined* that ecosystem," Kashmir spat. "I heard your people killed off some of these rare species, and you won't leave the island even though you've done irreparable harm!"

"We didn't kill off anything on purpose," Vitra countered. "It was the spiderbats." Drek licked his lips at the sound of that creature.

"When the first humans discovered this island," Vitra continued, "some spiderbats had stowed away on their ship, and thus came along with them. Those spiderbats made a home here, safe from their normal predators of the mainland. Unchecked, their population grew and grew. They hunted and eventually wiped out some endangered insect species native to this island… which was bad for those insects, but also meant less food for other animals, such as the owlvulture. This is a slippery slope, especially when every creature in this fragile ecosystem is already on the verge of extinction."

"This is all still the fault of humans," Kashmir pushed.

"Yes," Vitra replied, "which is why the towns of Claus and Blip were built: to redeem our mistake, and study this beautiful place. Almost everyone living in these two towns is a scientist – just like me and Borin. We're all doing our part to help bring balance back to the ecosystem, and to protect all the rare creatures still here from extinction."

"How can you say that when your potions contain dead ladybugmoths?" Kashmir cried. Snow started to form around the corners of her eyes as she spoke. "I loved those creatures as a kid! How could you slaughter them, especially when they're endangered?!"

"Sally Drewdyle's been breeding them like crazy over at the ladybugmoth sanctuary on the other side of town," Vitra countered. "The ladybugmoth is only considered threatened now… it's no longer endangered!"

Kashmir tilted her head. *Hmmm… Kashmir is listening!* Colb thought to himself. *She's talking with the human! This is good, yes? I'm proud of her.*

"Also, the ladybugmoth in that potion was already dead when I received it," Vitra continued. "I only recycle animals which have passed from natural causes. There's no reason to kill them for my research."

"So… I'd like to offer you this," Vitra said. She pulled out another ladybugmoth potion, and held it out. Borin stepped out of the way, and Colb mirrored him: opening the space between Kashmir and Vitra. "I'm sorry for tossing some explosive liquid on you… if you're hurt, can I heal you?"

"Um… I'm okay," Kashmir said. She seemed unharmed by the small explosion – her dress had some soot on it but hadn't ripped. Colb did notice the elf occasionally rubbing the ice-bandage over her crossbolt wound, but it would probably heal on its own over time.

"Rrghegh… I'll take some healing," Drek added, showing his neck to Vitra. It contained a half-healed frost blister from his first encounter with Kashmir. Vitra sucked up some of her potion with a small syringe, and applied it to Drek's wound – healing it instantly.

"Would you still like to see my experiment?" Vitra asked, picking up her vial of frothy pink potion and looking at Kashmir. "I think you might like it."

Kashmir looked at Colb, who nodded encouragingly. "Um… okay," she said, sounding calmer. She rubbed her eyes, wiping away the snow-tears that had accumulated during the emotion-filled conversation.

"Alright. What happened to that hammer?" Vitra asked.

Stibs walked up to her – happily skipping a little bit, with his freshly healed leg – and presented his woodworking hammer. Vitra accepted it, then kneeled to the ground. She placed Borin's metal tube into the clovergrass, then hammered it in place with the old goblin's small tool. "Thanks," she said, handing Stibs his hammer.

"Alright… now watch this," Vitra announced. The human poured her potion down the center of the metal cylinder. The pink froth cascaded along the interior of the tube, eventually soaking into the dirt beneath. After a few moments, a bright flower magically sprouted, poking out from the tube's opening. Mixed between its pedals, a lob of green plant matter formed into the shape of a toadroach.

"Instant flower!" Vitra announced.

"Nice," Borin grunted.

"Hmmm, where did that toadroach come from, yes?" Colb asked, pointing out the plant matter on the tip of the flower.

"It's not a real toadroach, no it is not," Vitra explained. "Rather, it's plant matter that *looks* like a toadroach, yes it is – and if I did my math correctly, it should be full of a concoction called garvine." Vitra looked up at Kashmir, who met her eyes with a cautious glance. "Now, garvine is an interesting solution I've come up with," Vitra continued. "After extensive testing, it has proven to be harmless to all known animals… *except for spiderbats.*"

Vitra pointed up into the sky, where a spiderbat had begun circling overhead. The human then took a step away from the flower, and urged the others to do the same. "As I explained before, spiderbats are an invasive species on this island, yes they are," Vita continued. "With no predators here, and only prey, the spiderbat population is going to keep growing until they wipe out a vast number of the endangered creatures on this island. How can we solve that? By engineering a predator to balance their population."

As the human, elf, and four goblins stepped away from the flower, the spiderbat took the opportunity to dive down, snatching the fake toadroach off the plant. As it flew away, it began convulsing midair, eventually losing flight and dropping to the ground. A new fake toadroach magically grew on the tip of the flower, replacing the lost one.

"Mm, it's a bit grim, yes it is, but this garvine flower is my and Borin's latest contribution to the research," Vitra explained. "While others are breeding endangered animals and improving their habitats, I'm tackling the source of our initial mistake: getting these invasive spiderbats to stop living unchecked on this island."

"So... you came here to help the endangered creatures of Jaiphione's Crescent?" Kashmir asked.

"That's right!" Vitra replied with a nod. Kashmir looked down at the garvine flower. She then looked over at Stibs and Drek, who had been freshly healed. Finally, she turned back to Vitra, whose armor shined with magic, and whom a magical winter foxferret seemed to love and trust.

"Hmmm, perhaps there are some good humans, yes?" Colb prodded, trying to put words to the thoughts he imagined Kashmir was thinking.

"...Alright," the elf conceded. "I'll admit we found *one* human that isn't terrible." Her shoulders, which had been tense since the moment she set foot on this island, lowered a little.

Kashmir adjusted her hair to cover her face, preventing anyone from making direct eye contact with her. "Um… I guess I apologize for attacking you, human," she continued, staring at the ground. "Um, Vitra, that is. You have a name. And… to both of you… Vitra and Borin… th-thank you for the work you're doing here. Like any elf, I care for Jaiphione's creatures. Anyone who cares for them as well is good as an ally in my book."

Hmmm! This makes me proud! Colb thought to himself. The chef goblin smiled, feeling warm inside as Kashmir apologized and thanked the scientists. *Hmmm! It looks like I finally got through to her!*

Chapter 15

LADLE TAVERN

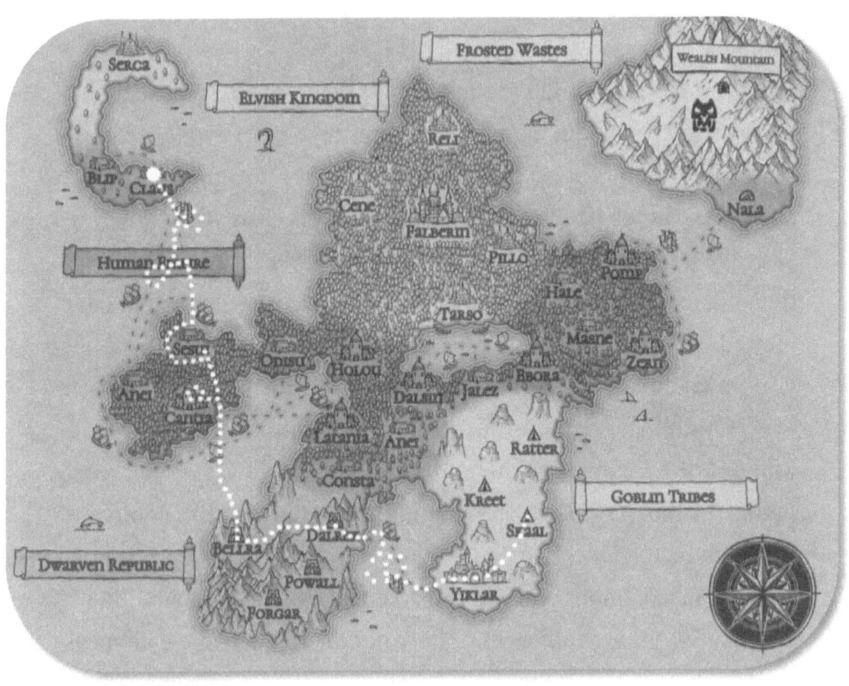

15. LADLE TAVERN

"Hurmph, while we're saying thanks, I'd like to say I appreciate my healed leg!" Stibs cheered.

"Rrghegh… I appreciate the healing too," Drek agreed, poking at his green neck.

"Hmmm," Colb mumbled. *This woman could teach me something, yes?* he thought to himself.

"27," Colb whispered, turning to his friend. "Could this pit stop turn into a day-long trip? I'd like to learn how to heal like Vitra can, yes?"

27 nodded, scanning the town with his eyes. "AaAaaaaahhhh, I'd like to try making some sales here, too, yes I would. A day-long stop sounds most reasonable; I'd love to approach some customers here, like I did in Cantia. If this is really a town of scientists, I'll bet they'd be interested in some of my wares." He then glanced at Kashmir, whose frosty composure seemed to have melted slightly after Vitra explained herself. "Also, I notice you've taken a liking to that elf," he continued.

"Hmmm, she reminds me of the children in Skaal, yes?" Colb replied. "She came here to drive the humans away… to freeze them, if necessary. I've been hoping to teach her a little empathy for them instead, yes?"

"AaAaaaaahhhh, you are just like Orta said, you know that?" 27 cheered with a smile. "So, how about this: since I can speak Hewmish, why don't I take Kashmir with me? I won't know what she's saying, but with her amulet, she'll at least know what *I'm* saying. We could tour the town together, and I could introduce her to all the different scientists while I'm meeting them myself. Perhaps that would enlighten her to the many different projects Vitra claims are helping the animals around here, yes it would? It might make her more comfortable with humanity, one person at a time, yes it might?"

Colb grinned. "Hmmm! That sounds great!" he rejoiced.

"AaAaaaaahhhh, most excellent!" 27 cheered back. The noble goblin clapped his hands together, and announced the plan to the team. Meanwhile, Colb went up to Kashmir, and explained why she should follow 27.

"Hmmm, I'm going to stay here for today, and try to convince Vitra to teach me to make medicine, yes?" Colb said. "Hmmm, but you should follow 27 around town, yes? He's going to seek out some of the human scientists, and introduce you – if you *listen* carefully, perhaps they'll show you how they're helping Jaiphione's Crescent, just like Vitra did? Hmmm! The humans messed up when they first arrived here, but it sounds like they're all working really hard to fix their mistake, yes? Perhaps someday, the crescent will be even *better off* than it was before they arrived, thanks to their experiments, yes? Isn't that nice?"

Kashmir put a bit of hair in her mouth, and chewed it. It flowed along her teeth like regular hair – Colb heard no crunching ice sound like he did when the elf ate food. "Um… I guess I'd be interested to see what else is happening here," she said. "So… okay."

With that, 27 and Kashmir broke off from the group, and head out to explore Claus. Stibs followed them, looking excited to test out his new leg on the town.

This left Colb and Drek behind at the laboratory. "Hmmm," Colb said, looking up at Vitra. "I'm sure you're quite busy… but I'm meant to be the medic for my group. As you can see, many of them came here wounded, because I had no idea how to help them. Could you teach me to make medicine?"

"Ehhhhhhhh," Vitra replied, tilting her head. "That's kind of a big commitment for the day. I just wanted to see what that elf was all about, and show you guys an experiment since you seemed interested. I've already down both those things, so I figure I'll get on with my day. It was nice meeting you, though!"

Colb frowned. "Hmmm… alright," he conceded.

"Rrghegh… wait," Drek said. "What if we paid you? Gave you some rare metal for your research?"

The mop of hair on Borin's head rose slightly with intrigue. He coughed, then replied in ratty Goblish. "What kind of rare metal?"

"Rrghegh… not this specifically, but how about a couple coins made of the same stuff?" Drek replied. He presented his shiny arrow, from his *Yiklar Bow of Returning Arrow* kit. "Rrghegh… but only if you teach my friend what he wants to know."

"Iridhodium…" Borin muttered. He leaned close to the arrow, as if to get a better look – although his eyes appeared to be blocked by hair as far as Colb could tell. "How many coins?"

"Two," Drek said.

"Six?" Borin countered.

"Three," Drek conceded.

"Five?" Borin replied.

Drek thought for a moment. "Rrghegh… I'll give you five coins, but you also must smith something for *me* today."

"Like what?" Borin asked.

Drek's teeth formed into a wicked smile as he reached into his cloak. He soon revealed some goldatinum coins he'd taken from the pirate ship. "I have chest full of goldatinum coins and precious gems," he explained. "I want you to turn some of the treasure into an object that will signify my might. Something to strike fear into enemy hearts when I become king of Ratter tribe. Rrghegh, maybe goldatinum dagger or something. I'm not sure, but if you can make something good for me – and if Vitra helps my friend with his thing – then, I'll give you five coins of the rare metal."

The dwarf stepped back in line with Vitra, and nudged her in the arm. Their armors reacted, setting off a quick spark. This startled the winter foxferret on the woman's shoulder, making it grow an inch larger and wider.

"Can you clear your schedule for today?" he asked.

"Aw, look what you did to Bitty!" the woman complained, picking up the winter foxferret from her shoulder. Her armor glowed to protect her hands as she pet the beast in a calming manner.

"Iridhodium's *really* rare," Borin burped, switching to Dwarvish so Drek couldn't understand him. "I could melt five coins down to make some very precise little tools. Please do this for me."

Bitty purred as the human stroked her hair, and shrunk back down to her original size. "Fine," Vitra said, placing the calmed winter foxferret back on her shoulders.

"It's a deal," Borin burped, switching back to Goblish. "Vitra will help your friend, and I'll make you something good."

Colb smiled at Drek, surprised and pleased that the friend had given up some treasure to help him. "Rrghegh… just give us a minute to grab the goods. We'll meet you back here," Drek announced. He pat Colb on the back, and head towards Claus port. Colb followed, then helped his companion carry the small-but-heavy treasure chest off the pirate ship and over to Vitra's Lab.

Colb spent the remainder of the day learning basic alchemy from Vitra, hoping to become proficient in some type of health potion before the group moved on to the Frosted Wastes. Drek spent his time silently watching Borin in the back of the lab, eagerly inspecting the dwarf's progress at every step.

At the end of the day, as Colb finished brewing his first simple health potion, the rest of his team knocked on the door of the lab. Vitra let them inside, and Bitty yipped at the three visitors.

"Hmmm, look at what I've made, yes?" Colb announced to the group as they entered the cold building. He held up a bubbling, clear potion. "This form of medicine has some similarities with cooking, yes?" he said with glee.

"Ah! It's very nice, yea?" Vitra praised. She flipped out her notebook, and turned to a page covered in notes. "Fun fact about Colb's potion: it's a slight modification to my original recipe. We've replaced the sliced tomatoroot with crushed daisywheat. By my calculations, it should work just fine – not a bad discovery! I suppose this afternoon wasn't a total loss for my research after all."

"Hmmm, I tasted the tomatoroot, and it was an odd mixture of sweet and bitter, yes?" Colb added sheepishly. "I made the suggestion because I thought it would make the potion taste better... so it could be consumed, instead of injected. I'm not sure I feel comfortable injecting others, yes? Hmmm, and I was surprised when Vitra approved my suggestion!"

"The tomatoroot was just in there to act like a sort of glue for the other ingredients," Vitra clarified. "Crushed daisywheat should work just as well for that, which is why I approved the idea. Colb's modification to my recipe should be consumable, and able to work just the same as my injected formula – not to mention, it doesn't taste half bad." She pat Colb's bald head. "If you keep up the ideas like that, you're on your way to becoming a decent alchemist, yes you are!"

"AaAaaaaahhhh, that's wonderful, Colb!" 27 cheered. "We had a most productive day, too! I've made some sales, Stibs ran circles around us with his newfound health, and Kashmir got to see lots of experiments!"

The elf pushed her hair over her face, masking her emotions. "Um… I did like seeing the ladybugmoth sanctuary…" she admitted.

Suddenly, a loud sizzling came from the back of the lab as Borin used his armor to cool down something he'd been working on. "Rhe! It's done! It's done!" Drek squealed with joy, hopping around in the back of the lab.

"AaAaaaaahhhh, you seem most excited, yes you do," 27 observed.

Drek pulled the hood of his cloak off his head, then looked up at the dwarf. "Gimmiegimmiegimmie!" he squealed as the Borin took a cooled mass of goldatinum and gems off the surface of his armor. The hairy dwarf burped, then placed the item on Drek's head.

"Ra-daa!" Drek shouted, scampering to the front of the lab to show off his new headpiece to the others. Atop his little green body sat a magnificently crafted goldatinum crown. Inlaid into it were some reddish-blue rubiamonds and bluish-green sappheralds from the pirate captain's stash. "Rrghegh, I'm one step closer to king of Ratter!"

Kashmir rolled her eyes. "Hmmm, you certainly look like it, yes?" Colb praised.

"Is that pure goldatinum?" Vitra asked, looking at Borin.

Drek nodded excitedly. "I told him it wasn't a good idea, but he insisted I don't mix in any other metals," Borin explained.

Vitra sighed. "Did you get the iridhodium coins he promised?" she asked. Borin nodded excitedly, his hair flailing as he did so. The alchemist sighed again.

"Alright little guy, I'm going to offer to do the right thing here," Vitra said, pulling a spray bottle of misty purple liquid out from her yellow duffle bag. "Pure goldatinum will bend and scratch over time. Let me enchant it with this to make it structurally sound, yea?"

Drek thought for a moment, then nodded, presenting the crown to Vitra. "Magic crown!" he cheered, as she sprayed it with the enchantment.

"Hm, there we go," she said as she finished spraying. Drek put the crown back on, and smiled at the accomplishment.

"Welp, looks like we're all done for the day," Vitra announced, packing up her duffle bag of potions. She then held out an arm, and Bitty jumped to it from the floor, climbing up onto the woman's shoulders. "It was fine meeting all of you. I appreciated seeing the elf's powers, I'm glad to have spread Tanja's good will by introducing someone new to alchemy," she continued, placing a hand on Colb's bald head, "and I'm glad Borin got some iridhoidum. However, the sun is setting, and I think it's high time we split ways."

"Wait… uh, don't you want to head to the tavern first?" Borin asked, switching to Dwarvish. "Today's that big special I was talking about, where everything's half price if you bring someone that's never been before!"

"Oy, I'd rather rest tonight," she replied in Dwarvish, stepping out the door. "Plus, you owe me one for helping you get that iridhodium today. You wouldn't want to be indebted to me double, right? Make sure nobody's left in the lab before you lock up." Bitty let out a quick goodbye *yip!* as the duo stepped out of the building.

Borin sighed, then started packing up his blacksmithing supplies. "What's a tavern?" Kashmir asked, her *Yiklar Amulet of Open Ears* having translated the Dwarvish for her.

Colb did a double-take. "Hmmm! What's a tavern?!" he exclaimed. "A tavern's exactly what I run back at my home tribe!

It's a place of good food, and complicated drinks, yes?"

Borin's hair rose with intrigue. "Uh… I haven't seen you guys around before," he burped, switching back to his rough Goblish. "You're new to Claus, I assume? Have you… uh, what's the word… have you guys come under the Ladle Tavern?"

"MMmMmmmm… what?" 27 asked.

"Uh… come through? No, visited. That's the word. Have you visited the Ladle Tavern?" Borin clarified. The goblins shook their heads. "Well, uh…" Borin burped. "Everything's half price today, but only for customers who've never been to the tavern before… and for the customer that referred them," he prodded. "Would any of you like to be my invitees, so we can all save some money tonight?"

"Hurmph, well it's probably best we don't set sail until morning, anyway," Stibs noted.

"Hmmm! I'd love to go," Colb cheered. "Just as long as we don't stay *all* night, yes?" he continued, glancing at 27.

"MMmMmmmm, yes, I did stay at a tavern little bit too long back in a human city… but I just love them!" 27 replied. "We should all go, yes we should!"

"Rrghegh… I see no reason to reject dinner alongside my royal blacksmith," Drek added, gleefully touching the crown on his head.

"Um… I am hungry, so I'll come, too… I don't have any money, though…" Kashmir muttered.

"AaAaaaaahhhh, I will cover your meal, yes I will," 27 promised. "In fact, I made much money with my kickback from selling many highest-of-quality goods today, yes I did. I'm feeling most generous after how far we've traveled together on this journey… plus, I know everyone but Drek is broke. I'll pay for food and one drink for everybody. AaAaaaaahhhh, and that'll include you, too, Borin!"

"Well! Alright then!" Borin rejoiced.

With that, the crew of six head to the Ladle Tavern for the evening. Colb found himself entering a dimly-lit building made from bismuthslate bricks, and filled with birchpine wood tables. The other customers in the tavern consisted of mostly humans, with some dwarves speckled in as well.

The crew enjoyed some good-quality, human-made meals and drinks, and shared stories with the dwarf blacksmith that had invited them.

Colb discussed the day he discovered a love for cooking, and how he established a tavern of his own back in Skaal. 27 discussed some stories from *Yiklar University*, including some lighthearted pranks he'd played on the teachers with his fellow students.

Borin described how he'd gotten into blacksmithing as a child, and the day he met Vitra – who ended up being an excellent partner, as her potion-based enchantments could elevate his work beyond that of other dwarves. Borin also revealed that, before building Vitra's Lab in Claus, he and Vitra had done a three-month excursion through the Frosted Wastes. This story particularly intrigued the goblins, as that's where they knew Wealth Mountain to be.

When 27 pushed Borin for more details about that journey, the dwarf went on to describe how Vitra first met Bitty in the Frosted Wastes, and how she spent days playing with the little creature while he worked on navigating the brutally cold region. Borin revealed that they ultimately failed in their mission of finding Tanja, but taming a rare winter foxferret seemed to satisfy Vitra, since she at least wasn't returning home completely empty-handed.

"Hmmm, your mission was searching for Tanja?" Colb asked.

"Vitra mentioned something about 'following Tanja's good will' when she taught me alchemy this afternoon, yes? What does that mean? Who is Tanja?"

"Ah, that's sort of a religion thing," Borin replied. "You'd need to know your Human Empire uh… what's the word… history? You'd need to know your Human Empire history for that one. If you want a quick lesson, I can tell you she's a human from Ebora who died around 300 years ago. Her full name was Jane Freda Tanja, but she just went by her last name, Tanja. Let's see… Tanja was famously the first human to combine magic and science into a single field of study, making her the founder of alchemy. She led construction on the town of Nala, which is a little village south of the Frosted Wastes. She spent much of her time in Nala because she liked exploring northwards in the snowy region. She was the first human to tame a winter foxferret, which she named Flufei. Let's see… what else… oh yea, and she was obsessed with… gosh, I don't think there's a Goblish word for it."

"Hmmm, do you know in another language?" Colb asked.

"Transmutation," Borin said, reverting to his native language.

"Basically, Tanja was obsessed with the art of trying to use magic and science to change cheap materials into rare and expensive materials," Borin clarified, switching back to Goblish. "Stuff like iridhodium, goldatinum, rubiamonds – you name it, she wanted to find a way to effectively create it. She theorized potion-making could achieve that gold, but never succeeded. Regardless, her invention of potion-making in general has been the focus of Vitra's career."

"Hmmm, if Tanja died around 300 years ago, why were you two looking for her?" Colb asked.

"Well, I say she died, but Vitra says her body was never found," Borin clarified. "I figure she ventured out into the Frosted

Wastes a little too far one day, and never made it back to Nala. It's a brutal place for certain. Vitra's got all sort of theories – maybe she invented immortality, or went into some sort of cryo-sleep… I think it's all nonsense, to be honest. Vitra's just *obsessed* with this historical figure."

"Hmmm, what do you mean by obsessed?" Colb asked.

"Well, I mean, look at Vitra, then think about the story I just said. Jane Tanja famously likes being referred to by her last name? Bam. Rachel Vitra goes by Vitra. Tanja goes into the Frosted Wastes and tames a winter foxferret? Bam. Vitra goes into the Frosted Wastes and tames a winter foxferret. Tanja invents alchemy? Bam. Vitra dedicates her life to alchemy. There's a lot of parallels – I mean, if you saw a picture of Tanja, you'd notice Vitra copies her hair style, her clothes… she's just *clearly* a big fan."

Kashmir cracked a little smile. "Vitra sounds a little wacko," she muttered.

"Well, you know how it is. Tanja's sort of got a cultish, religious following," Borin said, swirling his drink around as he spoke. "Lots of humans don't understand or like magic, and yet – Tanja is by *far* the most well-known person in Human Empire history. I mean, we're talking more famous than even the royal Cognemi family, and they've produced all the leaders since this empire was founded. Personally, I think the humans all find her interesting because of her quest to make rare materials out of common materials. Wealth always catches people's interest, doesn't it?"

"AaAaaaaahhhh, I cannot argue with that," 27 agreed, sipping his drink.

"Hmmm, so a lot of humans worship Tanja? As if she were a deity?" Colb asked. Borin nodded, shoving a daisywheat breadstick into his hair-covered mouth as he did so. "Do you?" Colb inquired.

"Nah," he said. "I'm not really into all that stuff... and if I were, I'd probably worship Maxten given where I'm from. He's a very famous dwarf, died something like 2,000 years ago, slaughtered a king, established the Dwarven Republic, blah, blah. If you ever visit the Dwarven Republic, people love him."

"Slaughtered a king? I could get behind that," Kashmir added.

Colb gave her a concerned look. "Hmmm, what about all this progress you'd made today, yes? Talking is better than fighting, yes?"

"Alright... yea," Kashmir agreed. "I'm just saying, royalty is dumb, so I get it. I think I'm allowed to have that opinion, as someone who has been marked as a traitor by a tyrannical queen of my own, just for doing what I thought was the right thing... which I didn't end up... even doing..."

Kashmir suddenly looked sick in the face, and put her head in her hands. She plopped her elbows onto the table, which made a crackling sound as it started to freeze.

"Oh, woa, what happened?" Borin worried.

"Rrghegh, no idea," Drek replied. "She only speaks in Elvish, so the three of us just kind of nod while Colb takes care of it."

"Well no, I understand Elvish too. I was just surprised she got so sad out of nowhere," Borin clarified.

"Hmmm, Kashmir? It's okay..." Colb comforted. "You can still come with us, yes? You don't have to stay here, or go home. It's okay that your plan changed, yes? That means that you grew, and learned more, yes?"

"I thought it was my *destiny* to save this island," Kashmir sniffled. "I assumed Jaiphione wanted me to come here, and kick out the humans... but now that I've seen them, I don't even feel like… like the humans should leave at all… and now there's nothing left for me to do…"

"Oy, Jaiphione? Sounds like another religion," Borin burped. "Look, kid, don't tell Vitra I said this… but don't spend your life trying to follow the will of some dead person that can't even talk to you."

"For your information… Jaiphione created the very island you're standing on," Kashmir huffed. Tears of snow dripped off her eyes and landed in small mounds on the table.

"Listen," Borin sighed. "When I convinced Vitra to give up on the Frosted Wastes, and we came to this place… our research skyrocketed. Honestly, you can tell she's much happier with the work we're doing here, and so am I. Just because Tanja loved the Frosted Wastes, doesn't mean that was the best thing for *our* research. Just because you believe this Jaiphione person created the island I'm standing on, doesn't mean it's your destiny to stand here, too."

"Well, I can't go home…" Kashmir whimpered.

"Hmmm, again, why don't you come with us?" Colb pitched. "Our next stop, coincidentally, is the Frosted Wastes, yes? That's not in the Elvish Kingdom, yes?"

"Oy, well there you go!" Borin said. "The Frosted Wastes… it's very cold there. Brutally cold. Someone like you is going to *love* that."

"…Yea?" Kashmir sniffled, looking up at Borin through snow-covered eyes.

"Oh yea, and hey – maybe you can pull a Vitra? Adopt yourself a winter foxferret?" Borin continued. "They're quite rare, but if you can befriend one, you'll find yourself with an intelligent and thoughtful creature by your side. They're pretty friendly, too, especially if you pet them frequently. Of course, normally you'd need protection to even touch them, like the armor I'm wearing, since their skin is colder than ice. Heh, but your skin's super cold like that, too. You probably never have to worry about frostbites, do you?"

"Um… no, I don't," Kashmir agreed.

"Well, then there you go! That's a purpose," Borin said. "Taking care of another creature, that's a great purpose right there. Doesn't even have to be a winter foxferret; anything from a climate *that* cold would probably get along with you just fine."

Kashmir sniffled. "I guess so… well, I suppose I don't have anything left to do here… and I'm dead if I set foot back on the Elvish Kingdom mainland… so, that sounds like a better plan than anything else I can think of." She rubbed the snow off her eyes, and glanced at Colb. "I'll go with you guys… thank you for inviting me."

Colb smiled. "Hmmm, we'd love to have you, yes?" he cheered. With that, Colb announced Kashmir's decision to the rest of the group in Goblish. The group toasted to the official fifth member of their team, then continued to share stories and enjoy food late into the evening.

A few hours after sunset, the group was ready to leave the Ladle Tavern. As his companions walked out the door, Colb tipped their server with the two goldatinum coins he'd found on the pirate ship earlier that day.

"I really appreciate you coming with me," Borin stumbled as the group left the tavern. He seemed a little tipsy from the vast number of drinks he'd ordered. "And the food and that one free drink, too. If you follow me back to the lab, I'll give you something for your trouble."

"Hmmm, I'll help you get to the lab, and get home, yes?" Colb offered. He hadn't sipped more than the one drink 27 bought for him today, and he wanted to share some kindness to this dwarf that had brought such a nice evening to the team. "I'll meet the rest of you at the boat, yes?"

The group of four nodded in agreement, then returned to their pirate ship, with Stibs helping Drek carry his small-but-heavy treasure chest along the way.

Colb led a wobbly Borin back the way they'd come, to the metal building with a complicated door. Borin opened it easily, having forgotten to lock it on their way to the Ladle Tavern, and led Colb inside the chilly room.

"Here," he mumbled, picking up a ragged sack. "Let's see…" The dwarf grabbed a telescope, a sheet of paper, and a random vial off Vitra's desk, then tossed them all into the sack. "There…" he said, handing the bag to Colb. "You like po… potions, right? You were making some today, so… so… here's one of our newest inventions for you," he hiccupped.

"Hmmm, thank you, yes?" Colb said, peering into the sack. The telescope was metal, with Borin's name etched into the side of it. The glass potion bottle contained a viscous, radiant white liquid. The sheet of paper appeared to be instructions, depicting a hand-drawn image of a human hand pouring the white potion all over the telescope.

"I live… uh… close," Borin hiccupped.

"Hmmm, let's get you home, yes?" Colb agreed. He shut the sack, tossed it over his back, and helped the hairy dwarf walk as he stumbled back to his nearby hole-in-the-ground house.

Colb then returned to the pirate ship, where the weary crew had already fallen asleep. Just like the night before, 27 had set up his *Yiklar Folding Cabin* for the goblins, while Kashmir slept beneath the stars. Colb quietly stepped into the cabin, making himself comfortable in the sleeping area.

Hmmm, this feels great, Colb thought to himself as he settled into bed. *We've got a boat, and a gift from Borin, and Kashmir joined the team, and I made a health potion with Vitra for the next time someone gets hurt… things seem to be going quite well, yes? We're off to the Frosted Wastes next, yes? Hmmm! Wealth Mountain, here we come!*

Chapter 16

CHAOS AT SEA

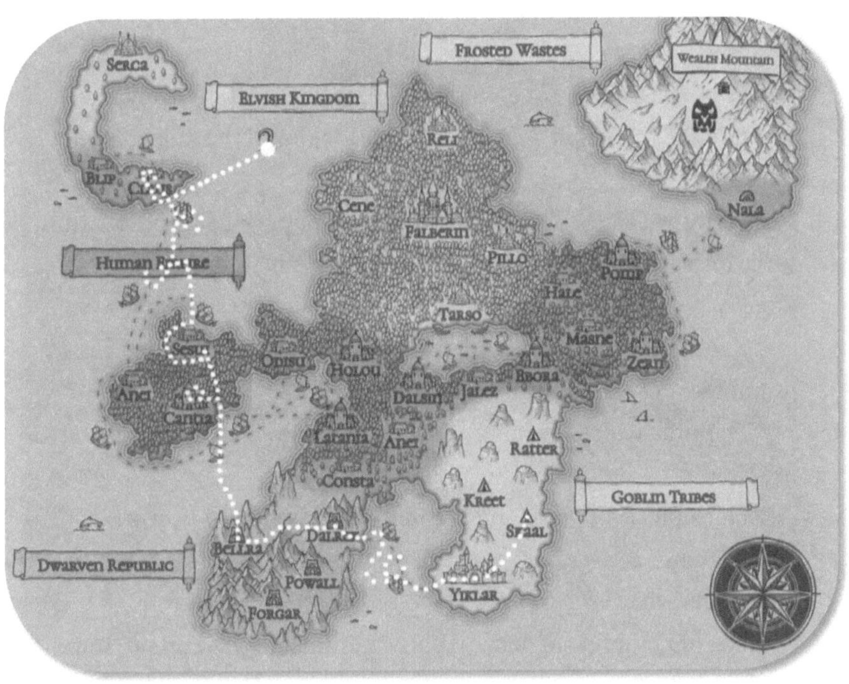

16. CHAOS AT SEA

As the sun rose over Jaiphione's Crescent, Colb, 27, and Drek stepped out of the *Yiklar Folding Cabin.* "Hurmph, so you're finally awake?" Stibs asked the crew.

The goblins looked up. Before them stood Kashmir and Stibs. Kashmir was toying with a small chunk of ice, watching with mild amusement as a cloudy mist flowed off it in response to her touch. Stibs was proudly hoisting a sail, skipping as he did so to demonstrate the wide range of motion his newly healed leg could perform.

"AaAaaaaahhhh, I see you two are up early! This I like to see, yes I do," 27 cheered. "Stibs, are you looking to be ship captain once more?"

"Hurmph, I sure am," Stibs replied, hopping up and down a little bit as he spoke. "If you three got up a little earlier, we'd already be well on our way!"

"Rrghegh, we get it, your leg's better and you feel great," Drek grumbled. "Doesn't mean I have to get up before sun does."

"Hmmm, we're up now, yes?" Colb threw in. "Ready to set sail!"

"Hurmph, well hold on," Stibs said, tying up a rope and approaching the goblin trio. "I would like to first make an announcement."

The old goblin signed, patting the side of the pirate ship. "Hurmph, this is our third time at sea together. As an experienced sailor, I would like to make one thing clear: usually, when you sail somewhere, the boat you leave on *makes it* to your destination along with you. Oddly, this has not been the case in *any* of our previous excursions. As elected captain of this ship, I say that's unacceptable."

27 raised his hand. "Hurmph, what, 27? You have a question?"

"MMmMmmmm, yes I do," the noble replied. "I noticed that every boat we've used so far, including today, was not Yiklar-made. Thus, we could not – and still cannot – be assured to have a boat of highest and most flawless of quality."

"Hurmph, are you calling the boat I made in two hours to be of low quality?" Stibs asked.

"Nononononono," 27 replied, "I am not! Although it did stink very fast due to fairly mild trauma, I would never suggest such a thing, no I would not. I am simply pointing out that Yiklar-made goods are very high of quality, and to lack goods of such high quality is a risk we all must assume, yes it is."

Colb gave a small round-of-applause to the noble's well-put point. "Hurmph, alright, whatever. The boat we have now is, admittedly, the nicest one we've had so far. Let's just make sure that we sail to the Frosted Wastes without a problem. We're going to travel northeast until we're over the tip of elf territory, and then we're going to go straight east until we hit snowy land. We're not stopping in the Elvish Kingdom…"

"Woo!" Kashmir interjected from where she was sitting on the main deck.

Stibs continued, "…and we're not letting anyone, or anything, board this ship. This is a clear-cut journey: we go to the Frosted Wastes, and we avoid everything that is not the Frosted Wastes." The crew nodded with understanding.

"Hurmph, alright. Now that that's done, let's get to business!" Stibs announced. Following their captain's orders, the crew split off to their different jobs on the Quartzelian Pirates boat. Together, the goblins got the ship on course for the Frosted Wastes.

Stibs took the wheel, navigating their journey with his *Yiklar*

Map of Finding Location. Drek stood at the boat's bow, watching the seas for danger ahead. Colb worked near the stern of the boat, in the *Yiklar Folding Cabin*'s kitchen, preparing a meal for the team. 27 patrolled the center of the vessel, checking for any ropes or sails that looked loose. Kashmir relaxed on the main deck, watching the sun gradually rise into the sky.

The morning's journey went well. The boat sailed northeast at a strong speed, and the waters looked to be clear all day. Even better, the weather was fine, with not a cloud in sight.

Around noon, Colb began making lunches for the crew. He mushed some dusty toadroach carcasses he'd found along the floors of the lower deck into a soft paste, which he then spread on some seagullfish fillets that Drek had hunted with his bow – ensuring to leave a couple of fillets plain for Kashmir.

Colb handed out the raw lunches to each member of the crew, eventually making his way to Drek. The crown-wearing goblin seemed alert, watching the waters carefully.

"Hmmm, I brought food, yes?" Colb cheered.

"Rrghegh… I saw dark shadow in distance," Drek announced, ignoring Colb's offer. "Unusual… I couldn't tell what it was."

Colb squinted his eyes. The waters looked empty to him. "Hmmm, I see nothing, yes?"

"Rrghegh… I swear I saw something," Drek exclaimed. The young goblin pointed out to the sea, which still looked barren to Colb.

"Hmmm," the chef muttered, setting Drek's lunch down on the floor of the deck. "I still don't see anything, yes? Hmmm, but maybe I have something that can help, yes?" Colb unhitched a ratty-looking sack from his belt. "Borin gave me this potion kit yesterday, yes? It came with a lens."

Colb pulled the metal spyglass out from his sack, and stared out at the sea with it. "Hmmm… I still don't see much, yes?" he muttered.

"Rrghegh… what is potion for?" Drek asked, inspecting the bag. "Can it make the telescope magic? Like how human enchanted my crown with spray bottle?"

"Hmmm, probably," Colb replied. He picked up the potion and inspected it. The flask contained a viscous, brilliant white liquid with small lettuceshrimp eyes floating in it. "I guess I'll do what the instruction sheet says, yes?"

Seeing that the paper depicted a hand-drawn image of a human pouring the white potion all over the telescope, Colb proceeded to dump his own potion onto Borin's handiwork. The liquid immediately flowed upwards, to the object's lens, then absorbed into it. Once the reaction seemed to be finished, Colb put his eye up to the telescope once again.

This time, the seawater looked as clear as air. The chef goblin could easily see an enormous, kraken-like beast hiding in the tides. It was covered in thick, black-stained feathers, and its eight tentacles joyfully vibrated as if excited to catch the pirate ship sailing towards it. Instead of a mouth, the monster sported a wide, yellow-tinted beak that looked sharper than a knife.

"Hmmm, stop the boat, yes? Stop the boat!" Colb yelled, raising his voice for the rest of the crew.

"Rrghegh, what? What?" Drek grumbled. The crown-wearing goblin snatched the telescope from Colb's hands, and took a look for himself. "Rrghegh! Stop the boat!" he loudly agreed. "There's a monster waiting to snatch us!"

"Hurmph, 27, drop anchor!" Stibs announced.

As the noble rushed to complete the order, Stibs jogged over to Drek and Colb. "Hurmph! What do you see?"

Drek handed the telescope to Stibs, the pointed out towards the sea. "Hurmph, this telescope's crazy…" Stibs mumbled as he put his eye up to the enchanted item.

"Hurmph! Good eyes," Stibs praised as he looked out at the sea with the eyepiece. "I'm impressed you two saw this. That's an octopusduck right there. They're almost invisible… waiting for ships to come too close, then gobbling them up. I've never seen a live one before."

A clinking chain sound could suddenly be heard as 27 dropped anchor. "Oh no…" Stibs grumbled.

"Hmmm, what?" Colb asked. "It's just sitting there, yes? We can just go around it, yes?"

"They're rather intelligent beasts," Stibs worried. "It looks like it's noticing our anchor dropped… and it's realizing we aren't planning to keep sailing towards it… and yep, now it's coming right for us. Uh oh, it's swimming really fast, too." Stibs handed the telescope back to Drek, then turned to face the elf sitting on the main deck. "Kashmir!" he ordered. "We're going to need some defense over here."

"Against what?" she replied in Elvish, not moving from her spot on the ground.

Within moments, an enormous, feather-covered tentacle reached out of the water with a boom, then latched onto the bow of the ship. Wood crunched and crushed as the boat lurched forwards, and started sinking into the sea.

Kashmir's ears perked up and she stood, staring at the now-revealed monster destroying their ship. After another second, the boat trembled, and a loud screeching, crunching sound came from the lower deck.

27 opened the door to the boat's basement, and stared wide-eyed down the staircase. "MMmMmmmm, there is large beak eating through bottom of the boat, yes there is," the noble

reported. "It's flooding down there. The ship's going to sink, yes it is. I'm going to pack up my *Yiklar Folding Cabin*, yes I am." The noble shut the door, and rushed to retrieve his mobile vacation house.

"Okay, okay, I can make this go away," Kashmir announced frantically. The boat suddenly lurched forwards again, making Kashmir slip on her own puddle of ice that had formed under her feet.

"Hmmm! Let me help, yes?" Colb commanded, rushing to Kashmir's side, and drawing his shield. "I'll hold you still while you blast the octopusduck, yes?"

"Hurmph, I take back what I said about the defense," Stibs retracted. "If the octopusduck has started consuming the lower deck, we're going to sink no matter what we do. At this point, it'd be best to abandon ship and get out of here. Drek, find the escape boats."

"Um… they're all gone," Kashmir worried, looking at Colb. "They were attached by ropes, and… and Stibs told me to cut all the ropes a few days ago… so pirates wouldn't be able to climb after us on the ship… I mean to say, I… I cut them all down when we were fleeing from the pirates…"

"Hmmm, there are none, yes?" Colb translated, raising his voice so Stibs could hear him. The old goblin let out some Goblish curse words in response.

"But… um… I can't swim," Kashmir added.

"Hmmm, it's okay, Stibs will figure something out, yes?" Colb comforted. "Maybe he can build us a raft, or we could buy something from 27?"

"No… I mean, I physically can't touch water," Kashmir clarified. "It always freezes. It's not ideal, but if I jump overboard, I think I can make us a way out of here."

"Hmmm, jump overboard?!" Colb cried. "With an octopusduck right here, that doesn't sound safe, yes?"

"Hurmph, everyone!" Stibs suddenly announced as a layer of water started pouring onto the main deck from the pirate ship's shattered bow. "Octopusducks like to eat wood. If we can construct a small raft of some sort, it should ignore us in favor of eating the bigger meal – that is, the pirate ship." He glanced at 27, who had just finished retracting his *Yiklar Folding Cabin*.

"MMmMmmmm, the *Yiklar Floating Cabin* does not float, no it does not," 27 said, pocketing his doorknob as he regrouped with the crew. "It would not make good raft."

Abandoning Colb, Kashmir ran over to what remained of the ship's bow, and put her hand in the thin layer of water that was flowing onto the main deck. It began rapidly solidifying into a block of ice. She then looked at the other goblins, as if silently asking them for permission to do something.

"Hurmph, what? You think you can make a raft like that?" Stibs guessed. Kashmir nodded. "Well obviously, go for it," he ordered. 27 and Drek nodded in agreement as well.

The young elf put her hands together, then dove off the side of the boat. "Woa!" the three goblins said in unison, running to the boat's railings to see where she had fallen.

Colb rushed to the ship's edge as well, dodging a falling rod of mapleoak wood as he did so. When he reached the rest of the goblin crew, he looked down into the sea. What he saw was Kashmir, staring back up at him. Below her, a wide iceberg had formed, breaking her fall, and keeping her out of the peppersalt waters. The ice-platform she sat upon looked solid, and was slowly but surely drifting eastward.

Kashmir waved her fingers welcomingly, gesturing for the goblins to join her. One-by-one, as the pirate ship crunched and sank behind them, the goblins leaped into the water and swam up to Kashmir's iceberg.

By the time it was Colb's turn, the pirate boat had sunk so low that he only had to drop a couple of inches before landing in the peppersalt sea. As his small body naturally floated in the dense waters, Colb swam with all his might, eventually making land on Kashmir's cold, slippery mound of ice.

Colb then looked back, watching as the pirate ship sank into the octopusduck's embrace behind him. "Hmmm, this is working!" he cheered. "It's ignoring us, yes? We're safe!"

"Hurmph, as I foresaw," Stibs added. "It's too busy eating the larger ship to notice we escaped! Not to mention, those things only like eating wood, from what I've read. It's not going to care about this iceberg."

Colb looked at Kashmir, her long bluish-black hair covering one of her eyes. "Hmmm, you were right, yes?" he praised. "I'm proud of you! Your quick-thinking got us out, and we didn't even have to fight, yes?"

"Um… thanks," Kashmir said, looking out at the waters before them. "Although, I can't really control where this thing goes. We're pretty much adrift at sea until we hit the next body of land, and I doubt it's going to be the Frosted Wastes."

As Colb translated this revelation to the others, Stibs pulled out his *Yiklar Map of Finding Location*. "Whereami…" he mumbled. "Hurmph, based on this map, it looks like landing in the Elvish Kingdom is very likely."

Kashmir let out an audible gulp. "I was worried about that," she muttered.

"Hmmm, but we're safe, yes?" Colb comforted. "It's better to be on land in your home kingdom than underwater with a monster, yes?"

"Um… I'm not sure if I agree with that," Kashmir worried. "Queen Eylbella is much scarier than that octopusduck."

Chapter 17

CAPTURED

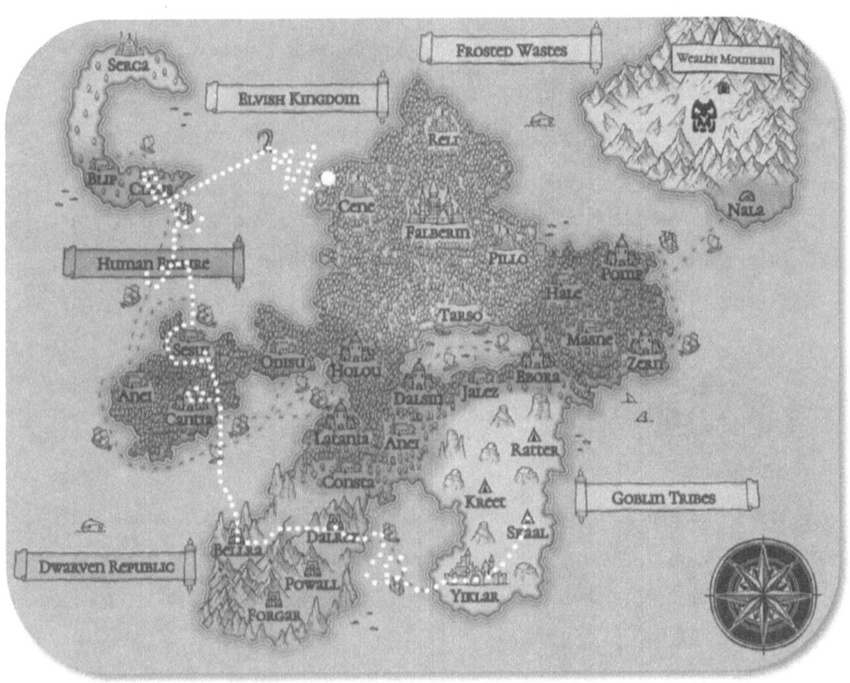

17. CAPTURED

As the team floated aimlessly at sea long into the night, Colb dozed off on the cool bed of ice.

After some time, he half-awoke to the sound of Elvish voices, feeling dazed and confused. Colb experienced a sensation of being lifted and moved, but was too drowsy to react. Everything seemed to be happening more quickly than he could understand it. Something was wrong.

An unknown amount of time later, after being set on the ground, the chef goblin had regained enough energy to look up. He noticed thick branches of goldatinum-colored leaves swaying in the air above him. *Hmmm... trees?* he thought to himself. *Did we hit land while I was asleep?*

Colb peered downwards, where he saw a mound of goldatinum-colored clovergrass underneath him. *I am on land*, he confirmed. *Hmmm, this is very beautiful clovergrass, yes? Did I die? Is this a dream?*

The chef next attempted to stand up, only to discover his arms and legs had been bound by rope. *Wait... this isn't right, yes?* he thought.

Colb blinked a few times and shook his head to wake himself up more. As his daze faded away, and his eyes started to focus, Colb noticed his friends sitting with him. They were all bound as well, and surrounded by elven guards.

These elves – who were more than twice the height of Colb – carried wooden blowguns and sharp, white-painted boomerangs. *Weapons!* Colb worried. *Hmmm! We must've hit the Elvish Kingdom while I was asleep, yes?! Have we been captured?!*

Colb looked outwards, towards the sea. At the shore's edge, a different group of elves with blue-colored skin, sharp-pointed ears, and long, flowing white hair were holding their hands out. As they did so, the water before them shifted, magically swallowing up Kashmir's iceberg. *Hmmm! This seems like no dream,* Colb realized.

Colb looked back at the guards surrounding him and his friends. They appeared to be answering to one particular elf, who looked quite different from all the others. This elf's natural skin was a mixture of white, black, and red lines, all twisting around each other as if someone had scribbled on their body with inks and paint. The elf also had a potent magical aura about them, which Colb could sense like waves of pressure through the air.

Colb looked around at his friends, to see how they were dealing with the situation. Stibs struggled against his ropes, which became tangled slightly in the backpack he wore. Drek sat proudly: tied up, but still wearing his glorious goldatinum crown, which had been left untouched by the guards. 27 looked absolutely confused and upset. Kashmir was simply staring at the ground, with defeat in her eyes.

Hmmm, we should get out of here, yes? Colb thought to himself. The chef goblin perked up his ears, hoping to get some information from the nearby elves that might help him escape – but as the guards spoke, Colb found their language foreign and impossible to comprehend. Confused, he looked down at his necklace. The *Yiklar Amulet of Open Ears* was still around his neck, but it didn't glow the way it used to. Instead, it appeared dull, more similar to the gemstones he'd purchased in Cantia than to an item 27 would sell.

Fighting against his bounds, Colb decided to carefully inch his way towards 27. He eyed the guards as he progressed, wary that they could attack at any moment.

"Hmmm, my *Yiklar Amulet of Open Ears* seems to be broken,

yes?" Colb whispered as soon as his noble companion was in earshot. 27 looked at him, then looked down at his necklace.

"MMmMmmmm, that is not good, no it is not," 27 muttered. "However, it is good to see you're awake, yes it is."

"Hmmm, what exactly happened to get us in this situation?" Colb asked. "I'm confused, yes?"

"MMmMmmmm, when we hit shore, these elves ambushed us immediately, yes they did," 27 replied. "One of them fired a blowgun dart right into your neck, and whatever it was tipped with seemed to prevent you from waking up. They fired one at me as well, but fortunately I managed to dodge it."

"Hmmm, I was wondering why the sounds of conflict hadn't woken me up," Colb murmured. He rubbed his shoulders against his neck, checking for the dart. A purple-colored needle came loose from his skin, and fell to the ground.

27 continued to recount the recent events. "After they attacked with darts, I tried to summon an Elvish-translated *Yiklar Catalog* to befriend and barter with them, yes I did," he muttered. "MMmMmmmm, but my *Yiklar Bag of Traveling Inventory* had gone dull, yes it had! Worse yet, Drek fired an arrow at the elves with his *Yiklar Bow of Returning Arrow*, and it didn't come back! It fell into the water, and now that beautifully crafted iridhodium arrow is gone for good!"

27 shook his head in disbelief. "MMmMmmmm, it's as if all magic has gone away, yes it is. There was nothing we could do, and the elves – they overwhelmed us. We never stopped struggling, but they still managed to tie us up one-by-one, yes they did."

"Hmmm, all magic has gone away?" Colb repeated.

"Look at Kashmir!" 27 continued, his eyes becoming crazed with anxiety. "Her hands have been bound, and she's not wearing any gloves! You'd think her bare skin would've destroyed those ropes by now, yes you would? Even her innate magic has disappeared!"

Colb looked over at the defeated young elf. Indeed, she was tied up without problem – even the clovergrass she sat upon looked perfectly unharmed. "Hmmm, not all magic has vanished, yes?" Colb countered. "Look out to the sea, yes? Hmmm, they're destroying our iceberg with magic, yes?"

Colb and 27 looked out towards the peppersalt tides. The group of blue-skinned elves had finished sinking the ice-platform, and appeared to be regrouping with their leader. Droplets of water magically flowed atop their skin as they walked, shimmering in the moonlight.

However, as the group got closer to their tricolored leader, this effect suddenly stopped: the droplets fell to the ground with a splash, and the blue-skinned elves appeared to dull and weaken.

"MMmMmmmm, not anymore – their magic is gone, too," 27 observed. "Perhaps there's something about this area that suppresses magic, yes there might be? MMmMmmmm… but my *Yiklar Bag of Traveling Inventory* stopped working while I was on the iceberg, yes it did, not while I was sitting here."

"Hmmm, maybe there's some sort of mobile magic-blocker, yes?" Colb theorized. He looked around. There didn't seem to be any large magical machines in the area… but the leader covered in black, white, and red scribbles certainty had a palpable presence. Each time that elf took a step, Colb felt a light ringing sensation in his ears.

"Hmmm, do all elves have powers like Kashmir?" Colb asked. 27 shrugged, giving him a *how-am-I-supposed-to-know* look. "Hmmm… perhaps that leader is blocking all magic, yes?" Colb continued. "The elf's skin almost looks like it's… wiggling the air, yes? Maybe that's disrupting the magic of anything that gets too close, yes?"

"MMmMmmmm, that is most interesting theory, yes it is," 27 replied, struggling against his bounds. "However, if that *is* the case, then we have big problem, yes we do. Without your *Yiklar Amulet of Open Ears*, how are we supposed to befriend and barter with these elves? Let alone fight them?"

Suddenly, some *mee-honk! mee-honk!* sounds grabbed Colb and 27's attention. The chef goblin craned his neck around to see a train of carriages riding up from inland. The vehicle was pulled by a duo of strange, wide-mouthed creatures. They looked a little like chickenhorses, but were tan, featherless, and three times bigger. They both sported a wide hump on their back.

Once the creature-drawn train came to a stop, the elvish guards started lifting members of the party and loading them into the backmost cart one-by-one. "Hurmph! Don't put me in this camelmule-drawn piece of garbage! Who do you think you are?!" Stibs complained as he struggled against the elves picking him up.

The elves soon shoved Colb into the cart, between 27 and Kashmir. All five members of the crew were packed into this single space, shoulder-to-shoulder. Once they were all in, and elf guard slammed the door shut, locking them inside the carriage-train's caboose.

Colb's left arm was touching Kashmir's skin: it felt warm, like the flesh of a goblin or dwarf. Kashmir continued to sit solemnly, not speaking a word.

"Hmmm, Kashmir?" Colb asked, looking at the child. Colb tapped his arm against hers, prompting the elf to look up at him. Her sky-blue eyes were wet with slush.

"Hmmm, are you okay?" Colb asked. "I hear we were ambushed – you didn't get hurt, yes?"

Kashmir shook her head, muttering some Elvish phrase. Colb got this impression that this was more of an *I-don't-understand-what-you're-saying* sort of head shake than an answer to his question.

"Hmmm," Colb muttered. He looked at Kashmir's neck. For once, her *Yiklar Amulet of Open Ears* was visible, as the frost constantly surrounding it had thawed – but the magic item looked dull and weakened, just like Colb's.

Hmmm. This is clearly the Elvish Kingdom, Colb pondered, having seen nothing but elves since waking up. "Hmmm, what's everything we know about the Elvish Kingdom?" Colb asked, turning to 27.

"MMmMmmmm, that is not long list," 27 said. "Let's see… there is queen, yes there is."

"Hmmm, a queen that's specifically angry at Kashmir, yes?" Colb added.

"Do we know why?" 27 questioned.

"Hmmm… I do, it's one of the first things she told me," Colb recalled. "Her father wanted to rally an army against the humans on Jaiphione's Crescent, but the queen wasn't having it… so she executed him, and banned his family from even thinking about that island ever again, yes? By leaving home and going to Jaiphione's Crescent, Kashmir became a traitor."

"MMmMmmmm, that's quite a problem, yes it is," 27 replied. "No wonder we've been captured."

"Hurmph, do we know anything else?" Stibs chimed in from the opposite side of 27. "That sounds like elvish rule-breaking squabbles that, frankly, we don't want to get involved in. We have a mission to finish, and we're not getting to the Frosted Wastes anytime soon as prisoners."

"Hmmm, well, perhaps we could guess where we're going,

yes?" Colb proposed. "Maybe to a prison? Maybe to talk with the queen?"

"Rrghegh, maybe to be executed," Drek grumbled from next to Stibs. "We need to escape."

"Hurmph! I couldn't agree more," Stibs added.

Colb looked back over at Kashmir. She was solemnly staring at the wooden floor of the carriage-train cart. Suddenly, this gave Colb an idea.

"Hmmm, I'm going to ask Kashmir where she thinks we're going," he announced. Colb wiggled one of his little green feet closer to where Kashmir was looking. Using his sharp yellow toenails, he meticulously etched a drawing of a cart holding five stick figures into the wooden floor. It looked like a child's drawing when he was done with it, but it was better than nothing.

Colb then drew three arrows from the cart, pointing at three different possible destinations: a crown, a gravestone, and a prison cell. Once he was done, he looked at Kashmir expectantly.

The elf blinked away her slushy tears, and surveyed the drawings. After a moment, she began to cry some more, shamefully pointing towards the crown with the tip of her shoe.

"Hmmm, I think Kashmir's expecting this train to bring us to the queen," Colb revealed to the others.

"MMmMmmmm, so we're going to see royalty?" 27 repeated. "With this anti-magic nonsense going on, my *Yiklar Bag of Traveling Inventory* will not work, no it will not. Otherwise, I would suggest we simply impress the queen with my many fantastic deals. Then, she would surely let us go and forgive Kashmir, yes she would."

"Rrghegh, that is not good plan," Drek countered. "If queen killed Kashmir's father, she might do the same to us. This may be death sentences. It's better to just find a way to escape now."

As Drek went back to surveying the cart for escape options, Colb sighed and looked back at Kashmir. Her brilliant blue-black hair looked jumpy and youthful – but she acted like a cowmammoth heading to slaughter.

Hmmm, Kashmir has an incredible number of years left to live, Colb thought to himself. *It's too early for her to perish anytime soon. I don't know what this queen will be like... and I can't even talk to Kashmir anymore... but right now, in my mind, I make this vow: no matter what, I'm not letting that queen end Kashmir's life. No today, not ever. Not as long as I have something to say about it, yes?*

Chapter 18

OUTSIDE OF FALBERIN

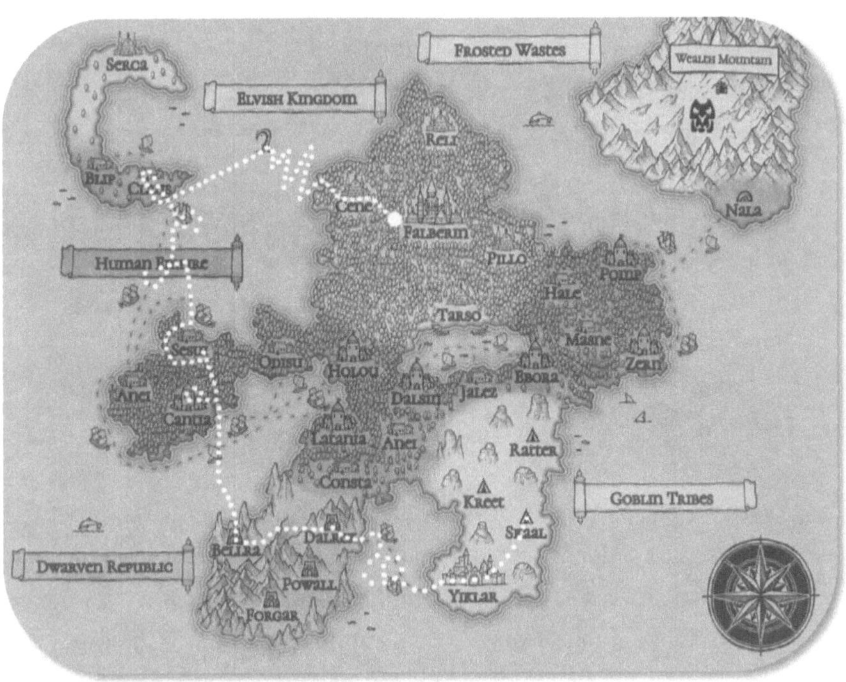

18. OUTSIDE OF FALBERIN

The carriage-train chugged along for a good few hours. The crew sat stiffly, uncomfortable as they remained bound in the dry wooden caboose. Suddenly, a light *snap!* sound came from Drek, as if some ropes had released their tension.

"Hmmm! What was that?" Colb asked aloud. Drek squirmed his way to the front of the group, showing off some shredded rope.

"Rrghegh… I freed myself," he announced. "Without knife or arrow, it took long time. Rrghegh, but with loose piece of wood on cart floor, I slowly wore away rope."

He snapped a sharpened slinter off the bottom of the cart, walked up to Stibs, and sliced the old goblin free. "Rrghegh… is also much easier to cut while not bound myself," Drek noted. The young goblin proceeded to cut 27, Colb, and Kashmir loose as well.

"Rrghegh… escape has begun. Let's jump out of cart," Drek announced with glee.

"Hurmph, I'm impressed!" Stibs praised. "Good job." He pat Drek on the back. The roguish goblin flinched at the sudden affection.

As the group prepared to dive out of the moving cart, some Elvish shouts suddenly came from further up on the carriage-train. The prisoners all reactively ducked their heads down.

"Hmmm, did they realize we've cut our bounds?" Colb asked in a harsh whisper. Kashmir's ears perked up, and her eyes widened as the Elvish guards continued to yell. She gave the goblin crew a panicked look, then pointed her finger at the gravestone Colb had etched into the floor.

Suddenly, the wooden cart split beneath them, as some heavy force smacked into the side of the carriage-train. The prisoners, guards, and anti-magic elf all toppled onto the road as the line of carts flipped over and shattered from impact. The camelmules neighed as their bounds to the front of the carriage-train snapped off, and they fled into the forest.

Colb, suddenly finding himself face-down in a field of goldatinum-colored clovergrass, sat up to see his surroundings. An impressive city of pewterorange, lemongranite, and marblelime (three of the rarest, most beautiful plant-based building materials known to exist) was just a five-minute walk away.

The armed elvish guards were shouting and mobilizing defensively. They looked to the tricolored elf for orders, but the terrified leader just turned and fled towards the nearby city. Similarly, all the blue-skinned water elves scattered into the forest, abandoning the remaining six weapon-wielding guards to fend for themselves.

Colb next peered upon the flipped-over line of carts, trying to figure out what these elves were so afraid of. Standing in the wreckage was a beastly thing: a pink-skinned mammal covered in splotches of yellow fur. Around its neck shined an enormous brown mane, which put even Borin's hair to shame, and a pair of long, razor-sharp teeth stuck out from its mouth.

"Hurmph – I didn't know those things were real! I think that's a lionpig!" Stibs exclaimed.

The monster let out a roar, then charged towards the six weapon-wielding elvish guards. The elves reacted by slashing at the air with their boomerangs, and firing blowgun darts into the monster.

The lionpig, undeterred by the weapons and unfazed by the darts, crunched an elvish leg with its nasty teeth, then bit another right in the throat. The other four began to back off, looking unsure of what to do.

"Rrghegh… this seems like great opportunity to escape," Drek observed.

"Hmmm, I think we should help them, yes?" Colb countered.

"Rrghegh… they are captors," Drek grumbled back. The young goblin straightened the goldatinum crown on his head as he spoke. "They work for evil queen. Right?"

"Right," Kashmir agreed. Colb turned, surprised to hear her response.

"AaAaaaaahhhh! Your necklace is lit up again, Colb!" 27 exclaimed, pointing at the glowing crystal attached to Colb's neck. "Does that mean you can understand what she says?"

Colb looked over at Kashmir. The necklace upon her neck was glowing again as well – and quickly becoming coated with frost. "Hmmm, I can. I think our magic is back, since tri-colored elf has run away, yes?" Colb observed. "Our theory must have been correct about that elf, yes?"

Sure enough, the wave-like field of anti-magic faded as the tri-colored elf retreated to the city. "Hmmm, with our magic back, we can definitely save these guards, yes?" Colb suggested.

The crew looked over at the six remaining elven guards, who at this point had all been crumpled to the ground by the raging lionpig. The pink creature next reared its head towards the prisoners, snarling with its flat snout. "Hurmph, I don't think we have a choice now," Stibs grumbled.

The lionpig kicked the dirt a couple of times, then charged towards Stibs. The old goblin pulled out his *Yiklar Shield of Reflecting*, and held it true. As the sprinting lionpig made contact with the device, it bounced off as if it had hit a spring, and crashed into the flipped-over carriage-train.

Meanwhile, Drek drew his *Yiklar Bow of Returning Arrow*,

then hesitated. "Rrghegh… I don't have my arrow anymore. I don't have any weapons!" he realized.

"Hmmm, I have this?" Colb suggested, tossing his *Yiklar Wand of Rainfall* to Drek. As the lionpig stood up from the wreckage, Drek shook the wand with ferocity, starting a rainstorm in the sky above.

"Rrghegh… I don't think this is going to do anything," Drek worried.

"No… I think I can do something with that," Kashmir muttered, looking at the raincloud. "Colb, get behind me with your shield."

As Colb knelt behind the purple elf, raising his shield, Kashmir aimed her hands up into the air and closed her eyes. Colb's ears popped as air rushed to the elf's palms, transforming into a frigid beam of clear liquid that fired into the air.

Before the lionpig could react, the thick droplets of water above it began to transform into dagger-like icicles upon contact with Kashmir's beam. These sharp icicles pierced its head and shoulders as they fell from above.

The beast let out a squealing roar, confused by the harmful weather, and began to back off towards the forest. "AaAaaaaahhhh, it's fleeing!" 27 cheered.

Suddenly, with a *whoosh!* sound echoing throughout the forest path, Drek's iridhodium arrow magically rushed into the scene from out of nowhere. The arrow pierced into the lionpig's skull, then abruptly curved through the air to return to Drek. The young goblin caught the arrow – which was soaking wet from the peppersalt sea – with glee. "Rhe, it came back!" he cheered.

"They killed it!" an Elvish voice suddenly rejoiced from nearby. Colb hustled over to the half-dozen elves that had crumpled to the ground. His ears perked up as he listened to them via his *Yiklar Amulet of Open Ears.*

"Our leader and comrades abandoned us," one of the six guards choked.

"These prisoners," another one continued, "they could have run too, but instead they fought. They've slain the lionpig!"

"You didn't deserve it!" Kashmir huffed, crossing her arms. "You should've left me and my friends alone in the first place!"

"You're the Quilliva kid," a guard countered. "The one that ran off to the human lands after the queen explicitly had her father executed, right? Of course we had to capture you. That's our job."

"Yes, I am Quilliva Kashmir," the purple-skinned elf admitted. "But you didn't have to capture my friends as well! I didn't even want to return to this stupid kingdom!"

"Hmmm! Now hang on," Colb interjected. *Hmmm, I don't want Kashmir incriminating herself any more than she already has,* Colb thought.

He looked down at the Elvish guards. Five were injured, and the sixth looked to have perished. "Hmmm, although they've made our lives a challenge, these guards need medical attention, yes?" Colb pitched to Kashmir. "We should bring them to the city nearby, yes? Worry about ourselves once we know the injured are safe, yes?"

The elf huffed. "They brought us all the way to the outskirts of Falberin, and you want to bring them inside?! That's where Queen Eylbella is! We need to get as far away from here as possible."

"Please don't leave us…" an elvish guard choked, looking up at Kashmir. "You say the goblin wants to bring us into Falberin? Let him! Please… if you do, I'll *personally* tell the queen what you all did here… we'll bring you to her step as heroes, instead of as prisoners! Maybe she'll even restore your family's honor?"

Colb translated the Elvish plea for the other goblins.

"AaAaaaaahhhh, I like the idea of visiting the queen as hero goblins rather than as prisoner goblins, yes I do," 27 noted. "If we can get the queen on our side, we could pass through the Elvish Kingdom without problem!" The other goblins nodded in agreement.

"Um… I don't know…" Kashmir mumbled. "That just seems like a bad idea…"

"Hmmm, it's going to be okay, yes?" Colb promised. "We'll no longer be prisoners, and I'll personally do everything I can to make sure the queen doesn't hurt you. This is a chance to talk things through with your enemy, and that's always a good thing, yes?"

"Um… fine," the young elf conceded. "It seems my associates like your offer. We'll bring all of you to some healers *on the condition* that you free us and proclaim us heroes to Queen Eylbella."

"Deal," the guard replied. The other guards nodded to the terms as well.

With that, the goblins got to work. Using 27's *Yiklar Floating Bed* as a stretcher, Colb and 27 lifted the battered and fallen elves off the ground. Meanwhile, Stibs and Drek carved off the lionpig's head as a trophy – further proof of their heroism for when it was time to meet Queen Eylbella.

With the guards lifted and a trophy acquired, the group made their way – willingly, this time – towards the Elvish Kingdom's capital.

Hmmm, this went well! Colb thought with joy. *The guards are thankful, battling the lionpig went well, and I feel like we're setting a good example for Kashmir by giving aid to our enemies, yes? Falberin awaits!*

Chapter 19

QUEEN EYLBELLA

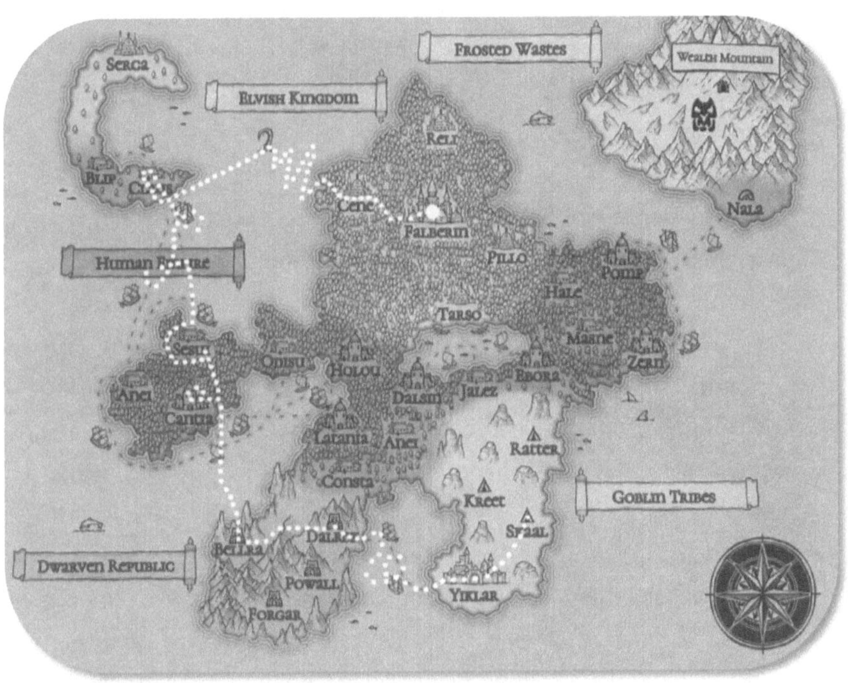

19. QUEEN EYLBELLA

As the team escorted the battered guards through the gates of Falberin, elves from the city quickly rushed in to assist with the transportation. Each elf looked vastly different from the previous – some had skin with a rocky texture, others were polka-dotted or striped. Many, but not all, emanated with unique magical energies.

The elves of the city led the team to a series of eight small huts, each built from marblelime: a plant-like stone, covered in smooth white bumps. From each hut exited a tall elf with pink-and-white swirling features around their eyes. These bright elves looked upon the fallen guards with kindness, placing their thumbs over the foreheads of the wounded.

With a sudden flash of pink light, each of the five wounded guards suddenly looked healthy as ever – a sight not unlike Vitra's potion healing Stibs in an instant back on Jaiphione's Crescent.

As the five warriors calmly dismounted the *Yiklar Floating Bed*, the eight healers bowed their heads somberly, chanting an elvish prayer for the fallen sixth guard. Having been bitten in the neck by the lionpig, he had entered Falberin already dead, and it seemed there was nothing more these healing elves could do for him.

Once the touching prayer – which requested Jaiphione to give grace and brightness to the fallen guard in his next life – was finished, a group of elves wearing red-and-purple robes lifted the body off the *Yiklar Floating Bed* and carried it away. As they left, 27 cautiously removed the covers from his levitating mattress, visibly uneased by the fact a dead body had been resting on his personal cot.

As 27 unfolded his *Yiklar Folding Cabin* and returned his magic bed to its rightful place inside, the five healed guards regrouped with the team – ready to fulfill their end of the bargain.

Once everyone was ready, the five guards escorted their heroes deeper into the elf-filled capital city. The crew eventually came upon a magnificent castle made of plant-based materials: thick marblelime walls, yellow-colored lemongranite columns, and vinelike pewterorange arches above each entrance and pathway. The castle felt alive, with plant-like citrus textures visible on every brick. The guards guided the prisoners through the pleasant-smelling fortress, towards the throne room.

"Hmmm, this is quite nice, yes?" Colb cheered, looking around at the plants and artwork surrounding him.

"Make no mistake – this is still a dire place," Kashmir murmured. Her sky-blue eyes looked a shade darker than normal as they darted around the room. The purple elf seemed to be searching for exits or signs of danger.

"Hmmm, we're being welcomed as heroes, yes? There's no reason to be enemies when you can be nice, yes?" Colb reminded.

"I know…" Kashmir muttered. "Still, we need to be careful. From what my father told me, Queen Eylbella can get furious in a moment. If we make her angry, it won't matter that we spared a few guards and killed a lionpig. Tell the others to never speak out-of-turn, and to never say anything rude or question something Queen Eylbella says. Only speak when spoken to, and remain agreeable and respectful."

Colb translated the purple elf's words for his companions, who nodded with understanding. 27 and Drek looked eager to impress the queen, as they adjusted their robe and crown respectively. Stibs was still lugging the lionpig's large severed head behind him, which occasionally dripped some blood onto the castle floor.

The guards led the crew into a royal area. This room was covered in magnificently detailed architecture, from an intricately carved timeline of previous rulers on the floor, to a magnificent throne made from marblelime and speckled with flakes of pewterorange in front of a large window. Elven guards stood stationed along the edges of the space: some armed with swords and daggers, others simply emanating with palpable innate magic.

Inlaid at the top of the queen's throne sat an attached glass orb filled with glittery green dust. A faint Elvish chant "Jaiphione, Jaiphione, Jaiphione…" could be heard lightly flowing from the spherical artifact.

Below the whispering orb sat an elvish woman, holding a fine lemongranite staff. She was adorned with the fanciest of green dresses, color-matched perfectly with the particles twisting and turning in the glass sphere above her head. Her skin was bright white like a fluffy cloud in spring, and her hair shined yellow like the morning sun. Her eyes were pure goldatinum, which flawlessly matched the crown set upon her head.

The group entered awkwardly, escorted by the team of guards from before. After they stepped into the room, Kashmir and the five guards performed a slight dance: an elegant elvish bow to address the royal queen.

The goblins watched these movements, then attempted to do the same. They flopped their arms around gracelessly, all four of them stumbling to the ground during their shaky attempts at the ritual.

When they were done with their pathetic greeting, the goblins stood quietly, waiting to be addressed before speaking – as Kashmir had requested of them.

"Your majesty," a guard suddenly announced, lowering his pointed ears as he spoke. "On our way into your city, we were attacked by a lionpig in the western forest. As our commanding officer retreated, and our magic-users left us for dead, these five heroes saved our lives. They slew the beast easily, then brought us to the Healing Eight for rejuvenation. The event resulted in one casualty, but it would have been six if not for these warriors."

Queen Eylbella sat silently, staring at the group. Stibs cautiously stepped forwards, placed the lionpig head on the ground before the queen, then stepped back in line with the rest of his crew without a word.

The queen looked down at the trophy expressionlessly, then turned her gaze back up to the crew before her. She tilted her head, and her voice soon entered everyone's minds telepathically. Colb shuddered with surprise as the queen's smooth words entered his brain, speaking fluently in his native language of Goblish.

"Quilliva! Step forward," Queen Elybella's voice commanded. Kashmir walked forward a small bit, bowing her head respectfully.

"I've heard that you left Tarso suddenly, traveling to Jaiphione's Crescent," the queen continued. "That's the very place your family wishes to wage war. What were you doing there?"

"I went there to… to hurt the humans," Kashmir admitted. "While I was there, I learned they weren't so bad. So, I changed my mind."

"You left to hurt the humans. The exact ones I explicitly barred your family from even *thinking* about?" Queen Eylbella replied. Her voice spat in Colb's head like a dwarven leader reprimanding a cowardly soldier.

"Um… yes," Kashmir confirmed. Her ears drooped as she stiffly admitted to her crimes before the queen.

"You've *clearly* performed treason by disobeying my direct orders for the Quilliva family to stop bringing attention to Jaiphione's Crescent. Avoiding war with the humans is a diplomatic nightmare, and your little escapade could have set us back decades. It seems my wishes were not made clear enough the first time. I should have you and your whole family executed for this."

"Rrghegh… that's stupid," Drek muttered.

"Excuse me!" Queen Eylbella gasped. Colb watched a look of horror seep into Kashmir's eyes.

"Step forward, goblin," the queen ordered. As her voice boomed in everyone's minds, the queen waved for Kashmir to retreat.

Kashmir silently stepped back into the group, and Drek waltzed forwards. "You *dare* call my policy stupid?" the queen demanded.

"Rrghegh… from what I've seen, she learned lesson already, and is strong fighter. To kill her would be waste of good elf," the crown-wearing goblin replied. The room went silent. Kashmir grit her teeth at the sound of Drek talking back to the queen.

"And who, pray tell, do you think you are?" Queen Eylbella spat. Colb adjusted his leather chestplate nervously, discomforted by the scene.

"Rrghegh… a hero. A warrior. That's what your own guards announced when we entered the room," Drek retorted.

"You think that scrappy little crown you're wearing allows you to speak over royalty?" Queen Eylbella demanded. Colb looked at the little goldatinum headwear sat upon Drek's head, which Borin had crafted from the pirate captain's treasure. It didn't look scrappy at all in Colb's opinion.

"Even a hero or warrior, would not DARE," she continued. The queen stomped her white staff onto the ground, and a resulting *BANG!* sound echoed throughout the chamber. "DARE speak to me like they own this place!"

Drek wrapped his arms silently in his cloak. Colb had a feeling the young goblin was preparing to draw his deadly iridhodium arrow. For a moment, silence sat frozen in the space like an ice chuck pressure-bound in the center of an iceberg. Some of the royal guards around the edges of the room began readying their swords and sharpened boomerangs, cautious of the scene.

Finally, to break the silence, Colb decided to speak out-of-turn. With a small voice, Colb replied, "Hmmm, but *he* is something more than just a hero or a warrior – he is goblin king, yes? This is why he can dare speak such a way, yes?" Kashmir snapped her head towards Colb with wide, are-you-crazy eyes.

"What, because he's wearing a little crown? You take me for a fool?" Queen Eylbella's telepathic voice spat in response. "*Everyone* knows that there's no king amongst the goblin tribes. You're nothing but a desert of decentralized, primitive beings that live in small wooden huts."

"Rrghegh," Drek said with a smile, removing his hands from his cloak. "No, your majesty… you are mistaken. I *am* king goblin. All goblin bow down to me."

Drek looked back at the other expectantly. Colb immediately dropped to his knees. Stibs and 27 hesitated, looked at the queen, looked at Drek's smug face, looked at each other, then also knelt.

"Rrghegh… and we only live in small wooden huts when we choose to. Others live in grand castles and magical cabins," Drek continued. He looked back at 27 expectantly. "Servant! Show her some proof," Drek ordered.

27 pulled the *Yiklar Folding Cabin* doorknob out from his pocket, and activated it, opening up the small building in an empty section of the throne room.

"Rrghegh… what more proof could you need?" Drek prodded. "I'm wearing an enchanted crown of pure goldatinum, my servant just pulled a house out of his pocket, and as your own guard stated, we *easily* defeated this lionpig that most of *your* servants fled from." Drek put his hand over the large lionpig trophy triumphantly. The head stood taller than his waist as it sat upon the floor. "Rrghegh… those things don't sound very primitive to me?"

"Hmmm… well, I was unaware of a kingdom amongst the goblins," the queen said, softening her eyes as her voice seeped into everyone's minds. "We thought you were separated into a series of tribes."

"Rrghegh… you speak of the old ways," Drek replied. "I united the tribes with my great might. Now, we are goblin kingdom. And I am king of kingdom."

"Hmmm, all hail King Drek, yes?" Colb threw in. Drek gestured to his little crown triumphantly.

"I see…" Queen Eylbella replied. "Well, the audience of another royal certainly outweighs my quarrel with your defending of one Quilliva Kashmir. Pray tell, your majesty, what brings you into my domain unsolicited?"

Drek hesitated, then glanced back at the other goblins for help. 27 moved within earshot of Drek and whispered, "AaAaaaaahhhh, this is good opportunity for Yiklar, yes it is. Say you are here to propose economic alliance between elves and goblins, yes you are."

Drek gave a slight smile to the queen, then walked backwards to be more in-line with 27. "Rrghegh… to propose eco-what?" he whispered through his smiling teeth.

"Propose economic alliance," 27 repeated quietly. Drek furrowed his brow a little bit.

"What are you muttering to your servant about?" the queen's voice sharply boomed into everyone's heads. "King Drek, what have you come to say to me? Answer me now." Drek stepped forwards again sheepishly, adjusting his crown as he walked.

"Rrghegh, yes, as I was saying… I am here for… rrg… to propose… rrg…" The crowned goblin glanced back at his friends again. 27 mouthed ec-on-om-ic towards the goblin, and Colb flashed a silvopper coin from his pocket as a helpful hint.

"To propose…?" Queen Eylbella prodded. Drek looked back at the queen.

"Rrghegh… to propose… rrg… Yes! To propose!" Drek's face lit up with an idea, and he dropped to one knee. "Rrghegh, as King Drek, I have come to propose marriage with Queen Elf-lady."

"What?" came as a simultaneous reply from a surprised Queen Eylbella, Stibs, 27, and Colb. One of the queen's guards whistled slightly at the announcement.

"Rrghegh… yes," Drek continued, standing back on two feet. "Rrghegh, I come to unite elves and goblins through marriage pact of goblin king with elf queen."

"…Me and you?" Queen Eylbella questioned skeptically.

"Yes," Drek responded with a nod. "Rrghegh. Me and you. Let's do this."

"I see…" the queen mumbled.

"Yes," Drek replied again. Colb mouthed what-is-the-plan-here to 27, who shrugged with a baffled expression.

"You know, I'm over 3,800 years old," Queen Eylbella countered.

"Ah. I like that," Drek replied.

The queen continued, "Considering you're a goblin, you look like you're probably… what? 25 years old?"

"Rrghegh, 20," Drek corrected.

"I see…" Queen Eylbella mumbled again.

"Rrghegh, right, you see… and you like what you see," Drek pushed.

Colb surveyed the room. Most of the queen's guards stood expressionlessly, professionally ignoring the conversation – but a few were wide-eyed, visibly unable to hide their interest in where this discussion was going. In contrast, Kashmir looked frozen with fear, like a deerdolphin that just swam into a seagullfisherman's net.

After a moment to gather her thoughts, the queen spoke again. "I apologize for insulting your crown. Now that I look at it again, it's quite nicely crafted."

Colb smiled. *Hmmm, if I ever see Borin again, I'll tell him Queen Eylbella said that, yes?* he thought. *I'll bet he'd get a kick out the royal compliment!*

Queen Eylbella continued, "Although I will most certainly outlive you, I will visit your kingdom in one calendar year. If I like what I see, I will consider your proposal."

"Rrghegh, that sounds most good, m'lady," Drek replied, tipping his crown. "Rrghegh… we have taken up enough time. My subjects," he gestured to the other goblins as he spoke, "and I shall now bid you farewell. I have very important king business overseas that I must be getting to. After that, I will return to goblin kingdom and prepare for your visit."

"This is acceptable," Queen Eylbella replied.

"Rrghegh… additionally, I will be taking the purple elf with me, should she wish to come, as she's the best warrior I've met from this kingdom," Drek continued. "Rrghegh, and you'll be granting her family back their honor… forgiving them for anything they've done in the past that you didn't like." Drek spun around, and gestured for everyone to follow him as he began walking out.

"Halt," Queen Eylbella's voice said. The face on her body had begun to frown. Drek stopped in his tracks. "Now, why should I allow that?" her voice boomed. "My kingdom shares an *enormous* border with the Human Empire. I've promised careful, thoughtful interactions with their Empress Cognemi to keep peace. The Quilliva's foolish actions this week put that all at risk – her family *cannot* go unpunished."

"Rrghegh… you promised the leader of the Human Empire that you would be thoughtful and careful?" Drek asked, turning around to make eye contact with Queen Eylbella. "I'll be sure to let her know that tying up kings, throwing them into carts, and treating them like *prisoners* is how you act thoughtfully around here."

"Now, I–" the queen defended, but Drek continued to speak.

"Rrghegh! When Empress Cognemi, Leader Glazeanvil, and Leader Boldpass ask me how my marriage proposal went, I'll be sure to let them know that *every* elf in this kingdom was a coward in combat, and treated me like scum. Every elf, that is, except for one – a powerful warrior named Kashmir. Rrghegh, so of course, Queen Eylbella went out of her way to *punish* that one elf, explicitly against my wishes. I'm sure they'd be interested to hear that," Drek threatened.

"You're allied with Empress Cognemi? With leaders from the Dwarven Republic as well?" Queen Eylbella inquired.

"Rrghegh, of course I am," Drek lied. "Rrghegh, and when I next see them, I would *love* to look the other way about how I've been treated in your kingdom… so long as you're not shooting down my most simple request, or continuing to treat me and my companions terribly from this point forwards."

"Of course not," Queen Eylbella's voice muttered. The queen shifted in her chair, making herself look more relaxed and welcoming. "As the Quilliva seems to have given a good impression of our culture to your majesty, they are yours to deal with as you wish from here on out. I will consider their slate clean from this day forwards." Kashmir's expression softened at those words.

"Additionally," the queen continued. "I will of course treat you, my suitor, and your companions with *utmost* respect from this point forwards. You said you have business overseas to attend to, correct? Allow me to offer a royal envoy to bring you across my lands, and some more transportation for once you reach the sea."

"Rrghegh, that's more like it!" Drek cheered. "Royal navigator... where should she bring us?" Drek looked over at Stibs. The old goblin frantically pulled out his map, scanned it, then mouthed Coast-Of-Re-li to the charlatan king.

"I'm headed off the coast of... Real... Wrell-ee?" Drek replied phonetically.

"I see," Queen Eylbella responded. "I'll order a royal envoy to bring you to Reli, and I'll have something similar to a boat prepared to bring you wherever you need to go from there. Apologies that you traveled so far without a royal envoy, by the way. Had I known you were coming, I would've prepared one to greet you before you even set foot in the Elvish Kingdom."

"Rrghegh, I am rather forgiving king, fortunately for you," Drek replied. "Your offering is accepted. We will leave now. Rrghegh... I'll see you one year from today in my kingdom's capital, Ratter." Drek bowed awkwardly, then together with his team, waltzed right out the castle doors. They were free, and the journey to the Frosted Wastes – and by extension, to Wealth Mountain – was back on.

As the team exited from the castle doors, everyone looked around at each other, wide-eyed with surprise at how well that interaction had gone.

"Hmmm! That was fantastic, Drek!" Colb cheered.

Stibs slapped the crown-wearing goblin on the back. "Hurmph, good show!"

"Um… tell Drek I appreciate what he did back there," Kashmir muttered. Colb translated her words, nudging Drek's arm with glee as he did so.

As a group of elvish royal servants mobilized to rapidly prepare a vehicle for Drek and his team, 27 made a cheerful announcement to the group. "AaAaaaaahhhh, we're off to the Frosted Wastes, just like we planned!" he said. "For Wealth Mountain!"

"Hurmph! For the Kreet tribe!" Stibs rejoiced.

"Hmmm! For all the tribes, yes?" Colb threw in.

"Rrghegh, for my Goblin Kingdom that I'm planning to make!" Drek cheered, lowering his voice as he spoke, so as not to reveal his falsehoods to any nearby elves that might know Goblish.

Kashmir smiled. "For seeing the world, finding my purpose, and maybe to meet a winter foxferret like Borin suggested!" she added.

"Hmmm, you don't *have* to come anymore, unless you want to, yes?" Colb reminded Kashmir. "We'd love to have you come with us – but your family is forgiven. You can choose to stay here if you wish!"

"I'm glad my family's safe… but I'm sick of living in this kingdom. I want to see what else is out there," the young elf replied to Colb. "I've got thousands of years to sit around with my family… for now, I want to keep exploring. My destiny turned out *not* to be on Jaiphione's Crescent, so I want to go find it somewhere else!"

"Hmmm, then welcome aboard!" Colb cheered with a smile.

Hmmm, I love my team! the chef goblin thought as he watched

Queen Eylbella's servants prepare a royal vehicle. *Everything's coming together for us now, yes? Finally: Wealth Mountain, here we come!*

Chapter 20

TOWN OF TUNES

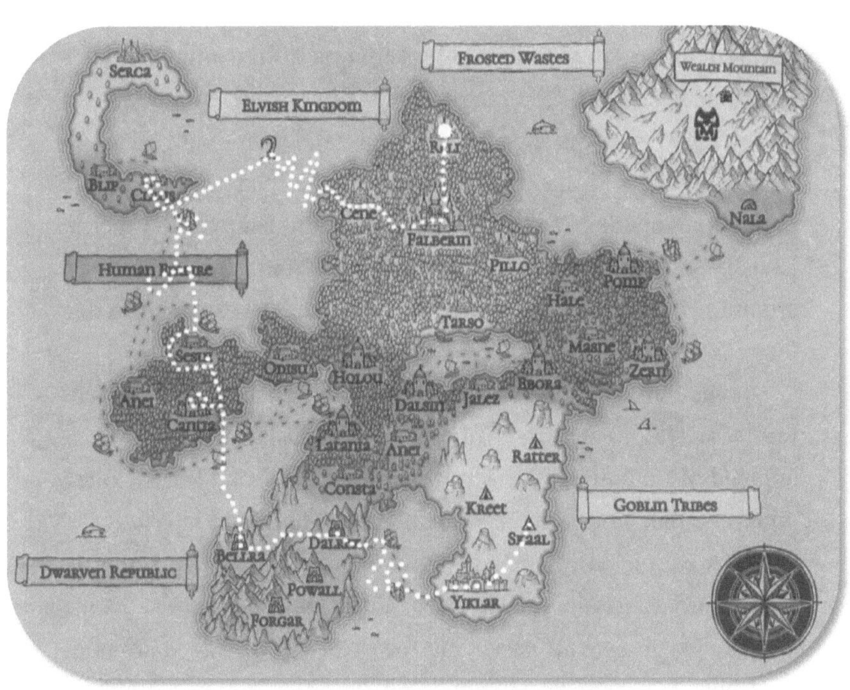

20. TOWN OF TUNES

In stark contrast to the cramped prison cart which brought the crew into Falberin, the gang left the city in style, riding as passengers of a cozy longwagon prepared by some of the queen's servants. This stylish vehicle was 120 feet long, with an interior covered in silk fabrics even smoother than 27's attire. Although it was camelmule-drawn, the front of the longwagon had been adored with an assortment of flowers, which both visually blocked the passengers from seeing the camelmules, as well as fragrantly covered up any smell that might be coming off the animals.

Along the roof of the longwagon sat twelve elven guards: six non-magical warriors sporting weaponry and armor, and six robe-wearing elves with their innate magic at-the-ready to protect the goblin king inside. As the dozen guards mumbled to each other in Elvish, Colb toyed with the glowing *Yiklar Amulet of Open Ears* around his neck, pleased to see none of the elves assigned to this longwagon had the ability to block magic.

As the long vehicle traveled out of Falberin and towards Reli, the team was treated to a fine meal of elvish delicacies. They enjoyed bisonquail steaks, lettuceshrimp salads, and brassleaf tea with rabbitbee honey and cowmammoth milk mixed into it.

After eating, Stibs and 27 took the remainder of the trip as an opportunity to get some rest. Drek, Colb, and Kashmir sat awake a bit longer, however, surveying the brass-tinted leafy shrubs of the Elvish Kingdom passing by.

As Drek polished his crown against a silk pillow, he looked at Kashmir and tilted his head. "Rrghegh… what is Quilliva?" he asked after a moment.

Kashmir looked up from a window. Colb's ears perked up, and he scootched himself closer to the two, ready to translate her

Elvish responses for his friend. "Queen elf-lady called you Quilliva, but you called yourself Kashmir," Drek clarified.

"I am Quilliva Kashmir. That means Kashmir is my name, and Quilliva is my family name," Kashmir responded.

"Rrghegh, goblins don't have family name," Drek replied after listening to Colb's translation.

"Hmmm, I'm just Colb, yes?" Colb added. "I have sister, but she is just Vrel. Our bond is just called sister and brother, yes?"

"As a name, Quilliva represents my family in Tarso," Kashmir explained. "Along with myself, it refers to my older sister Quilliva Vekoona, my mother Quilliva Feshminnah, and my father Quilliva Marinoe. We're bound by the name Quilliva, because anything that one Quilliva does will reflect upon all four of us."

"Hmmm, what are they like?" Colb asked.

"Kind of like me, I suppose," Kashmir responded. "My father was brave and decisive. He was working as a guard in Tarso when he met my mother. She fell into a sacred lake south of our town, and didn't know how to swim. He was nearby, pulled her out, and the rest was history."

"Hmmm, but the water would've frozen when your parents touched it, yes?" Colb asked.

"No," Kashmir replied. "My father never had any innate magic. My mother does have power over cold, but not enough to freeze something. She passed her ability down to Vekoona and myself, but I'm the only one that destroys everything I touch. Feshminnah and Vekoona both just make things a little colder."

Colb continued to translate Kashmir's words as the conversation went on.

"Rrghegh... you said you dislike royalty," Drek reminisced. "Do all Quilliva feel this way?"

"Well, obviously executing my father didn't improve our

opinions of Queen Eylbella," Kashmir huffed.

"Rrghegh… what about other royalty?" Drek asked.

"Even before my father's passing, our whole family felt uncomfortable with the idea of an elf being born into power," Kashmir answered. "My father was the most outspoken against the concept of royalty, but all four of us would sometimes joke about moving to the Dwarven Republic as a family. We wouldn't know any of their customs, or even their language, but at least the leaders there must prove themselves to be elected."

"Rrghegh… what about very first elf ruler? They weren't born into power," Drek pointed out. "They couldn't have been, if they were first. They must've proved themselves by uniting your people?"

"That's true… but as soon their child succeeded them, a millennium of unworthy, born-into-power rulers began," Kashmir countered. "So, still not very good."

"Hmmm, you said your family thought about leaving the Elvish Kingdom, yes?" Colb threw in. "Why didn't they?"

"My mother says that moving away without a valid reason would be frowned upon," Kashmir huffed. "We would be shunned by our own people if we ever wanted to come back."

"Rrghegh, queen elf-lady said Quilliva are mine to deal with," Drek recalled. "Does that just mean Quilliva Kashmir, or the whole Quilliva family?"

Kashmir poked at a nearby silk pillow, ripping holes into it with her frosty touch. "Knowing the queen, she meant my whole family. She views her subjects more as family units than as individuals."

"Rrghegh… couldn't I order your family to move anywhere you want, then? Other elves can't frown at you for following orders of mighty king."

Kashmir smiled. "You aren't really a king, though," she replied. "Once you're found out, the queen would demand we all move back or be banished forever. Come to think of it, one she finds out about you, she might even retract her forgiveness and restoration of my family's honor…"

"Rrghegh, well that's not going to happen, because I'm not *going* to be found out," Drek countered. "I will make myself real king before queen elf-lady visits Ratter next year. I will become rich, bring my fortune to Ratter, and unite the tribes with my great might before she even realizes I lied."

Kashmir let out a worried sigh. "If you think you can do all that before you're found out, then yes, I'm sure the rest of my family would enjoy an amicable excuse to move out of this place. One that doesn't result in us all being exiled or killed."

"Rrghegh… I will do all that," Drek promised. "Rrghegh, and you know what? I won't have child, either. My system will be better. I'll choose the most worthiest goblin to succeed me. Someone who came from the guts of Ratter, just like I did. I'll find a lowly thief that knows they could be something more, and take them under my wing so they have a chance to prove themself."

"Your dreams are even bigger than mine," Kashmir observed.

"Rrghegh, my words are no dream – they are facts of what I will do," Drek challenged. "Rrghegh, watch: Colb, would the Skaal tribe like to join the Ratter tribe in my goblin kingdom?" Drek pitched.

"Hmmm, I could bring the idea to the elder, and put a good word in for you, yes?" Colb replied.

Drek smiled, his yellow tongue gliding across his razor-sharp teeth. "Making progress every second," he announced, getting a small smile out of Kashmir.

"Well… your ideas sound interesting, Drek," Kashmir

muttered. "Regardless of how they turn out, thank you again for what you did back there… seeing you talk back to the queen was scary, but I think she was seriously considering executing me before you talked her out of it. So, I… um, appreciate that. That, and the fact you bought a year of peace for my family. Perhaps a lifetime of peace, if you do manage to become a king, or at least keep the ruse going."

Colb glowed as he translated these words, feeling so proud of the young Kashmir for sharing her feelings with Drek like this.

"Rrghegh, you're welcome. Queen was being dumb and unreasonable… it only made sense for me to point it out. Rrghegh, and I assure you – your family will see a lifetime of peace. I'll order their relocation to *wherever* you want as soon as we finish looting Wealth Mountain, and I'll most certainly establish my goblin kingdom before next year. You have nothing to fear!"

"Thanks," Kashmir replied, cracking another smile at Drek's reassurance. With that, she turned back to the window, quietly gazing at the numerous brassleaf shrubs lining the woodland path.

The rest of the journey to Reli was relaxing and comfortable. The longwagon had no issues moving through the forest, and the dozen rooftop guards warded off any dangerous animals that might have otherwise considered approaching the travelers.

As the longwagon approached the village of Reli, the crew awoke to a symphony of music. "AaAaaaaahhhh, we must be close, yes we must be!" 27 proclaimed, jumping to his feet and dancing along with the tune. "I hear a symphony of song welcoming us, yes I do!"

"It's not for us," Kashmir replied with Colb translating for her. "That's just what Reli sounds like. A large population of Reli focuses their magic through instruments and song."

"AaAaaaaahhhh, magic through instruments? That is good

idea for a Yiklar product, yes it is," 27 cheered.

As the longwagon entered Reli, the crew looked out the windows to survey the villagers. Sure enough, just about every elf in sight was holding an instrument, playing in harmony with their fellow elves. This combined effort across the entire town mixed into one miraculous, ever-shifting, non-stop song.

Colb watched as an adult elf with shiny sappherald earrings and lustrous red hair played along on their banjo. Every time they strummed the instrument, a burst of wind flew out from their hands, launching leaves around them into the air.

Elsewhere, an elderly elf with curly gray hair played along to the tune on a wooden flute. With each note she blew, a new beautiful flower magically sprouted in her garden. "Hmmm, this is quite amazing, yes?" Colb muttered in astonishment.

Colb looked around some more, eventually landing his eyes on a young elf tapping a small drum down a nearby street. His music didn't seem to be creating any magical effects, yet he was undeterred from contributing to Reli's continuous song.

After a few moments, the drum-playing boy suddenly tripped, dropping his drum and scraping his knee. A girl about the same age as him rushed over, playing a healing tune for him on her slide whistle. As she blew on the little instrument, the red scrape along the boy's leg sealed up, and the swelling went away.

The camelmule-drawn longwagon continued to trudge through Reli until eventually coming to a stop on the northeastern shore of the Elvish Kingdom.

The crew exited the longwagon, and with some prompting from the dozen royal guards, approached the watery shore. Once they were close to the sea, the youngest of the royal guards – probably only a hundred years or so older than Kashmir – pulled out a green ocarina and stepped past them, into the water.

The guard's light blue hair glistened below the rising sun as she gracefully held the green instrument up to her lips. She began to softly exhale and move her fingers, contributing to the continuous, beautiful melody of Reli with her ocarina.

A quartet of spring robinfinches flew in from nearby, singing along to her music and perching on her shoulders. This warm scene of companionship reminded Colb of the alchemist Vitra, whose winter foxferret pet liked perching upon her shoulders as well.

"Ragh, welcome to Reli," the guard suddenly said in Goblish, looking up from her ocarina. She then danced with a ballerina-like bow aimed towards Drek. At the end of her bow, she blew lightly into her instrument, and the spring robinfinches upon her shoulders lowered their heads in bow as well.

The crew stared at the elf as she continued to lower her head. After about ten seconds, Kashmir summoned a small chunk of ice, and flicked it into Drek's side. "Rrghegh… uh, oh! …At ease," he said to the elf. She elegantly stood back up, watching the crew with her calm, pink-colored eyes.

"Rrghegh… what uh… what er, is your name?" Drek asked.

"Ragh, I am Oceanbreeze Trisgwn," she replied in fluent Goblish. "I'm a member of the royal guard, and your envoy for this evening. Her majesty sent me with you because I was born and raised here in Reli."

"Rrghegh… miss elf, er, Trisgwn," Drek replied, adjusting his crown. "What… brings you, er, to my domain unsolicited?"

"Hurmph, this isn't your domain," Stibs whispered sharply to Drek.

"MMmMmmmm, I don't think he knows what domain means," 27 added quietly.

"Rrghegh… I don't know what unsolicited means either,"

Drek admitted softly.

"Ragh… there are two reasons Queen Eylbella chose to place me here today," Trisgwn announced in reply. "I am here both for my fluency in your native tongue, and for my ability to summon your ride." The elf then held her ocarina at-the-ready, and stepped further backwards into the water. As she played, the spring robinfinches flew off her shoulders, and five rubbery brown creatures swam up to her from nearby in the sea.

"Ragh… these are deerdolphins," Trisgwn cheered, patting one of them on the nose. "They're very intelligent creatures, although also quite skittish. They need to breathe air to survive, so they always swim right at the surface of the water."

"Rrghegh, okay," Drek mumbled, scratching the skin under his crown with one of his clawed hands.

"Ragh… I've summoned them so you can ride them wherever you'd like," Trisgwn clarified. "They're faster than boats, and much more intelligent, too."

"Rhe! I see," Drek exclaimed with understanding. "Then we'll be off to the Frosted Wastes to take care of my kingly business," he announced.

"Hurmph, took us long enough!" Stibs added.

Trisgwn played another song, which seemed to keep the skiddish deerdolphins calm as more royal guards trudged into the water and snapped white-colored saddles onto their bodies.

Once each deerdolphin was properly equipped, the royal guards helped the goblins mount them. Next, Colb watched cautiously from atop his rubbery steed as a guard wrapped Kashmir in an elven blanket, then carefully placed her upon the fifth deerdolphin's saddle. Much like Kashmir's dress, the blanket appeared to be immune to her frosty powers – thus protecting both the deerdolphin she sat upon, and the water around her, from freezing.

Once everyone was settled onto a deerdolphin, Trisgwn let out a complicated tune on her ocarina, to which the creatures perked their rubbery ears. Once Trisgwn finished playing her musical message, each of the aquatic steeds let out a small bellow of understanding, then zoomed off into the distance, carrying their five passengers towards the isolated Frosted Wastes. With his green ears flapping in the wind, Colb looked out to the vast sea before him, excited to finally be approaching the legendary Wealth Mountain.

Chapter 21

VOYAGE OF DESTINY

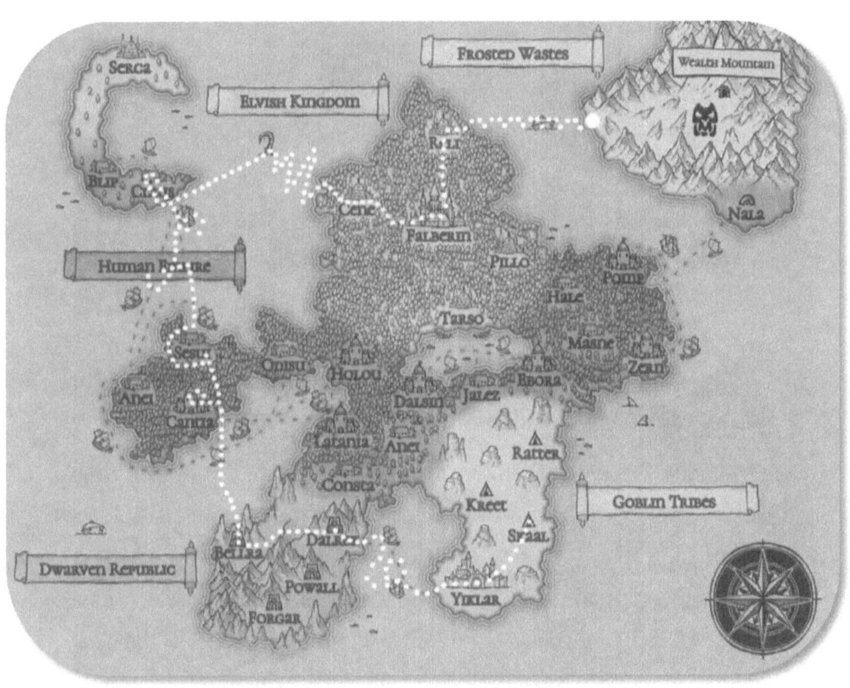

21. VOYAGE OF DESTINY

The school of deerdolphins sped across the water all day, eventually reaching the Frosted Wastes at nightfall. After the crew dismounted their steeds, the rubbery creatures grouped together to preserve warmth in the chilly waters.

"Hmmm, thank you for the trip, yes?" Colb called out to the deerdolphins. A few of them let out soft squeaks as they fell asleep near the shore's edge.

"Hurmph, I don't think they understand Goblish," Stibs chuckled.

"AaAaaaaahhhh, but it's nice of Colb to have thanked them anyway," 27 said. The noble goblin activated his *Yiklar Folding Cabin* as he spoke. "I'm sure they could sense the sentiment, yes they could."

"Rrghegh, it's cold here," Drek complained with a shiver.

"Seems fine to me," Kashmir cheered, diving into a pile of snow. The young elf nearly disappeared as her white dress camouflaged her amongst the blankets of frost.

"Hurmph… whereami?" Stibs mumbled, pulling out his *Yiklar Map of Finding Location*. A brilliant light flashed onto the map, forming into a point on the western coast of the Frosted Wastes. Suddenly, out from the dot, the lights started to crawl eastwards, displaying a path through the mountain range and up to a cave entrance clearly marked as "Wealth Mountain." Below the cave entrance sat a dangerous-looking mark of a monster.

"Hurmph, that's convenient," Stibs announced. "1 laid out exactly where we need to go. It'll probably take a couple days to walk this path – and the Frosted Wastes certainty doesn't have ideal conditions for walking – but if we take occasional breaks in 27's cabin, I think we'll be alright."

"Rrghegh, I'm ready to find that goldatinum and start my kingdom!" Drek cheered.

"Hmmm, we can't forget about the howling sound that 1's oracle heard, yes?" Colb worried. "The sound that might be linked to some horrible monster in this area, yes? Hmmm, we shouldn't get careless, yes?"

"Rrghegh, did you forget about our superweapon?" Drek countered.

"AaAaaaaahhhh, that's right!" 27 cheered, holding up the *Yiklar Spear of Irreversible Death.* "Nothing can stop this!"

"Rrghegh, I meant our other superweapon," Drek said, pointing his gnarly green finger at a pile of snow nearby.

"This is literally the best place I've ever been," the muffled voice of Kashmir exclaimed from under it.

"Hurmph, with Kashmir's powers, 27's spear, and my ingenuity, nothing's going to get in our way, Colb!" Stibs agreed.

"This seems like the last leg of our journey together, and I've come to care deeply about all of you," Colb clarified. "Hmmm, I just don't want any of my close friends to get hurt, yes?"

"AaAaaaaahhhh, then let's take a nice rest out from the cold," 27 pitched, opening the door to his *Yiklar Folding Cabin.* "That way, we'll start our journey with fresh minds and warm bodies, yes we will. The perfect combination to keep ourselves sharp and safe!"

The crew nodded, pleased by 27's plan. With that, the goblins head into their climate-controlled *Yiklar Folding Cabin.*

As the goblins shared a quick dinner to end off the day, Kashmir built a bed of snow outside. When Colb left to check on her, the young elf announced that she wanted to spend the night a "comfortable snowbank," rather than inside the cramped, goblin-sized cabin.

Once it was time for bed, Colb pulled his cot over to a window, such that he could watch over Kashmir as she slept amongst the elements. As Colb looked out along the vast wasteland of snow beyond the glass, he reflected on his journey so far – the friends he'd made, the places he'd seen, and the distance he'd traveled. *Hmmm, it's hard to believe we've almost made it to Wealth Mountain!* he thought to himself. *Although this landscape is foreign and scary, I find myself eager to explore it with my good friends, yes? Wealth Mountain, here we come!*

With that, Colb laid down on his side, watching Kashmir through the window until he drifted off to sleep.

When morning came, a spark of excitement flew around within the goblin crew. Even Drek jumped out of his beanbag chair at the first sign of sunlight, exclaiming "Rhe rhe, soon I'll be rich!" as he did so.

"Hurmph, look at you! The first one awake, eh?" Stibs cheered, rubbing his eyes as he sat up.

Colb turned to the window, where he saw Kashmir waking up under beams of sunlight spilling over the horizon. "Hmmm, off to Wealth Mountain, yes?" he rejoiced.

"To Wealth Mountain!" the other goblins cheered in reply.

The group quickly gathered up their things, and began their long trudge northeast through the snow. As they moved, Colb and Kashmir kept an eye out for any winter foxferrets that might consider befriending the purple-skinned elf.

As expected, the cold air of these Frosted Wastes took a toll on the goblins, requiring them to periodically stop and rest in the climate-controlled *Yiklar Folding Cabin.* The Frosted Wastes were a cold and barren place, filled with dull, stick-like stones protruding up from the ground. The bright morning sun reflected off the snowy landscape with a blinding white hue, making it hard for the goblins to look upwards at the mountain range ahead of them.

The journey took three days of walking in total, slowly wearing away at the spirit of the travelers. Nevertheless, the potential of fortune, destiny, and new winter foxferret friends ahead kept everyone moving, excited for what the future had in store.

Stibs walked in front, navigating for the others with his *Yiklar Map of Finding Location*. As the third day of travel entered late afternoon, the old goblin spoke fondly of their progress. "Hurmph, look at that!" Stibs exclaimed, pointing out an exceptionally tall summit in the mountain range nearby. "That's got to be Wealth Mountain. There's only another mile to go, and we should find some sort of cave entrance to the goldatinum."

Colb, who had generally been focusing his weary eyes downwards to avoid the sun's reflection off the arctic landscape, now finally glanced up to see what Stibs was pointing out. Sure enough, a glimmering peak stood before him, two times taller than all the other mountains in the Frosted Wastes. A thick stream of ice curved down along Wealth Mountain's summit, like an extravagant waterfall that had been frozen in time.

"Rrghegh... maybe we rest for today, and get goldatinum tomorrow," Drek replied with a shiver.

"I could keep going," Kashmir added smugly. Colb shook his head, deciding not to translate her reply to the freezing Drek.

"Hurmph, I'm pretty cold too, but I think we could make it another mile," Stibs countered.

GGGgggggrgrrrorrooooooooooooooooooooooo! a low, pained howl suddenly echoed throughout the mountain range. Immediately, the wind started to pick up, knocking Drek off his feet and covering the rest of the team in a veil of sleet.

"Hmmm... what... what was that?" Colb worried, shivering

from both cold and fear and he pushed the ice off his armor.

"MMmMmmmm, that sounded like horrible, deep howl to me, yes it did," 27 announced, drawing his *Yiklar Spear of Irreversible Death.* "Kind of like what 1 warned us about, after listening to the good oracle 67…"

"It sounds like something screaming in pain," Kashmir muttered.

Another loud *GGggrrrrggrooooool* cried throughout the mountain range. A rough blizzard started to pick up, and a swirling vortex of snow touched down at the base of Wealth Mountain – less than a mile away from the goblin.

"Hmmm! Is that a snow tornado?!" Colb exclaimed. "Did the howling cause that?!"

"Hurmph, maybe we *have* gone far enough for today," Stibs retracted.

The blizzard started to pick up as the howling continued, making it so Colb could no longer see his friends, nor track the icy vortex that had touched down in the distance.

"Hurmph! Everyone follow my voice!" Stibs shouted. Colb's ears perked up as he listened. Suddenly, Drek came back into view, having lit a torch with his tinderbox. The young goblin held one of his hands over the flame protectively, shielding it from the assailing snow.

"Rrghegh, where are we going?" Drek called out.

"Hurmph, I saw a small cave about a quarter mile back," Stibs shouted. "Let's retreat to that so we have some shelter, then rest and regroup. Move, move!"

With that, the crew fled westward, away from the freak weather event beneath Wealth Mountain. Everyone called out their own names periodically, to ensure nobody had gotten lost or sucked up by a tornado.

Stibs successfully led the group to a small cutout in another mountain, where everyone could finally get out of the snow and see each other again. As the team panted, looking around to make sure nobody had been lost, 27 activated his *Yiklar Folding Cabin.*

"MMmMmmmm… that was scary," the noble announced. "AaAaaaaahhhh, but that was good thinking with this cave, Stibs, yes it was. The *Yiklar Folding Cabin* should be safe under this shelter… if that icy vortex comes by, we'll be glad the cabin's sitting in a cave instead of out in the open, yes we will be."

With that, the crew piled into the cabin. Even Kashmir was quick to squeeze into the safe building, rather than sleeping outside like she had done for the past few nights of travel. The team rushed to the cabin's living area, silently taking a moment to gather their breath and think about what they'd just witnessed.

"Hmmm! Those weather events *definitely* happened right after the howling, yes?" Colb said after a moment.

"Rrghegh, and did you see how it got way worse after the second howl?!" Drek added.

"MMmMmmmm… let's not get ahead of ourselves, gentlegoblins," 27 countered. "Maybe that howl was just… sound of wind going through mountains? Maybe weather event was happening anyway, yes it was, and howling was just part of it?"

"It sounded like some huge creature screaming out in pain," Kashmir muttered.

"Hurmph… I may be new to visiting this region, but I've read a lot about nature and weather," Stibs said. "I've never heard of weather that sounded like a… like a monster like that. If anything, that reminded me of the, uh… the… the, that summer antlizard's screech back in the Dwarven Republic. You guys remember that? That ear-piercing screech?"

"Hmmm! It sounded a bit like a furnace, yes?" Colb

reminisced.

"Rrghegh, I remember that," Drek agreed. "The summer antlizard was huge. It lived in a mountain range, and it could breathe lava... and look where we are now. We're in another mountain range, we're hearing another screech, and it seems like the very elements have turned on us. This *must* be another super monster."

"Hurmph, but this time, we don't have an army with us," Stibs grumbled.

"MMmMmmmm, but we do have the *Yiklar Spear of Irreversible Death* for a change," 27 noted. "A super monster seems like an ideal foe to use it on, yes it does. 1 certainly thought of everything when he gave us this gift!"

"What about helping our enemies?" Kashmir asked, looking at Colb. "Whatever out there sounds like it's very upset. Maybe we can reason with it?"

"Hmmm, Kashmir thinks we should try reasoning with the monster... perhaps helping it, since it sounds like it's in pain, yes?" Colb translated. "I agree, yes?" he added.

"MMmMmmmm... I don't know. We're all exhausted; why don't we have a meal, get some sleep to clear our minds, and come up with a plan in the morning? Perhaps the blizzard will have even subsided by then, yes it perhaps will have."

As usual, 27 had a point. Everyone agreed to stop talking about this potential new threat for the night, and prepared themselves for bed.

Colb made a meal for the team with scraps and leftovers from the kitchen, then plated everything in the dining area.

"No matter what happens, tomorrow we really will finish our quest, yes?" he announced, trying to lighten the mood as everyone grabbed a seat.

"Rrghegh… tomorrow my kingdom begins," Drek agreed.

"Hurmph, I'm just glad we're finally finishing this up. It feels like we took the longest, most inefficient route to the Frosted Wastes," Stibs grumbled. "If we took a boat straight from Yiklar, we could've completed this journey three times in a row at this point."

"AaAaaaaahhhh, but you must remember the Yiklar way, Stibs!" 27 countered.

"Hurmph, I'm from Kreet," Stibs retorted.

"Quality defeats quantity: that is the Yiklar way!" 27 clarified. "It is better that we took a long journey, during which we made many friends, than if we had taken some short ones. I feel that our adventure has been one of the highest quality. Much like I am honored to sell the most flawlessly crafted goods from the Yiklar tribe, I, too, am proud to have traveled on such a life-changingly high-quality journey with the four of you, yes I am."

Kashmir cracked a small smile as she munched on her meal. Colb's eyes lightened, pleased to see Kashmir feeling joy from 27's words.

After they finished their meals, Kashmir sauntered over to the living area, where she slumped down on the couch – which immediately became frostbitten upon contact with the cold elf. The four goblins retired to their sleeping area, curling up on their little cots to rest for a potentially life-threatening encounter in the morning.

Chapter 22

THE YIKLAR WAY

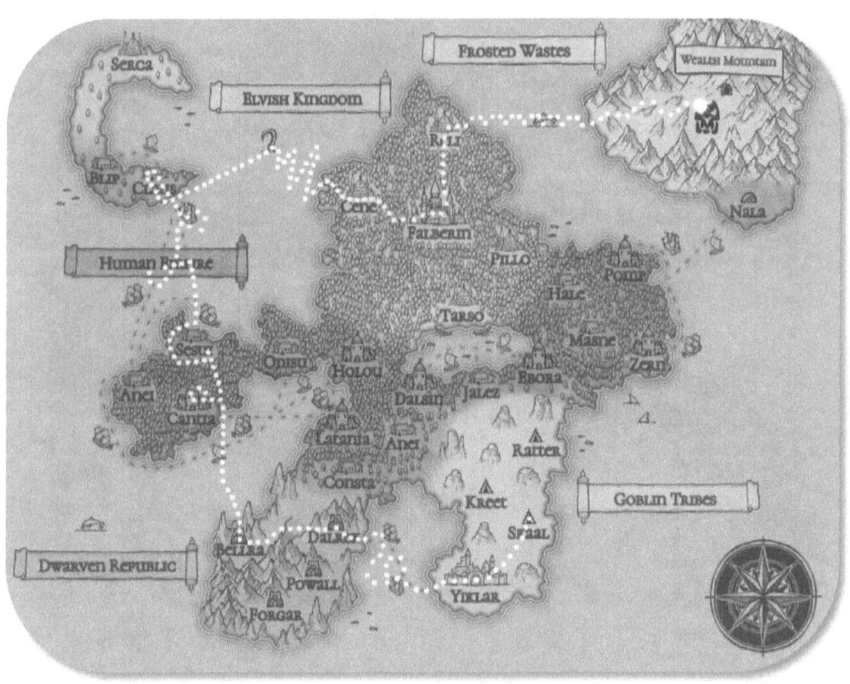

22. THE YIKLAR WAY

As morning arrived, the goblin crew's excitement to finish their quest came mixed with anxiety about facing the threatening howls outside. Colb went straight to the kitchen after he woke up, cooking a meal to calm his nerves. Stibs sat in the center of the dance floor, drawing out a combat plan with some ink and an old sheet of paper. 27 danced next to him – although the disco ball was turned off – getting out his last-minute jitters like Colb.

"Hurmph! What equipment do we all have?" Stibs asked the room. "It'll be easier to make a plan if I can see everything available to us." The old goblin started a pile on the dance floor next to himself with his blowgun, his *Yiklar Blowgun Darts of Freezing*, and his *Yiklar Shield of Reflecting*.

Colb paused his meal-making process in the kitchen, and walked over to toss his *Yiklar Wand of Rainfall*, the shield he'd gotten from Skaal, and the healing potion he'd made back at Vitra's Lab into the mix. "Hmmm, I'm wearing this too, yes?" he added, gesturing to his leather armor.

"Hmmm, I also have this," Colb said, placing a telescope into the pile. "Borin gave it to me, yes? It's what we used to spot that camouflaged octopusduck in the sea, back on the pirate ship."

He put his hands in his pockets, feeling around. "Hmmm, and one silvopper coin. I found it in a fountain, back in Cantia with 27. I'm not sure why, but I suppose I've been holding onto it all this time for good luck, yes?"

"Hurmph… this is some good stuff," Stibs grumbled, looking over the supplies. He didn't seem particularly interested in the silvopper coin, so Colb kept it in his pocket.

"AaAaaaaahhhh, and I have the *Yiklar Spear of Irreversible Death*," 27 threw in. "I've got my Yiklar *Bag of Traveling*

Inventory as well, yes I do, in case we want to buy something?"

"Rrghegh… bow and arrow…" Drek mumbled from his beanbag chair.

"I just have myself," Kashmir muttered from the living room. She was sitting cross-legged on the couch, with the tip of her head touching the cabin's goblin-height ceiling.

"Hurmph, alright," Stibs muttered, looking over the team's assets. "We should buy something from 27, perhaps an item to help protect whoever holds the spear. Another shield, maybe."

"AaAaaaaahhhh, buying something sounds like most excellent idea!" 27 cheered.

"Hurmph, Drek? Don't you have a treasure chest of money somewhere around here?" Stibs inquired.

The goblins looked over at Drek, who hadn't moved from his spot on the beanbag chair. "…NO," he grumbled. "Rrghegh… all funds were used up to make crown," he clarified.

"Hurmph, I specifically recall helping you carry that treasure chest back to the pirate ship *after* your crown was already made," Stibs countered. "There were definitely some coins left in it."

"Rrghegh… fine, fine," Drek admitted. The goblin flopped onto the ground, then pulled his treasure chest out from behind the beanbag chair. "You have to buy something for me," he grumbled, pulling out a small handful of iridhodium coins. He slid them towards the dance floor, then closed his chest and hopped back into the beanbag chair.

Stibs picked up the dozen iridhodium coins and presented them to 27. "Hurmph… what can these buy?"

"AaAaaaaahhhh," 27 said, lowering his voice a little. "Just one iridhodium piece is quite rare to come by, and highly valued since it's an important material in some Yiklar-made goods… combine those coins with what I've got left in my *Yiklar Bank Account*, and we can afford some most excellent items, yes we can." Stibs smiled, tossing the iridhodium coins next to the pile of equipment.

With that, the goblins got to work. While 27 rifled through a *Yiklar Catalog*, looking for products that might be useful, Stibs worked to organize the weapons they already had. Colb returned to his meal-making process nearby, throwing ideas around with Stibs as he cooked.

"Hurmph, I don't think we want to magically summon more ice if we're in a blizzard," Stibs mumbled, pushing his *Yiklar Blowgun Darts of Freezing* to the side.

"Hmmm, the *Yiklar Wand of Rainfall* might be a bad idea too, yes?" Colb noted. "We don't want to worsen the weather if it's already terrible, yes?"

"Hurmph, do we have anything that could help us see through a blizzard?" Stibs inquired.

"Hmmm! Perhaps the magic telescope that Borin gave me, yes?" Colb pitched.

"Hurmph, you're right! I'll bet that will work," Stibs agreed. "I wish we had more than one!"

"AaAaaaaahhhh, I think I could help with that," 27 said. The noble wagged his finger as he flipped to a specific page in the *Yiklar Catalog*. He opened the booklet to a picture of dark blue goggles with light purple swirls painted along the frames.

"These are *Yiklar Goggles of Vision in Darkness and Harsh Conditions*," 27 cheered, presenting the page to Colb and Stibs.

"That's an awful name," Kashmir threw in from the other side of the cabin.

"MMmMmmmm, what did she say?" 27 asked, looking at Colb for a translation.

"Hmmm, nothing," Colb lied. "Those goggles look perfect, yes?"

"AaAaaaaahhhh, yes, they are most perfect – and they happen to be on extra special good deal offer today, too! That means they're less than half what they normally cost – we can easily afford more than one if we buy them soon!"

After some more deliberation, the three goblins came to an agreement on what to buy. As Colb called everyone into the dining room to enjoy a morning meal, Stibs began to make some purchases with 27.

Colb placed a plate of fried toadroaches onto the table for the goblin crew. For Kashmir, he instead presented a blanched tomatoroot, which he'd held onto from his brewing lesson in Vitra's Lab. He'd carefully seasoned it to counteract the bitterness of the vegetable, and had carved a little smile into it to brighten Kashmir's day.

"AaAaaaaahhhh, thank you for your purchase!" 27 cheered as he poured a pile of coins into his bag, then pulled out four pairs of *Yiklar Goggles of Vision in Darkness and Harsh Conditions*.

"Hurmph, these will keep your vision sharp if another blizzard starts up," Stibs announced as 27 handed out the eyepieces. A line of frost encrusted the frames of the goggles as Kashmir placed a pair over her eyes.

"Hmmm, and I'll just be using my telescope, yes?" Colb threw in, holding up the metal object that Borin had given him.

Next, 27 summoned a *Yiklar Shield of Reflecting*, and handed it to Colb.

Stibs grabbed a fried toadroach, tossed it into his mouth, gulped it down with some water, then made an announcement to the team. "Hurmph, our plan is simple: whatever's out there is probably too strong to fight, so we're just going to avoid it altogether and sneak into Wealth Mountain. If we get attacked, we'll have two magic shields to defend ourselves, and 27's spear if we're forced to strike back."

The team nodded in understanding of the plan, then resigned to finishing their meals in silent thought, mentally preparing for the events to come.

Colb sweat as he chewed on his toadroaches, thinking about the snow tornado he'd briefly seen the night before. *Hmmm, I hope everyone's going to be okay, yes?* he thought to himself. At the same time, a little part of Colb couldn't help but feel excited to finally see how much goldatinum was hidden inside the mysterious Wealth Mountain. This mixture of anxiety and excitement swirled around in his stomach, making it difficult to eat.

Once the meal was finished, the group carefully made their way outside. As 27 compressed his *Yiklar Folding Cabin* back into doorknob form, Colb gulped, looking out at the vast wasteland of snow before him. The blizzard had dissipated since the previous night, but the emptiness of the Frosted Wastes still wasn't a welcoming sight. The crew exchanged a few nervous glances, then together trudged forth into the unknown danger.

As the team came within one mile of Wealth Mountain – around the same area they had retreated from some twelve hours ago – they were met with a low *GGggggggrrrrggggrooooooooo!* in the distance. The noise continued, growing louder as they walked closer. Colb and Stibs stood in the front, holding up their matching magic shields anxiously.

Snow began pelting the team from above, coating everyone in cold white powder. As a blizzard started up, becoming rapidly too thick to see through, Colb held his magic telescope up to his eye with a free hand.

His vision immediately cleared, showing a detailed picture of Wealth Mountain in the distance. The base of the peak contained a tantalizing cave entrance, which was surrounded by a couple icy tornadoes that had just touched to the ground.

"Hmmm! I think I see a way into the mountain, yes?" Colb cheered.

"Rrghegh! What are we supposed to do about that?!" Drek exclaimed.

"Hmmm! You can see the tornadoes too, yes?" Colb shouted over the storm.

"Who cares about the tornadoes?!" Drek cried out. "Look up!"

Colb moved his telescope skywards, towards Wealth Mountain's summit. As his eye approached the clouds, he soon noticed an enormous four-legged beast covered in white fur looking down upon him.

The monster, which had a triangle-shaped jaw and a set of intimidatingly dark eyes, was perhaps a mile taller than Wealth Mountain itself. The colossal beast, which had been cloaked by the blizzard around it, stood with a mighty paw over Wealth Mountain's summit, and had locked eyes with the five adventures.

GGGggggggggrrrrrrrrgggggggrrrooooooooooooo! it howled at the team, as an entire blizzard erupted from its mouth. Colb and Stibs held strong, their magic shields reflecting the brute force of the air as waves of pressure shockwaved throughout the mountain pass.

"Hurmph! It already sees us!" Stibs exclaimed.

"Why's it so angry?" Kashmir called out.

"Hmmm! Kashmir's wondering why it's so angry, yes?" Colb translated at the top of his lungs.

"Rrghegh! It's probably hungry and wants to eat us!" Drek shouted in reply.

GGGgggggrrrgrrooooooooooooo! the beast raised its head high into the sky, letting out another pained howl into the atmosphere.

"MMmmMmmmm, if it's hungry, let's give it food?" 27 pitched.

"Hmmm! We're running low on food just for ourselves, yes? What could we feed it?" Colb yelled back.

"Hurmph, everyone! I have an idea," Stibs shouted. "The mountain's only a mile away. Drek and I should split off, flanking around the side of the monster. When we do that, Drek can distract the beast with his arrow while I guard him with my shield. Meanwhile, you three can continue with the original plan. Sneak into the mountain, grab as much goldatinum as you can, and get out. Then, rinse and repeat until the mountain's empty, while Drek and I keep the beast out of your way. Got it?"

"Hmmm, what if the goldatinum's stuck in the mountain, and we need time to mine it free?" Colb asked at the top of his lungs. It was a struggle to be heard over the harsh winds the monster had summoned.

"Hurmph, chop out whatever you can with 27's spear if you have to. We'll distract the beast as long as we can, but this is a mission of speed," Stibs shouted back.

"Hmmm, okay!" Colb called out. The rest of the team affirmed the plan as well.

"Rrghegh… see you in a bit," Drek said, patting Colb on the shoulder. The old and young goblin duo then broke away from the group, marching off to prepare their distracting attack.

As Stibs and Drek ran off, Colb put the telescope back up to his eye, watching the colossal creature intently. It seemed to be glaring at Drek and Stibs, perhaps angered that the two goblins were approaching it.

"MMmMmmmm, this is working. The monster isn't focused on us, no it is not," 27 piped up. "We should get on with our sneaking, yes we should."

Kashmir stepped in front of Colb, pulling her dress outwards to make herself look as big as possible. "Maybe we'll blend in with the snow a bit better if I'm in front with my white dress?" she pitched.

"Hmmm! That's a good idea, yes?" Colb agreed. He then turned to 27. "She's going to camouflage us with her dress, yes?" he translated.

"MMmMmmmm, okay," the noble said, gripping his spear. 27's hands looked strained and veiny, as if he were holding onto the weapon for dear life.

"Hmmm, off we go," Colb muttered.

The chef goblin held up his shield, and with Kashmir leading the way, the trio began to trudge in a straight line towards the base of Wealth Mountain.

As they walked, the monster howled into the sky with another wretched *GGggrrrrrrgggroooooooooo!* and looked more and more furious as Drek and Stibs approached it.

Once Colb, Kashmir, and 27 were within a minute's walk of Wealth Mountain's entrance, a fleck of iridhodium flew out from Stibs and Drek's position. The shiny arrow made a direct hit at the side of the beast's head, causing it to erupt with an enraged growl that echoed throughout the region like an earthquake.

With a single step, the beast took its paw off the summit of Wealth Mountain, and stomped onto the ground about 500 feet away from Colb. Three more icy tornadoes spawned right next to the city-sized foot.

"Go go go," 27 ordered. Panicked by the tornadoes, the trio picked up their pace, rushing to the cave entrance. As they did, they could hear the *BOOM!* of another paw stepping closer to Drek and Stibs.

Once the trio successfully reached the snow-covered cavern, they looked around expectantly. There was no goldatinum to be seen – but a clear path leading deeper into Wealth Mountain did sit before them.

Colb looked back with fear in his eyes. "Hmmm! We can't go spelunking now, yes?" he cried out. "That thing's about to kill Drek and Stibs! There's no way they'll last more than a minute!"

27 looked down at the *Yiklar Spear of Irreversible Death* between his palms. "MMmMmmmm, I can think of one solution," he confided.

Colb nodded, then looked over at Kashmir. Her eyes were covered with snowy tears as she, too, nodded in agreement with 27's plan.

"Hmmm, I'll cover you with my shield, yes?" Colb promised to 27. He then pondered what the young elf should do. *Hmmm, it might be best for Kashmir to stay in this cave,* he thought. *I know she's a fighter, but I'm worried Drek and Stibs might die if our plan with this spear doesn't play out well. I don't want her seeing that, yes?*

"Kashmir... you stay here, yes?" Colb requested. "Hmmm, I don't want you getting sucked into a tornado... plus, if 27 or I get sucked into one, or flung somewhere... then... we need *you* to watch where we land from the safety of this cave. Hmmm, so you can find us once the storms calm down, yes?" he said, giving her a task to ensure she wouldn't follow them into danger. "Stay in this cave, and don't take your eyes off me and 27.

Kashmir nodded again, putting a hand over her mouth as snow rolled down her face.

"MMmMmmmm, okay, it's now or never, yes it is," 27 said. Colb and 27 shared a brief hug of reassurance, then rushed out together, back into the cold.

For Colb, the next few moments rushed by like they happened in under a second. Holding his shield high to protect 27 from the mighty winds, he ran straight into the face of danger, getting the

noble goblin as close as possible to the beast's fur-covered foot –
without getting too close, else they might lose their own footing
against the pull of the snowy vortexes nearby.

"Hmmm! I think this is as close as we can get, yes?" Colb
shouted, as he started to feel the pull of the tornadoes against his
skin.

27 let out a deep breath, stretching his arms. "I think I can make
this shot, yes I can," he said, sizing up the distance to the monster's
foot.

"Hmmm! Throw it before the monster takes another step, yes?
Otherwise, the foot might go too far away," Colb advised.

27 rubbed his hands together, then lifted the *Yiklar Spear of
Irreversible Death* high. "For Yiklar! Or… or something! I don't
know. I'm not a warrior, no I am not," he said, chucking the spear
with all his might towards the beast's enormous leg.

The dark blue weapon whirred majestically through the sky,
aimed perfectly at the back of the monster's limb… until a nearby
snow tornado pulled it off-course.

The freak weather event ripped the spear off its trajectory with
a powerful gush of wind. The weapon began to fling wildly around
in the air, orbiting the snow-filled vortex.

Before Colb could tell what was happening, the *Yiklar Spear
of Irreversible Death* suddenly broke free from the storm's grasp,
flying straight and true… back in the direction from which it had
been thrown.

The *Yiklar Spear of Irreversible Death* flung back to 27 at an
incredible speed, piercing into the goblin's torso. Before Colb
could even comprehend what he was seeing, Kashmir let out a
blood-curling scream from the cave entrance behind him.

"TWENTY-SEVEN!!!" the purple elf cried out in horror.

Ggggrrrrggrrrrrooooo! the beast howled in reply. Its

massive ears straightened into the sky as it reared its head, now looking down at the intruder in Wealth Mountain's cave entrance.

Another fleck of iridhodium shot from Stibs and Drek's position, but this time the monster ignored the sharp strike, seeming blinded by rage as it glared down at Kashmir. The beast reared its massive jaw, and blew a storm of hail towards the elf.

Massive chunks of ice smashed into the face of Wealth Mountain, causing a cave-in. "KASHMIR!" Colb shouted, turning to look back at the young elf with his magic telescope. The eyepiece revealed a mess of snow and ice rapidly covering the entrance to the cavern, permanently locking the young elf inside Wealth Mountain's jaw.

Hearing another growl, Colb moved his gaze to the beast. It was looking furious, snarling as it towered above Colb. Another arrow flew at it from Drek and Stibs, but it didn't seem to care.

"Hmmm! Kashmir!" Colb worried, too frazzled to know what to do. *Now she's trapped in the mountain! Hmmm! I shouldn't have told her to stay in there!* he thought.

The chef goblin then looked down at his noble companion, who had fallen limp in the snow. His body had been skewered by the dark blue spear. "27!!" Colb shouted, finally comprehending the reality of this moment.

A small explosion came from where Drek and Stibs were positioned, and a wide boulder sailed through the sky as a result. The boulder bashed the beast in the side of the head, splitting into pieces as it hit. The monster howled with rage, shifting its focus back to them.

With the beast successfully distracted by Stibs and Drek, Colb rushed to the side of his good friend. "27?" Colb whimpered, holding up his *Yiklar Shield of Reflecting* against the windy conditions.

27 stayed limp, the *Yiklar Spear of Irreversible Death* embedded deep in his body. Black tendrils of energy were visibly pouring out from the spear, flowing across the noble goblin's skin in a pattern not unlike that of a spiderbat's web.

Colb frantically pulled his homemade healing elixir off his belt, and poured it down the goblin's throat. "Hmmm, come back… come back…" he cried.

27's neck glowed as the potion dripped down his esophagus. The black tendrils along his skin seemed to react violently, twisting and curling as if being assailed by an enemy.

27 suddenly let out a cough, and half-opened his eyes. "MMmMmmmm… I am here…" he softly groaned.

"Hmmm! The potion's working!" Colb rejoiced.

"MMmMmmmm… it's taking away some of the pain," 27 reported. "…Thank you… but… it will not save me."

The black tendrils of the *Yiklar Spear of Irreversible Death* began to dance along his skin, shimmering and darkening as a magic battle of healing and death ensued inside 27's body.

"Hmmm! That is not true!" Colb cried out, frantically checking his pockets for more items. All he could find was the silvopper coin he'd pick up from a fountain back in the Human Empire.

"Yiklar Spear of Irreversible Death… it is simply…" 27 coughed up a little bit of green blood as he spoke, staining his beloved silk clothing. "It is simply… too highest… of quality," he finished.

"Surely this can be undone somehow, yes?!" Colb cried, shaking the empty health potion bottle to pull out any last drops he might've missed.

"This is a Yiklar-made item we're talking about…" 27 replied. "Its only flaw… is that it's… so very without flaw…" 27 smiled slightly, as if proud of his tribe's handiwork to the very end. "It promises irreversible death… and a promise made is a promise kept…"

The web of black tendrils began slowly spreading again, as if starting to overcome the resistance Colb's health potion had wrought.

"Listen to me, Colb…" 27 muttered, life fading from his eyes. "I think… I… I understand… 1's secret… to… investing…" Colb began to cry harder, feeling unnerved by 27's sudden harkening back to his roots – something that might imply the noble goblin was having his life flash before his eyes.

"Investment… is to believe in someone… someone worth believing in… like this team…" 27 coughed again, his throat turning drier and coarser with each word. "…a team of good friends… far outweighs the… value… of money…"

The black tendrils flowing from the *Yiklar Spear of Irreversible Death* had now flowed as far as 27's knees. The noble shut his eyes, and his face began to wrinkle.

"Hmmm! We can't do this without you!" Colb cried. "One goblin from each of the four tribes – those were your words, yes?! If you leave now, there will only be three goblins… so, you can't leave. You can't leave yet, yes?"

"…Oh, Colb…" 27 muttered. His voice sounded quiet and ethereal, and his blackened body looked limp and dry. Colb struggled to tell if this was even 27 talking, or just his imagination stretching out the noble's final moment.

"…Three goblins is plenty…" the voice whispered.

"Hmmm… because there is no need for more, yes?" Colb agreed softly. "Quality defeats quantity, yes?" Colb could swear the noble's body cracked a smile at those words. "…That is the Yiklar way," Colb finished. With that, Colb gazed upon 27 fondly, until his tears blocked his vision too much to continue looking.

Chapter 23

WEALTH MOUNTAIN

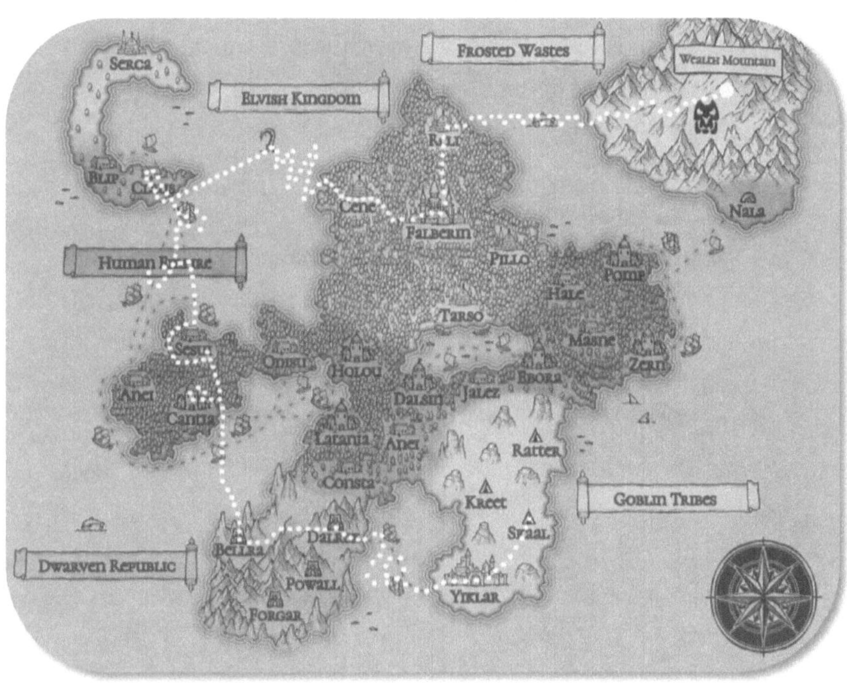

23. WEALTH MOUNTAIN

"TWENTY-SEVEN!!!" Kashmir cried out in horror as she watched a spear, which visibly radiated with death magic, skewer the noble goblin.

Grrrrrrggrrrrrrrroooooo! *CRUNCH! BANG! THUMP!* Shocked and alone, the purple elf suddenly found herself trapped within the cave system of Wealth Mountain.

"Hey!" Kashmir shouted, pounding against the icy blockade with her fists. "Let me out!"

With bits of snow covering her eyes, the elf frantically scanned her surroundings for options. After a moment, she opened her fists towards the blockade, closed her eyes, and opened her hands.

Go away! she thought, as a blast of liquified air shot from her fingers, knocking her to the ground.

Kashmir skid across the cave floor, eventually bumping into an icy stone wall. When she opened her eyes, the blockade was still there – perhaps a little stronger, even, as she'd imbued it with yet another layer of ice.

This isn't fair! Kashmir thought to herself, standing back up. *All four of them are going to die out there! I think one already did…*

Kashmir sniffled, fiddling with her goggles to wipe some snowy tears away from her eyes. *I won't even be able to see where Colb lands if a tornado sucks him up… I promised I'd watch for him…* she thought.

Kashmir sat down, looking at the floor in defeat. The icy cave made a slight crackling sound in response to her particularly cold body sitting upon it.

After a few moments of Kashmir sitting on the ground and feeling utterly alone, a mighty stomp shook Wealth Mountain from outside. *The monster's on the move...* Kashmir thought to herself.

Another stomp emanated from outside, jiggling the cave system around her. She heard some *CRUNCH!* and *SMASH!* sounds as rocks broke free from the cave ceiling in response to the tremor.

Suddenly, a faint voice echoed from further down into Wealth Mountain. Kashmir's necklace glowed as it fluently translated the words to Elvish.

"...#348. A ball of red yarn. The ball of yarn reacted strangely to the tincture, fraying immediately and turning yellow. Further testing..."

Kashmir's pointed ears perked up, surprised to hear another voice in the cave with her. "...Hello?" she called out, standing up. "Colb?" She listened carefully for a response, cupping a hand to her ear.

"...another update, Flufei has stolen the ball of yarn, and hidden it when I wasn't looking. Fortunately, this version of the potion isn't toxic, so she should be okay. However, I wasn't done with my..."

"Hello?" Kashmir called out again, confused by the voice. It was definitely coming from deeper in the cave. "Who are you? Do you know a way out of here?"

Following the sound, Kashmir stepped deeper into Wealth Mountain's interior. Although the cave pathways were pitch black, she could see the rocks and ice around her in great detail thanks to the *Yiklar Goggles of Vision in Darkness and Harsh Conditions* stuck to her face.

"...next up was experiment #349. A wooden toy train. The train reacted violently to the potion, immediately dissolving into a puddle of brown goo. I have no idea why..."

As Kashmir hustled deeper into the cave system, the voice got louder and louder. Suddenly, she tripped, falling to the ground and scraping her knee.

Ow! she thought, pulling up her dress to check on the wound. *What did I just trip on?*

When she looked back, a chunk of goldatinum shimmered in her magically-enhanced vision. She crawled over to it, picking it up. The object was shaped like a brick of marblelime, but felt as if it were made of solid goldatinum. *That's weird...* she thought.

"...we have experiment #350. A stem of living daisywheat. As expected, this one seems to have worked. The plant instantly turned a sharp goldatinum color, and scratches at a level four. This is consistent with previous experiments on biological material..."

Kashmir's ears perked up at the continuing sound, and she dropped the goldatinum brick. "Who are you?" the elf called out again. "I just watched someone die… I'm not in the mood for you to be all mysterious right now!"

Kashmir continued to march down the cave path, eventually reaching an open chamber that was filled with goldatinum. "Um… what? Hello?" Kashmir called out again.

Before her stood a chilling display of wealth. Thousands of life-sized, intricately carved goldatinum statues littered the space. From tall vinelike pewterorange archways to detailed spiderbats, each art piece looked more realistic than the last – and it all appeared to be carved from pure goldatinum.

Notably separate from the others, a goldatinum statue of a human stood alone at the center of the room. The statue had been placed next to an old, rotten, wooden desk. Kashmir approached the art piece, investigating its face. The statue depicted a woman with short-cropped hair. She had been carved with a look of horror in her eyes. Her teeth were grit, her stance was stiff, and she was holding a hollow potions bottle, which appeared to have a large crack in it.

Oddly enough, only the human part of the statue had been carved in goldatinum. Her clothing, glass potion bottle, and spectacles were all made of their normal respective materials – albeit the objects were rather old and tattered.

"...next up is experiment #351. A living spiderbat. I kind of feel bad about this, but I just sort of opened the cage and dumped the potion all over it. Immediately, the spiderbat turned solid goldatinum. I've already done extensive follow-up testing, and verified that everything – even its internal organs – are entirely solid goldatinum..."

Kashmir looked down, as the mysterious voice was now coming from her feet. Under the desk sat a small, rectangular device.

Kashmir donned her mittens, then reached down to pick it up. She clicked a button at the top of the rectangle, which made the voice suddenly stop talking.

Oh... she thought to herself. *Nobody's actually down here.* The elf sighed, looking around at the detailed statues surrounding her. *27 would've loved this*, she thought. *All the goblins would love this... I hope they aren't dead.*

Kashmir kicked a piece of goldatinum on the ground, frustrated with her situation. *This is stupid. Who put all this stuff down here? Why did we come all this way for it? I feel like I didn't find my destiny, I didn't find a winter foxferret, and I can't even keep my new friends safe.*

Kashmir sniffled, sitting down on the ground. *Now I'm all alone, too,* she thought. She clicked the button on the rectangle again, hoping that another voice might at least soothe her loneliness in this inescapable cave system.

As the voice started back up, Kashmir's *Yiklar Amulet of Open Ears* glowed with understanding, illuminating the cave chamber with a soft white light as it translated the foreign words.

"...alright, that's it for today. Wanna say anything Flufei? ...Grooo!...That's a good girl! Alright, that's it from me. This is Tanja, signing off..."

Click! Kashmir turned off the rectangle, wanting silence as she fished for a memory in her head. *Tanja...? Where did I hear that name before?*

She looked up at the goldatinum statue next to her. It was clearly a human woman. *The only human I know much about is Vitra...* she thought. *Vitra... Vitra... the crazy alchemist with a winter foxferret named Bitty. The one with the dwarf friend... Borin... who said that they spent... oh! Spent months in the Frosted Wastes, looking for Tanja!*

Kashmir stood up, and began to pace around as she thought. *Looking for Tanja, the inventor of alchemy... a woman who loved the Frosted Wastes, had a pet winter foxferret named Flufei, and was obsessed with trying to turn cheap materials into expensive materials!*

Kashmir looked over at the goldatinum spiderbat statue she'd seen when she first walked in. She now noticed it had been sawed open, revealing a detailed set of goldatinum lungs, a goldatinum heart, and other internal organs – all carved flawlessly in goldatinum.

An artist wouldn't carve a bunch of internal organs for a statue, then seal them inside where they would never be seen! Kashmir thought. She turned, looking back at the statue of the human woman.

"Tanja...?" she muttered. Kashmir took off a mitten, and put her hand to the woman's cheek – causing frost to creep over the smooth goldatinum face.

Kashmir looked down at the rectangular device in her other, mitten-wearing hand. "I think you dropped this," she said, placing the device in Tanja's goldatinum grip.

Kashmir looked around the cave, investigating the other statues. "I don't see any goldatinum winter foxferrets around here…" she muttered. "Or even a skull and bones. What happened to Flufei? Could Flufei still be around somewhere? How long do winter foxferrets even live?"

Again, Kashmir thought back to her conversations with Vitra and Borin, back on Jaiphione's Crescent. *What do I know about winter foxferrets… well, Bitty clearly loves Vitra, so it's fair to assume Flufei felt similarly about Tanja. Whenever I attacked Vitra, or something bad happened, Bitty would retaliate by sneezing some snow at me, or growing a few inches in size. What was up with that? I think Vitra said they shrink when they're relaxed, and grow when they're upset?*

Kashmir looked back at Tanja, whose terror-stricken expression could only be that of a scientist that just made a life-ending mistake.

Winter foxferrets get attached to their owners, and grow in size when they're upset… so, how big would Bitty grow if she watched Vitra die from an experiment gone wrong? Kashmir pondered.

The purple elf looked up at the cave ceiling, which trembled slightly as the beast took another mighty step outside. The colossal beast… the one with a white winter coat, four fluffy paws, and a long snout. The monster that stood guard at the entrance to Wealth Mountain, which is the grave site of… of Tanja, its beloved owner.

"…The monster's just Flufei," Kashmir muttered as the realization hit her. With snowy tears entering her eyes, Kashmir turned to the statue of Tanja.

"That beast outside is just your pet!" Kashmir exclaimed. "Your pet winter foxferret is killing my friends just because she's upset that you died!" The young elf kicked the statue's leg, creating a slight dent in the goldatinum.

"You need to fix this!" she shouted at the statue. "I know how this works! A bunch of the humans worship you, just like all the elves worship Jaiphione! That means you should be able to grant a miracle or something, right? Jaiphione saved a whole island's worth of endangered animals *after* she died. The least you can do is save a small band of goblins!"

She kicked the statue again, crying from the overwhelming situation. "At least unblock Wealth Mountain so I can leave…" she murmured. "…maybe I can reason with Flufei, now that I know who she is…"

Kashmir sat down, once again resigning herself to stare at the floor in defeat. It didn't matter if she figured out the mysteries surrounding this place; she was still sealed in this cave system, and there was nothing she could do to save her friends.

Until a moment later, when a faint Hewmish whisper started echoing within the cave chamber.

"…Tanja, Tanja, Tanja…" a faint chant began.

Kashmir looked up, curious to see if the rectangular object had somehow started talking again. However, the rectangle no longer existed – it was warping, transforming into a sphere of radiant magical energy.

Kashmir jumped to her feet, getting a closer look at what was happening. "…Tanja, Tanja, Tanja…" the object chanted, becoming rounder and more magical by the second.

When the transformation was complete, the rectangular device had become a hollow, glass sphere filled with twirling, glittery, goldatinum-colored dust. Kashmir could immediately sense a potent magical hue about it, not unlike what she felt in the presence of Queen Eylbella, who famously kept Jaiphione's

Miracle Orb inlaid into the throne she sat upon.

Kashmir lifted the glowing object out of Tanja's goldatinum hands, inspecting it carefully. The orb was completely immune to the purple elf's icy touch – not even a small layer of frost grew over the item as it sat upon Kashmir's bare skin.

"Are… am I holding Tanja's Miracle Orb right now?" Kashmir asked.

"…Tanja, Tanja, Tanja…" the orb whispered in reply.

"Wow, I'm kind of talking to a dead person…" Kashmir muttered. "Or… a goddess? I guess?"

She shook the sphere, watching the goldatinum flecks of dust mix around in response. "I… guess I can make a wish, right? That's how you work?"

"…Tanja, Tanja, Tanja…" the orb continued to whisper.

"Okay… that's not really helpful. Hmmm…" Kashmir paused, thinking carefully for a moment. "My mother says that Jaiphione's Miracle Orb only works once every thousand years. Jaiphione sits behind the queen today, but if Queen Eylbella decides to make a wish using that orb, then the magic will fade for a century. Is it fair to assume this is sort of the same situation?"

"…Tanja, Tanja, Tanja…" the orb muttered.

"Yea, Tanja Tanja Tanja. Okay. I'm not going to waste this wish," she said, tucking Tanja's Miracle Orb under her arm. "If anyone deserves to see you before your magic vanishes for a thousand years, it's Flufei. She's bigger than this mountain, and she's been howling in pain – in grief, rather. I'm going to bring you to her."

With the magic item tucked under her arm, Kashmir hustled back to Wealth Mountain's ice-covered entrance. *I don't know how I'm going to get past the ice blockade, but I'm going to find a way*, she thought. *I need to bring Tanja's final gift to Flufei.*

Help your enemies, instead of hurting them. That's what Colb taught me to do, and in my gut, I know it's the right way to end this.

Chapter 24

TANJA'S MIRACLE

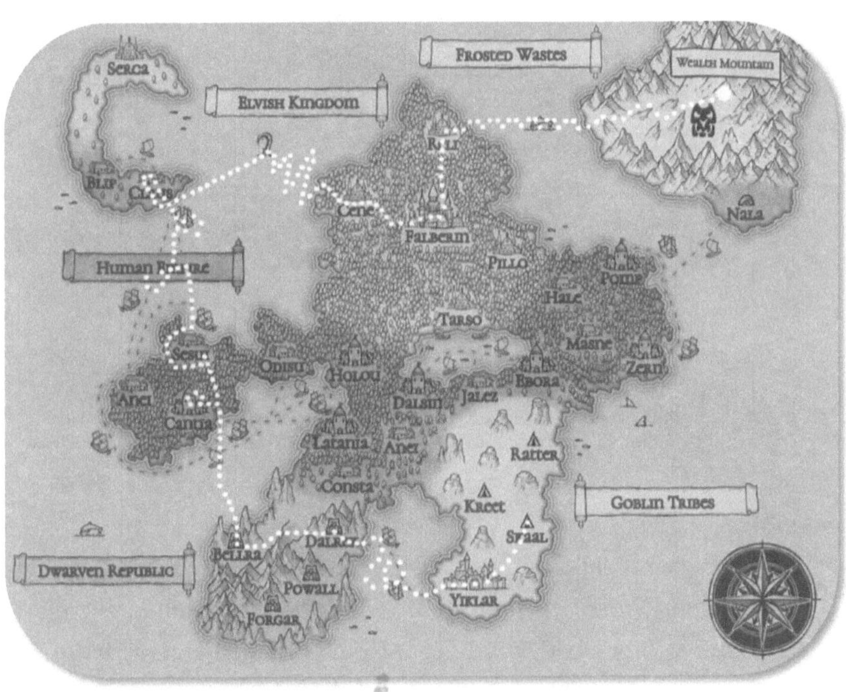

24. TANJA'S MIRACLE

Colb wiped tears from his eyes as he gazed upon 27's blackened corpse. *Hmmm... Kashmir's in trouble*, he thought, finally breaking his eye contact from 27 and looking back at the caved-in cavern with his telescope.

He then turned his gaze to the beast behind him. *Drek and Stibs are, too... everyone is in trouble! Hmmm! This whole journey has taken a turn for the worse...*

Colb scanned his surroundings, looking for options. Something to do. Some way to help. Some action he could take to prevent more deaths from happening around him.

Colb sadly looked down at his beaten friend. The *Yiklar Spear of Irreversible Death* appeared dull and weakened. He reached out, but the weapon crumbled to dust before he could even touch it. A thin layer of 27's green blood bubbled up from his wound as the disintegrating spear unblocked it.

Hmmm... I wish 27 were still here, Colb thought as he kneeled next to the corpse. Colb shivered, his legs freezing as his pants became saturated with wet snow. *27 would know what to do, yes? He'd probably pull some grand solution out of his bag, and give it to me...*

More tears welled up in Colb's eyes as he stared upon his companion. The *Yiklar Bag of Traveling Inventory* stood out on the noble goblin's body – a bright splotch of red in an otherwise dark, black-and-green scene. "Hmmm..." Colb muttered.

The chef goblin leaned next to 27, and removed the red sack from the noble's belt. He put his small green hand in the sack, and felt around. All he could sense was fabric – as if this bag had nothing special about it.

"Hmmm! I need some help!" he shouted, putting his face into

the bag. "Can you hear me, 1? We need help! 27 is dead, and… and someone is locked behind a cave-in, and… and we wasted the spear, and two goblins are fighting an insurmountable monster! Hmmm! Can you hear me?"

Colb pulled his head out of the bag, frustrated by the lack of response. *Hmmm… how does 27 use this?* he thought.

Colb scrounged around in his pockets, then pulled out the silvopper coin he'd gotten from a human fountain long ago. *He usually puts money in it, right?*

Colb held his silvopper piece close to the *Yiklar Bag of Traveling Inventory*. The red sack began to glow, as if enticed by the nearby currency.

Ggggrrrrrrrrggrrooooooooooooo! the monster lashed out nearby. Colb heard an avalanche of falling rocks, and felt the world shake as the beast took another step.

Stibs and Drek are doomed! Colb thought, shivering. *I need this to work now!*

Colb held his silvopper coin closer to the bag, and felt a tug – as if the bag were pulling on him, trying to absorb the coin.

Hmmm… Colb thought. He reached into 27's robes, and searched the noble's pockets, eventually pulling out a *Yiklar Catalog*. He ripped off the front cover, and flipped it over to reveal a relatively blank sheet of paper.

"Hmmm, I'm sorry 27," Colb muttered. Closing his eyes, he dipped a finger into the noble's fluid-filled wound. Once his hand was sufficiently covered in his deceased friend's green blood, Colb scrawled out a simple Goblish message onto the parchment:

Hmmm, at mountain

27 died

We're not strong enough

Please help

He then stuck his silvopper coin in the middle of the note, and folded up the sheet around it. "Hmmm… please work… please work…" he mumbled, placing the bundle into the *Yiklar Bag of Traveling Inventory*.

The magic bag glowed with excitement as Colb placed the parchment-wrapped silvopper coin into it. Within moments, the bundle disintegrated into the red sack – presumably, transported to the *Yiklar Factories*.

Colb let out a sigh, relieved to see his message appeared to have followed the coin to Yiklar. However, his sigh was cut short, as the beast stomped again – shaking the world and filling Colb with even more anxiety.

"Hmmm! Come on… come on…" he mumbled, glaring at the red sack. He gave the bag a sharp little slap. "Drek, Stibs, and Kashmir's lives depend on you giving me something, yes?" his voice choked up, and his eyes filled with tears as he begged the bag for assistance. "Give me *something* to turn the tides here, yes?!"

The bag sat in the snow, emotionless, for what felt like eons. Eventually, it began to vibrate. "Hmmm!" Colb exclaimed, holding his hands out in front of the bag.

Two small goldatinum gauntlets suddenly launched out from the magic sack, landing in Colb's hands. One of them had a note attached, which contained a message quickly scribbled in Goblish:

This should make you stronger

Sincerely 6,928

(A Yiklar Factories Worker)

Hmmm… okay, Colb thought, donning the gloves. He looked up at the monster as he put the metal gauntlets over his blood-covered fingers.

Grrrggggrrrrroooooooo! the beast growled as it stomped once again. The force of its step triggered another snow tornado to spawn in the distance, and a small avalanche of even more snow to pour out over the blockade of Wealth Mountain's cave entrance.

"No!" Colb cried, looking back at the last place he'd seen the young elf. "Kashmir…"

He thought about the young children of Skaal. How scared they would feel, to be buried alive beneath a mound of ice while the adults of the tribe were slaughtered by a beast beyond their reach. "I'll save you, Kashmir…" he promised.

Suddenly, as Colb donned the second gauntlet, a warm sensation shot through his arms and legs. With a *POP!* his muscles quadrupled in size across his body, and he grew a foot taller.

Colb stood awkwardly, his leather armor creaking as it adjusted to his new six-pack. "I'll save you, Kashmir…" he mumbled again, breaking out into a sprint towards the ice-blockade.

Gravity felt like nothing as Colb's powerful legs pushed him off the ground, making short work of his hustle to Wealth Mountain's entrance.

"Hmmm, I'll save you, Kashmir…" he promised again as he reached the blocked entrance to Wealth Mountain. Colb pushed a gauntlet-covered hand into a chunk of ice covering the cave, and grabbed into it as if he were taking the heart out of a chickengoose carcass.

Colb tugged, easily pulling a building-sized block of ice away from the cave entrance. He tossed it behind him without a second thought, and a resulting *BOOM!* echoed throughout the mountains as it crashed onto the ground.

He reached into the blockade again – with both hands, this time – and ripped off not only the rest of the ice, but a chunk of Wealth

Mountain, with it.

"Kashmir!!" he shouted, vaulting the 500-foot mound of ice and stone into the distance.

He poked his head into Wealth Mountain's cave, where he saw the young elf staring back at him. She had a bright orb filled with goldatinum dust tucked under her arm. It reminded Colb of Maxten's Miracle Orb – the glittery object that enchanted the *Yiklar Spear of Irreversible Death* back when the goblin crew had visited Bellra.

"Is that you, Colb?" Kashmir questioned, squinting at the muscular goblin. Colb nodded, taking a step towards her. The ice beneath him crinkled under the weight of his powerful step.

"Um, okay… then, you need to get me to the beast. Right now," the elf ordered. "I have a way to calm it down."

"Hmmm! Okay," Colb agreed, trusting Kashmir's judgement. He offered her a metal-covered hand, which she grabbed onto. He felt a chill cover his fingers as a layer of frost formed over his metal glove.

Colb lifted the elf over his head with a gauntlet-covered hand, and held a magic telescope to his eye with the other. "Hmmm! Hold on tight, and I'll get you in close, yes?" he promised.

"Perfect," Kashmir agreed.

Colb stepped back out into the wind, and pointed his telescope towards the fluffy monster. It seemed to have stopped attacking Stibs and Drek for the moment, instead looking perplexed as it stared at the 500-foot mound of ice and stone Colb had vaulted into the distance.

With Kashmir holding onto his glove, Colb leaped into a sprint, his powerful legs bounding across the snow. "Fluefei!" Kashmir shouted as Colb carefully weaved around a valley of tornadoes and falling snow. "Come here, girl! I have a gift for you!"

The monster sneezed, causing a shockwave of air to shoot across the mountain pass. Colb held strong, his powerful feet digging into the snow as the wave of pressure pushed against him. He shivered from the cold, but continued to trudge forwards, determined not to let Kashmir down.

As the shockwave subsided, Colb picked up his pace again, bounding across the snow at full speed. "Flufei!" Kashmir screamed, holding up her glittery orb. "This is Tanja. She's here for you!"

The monster turned its head to face Colb. It looked more curious than angry as it investigated Kashmir's display.

"Tanja, Tanja, Tanja…" Colb could hear the orb whispering softly above his head.

"Hmmm… Tanja?" Colb muttered, looking up at Kashmir. "That's the human that Vitra was searching the Frosted Wastes for, yes?" he shouted.

Kashmir nodded, but kept her eyes on the monster. "Tanja died inside Wealth Mountain," the elf explained. "Her pet, Flufei, must've been so upset by Tanja's demise, that it grew as large as it could – making it too big to even visit Tanja's final resting place."

"Hmmm! That's a winter foxferret?!" Colb exclaimed.

"Just like the one that sneezed snow from Vitra's shoulder," Kashmir confirmed.

The beast lowered its head, sniffing Kashmir with its colossal, black nose. Colb dug his feet into the snow, struggling to hold his stance against the beast's mighty sniff.

"It's okay, Flufei. Tanja's here…" Kashmir announced, holding up the orb as high as her arms would allow. The monster leaned in closer, placed the edge of its enormous chin over Tanja's Miracle Orb, and closed its eyes.

"Tanja, Tanja, Tanja…" the orb whispered. The voice was soft and feminine, repetitively speaking the chat in calm Hewmish. The monster's expression seemed to soften with recognition.

"This is Tanja," Kashmir reaffirmed. "She's here for you." The monster let out a soft hiccup, and began to shrink rapidly. Colb felt a popping sensation in his ears as the air pressure shifted, flowing in to replace where the creature's colossal body had once been.

The beast shrank smaller and smaller until it was about the size of Kashmir's leg. As this happened, Colb set Kashmir on the ground, and the elf lowered her stance, keeping Tanja's Miracle Orb in-line with the creature's chin.

"Hello, Flufei," she muttered once the winter foxferret had ceased shrinking. Kashmir cautiously pet the creature on its head, as it nuzzled against Tanja's Miracle Orb.

Suddenly, the goldatinum glitter drained from the orb, leaving an empty glass sphere in Kashmir's hands. An ethereal blue light began to shine next to Flufei.

"Hmmm! Is that supposed to happen?" Colb asked.

"I think Flufei just used the miracle," Kashmir replied.

The blue light darkened and twisted, forming into the shape of a human woman with short-cropped hair. The ghostly form adjusted her spectacles, then reached down to let Flufei sniff her hand.

"You look like Tanja," Kashmir muttered. Colb squinted at the ethereal form standing before them. "Are… are you Tanja?" the elf inquired.

The ethereal form glanced at Kashmir, giving her a small nod. Flufei let out a soft winter foxferret squeak, nuzzling her head against the ethereal form's legs. Unfortunately, Flufei's fluffy head went right through Tanja's ghostly form.

Flufei whined, visibly discomforted by her inability to touch Tanja. The ghost looked down at Flufei regretfully, then looked over at Kashmir again.

The ghost stepped forwards, putting a hand on Kashmir's shoulder. For the first time ever, Colb noticed a shiver run down the cold elf's spine.

"Thank you for finding me..." the ghost muttered in an unearthly whisper. *"I sense greatness within you..."*

"Um... thank... thank you," Kashmir whispered back.

The ghost reached for Kashmir's hand, gesturing for Kashmir to move it. The elf obliged, and Tanja led the hand to Flufei's head.

Kashmir pet the winter foxferret, prompting the creature to give Tanja a perplexed look. *"It's okay to move on..."* the ghost whispered, smiling at the pet. *"You have a very long lifespan, Flufei... find other creatures to love you, just as I once did..."*

Flufei huffed, as if insulted by the command. The ghost returned the huff with a knowing look, which seemed to sway the winter foxferret, as it agreeingly pushed its head into Kashmir's hand.

"Will you take care of her...?" the ghost whispered, staring at Kashmir. *"With your elvish lifespan, you won't vanish from her in a blink, like I did... not to mention, your magic lets you pet her without getting hurt, and vice versa. You two are a perfect match..."*

Kashmir smiled, scratching Flufei behind the ear. "Okay," she agreed.

"Hmmm, I guess you *did* have a destiny here, yes?" Colb cheered as he looked at Kashmir.

"I love these Frosted Wastes... I wish more people would live here, like I did..." Tanja's ghost muttered, looking around at the

wasteland.

"I'd love to live here," Kashmir agreed. "This is a nice place. I could imagine a whole society in these mountains. Where anyone is welcome, and only those who earn their place get to be leaders."

The ghost smiled. *"I was right when I sensed greatness in you..."* she mumbled. *"You know what? Let me see if I can help to bring life to this beautiful land..."*

The ghost stepped back, and raised her arms into the sky. Suddenly, the ground shook and rotated, knocking Colb and Kashmir off their feet.

Wealth Mountain suddenly crumbled into the ground, taking Tanja's physical corpse and all her experiments down with it. Next, a small village of igloos sprouted up where that largest peak had once stood. Half of the igloos were large enough to fit an adult elf. The other half were a little too small, even for an adult goblin.

A new path appeared next, cutting through the mountain range. A loud collective squeaking echoed outwards from it. Hundreds of small winter foxferrets started to pop out from the snow along the path. The creatures excitedly rushed towards the magically summoned village, each claiming one the smaller igloos that had been formed.

"A paradise..." whispered the ghost. *"My first big miracle! Take good care of it... Give these igloos away to people that might love the winter foxferrets like we do..."*

"I will," Kashmir promised, scratching Flufei's sides. "I'll bring my family... and some humans, and dwarves, and goblins, too. Everyone will be welcome in your miracle."

"Thank you..." the ethereal figure replied. *"I'll return in a thousand years, to give another miracle to someone that needs it... Until then, I wish you the best..."*

The ethereal form faded away, leaving behind nothing more

than an empty orb in Kashmir's hands. Flufei nuzzled Kashmir's legs affectionately.

With the ghost gone, Colb's mind returned to his tasks at hand. He lifted the magic telescope to his eyes, and looked out at the Frosted Wastes. He breathed an immediate sigh of relief as he noticed Drek and Stibs. They looked a little worse for wear, but otherwise alive and well as they marched through the snow to regroup with the rest of their crew.

"Hmmm! Drek and Stibs are okay, yes?" he announced. Colb took off his magic gauntlets, and his muscles returned to their normal size. "Hmmm, things might just turn out okay, yes?" he hoped aloud.

Once the team fully regrouped, they inspected and explored the town Tanja had created. As they did so, they swapped stories regarding what had happened over the past hour. The mood was soured upon realizing their team ended up one member short, but spirits rose again slightly when they performed a beautiful funeral for 27 the next morning.

Kashmir and Stibs spent the following week carving an elegant ice sculpture for 27 near the area where he passed away, which brought tears of joy to the eyes of the three goblins.

As the week came to an end, the goblins prepared to return to their respective tribes from the frigid town. Their pockets were empty, but their hearts were filled with stories to share.

Well, almost empty – they'd recovered 27's *Yiklar Folding Cabin*, and with that, Drek was able to keep the remainder of the small fortune he'd recovered from the Quartzelian Pirates. Given that fortune, the nice crown on his head, and the vast experience he'd gained during this journey, Drek felt ready to finally pursue his dream of establishing and ruling over a goblin kingdom once he returned home.

Stibs pat Drek on the back like a proud old father, and looked over the team before him. "Hurmph, I've lived a long life… for a goblin," he added, glancing at the 482-year-old elf. "Hurmph, but most of my life pales in comparison to what I've experienced over these last few months. I'll admit, I came into this group a little full of myself. Thinking I could do everything best on my own. It seems I was wrong – and if I could go back, I'd change nothing about this team. Thanks, all of you, for having my back, and for giving this old goblin a chance to see the world."

"Rrghegh… thank you for your experience and wit," Drek replied. "Rrghegh, and uh… your fighting. You did good job."

"Hurmph, you did a good job, too," Stibs replied, ruffling the crown on Drek's head.

"Thanks for teaching me so many things, and for helping me find my destiny, Colb," Kashmir added. "Tell the others I thanked them for being so welcoming, too."

Colb smiled, silently affirming the first part of her statement. "Hmmm, Kashmir says thank you for welcoming her into our team," he translated.

"Hurmph! We'd all have died to that octopusduck if it weren't for you," Stibs countered.

"Rrghegh, or the hawkbear," Drek added.

"Hmmm, or the winter foxferret just now," Colb threw in.

The three goblins smiled at the elf. "There *is* greatness within you, and you'll do amazing things here, yes?" Colb cheered.

Colb then turned to the other goblins. "Hmmm, and I'm glad I broke out of my shell, and became a better medic for the team, yes? Thank you both for spending these last few months with me, from the beginning of the journey all the way to the end," he said. The two goblins smiled, nodding in reciprocation of Colb's words.

"Hurmph, I suppose it's time we start heading home," Stibs

noted after a moment.

The chef goblin signed, looking around at the icy village around him. "Hmmm, I wish we had gotten out with some of that goldatinum before Wealth Mountain disappeared. To bring home for our tribes, yes?"

"Hurmph, it'll be okay," Stibs said, patting Colb on the back. "We'll help each other in tough times, and make things work one day at a time."

With that, the goblins said their farewells to Kashmir, and packed up their items. However, as Colb grabbed some of 27's equipment to bring it home, he found something unexpected sitting inside the *Yiklar Bag of Traveling Inventory*.

"Hmmm! I found an envelope in 27's magic bag," Colb announced. "It must be a letter from Yiklar, yes?"

Kashmir, Drek, and Stibs gathered around the chef goblin as he read the letter aloud:

To the friends of 27:

AaAaAaAaaAaAhhhhh, this letter is from me: 1, the leader of Yiklar!

MmMmMmMmMmmmm, Colb's blood-drawn message about 27's death was brought to my attention immediately, yes it was. Since then, our good oracle 67 has been watching over you with her most rarest Yiklar Telescope of Extrasensory Discovery, and giving me live updates on how your battle with Flufei played out. I was glad to hear that it turned out most favorably – even with the loss of Wealth Mountain's fortune.

If I could say one last thing to 27, I would tell him how unimaginably impactful his journey to Wealth Mountain turned out to be, even without any goldatinum to bring home in the end. You've all been away for quite some time, so I imagine you have no idea what's happened. In short, the friends and good customers you've all found during your journey have far surpassed the value of a goldatinum piece.

It all started in Dalrek and Bellra, where you helped an army defeat a summer antlizard using Yiklar-made items. This led to a renaissance of renewed interest in goblin-made goods from the Dwarven Republic. That alone boosted our economy enough to fix our immediate concerns, and begin our process of healing the other tribes.

But you all weren't finished, no you were not. You next went to the Human Empire, where 27 made the first goblin-to-human sale in history. This has completely changed goblin-human diplomacy forever.

Word of 27's interesting products spread across the Human Empire like a wildfire, leading to swarms of humans bringing business to all the goblin tribes.

Of course, the Yiklar tribe has been booming. Not just dwarves, but now humans, too, are purchasing our highest-of-quality items as fast as we can produce them.

The Skaal tribe has benefitted as well, selling hospitality and cheerful friendship to any human that passes through on their way to Yiklar. As a result, the Skaal tribe has been glowing lately – every goblin child has a toy and a home, and nobody goes to sleep on an empty stomach. I hear Colb's Tavern has been doing fantastic under his sister's leadership, too!

The Kreet tribe has similarly found great success with the humans. They're quickly becoming famous in the Human Empire for their intricately designed woodcarvings and other handmade knick-knacks. The Kreet goblins seem delighted to share their handiwork with the world, and the booming business has lifted them out of poverty as well, yes it has.

In their own way, the Ratter tribe has been thriving most of all. They've become a powerhouse in exporting crime-based services for the sketchiest nobles of the Human Empire. These days, goblin-to-goblin crime is virtually gone from the Ratter tribe, as everybody would rather make money from the humans than hurt each other. I can't say I agree with Ratter's business practices, no I cannot, but I'm glad to see the tribe doing so well for itself.

I even heard a rumor that you've all befriended the queen of the Elvish Kingdom, or something along those lines. I can't even fathom how much a connection like that could benefit our four humble tribes.

Anyway, I've written enough. Your accomplishments speak for themselves, and you should all be most proud, yes you should be.

With the news of 27's death, many here in Yiklar have begun to worship him as a deity of commerce, friendliness, and good service. His impact on us will never be forgotten. As for the rest of you, we look forward to giving a hero's welcome when you return home.

Most excellent work, all of you. Thank you for everything you've done for us, and for your tribes.

Cheers,

– 1

"Hmmm! This is wonderful!" Colb cheered, crying with joy. Kashmir and the other goblins teared up as well.

"Hurmph! 27, our goblin deity. What do you think of that?" Stibs chuckled.

"Rrghegh, if that's true, I think 27 should give us a free miracle! That's what I think!" Drek joked. "Free stuff! Free stuff!"

Suddenly, 27's *Yiklar Bag of Traveling Inventory* began to

glow and warp. Colb reactively dropped it to the ground, and took a step back.

The red bag shifted and twisted, transforming into a hollow glass sphere. Glittery particles – the same red shade as 27's beloved *Yiklar Bag of Traveling Inventory* – immediately began to appear inside the sphere, swirling around majestically.

"Woa…" Drek mumbled.

"That… is that *27's Miracle Orb*?!" Kashmir exclaimed. "Wow… 1 must not have been kidding when he said goblins had started worshipping the guy. He's already a full-fledged deity, just like Tanja or Jaiphione!"

Colb picked up the orb, inspecting its smooth surface. "…27…27…27…" it whispered in a familiarly friendly Goblish voice.

"Hurmph, well there's your wish, Drek," Stibs observed. "That's a fast-track to starting a kingdom if I've ever seen one."

Drek cautiously walked up to the orb, placing a small hand on Colb's back. "Rrghegh… I want to make the kingdom myself. The right way, using all the experience I've gotten from this journey. I will *earn* my way to establishing a throne." Drek glanced at Kashmir with a smile as he said that.

"Rrghegh… plus, I was joking that I wanted miracle. I don't need it. Colb, you should have it," Drek declared.

"Hurmph, I agree. I've lived my life, and lived it well. There's nothing more I really need," Stibs noted. "I'm more than happy yielding the wish to Colb."

"I pretty much already got my miracle from Tanja," Kashmir added. "This one's all yours, Colb."

"Hmmm," Colb muttered, inspecting the twirling red flakes within 27's Miracle Orb. "When Flufei had an opportunity like this, she wished for Tanja. Well, I wish for 27… I want to see him again, yes? Hmmm, I wish for one last conversation with my friend, so we can all say goodbye, yes?"

Immediately, the red glitter drained out from 27's Miracle Orb, leaving it empty and a little bit lighter. Moments later, a blue, ethereal form of a goblin fazed into existence.

"AaAaaaaahhhh, I do have some afterlife to be getting to, but I think I can spare an hour to chat!" the ghost said with a smile.

AaAaaaaahhhh, thank you for reading!

362

DON'T WANT THE STORY TO END?

Explore the world of *Wealth Mountain* to your heart's content with your favorite roleplaying game and a copy of the *Yiklar Book of Roleplaying Game Enhancement*. Check it out! It's real! You can find the easiest places to buy it at www.Yiklar.com!

We also have the *Yiklar Trading Card Game*, an adorable card game that's easy to learn and fun to play. The game was created by the author of *Wealth Mountain*, and features adorable drawings of all the creatures and many of the characters in this novel. You can find the best places to buy the *Yiklar Trading Card Game* at www.Yiklar.com as well.

Any other stuff that makes sense to be there – from future novels set in the world of *Wealth Mountain*, to new highest-of-quality goods published by the great goblin minds of Yiklar – will be posted on www.Yiklar.com as well, so keep an eye out!

Bonus!

The remaining pages in this novel are a flipbook!

Quickly flip through pages 367 – 407 to watch the map track the goblins on their journey across the world.

Bonus!

The remaining pages in this novel are a flipbook!

Quickly flip through pages 367 – 407 to watch the map track the goblins on their journey across the world.

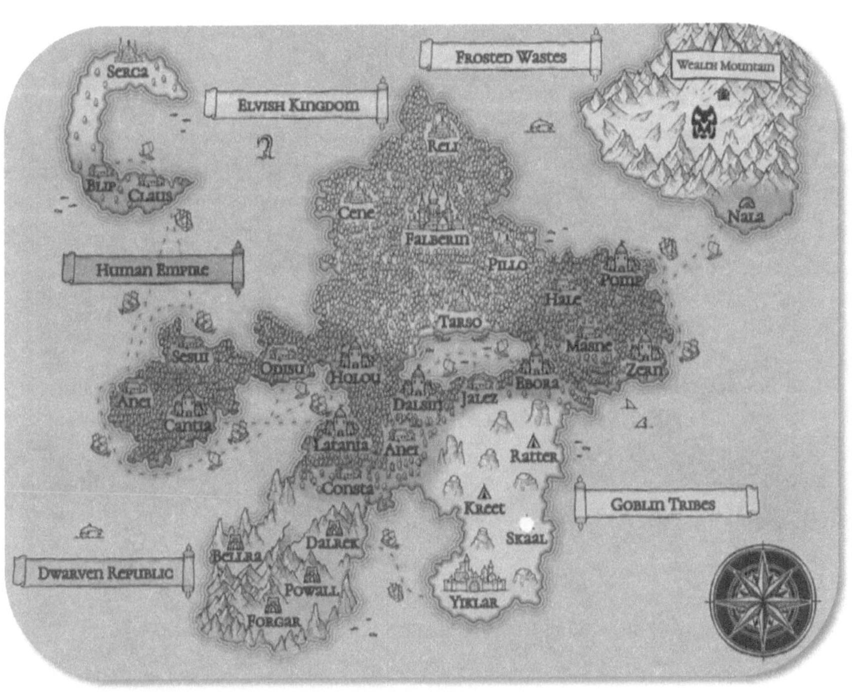
Serca
Frosted Wastes
Wealth Mountain
Elvish Kingdom
Reli
Blip
Claus
Cene
Falberin
Nala
Pillo
Human Empire
Pomp
Hale
Tarso
Masne
Zeri
Sesui
Odisu
Holou
Ebora
Anei
Dalsin
Jalez
Cantia
Latania
Anei
Ratter
Consta
Kreet
Goblin Tribes
Skaal
Dalrek
Bellra
Dwarven Republic
Powall
Yiklar
Forgar

Bonus!

The remaining pages in this novel are a flipbook!

Quickly flip through pages 367 – 407 to watch the map track the goblins on their journey across the world.

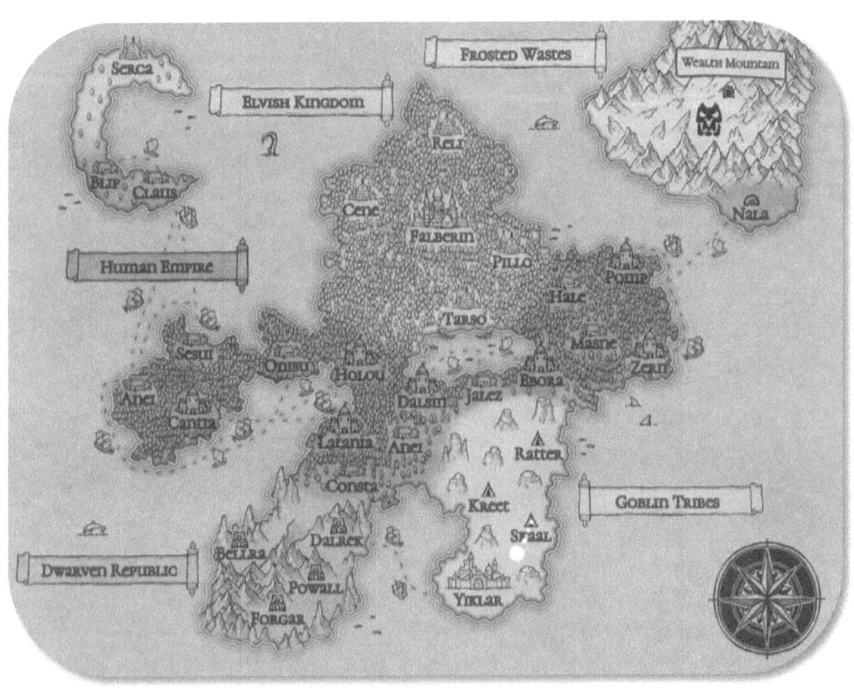

Frosted Wastes
Wealth Mountain
Serca
Elvish Kingdom
Reli
Blif
Claus
Cene
Falberin
Nala
Pillo
Human Empire
Pomp
Hale
Tarso
Masne
Sesui
Odisu
Zeril
Holou
Ebora
Anei
Jalez
Dalsin
Cantra
Latania
Anei
Ratter
Consta
Kreet
Goblin Tribes
Spaal
Dalrek
Bellra
Dwarven Republic
Powall
Yiklar
Forgar

Bonus!

The remaining pages in this novel are a flipbook!

Quickly flip through pages 367 – 407 to watch the map track the goblins on their journey across the world.

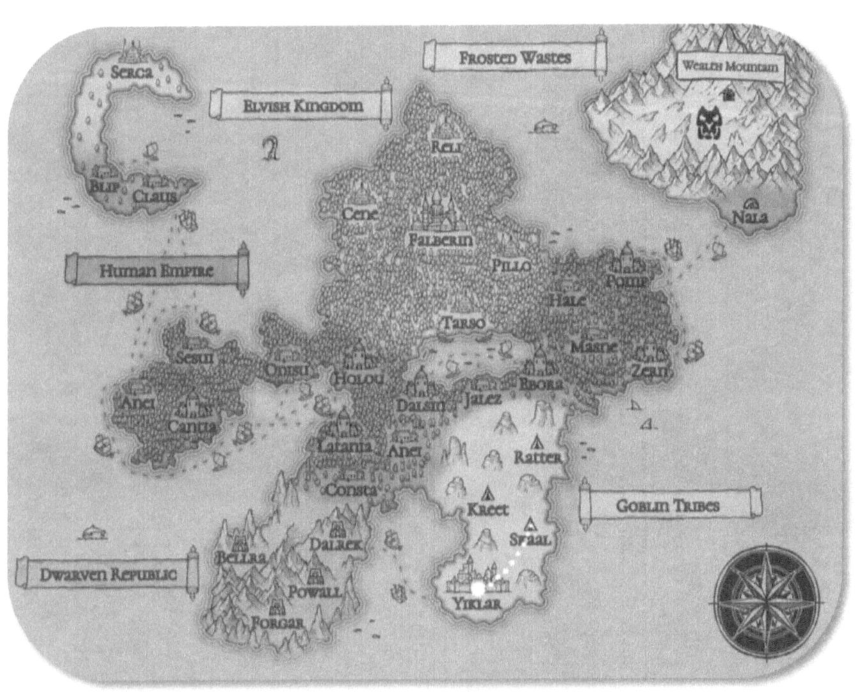
Serca
Blip
Claus
Elvish Kingdom
Frosted Wastes
Wealth Mountain
Nala
Reli
Cene
Falberin
Pillo
Pomp
Hale
Human Empire
Tarso
Masne
Zean
Sesui
Onisu
Holou
Rbora
Anei
Dalsin
Jalez
Cantia
Latania
Anei
Ratter
Consta
Kreet
Goblin Tribes
Spaal
Bellra
Dalrek
Dwarven Republic
Powall
Forgar
Yiklar

Bonus!

The remaining pages in this novel are a flipbook!

Quickly flip through pages 367 – 407 to watch the map track the goblins on their journey across the world.

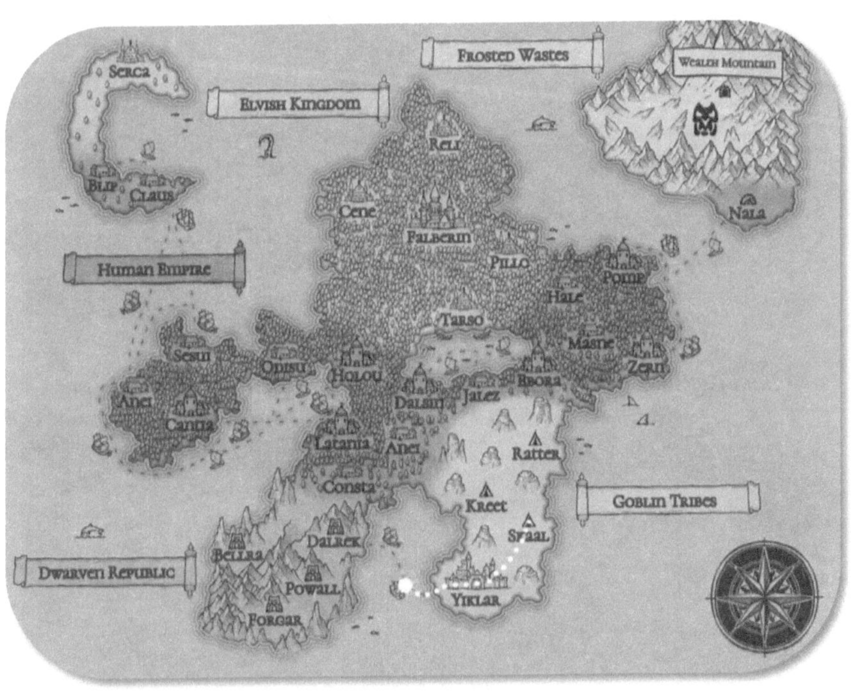

Frosted Wastes
Wealth Mountain
Serca
Elvish Kingdom
Relr
Blip
Claus
Cene
Falberin
Nala
Pillo
Pome
Human Empire
Hale
Tabso
Sesui
Masne
Odisu
Holou
Zeru
Aner
Rbora
Dalsir
Jalez
Cantia
Latania
Aner
Ratter
Consta
Goblin Tribes
Kreet
Bellra
Dalrek
Sraal
Powall
Dwarven Republic
Forgar
Yiklar

Bonus!

The remaining pages in this novel are a flipbook!

Quickly flip through pages 367 – 407 to watch the map track the goblins on their journey across the world.

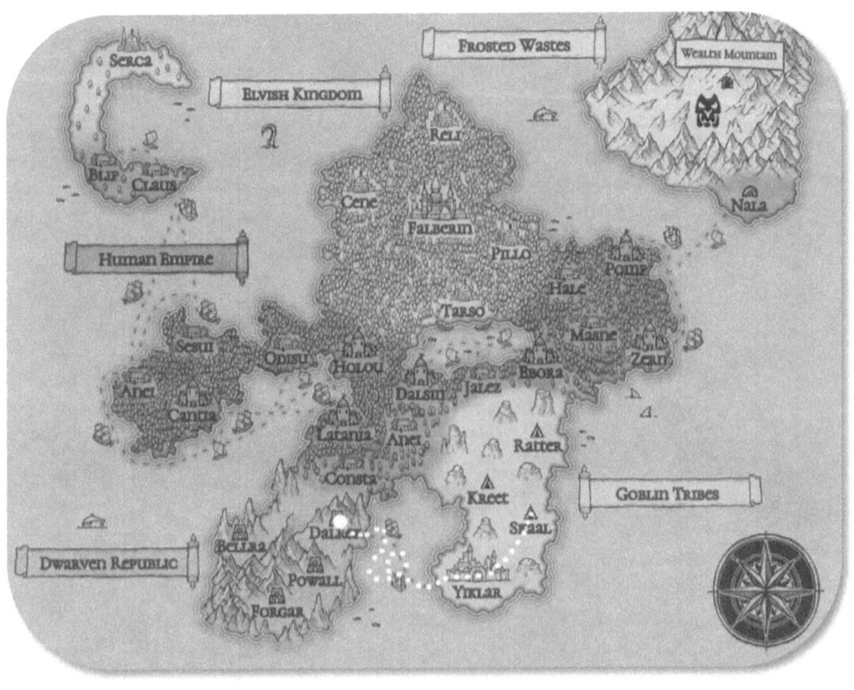

Serca
Elvish Kingdom
Frosted Wastes
Wealth Mountain
Blif
Claus
Reli
Cene
Falberin
Nala
Human Empire
Pillo
Pomf
Hale
Tarso
Maane
Sesui
Zerit
Odisu
Holou
Ebora
Anei
Jalez
Dalsin
Cantia
Anei
Latania
Ratter
Consta
Kreet
Goblin Tribes
Dalarr
Spaal
Bellra
Dwarven Republic
Powall
Yiklar
Forgar

Bonus!

The remaining pages in this novel are a flipbook!

Quickly flip through pages 367 – 407 to watch the map track the goblins on their journey across the world.

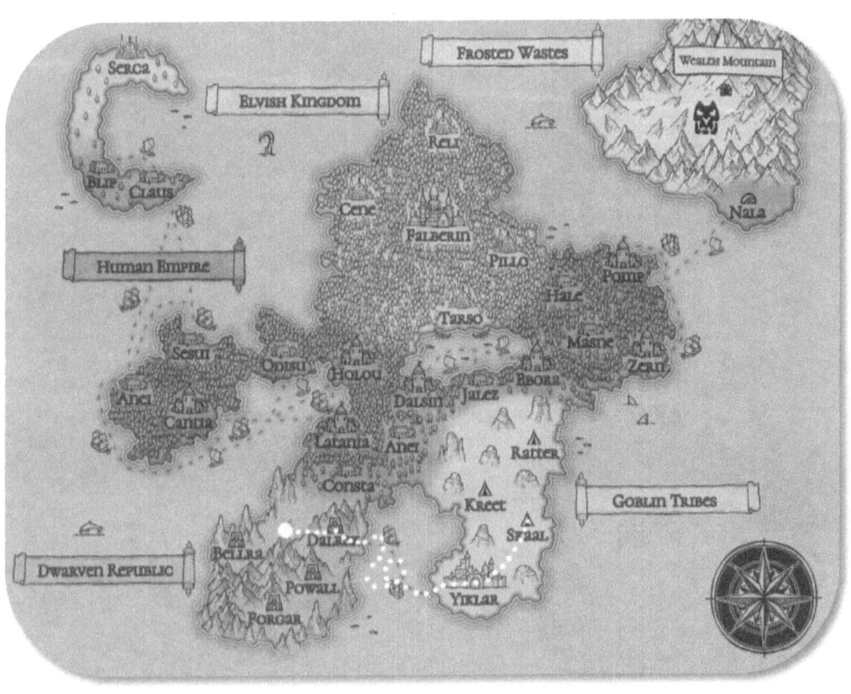

Serca
Elvish Kingdom
Frosted Wastes
Wealth Mountain
Blip
Claus
Cene
Relt
Falberin
Pillo
Pomp
Hale
Nala
Human Empire
Tarso
Masne
Zerit
Sesti
Odisu
Holou
Rbora
Anei
Cantia
Dalsit
Jalez
Latania
Anei
Ratter
Consta
Kreet
Goblin Tribes
Bellra
Dalac
Svaal
Dwarven Republic
Powall
Yiklar
Forgar

Bonus!

The remaining pages in this novel are a flipbook!

Quickly flip through pages 367 – 407 to watch the map track the goblins on their journey across the world.

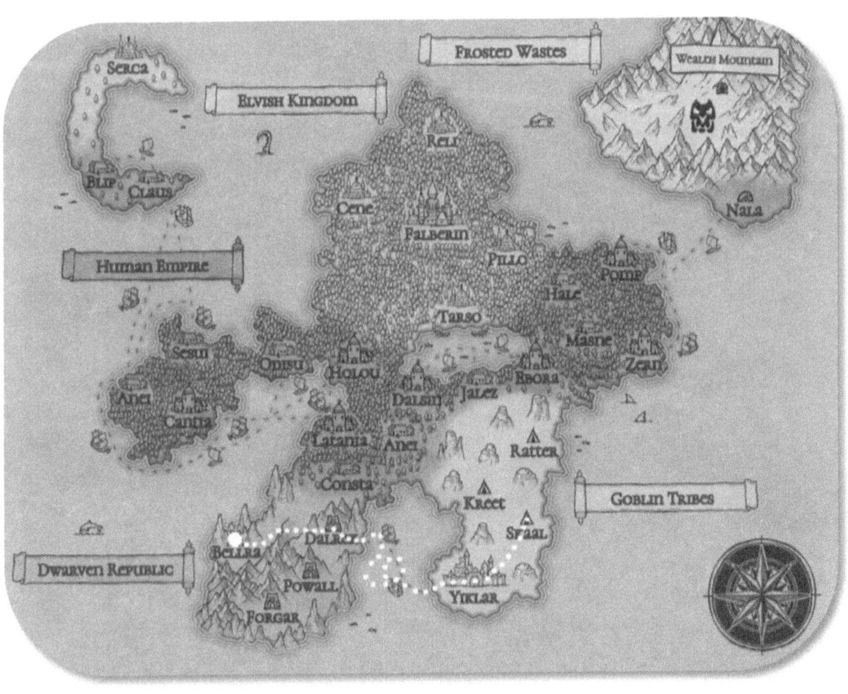
Serca
Elvish Kingdom
Frosted Wastes
Wealth Mountain
Blip
Claus
Cene
Reli
Falberin
Nala
Human Empire
Pillo
Pome
Hale
Tarso
Masne
Sesui
Odisu
Holou
Ebora
Zean
Anci
Dalsin
Jalez
Cantra
Latania
Anei
Ratter
Consta
Goblin Tribes
Kreet
Sraal
Bellra
Dalaz
Dwarven Republic
Powall
Yiklar
Forgar

Bonus!

The remaining pages in this novel are a flipbook!

Quickly flip through pages 367 – 407 to watch the map track the goblins on their journey across the world.

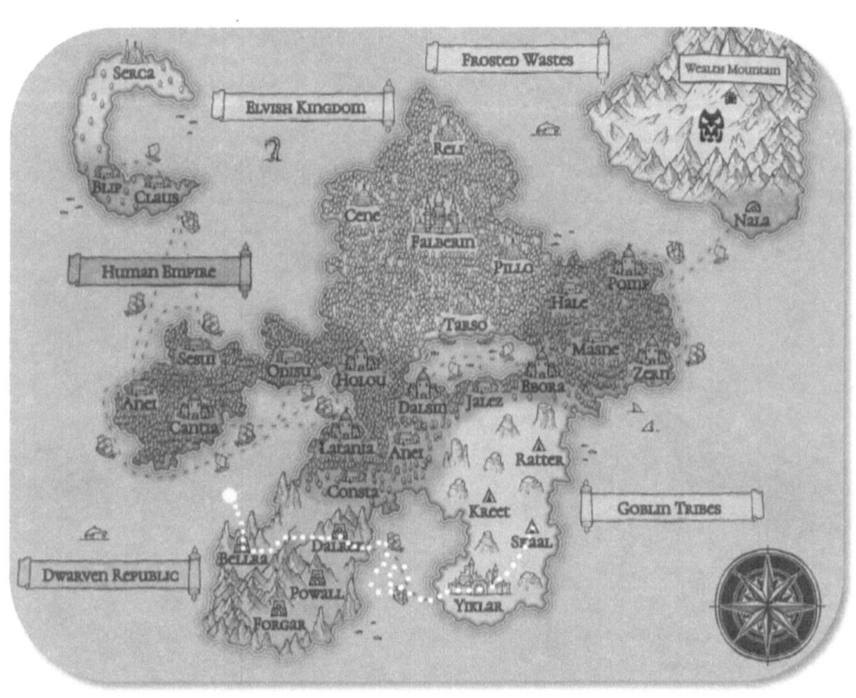
Serc2
Frosted Wastes
Wealth Mountain
Elvish Kingdom
Reli
Blip
Claus
Cene
Falberin
Nala
Pillo
Human Empire
Pomp
Hale
Tarso
Masne
Sesti
Odisu
Zern
Holou
Ebora
Anci
Jalez
Cantia
Dalsin
Latania
Aner
Ratter
Consta
Goblin Tribes
Kreet
Bellra
Dalacr
Spaal
Powall
Dwarven Republic
Forgar
Yiklar

Bonus!

The remaining pages in this novel are a flipbook!

Quickly flip through pages 367 – 407 to watch the map track the goblins on their journey across the world.

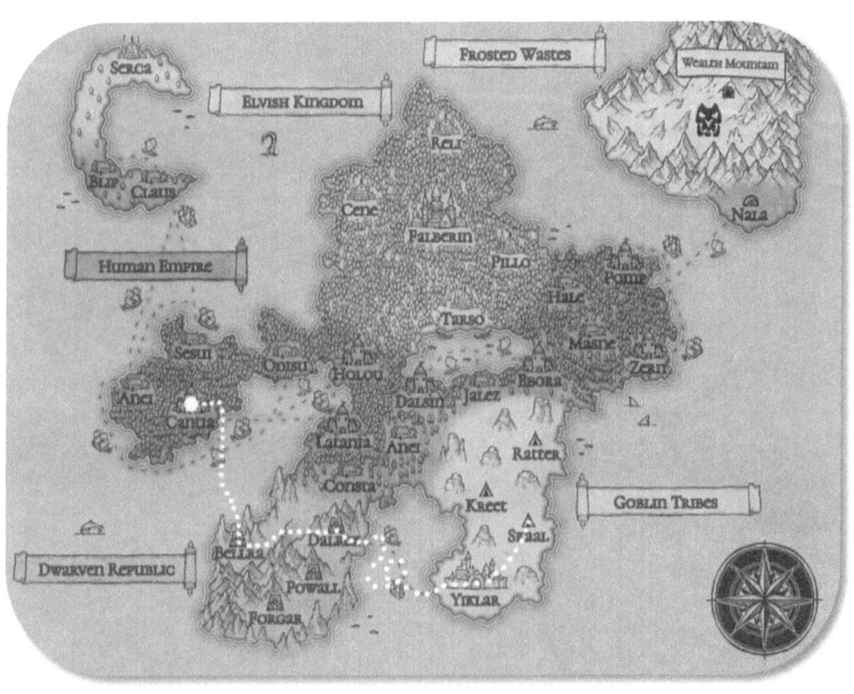

Serca
Blip
Claus
Elvish Kingdom
Frosted Wastes
Wealth Mountain
Nala
Relt
Cene
Falberin
Pillo
Pomp
Hale
Human Empire
Tarso
Masne
Zerit
Sesui
Odisu
Holou
Rbora
Anci
Dalsin
Jalez
Cantia
Latania
Anei
Ratter
Consta
Kreet
Goblin Tribes
Bellra
Dalack
Sraal
Dwarven Republic
Powall
Yiklar
Forgar

Bonus!

The remaining pages in this novel are a flipbook!

Quickly flip through pages 367 – 407 to watch the map track the goblins on their journey across the world.

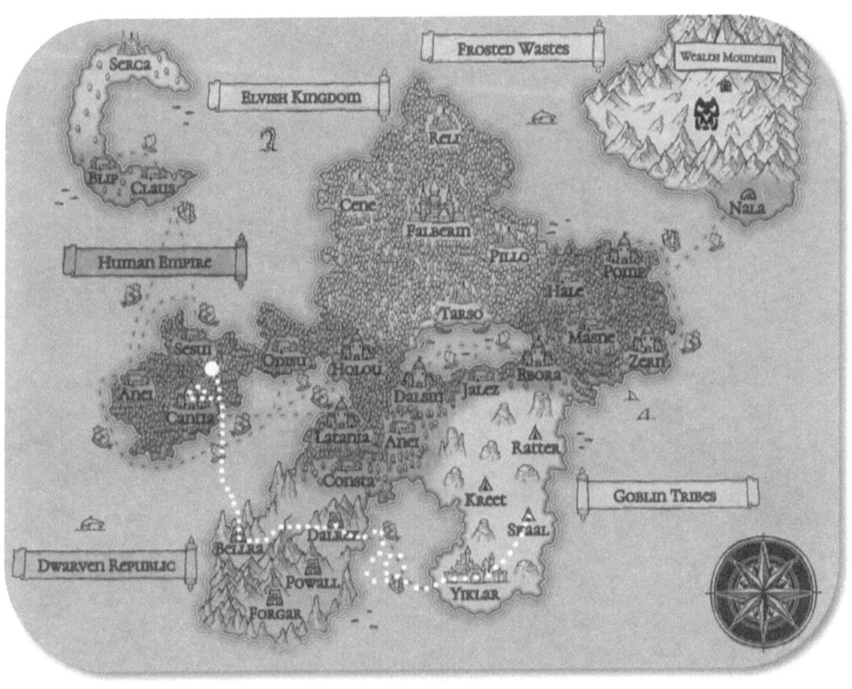

Frosted Wastes
Wealth Mountain
Serca
Elvish Kingdom
Reli
Blip
Claus
Cene
Nala
Falberin
Human Empire
Pillo
Pome
Hale
Tarso
Masne
Sesui
Opisu
Zeut
Holou
Rbora
Aner
Dalsii
Jalez
Canna
Ratter
Latania
Aner
Consta
Kreet
Goblin Tribes
Sraal
Dalacr
Bellra
Dwarven Republic
Yiklar
Powall
Forgar

Bonus!

The remaining pages in this novel are a flipbook!

Quickly flip through pages 367 – 407 to watch the map track the goblins on their journey across the world.

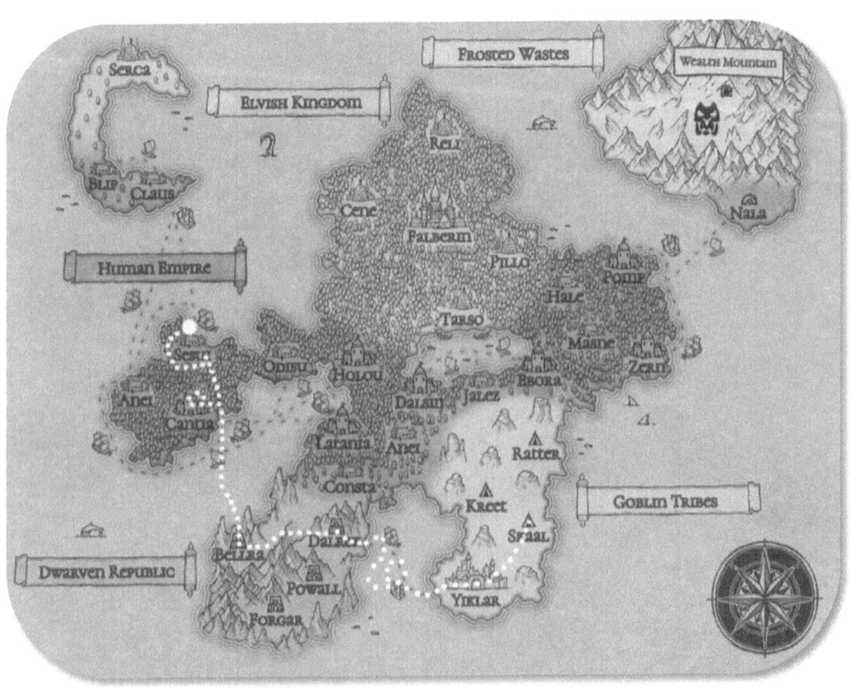
Frosted Wastes
Wealth Mountain
Serca
Elvish Kingdom
Reli
Blip
Claus
Cene
Falberm
Nala
Pillo
Pomp
Human Empire
Hale
Masne
Tarso
Sesru
Odisu
Zcari
Anci
Holou
Rbora
Cantia
Dalsin
Jalez
Latania
Anei
Ratter
Consta
Kreet
Goblin Tribes
Bellra
Dalecer
Spaal
Dwarven Republic
Powall
Yiklar
Forgar

Bonus!

The remaining pages in this novel are a flipbook!

Quickly flip through pages 367 – 407 to watch the map track the goblins on their journey across the world.

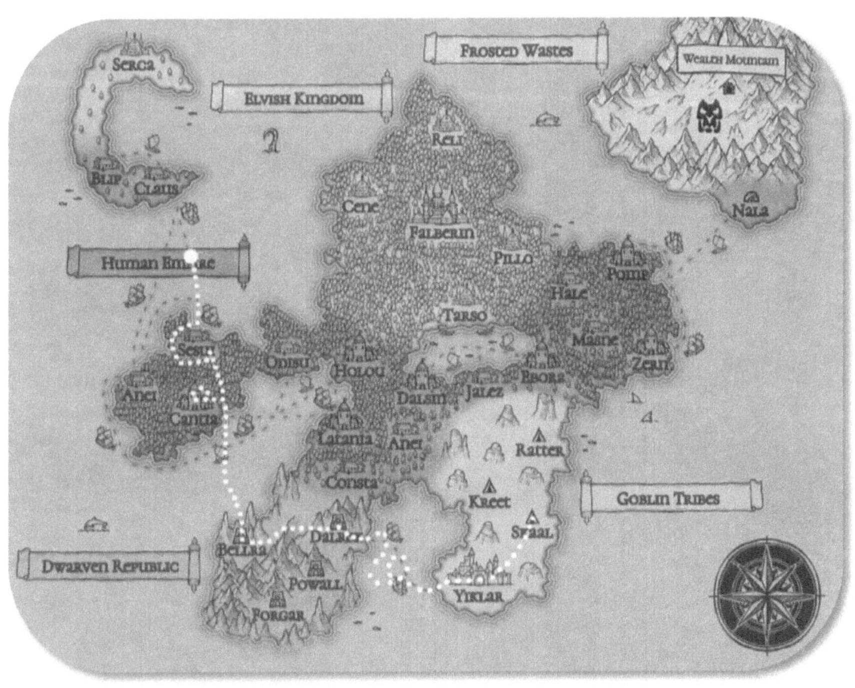
Serca
Blif
Claus
Elvish Kingdom
Frosted Wastes
Wealth Mountain
Reli
Cene
Falberin
Nala
Pillo
Human Empire
Pomp
Hale
Tarso
Sesu
Masne
Odisu
Holou
Zean
Anei
Ebora
Cantia
Dalsin
Jalez
Latania
Anei
Ratter
Consta
Kreet
Goblin Tribes
Dalai
Bellra
Spaal
Dwarven Republic
Powall
Golin
Forgar
Yiklar

Bonus!

The remaining pages in this novel are a flipbook!

Quickly flip through pages 367 – 407 to watch the map track the goblins on their journey across the world.

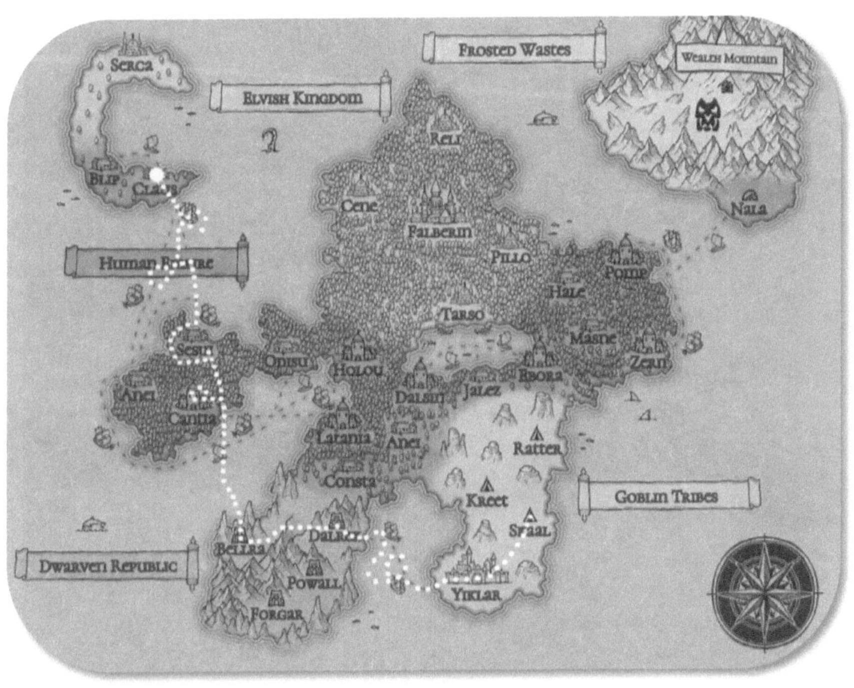

Serca
Blip
Claus
Elvish Kingdom
Frosted Wastes
Wealth Mountain
Nala
Reli
Cene
Falberin
Pillo
Pomp
Hale
Human Empire
Tarso
Masne
Zeun
Sesin
Onisu
Holou
Rbora
Jalez
Anci
Cantia
Dalsit
Larania
Anci
Ratter
Consta
Goblin Tribes
Kreet
Bellra
Dalsit
Sraal
Powall
Dwarven Republic
Forgar
Yiklar

Bonus!

The remaining pages in this novel are a flipbook!

Quickly flip through pages 367 – 407 to watch the map track the goblins on their journey across the world.

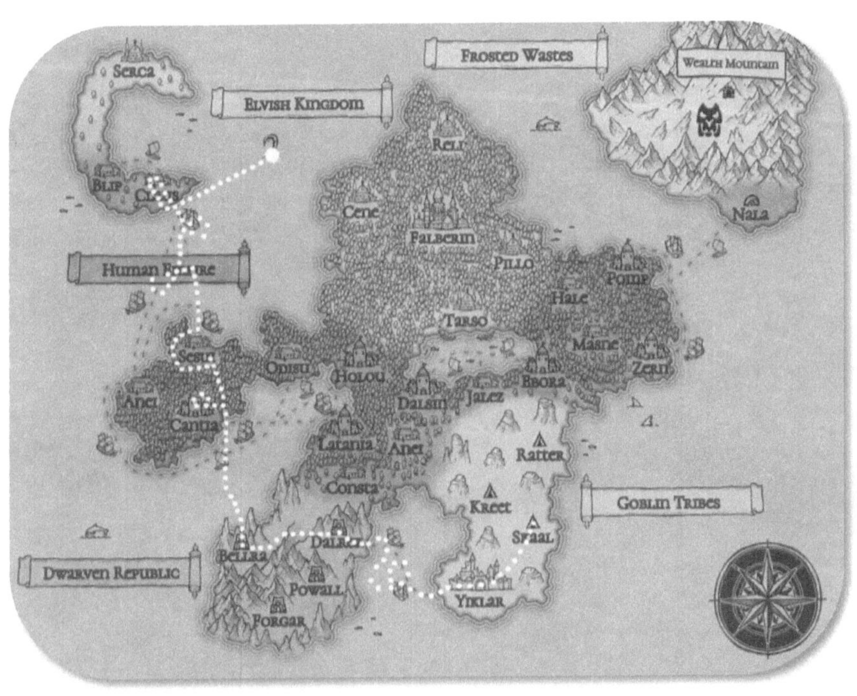

Frosted Wastes
Wealth Mountain
Serca
Elvish Kingdom
Reli
Nala
Blip
Clovs
Cene
Falberin
Pillo
Pome
Human Empire
Hale
Tarso
Masne
Zerit
Sesun
Opisu
Holou
Ebora
Anci
Dalsin
Jalez
Cantia
Aner
Ratter
Latania
Aner
Consta
Kreet
Goblin Tribes
Spaal
Bellra
Dalaer
Dwarven Republic
Powall
Yiklar
Porgar

Bonus!

The remaining pages in this novel are a flipbook!

Quickly flip through pages 367 – 407 to watch the map track the goblins on their journey across the world.

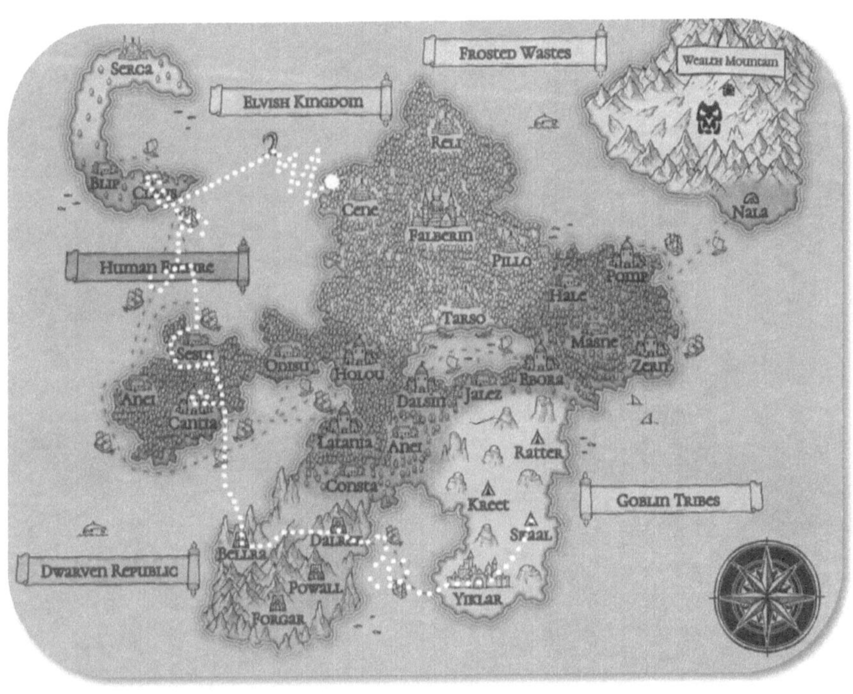
Serca
Frosted Wastes
Wealth Mountain
Elvish Kingdom
Blif
Cloes
Cene
Relt
Falberin
Nala
Pillo
Pomp
Human Future
Hale
Tarso
Masne
Zean
Sesu
Odisu
Holou
Ebora
Anci
Dalsu
Jalez
Cantia
Latania
Aner
Ratter
Consta
Kreet
Goblin Tribes
Swaal
Bellra
Dalacr
Dwarven Republic
Powall
Yiklar
Forgar

Bonus!

The remaining pages in this novel are a flipbook!

Quickly flip through pages 367 – 407 to watch the map track the goblins on their journey across the world.

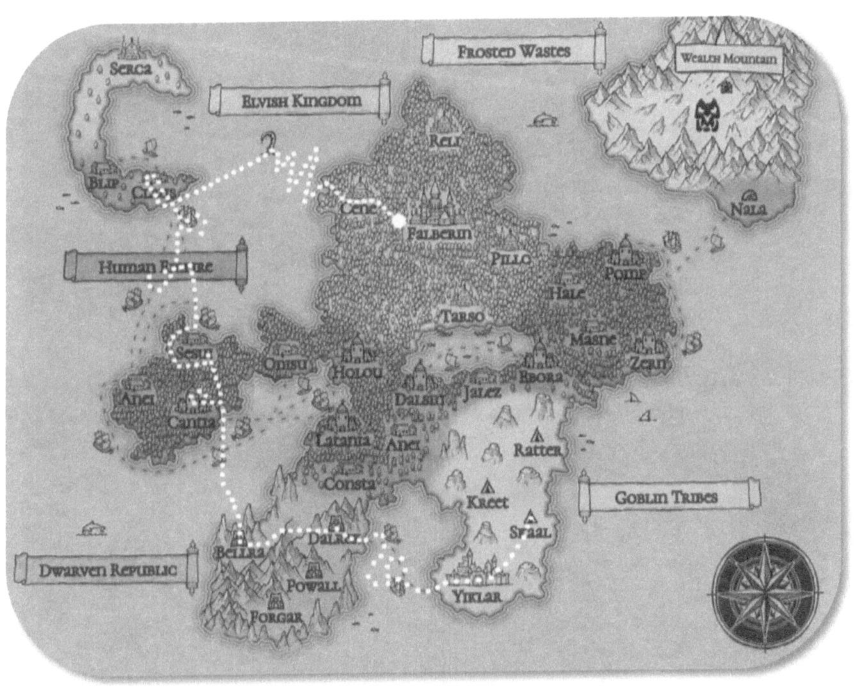

Serca
Blip
Cloos
Elvish Kingdom
Frosted Wastes
Wealth Mountain
Relt
Cene
Falberin
Pillo
Pome
Hale
Nala
Human Empire
Tarso
Masne
Zean
Sesut
Onisu
Holou
Rbora
Jalez
Anci
Dalsti
Anet
Latania
Ratter
Consta
Kreet
Goblin Tribes
Bellra
Dalect
Sfaal
Dwarven Republic
Powall
Yiklar
Forgar

Bonus!

The remaining pages in this novel are a flipbook!

Quickly flip through pages 367 – 407 to watch the map track the goblins on their journey across the world.

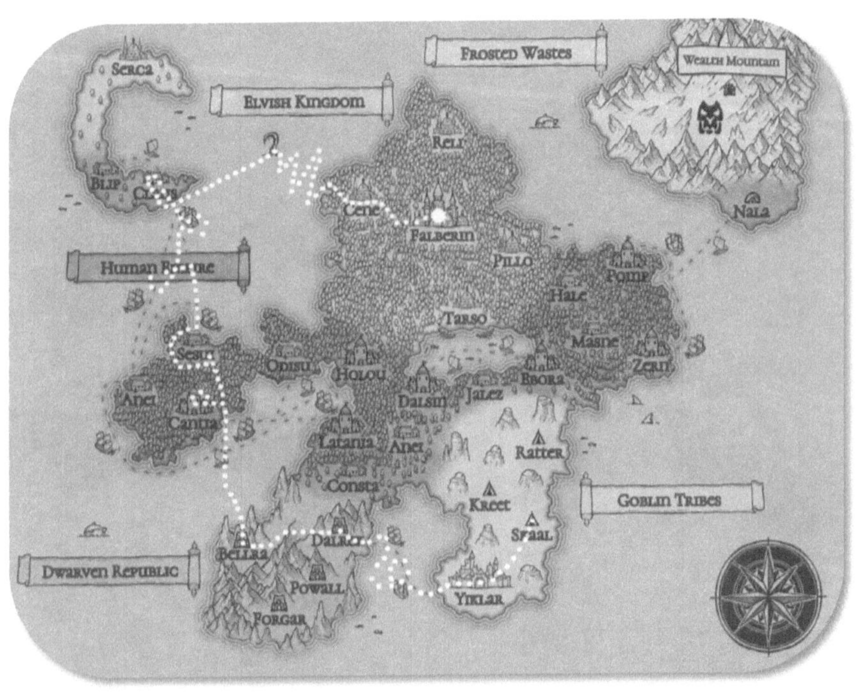
Serca
Elvish Kingdom
Frosted Wastes
Wealth Mountain
Blip
Claus
Relr
Cene
Falberin
Nala
Human Empire
Pillo
Pomp
Hale
Tarso
Masne
Zerit
Sesin
Odisu
Holou
Esora
Anei
Canna
Dalsin
Jalez
Latania
Anei
Ratter
Consta
Kreet
Goblin Tribes
Bellra
Dalrur
Spaal
Dwarven Republic
Powall
Yirlar
Forgar

Bonus!

The remaining pages in this novel are a flipbook!

Quickly flip through pages 367 – 407 to watch the map track the goblins on their journey across the world.

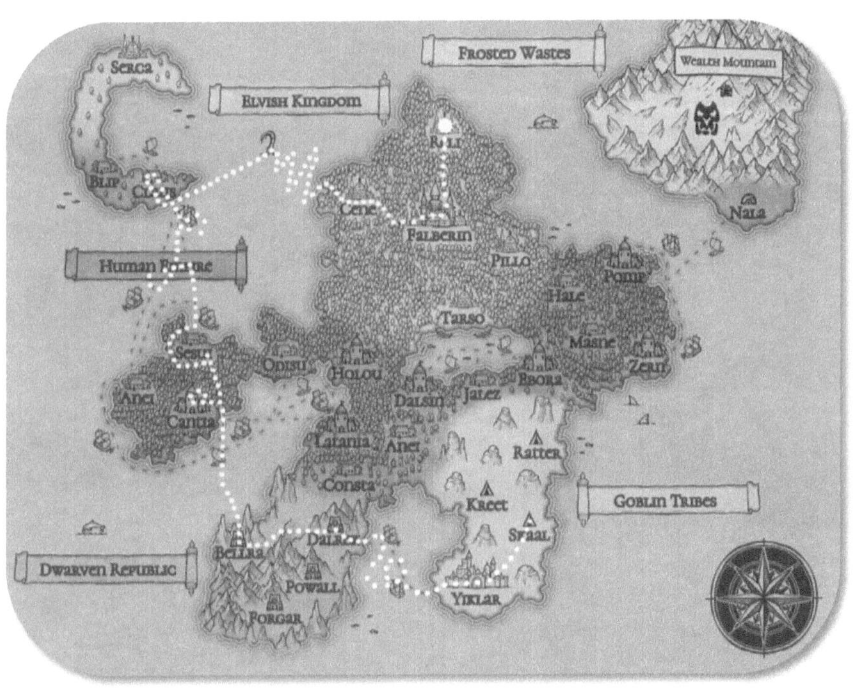

Frosted Wastes
Wealth Mountain
Serca
Elvish Kingdom
Rell
Blip
Claus
Cene
Falberin
Nala
Pillo
Pomp
Human Empire
Hale
Tarso
Masne
Zerit
Sesu
Odisu
Holou
Rbora
Anci
Dalsin
Jatez
Cantia
Latania
Anei
Ratter
Consta
Kreet
Goblin Tribes
Spaal
Bellsa
Dalacr
Dwarven Republic
Powall
Yiklar
Forgar

Bonus!

The remaining pages in this novel are a flipbook!

Quickly flip through pages 367 – 407 to watch the map track the goblins on their journey across the world.

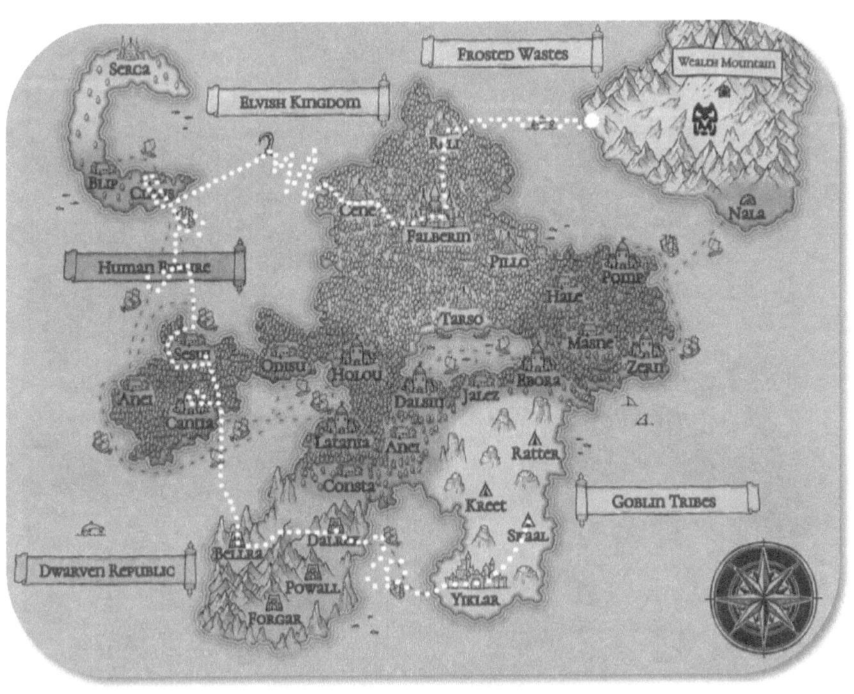
Frosted Wastes
Wealth Mountain
Serca
Elvish Kingdom
Ralu
Blip
Claus
Cene
Falberin
Nala
Pillo
Pome
Human Empire
Hale
Tarso
Masne
Sesui
Odisu
Holou
Rbora
Zeaii
Anei
Dalsii
Jalez
Canua
Latania
Anei
Ratter
Consta
Kreet
Goblin Tribes
Sraal
Bellra
Dalrei
Dwarven Republic
Powall
Yiklar
Forgar

Bonus!

The remaining pages in this novel are a flipbook!

Quickly flip through pages 367 – 407 to watch the map track the goblins on their journey across the world.

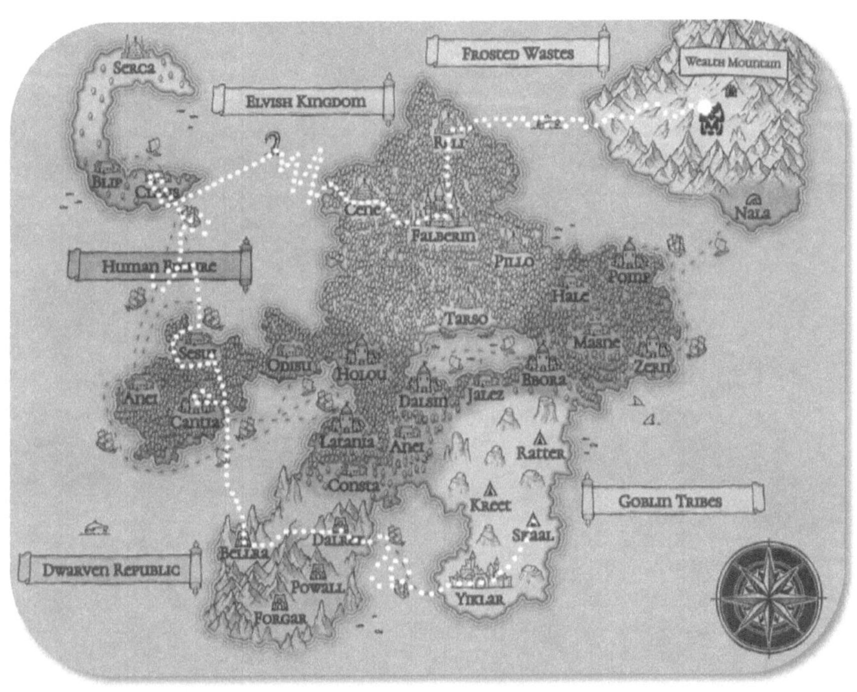
Serca
Frosted Wastes
Wealth Mountain
Elvish Kingdom
Blip
Clars
Cene
Rali
Nala
Falberin
Pillo
Pome
Human Empire
Hale
Zerit
Tarso
Masne
Sesin
Odisu
Holou
Ebora
Aner
Dalsin
Jalez
Cantra
Aner
Ratter
Latania
Consta
Kreet
Goblin Tribes
Spaal
Bellra
Dalaci
Dwarven Republic
Powall
Yiklar
Forgar

Bonus!

The remaining pages in this novel are a flipbook!

Quickly flip through pages 367 – 407 to watch the map track the goblins on their journey across the world.

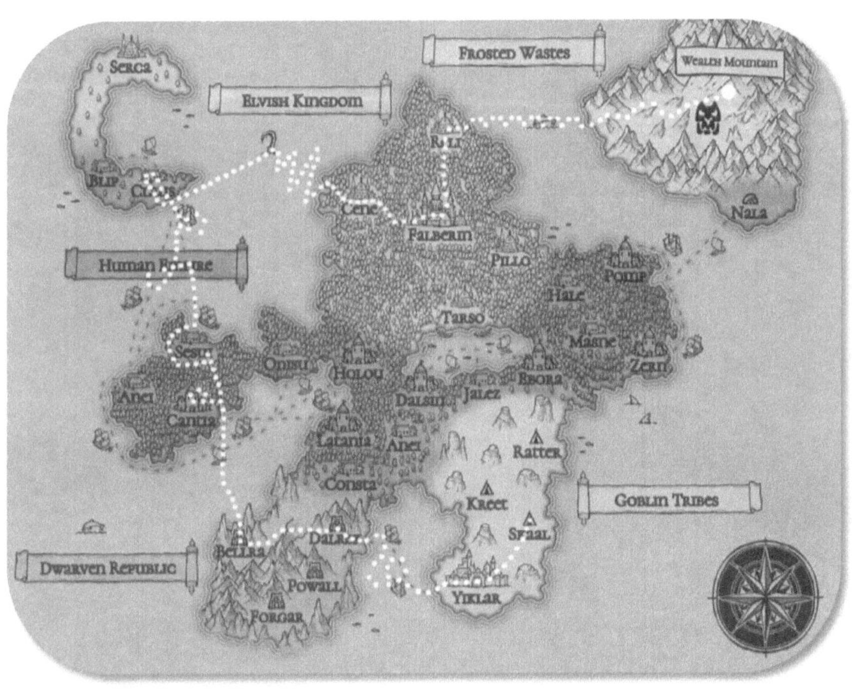

Serca
Frosted Wastes
Wealth Mountain
Elvish Kingdom
Blip
Claus
Cene
Rali
Falbern
Nala
Human Empire
Pillo
Pomp
Hale
Tarso
Masne
Zerit
Qnisu
Holou
Ebora
Anei
Dalsin
Jalez
Cantia
Ratter
Latania
Anei
Consta
Kreet
Goblin Tribes
Dalezi
Sfaal
Bellra
Dwarven Republic
Powall
Yiklar
Forgar